land/space

An Anthology
of Prairie Speculative Fiction

Edited by

Candas Jane Dorsey

and

Judy Berlyne McCrosky

TESSERACT BOOKS

an imprint of
The Books Collective

Tesseract Books and The Books Collective acknowledge the ongoing support of the Canada Council for the Arts and the Edmonton Arts Council for our publishing program. The editors also thank the Saskatchewan Arts Board and an anonymous donor for their contributions, which assisted in the preparation of this Anthology. The editors with to thank Norman Yates and his Land/Space series of paintings for the inspiration for the title of the anthology. Thanks to Ingénieuse Productions, and Kim Lundquist of Priority Printing.

Editor for the Press: Candas Jane Dorsey.
Cover painting by Robert Pasternak.
Cover design by Totino Busby Design.
Page design and typography by Ana M. Anubis.
Printed by Priority Printing Ltd., Edmonton.

The text was set in Adobe System's *Utopia*, an Adobe Originals text face designed by Robert Slimbach in 1989. It combines the vertical stress and pronounced stroke contrast of eighteenth-century Transitional types like Baskerville and Walbaum with contemporary innovations in character shapes and stroke details. The headlines are set in *Kino*, a "serifless Latin" designed by Martin Dovey in 1930 for the Monotype Corporation; section dividers are from David Hirmes' *Crop Circle Dingbats*.

Published in Canada by Tesseract Books, an imprint of
The Books Collective
214-21, 10405 Jasper Avenue
Edmonton, Alberta T5J 3S2.
Telephone (780) 448-0590   Fax (780) 448-0640

Canadian Cataloguing in Publishing Data

Land/space

ISBN 1-895836-92-1 (bound). — ISBN 1-895836-90-5 (pbk.)

1. Science fiction. 2. Fantasy fiction. 3. Prairie Provinces—Literary collections. I. Dorsey, Candas Jane. II. McCrosky, Judy, 1956-
PN6120.95.S33L36 2002   813'.08760832   C2002-910878-0

Contents

Foreword

A Prairie by Any Other Name...

People have shaped their surroundings for thousands of years. We have cleared land, paved over it, and redirected waterways. Deserts have been made to bloom, and animals and plants now flourish in climates previously unknown to them. Human beings have long sought to recreate the world in their image, visualizing an environment that exists to nourish our species.

Does this mean that we truly are masters of all we survey, with dominion over our physical surroundings? No. Like it or not, despite all efforts, there are aspects of our world that are simply too large or too powerful for us to change. People cannot stop the tides from ebbing and flowing, nor can they turn off the stars. And, geographical environment can still shape us. Urban or not, people are aware of the physical world around them and while we have affected great change on it, it has also affected us.

In addition to forming a changed physical environment for ourselves, people have created a different sort of environment, one that encourages bonds among people who share various identifying features. People feel most comfortable with others like themselves and so race, religion, and political vision have led to the development of nations. National boundaries, as we know well, are subject to change, and people within any one set of boundaries are not necessarily living together in peace, but people do seem to want to have an entity, larger than themselves as individuals, to call their own. People want the freedom to live within the country of their choice. While the reasons for this choice vary, there is a clear understanding that the country one lives in has an effect on our lives.

In North America, we live in countries that encompass a wide variety of geographical terrain. With which do we identify more strongly, the political or the physical? What plays a greater role in creative development, intangible affiliations with nation and culture, or the tangible world around us? Does living in a similar physical environment overcome the differences between nations and manifest itself in common themes, style, and imagery among writers who share a geography but not a country?

This anthology explores this question. The editors chose to focus on prairie, or plains, or grassland, (all called prairie from now on), in part because we live in prairie provinces, and are familiar with Canadian literature and how prairie writing both differs from and is similar to literature written by people living in other parts of our country. We chose to conduct our exploration through speculative literature, because an examination of the effects of environment is a common theme within this body of work. Also, while there is a common perception that speculative fiction deals with characters who live in the future or in a currently unknown society, these stories demonstrate a strength in the portrayal of peoples and societies of today. Contemporary issues, when viewed from the unusual and new perspectives of speculative literature, often provide revealing insights that can enhance readers' understanding of those issues. Candas and I both write speculative literature and are excited by this exploration of how an environment and a literature, both of which we love, come together.

This book includes work by writers who live or have lived in Canada, the U.S., and Australia. Although not all of it is set in the prairies, the stories and poems share common features. Let's have a look at some of these features.

Many of the works contain images of huge sweeps of grassland, and of roads. This is no surprise, considering that prairie consists of huge sweeps of grassland, or land that used to be grassland, periodically sliced by roads. Characters often feel trapped and lonely, surrounded as they are by a landscape that looks the same in all directions. Roads are of tremendous importance, for they serve as the only tangible sign that something different, whether better or worse, might exist.

Roads can be more than a means to an end, though. They are sometimes an environment in of themselves, since in an unchanging landscape, the journey itself might matter more than the starting point or destination.

Images of beauty are found throughout the book. The prairie's beauty is often subtle, one might have to work to find it, but it is there. Skies that seem to hang so near to us but which stretch so far, the sheer number of different shades of green and gold, the sunset light that's so rich it feels as if one can touch it, these and other images are inescapable within the prairie landscape. Beauty exists, not always where people expect to find it, and sometimes in forms other than the obvious, but it is there, a deep pool to refresh those who find it.

Beauty is found not only in the landscape, but also through connections with other people who share life on the prairie, and bonds between people are a frequent theme of the stories and poems. People need each other. Humans are social beings, but the bonds that can grow between individuals who work together to survive in a difficult environment can become almost mystical in their strength. The prairie is huge and sparsely populated. Bonds are formed from friendship or love, and sometimes are tinged with less pleasant emotions, but no one can live here without becoming part of the web of relationships.

Connections exist between people, but also between people and the land. It's difficult to live in a place where the land is so obvious, where it shows itself no matter where one looks, without forming some sort of intimate bond. People need the land, to provide food and shelter, but also for its spiritual essence. And while the people tend the land, it can also nurture those who live on it. The land's love can be explicit, sometimes spoken in voices that can be heard, or it can be less tangible, discovered by people who discover growth in themselves even as they tend the growing things that surround them.

Sometimes, though, despite our connection to the land, there is simply too much of it. Standing in the middle of untouched prairie can be like being in the middle of an ocean, out of sight of all land, surrounded by nothing but waves. The fact that the waves are blue in the ocean and golden on the prairie doesn't diminish the fact that they can both seem overwhelming. It's easy to get lost, both physically and intellectually, in a land that is so big and changes so little. The land is a force to be reckoned with, has a distinct personality, becomes almost a character, participant in the works in the anthology.

What have we learned about external influences on creative writing environments such as nation and geography have an effect? The answer is yes, do, and it appears that the physical environment of the prairie has a strong influence than does the political entity.

Nation does have an effect, though. Here's a summary of the variations within this book between Canada, the U.S., and Australia:

While all three countries explored issues of the harsh environment and feelings of being trapped by said environment, the Americans tended to include themes of rebellion, exploration, and the desire to escape more than did the other two countries. Canadians were most similar to Australians, in that their concerns included false hopes, vulnerability, the need to adapt to change, people as part of the land, and loneliness. Canadians, though, were the source of most of the writing that dealt with hope, the land caring for the life on it, and the need for connections, both with the land and with other people.

It thus appears that Americans are once again living up to their image of a nation of strong-minded individualists who refuse to knuckle under, and who are not afraid to impose their will and change their environment to suit their needs. Australians and Canadians feel more vulnerable, more at the mercy of the size and the harsh life imposed by their prairie. Australians are strong individuals, but their land is powerful, so overwhelming it imposes its will on people rather than the other way around. The Canadian view is less bleak, and Canadians show a willingness to adapt, and to work with their environment. They are more aware of the beauty that surrounds them and of the ties that bind people to land and land to people. At the same time, though, they are lonelier and more in need of tangible connections with each other.

Overall, when reading through the works in this anthology, the stories and poems show that there are far more similarities engendered by shared geography than there are differences caused by separate cultural and national environments. The same atmosphere flows through the works, just as wind-blown ripples in tall grass look alike no matter the borders within which the grass grows. The editors, before working on this book, were comfortable discussing and defining a Canadian prairie literature, but we now can take this a step further and find a larger, more global, scope for writing born of the prairie.

This literature focuses on characters who are not total masters of their fate, despite the power humans have exerted on their planet. The landscape is not inert, it contains and nurtures life, but it is also an entity itself, with both spiritual and physical personality. The land is not dead, meaning unresponsive, it acts and reacts as it sees fit. If the people who live within its body do not learn to adapt and to live according to its rules, they are faced with either extinction or the choice of leaving. The land, though, is not only cruel and unforgiving. Those who learn to live with it, as part of its natural environment, those who form connections with it and thus live in harmony with the land and the other life it nurtures, are blessed with the prairie's beauty, natural bounty, and, dare I say it, love.

Judy Berlyne McCrosky

SPACE

Lia Pas

the space i think of now is a wide one   an open one
the space i think of
deep in the space that is deep
is wide now
is open now
is the openness now
is open
is sky
is wide
is green

the moment races now
brings the closeness here
brings the beginning to a place   here
brings the way
here home here within here

these are spaces of the mind that open
aware that the openness is
is always
is the way
is the wide open
is space
is space

°°° ° °° °°° °°° °°° ⎤ °°° °° ° °°° °° ° °
°°° °°° °°° °°° °°° °°° °°° °°° °°° °° °°° °°°

Mormonism and The Saskatoon Space Programme

Hugh A.D. Spencer

"Those Mormons… either coming back from a church meeting or heading out to another one!"

The dominant memory of my uncles was of a bunch of bald-headed guys sleeping in my grandparent's living room just after lunch between the times scheduled for Priesthood meeting, Sunday school and Sacrament. They were all on the same rather busy schedule of worship, and having dealt with some of the day's physical and spiritual needs they would grind out some snores.

Impressive snores they were. It was like they were impersonating every diesel tractor that rolled its way over a Southern Alberta sugar beet farm.

My dad assured me that I only had four uncles and six great-uncles but when I heard that choir of nasal blasts I was sure I had at least two thousand of them.

All of them were wearing brown or gray suits ordered from the Magrath Trade Goods store. The suits were actually able to bend at the knees and elbows, which I found particularly amazing because the fabric was some kind of combination of raw wool, sandpaper and rusting plate steel.

They completed the fashion statement by wearing work boots with their suits. Out of respect for the deity they actually washed and polished them but this was the same footwear that trampled its way through cow shit for the other six days of the week.

Some of my uncles were bachelors, some were married. I would occasionally bump into my cousins who claimed some connection to one of them but I could never get most of my uncles to stay awake long enough to explain who belonged to who.

After a while, my grandma would wade into the sea of snores and announce:

"Time to go to church."

This stimulated some kind of classically conditioned response uncles would twitch, blink, brush back their non-existent hair and up out of their chairs.

"Come on, kid," my Uncle Weston (who always woke up the faste would whisper to me. "It's Testimony this week."

Great, I would inwardly sigh.

Testimony Meeting. Everybody would remind each other that Joseph Smith was indeed a prophet of God, the Book of Mormon was the revealed truth, and that socialized medicine was the vanguard of communism. Sometimes at closing, the presiding Bishop would remind us that Evil is Bad.

God, those summers in Southern Alberta. So long, so boring, so painful.

○○○   ○○○   ○○○

"Q: Why does Saskatchewan have rats and Alberta have Mormons?
A: Saskatchewan got first choice."

○○○   ○○○   ○○○

Usually, Uncle Weston drove me back home to Saskatoon. Unlike my other uncles, he didn't work on a farm and seemed to have more free time. He was some kind of a free-lance pilot and actually served with my dad in the RCAF during World War II. Consequently, Uncle Weston and my dad were the only good drivers in the family.

Not that you would notice in the ancient Dodge station wagon he used to drive.

I'm not sure if that model was even equipped with suspension and the engine's combustion wasn't all that internal. We kind of wheezed and exploded our way along the Transcanada Highway.

I was trying to read some Heinlien novel, I think it was *Revolt in 2100*, but all the bouncing was making it pretty hard work. I had to pause every minute or two to re-focus my vision.

"Good book?" Uncle Weston asked as he peered out the gravel-pitted windshield.

"It's okay," I mumbled. This as about as enthusiastic a thirteen year-old Western Canadian kid gets if he isn't into hockey or football. In truth, I was loving the book. I really wanted to like Heinlien's relaxed ultra-competent heroes and those "racy" bits were pretty damn exciting.

Hey, I was thirteen.

"Don't know the author," Uncle Weston said. "I was more of a *Mechanics Illustrated* reader when I was your age."

"Uh, huh."

This would explain the huge pile of yellow pulp magazines in the labourers' cottage on my grandparents' farm. I'd read them all two summers e fact that just about every piece of technology described was obsolete or impractical (when was the last time you took a ride on personal autogyro?) didn't bother me all that much. I was just delighted ind something to read that wasn't related to religion or animal husbandry.

"But I sometimes think I ought to read some science fiction once in a while."

"Uh, huh."

This was the bulk of our conversation for about six hours.

We weren't making very good time so the sun was setting as we passed through the "city" of Swift Current.

"Pit stop," Uncle Weston announced. He pulled into a Husky station and we sat in the Dodge while we gassed up.

"You aren't enjoying your time at the farm, are you?" Uncle Weston asked.

"Well…" I was feeling too tired to be anything but honest. "All I seem to do is dig weeds and go to church."

"You don't like farm work?"

Actually I didn't mind it that much. There was a direct quality to digging around in the earth that was strangely satisfying. Maybe it just made me too tired to think.

"That's okay," I said.

"So it's church you're not too keen on."

"It just seems to go on forever," I said. "And some of what they say is a little hard to believe."

Uncle Weston sighed. "Well," he said softly. "Your father would probably agree with you there."

"Do you believe everything they say?" This was a pretty dangerous question for me—if Uncle Weston took it the wrong way he might feel obligated to spend the next two hours in the Husky parking lot bearing his testimony.

I was lucky. He just nodded his head:

"I fulfill my obligations and attend church and priesthood meetings when appropriate."

Even then, that struck me as a rather interesting answer.

"We've driven far enough today," he said.

So we agreed to camp at a nearby Provincial park and come home a day late. My dad probably wouldn't even notice and I think Uncle Weston felt a little guilty with the realization that the fun quota of my summer vacation had been rather low.

Now, I'm sure there must be some tremendously rare and scientifically significant species of weed near our campground because it certainly wasn't designated as a Provincial Park on the basis of its natural beauty. It looked

like an abandoned landing strip with a couple of picnic tables, some rust
climbing structures and a wooden shed with male and female stick peopr
on the doors.

Uncle Weston rolled the station wagon to a stop next to a small gravel bed
with steel label at one end:

Lot 52.

"This is a great place," he said as he yanked on the parking brake and
opened the door.

"Really?" If any kid spoke to me with as much sarcasm as I did back
then, I think I'd punch him in the head.

I doubt that Uncle Weston even noticed.

"Sure thing," he answered. "Your father and I would stay here when we
were hitch-hiking to P.E.I."

He was referring to the time when he and my dad were training as pilots
at the RCAF base in Summerside. The War ended before my dad saw any
combat duty but apparent Uncle Weston flew some missions. I use the
word "apparently" because I had to pick this information up second hand—
neither of them would talk about what happened to them at that time.

We made a small fire in the flaking iron box next to one of the picnic
tables and warmed up some canned beans and Spam which we ate by
tilting our bowls and making small poking motions with our jack-knives.

"Very tasty," Uncle Weston smacked.

I wasn't sure what surprised me more—the fact that Uncle Weston liked
this food or that he hadn't bother to bless it before we ate.

Blessing the food was a huge deal at my grandparents' house. We actually
had to kneel next to our chairs while my grandfather gave the benediction—
and this would go on for what seemed like six hours while the spirit moved
him to comment on our performance on the farm.

I wasn't exactly complaining that Uncle Weston had missed this ritual step
in the day. Ordinarily, missing out on the blessing would have been quite
welcome.

But with beans and Spam I wondered if we might want to seek divine
protection from food poisoning.

"Do you know what we need right now?" Uncle Weston was studying
the rapidly separating fluids in his plastic bowl.

"Ummm?" Immediate medical attention? A sudden and unstoppable
desire to keep on driving? These and other suggestions occurred to me as
my uncle walked over to the Dodge and opened the trunk.

"Your grandfather used these as rations during World War I." Uncle
Weston removed a khaki-coloured tin can, about the size of my head, from
the trunk. "I wonder if it's still edible."

He cranked on the can opener to reveal what was inside.

It was a shock.

Bread.

Tinned bread that was over half-a-century old. The ends of the loaf were marked with the rings of the tin can.

Uncle Weston, using some effort, tore off a piece of bread to soak up the bean and Spam juice in his bowl.

"It's pretty good," he said speaking through the ancient but freshly chewed mass in his mouth.

I was fascinated by the concept of bread in a can, so I tried some. At best, I can describe its taste as… yeasty.

But it didn't kill us.

When it was time to go to sleep I lay down on an air mattress set under a pup tent that was also a bit of grandfather's military surplus kit.

While we were setting all this up, Uncle Weston's conscience must have been bothering him because he started going on about how important it was for my grandparents to see me in the summer and how it gave my dad a chance to deal with some of the more difficult parts of his research… and jeez whiz, weren't we having all kinds of fun right now?

But at least he wasn't telling me how important it was for me to keep going to church and how I ought to be preparing for my mission calling. That was my grandmother's version of good night, sleep tight.

Maybe he did start talking about church, but I'd fallen sleep by then.

"… This is a signal… "

I heard something. Something very soft and faraway.

"Uncle Weston?" I was awake now.

"… this is a signal… "

The sound had a weird metallic quality, sort of like robot ghosts whispering at you.

"… a signal on continuous broadcast… "

I looked out of the end of my pup tent and saw Uncle Weston sitting in the dark at the picnic table.

"… from the Galactic Core… I'm sending this through a worm-hole in the hope that you will receive in real-time… "

Uncle Weston's face was glowing green from the lights of some kind of big transistor radio. Its workings were exposed at the back and I could see a cluster of oddly-shaped vacuum tubes.

"… I am transmitting from a solar system of 57 planets… "

Every once in a while Uncle Weston would adjust a dial on the radio.

"… all uninhabited, but 11 were abandoned by some form of sentient life…"

After listening this long, I decided that the voice on radio w⟍ human, but it wasn't very happy about what it was reporting.

"… desolation… nothing but desolation… "

Eventually the voice became unintelligible, the few remaining w⟍ were eventually submerged in wave after wave of static.

After a while he turned off the radio.

"Uncle Weston?" I called out into the darkness.

I wasn't able to see the expression on his face.

"You heard that?" he asked.

"Some."

I heard the sound of him picking up the radio and walking over to the trunk of the car.

"Time to get back to bed."

In the morning, as we made the last stretch of highway between Biggar and Saskatoon, Uncle Weston told me that he was listening to an old radio play.

"I thought I'd try some of your science fiction."

"Sure."

"Do you like my home-made receiver?" he laughed, a little feebly I thought. "A project from my *Mechanics Illustrated* days."

Right. You see green-glowing radios that pick up signals from space in every prairie household.

"Looks nice." Was what I said.

"I think I was picking up a station down around Great Falls… in Montana."

Montana. With 57 planets.

Of course.

"This is CFQC, broadcasting from the potash capital of the world!"

Growing up in Saskatoon probably prepared me for life in outer space. It was an alienating experience at times.

In Southern Alberta, those towns with strange names like Magrath, Taber and Cardston where my grandparents dug irrigation ditches and built temples, the Mormons had their own communities. These towns were all trapped in orbit around Calgary, Fort McLeod and Lethbridge but they were places where we pretty much called the shots. Or at least people who were "like us" called the shots.

But Mormons were a minority, "one of those peculiar religions" in Saskatchewan.

There weren't too many connections between Salt Lake City and the Ukraine and the President and Prophet of the LDS Church hardly ever praised the policies of the CCF.

..y, my parents and myself, moved to Saskatoon when my dad
..his position at the Prairie Regional Laboratory at the University.
.. doing research on two substances that Saskatchewan had in
..dance: potash and uranium.

Most people on this prairie are at least aware of uranium. They know that
uranium has something to do with nuclear weapons and radioactivity.

Potash is only world-famous in Saskatoon. For those of you who don't
know, potash is a quartz-based mineral which was mined in large quantities
and used in fertilizer additives.

By the time I was thirteen, I'd figured out that what my father did for a
living had something to do with fusing uranium and potash but that was
as far as it went. I knew he had some kind of secrecy agreement with the
Federal Government.

Not that my dad ever tried to conceal the wonders of science from me.
He worked every weekend and on the Saturdays when he wasn't at the
reactor site he would let me play in the PRL building. This started when I
was about seven and a lot cuter; lots of the technicians and graduate
students were really nice to me. They would help me look through
microscopes, let me turn the switch on the oscilloscopes, and move around
some of the luminescent minerals under and ultra-violet light.

One technician even had this tabletop dynamo that fired off bolts of
lightning like those old Frankenstein movies. I had no idea what it was
doing in the lab but I certainly thought it was cool.

It was great, like growing up in your own personal science centre.

My Sundays, alternatively, were dedicated to religion.

The related activities were not something that my dad would participate in.

"Because I gave your mother my word… " he would invariably say as I
would squirm into my Sunday clothes.

I was decked out in a suit that was three sizes too big, a cardboard white
shirt and a clip-on tie. Dad was wearing his regular lab clothes: Hush
Puppies, pants with patches on the knees, and a checked short-sleeved
shirt with a slide rule and about 50 pens in the front pocket. He was wearing
that because he was going to the lab, I was going to church. Hell, I looked
like the grown-up and he looked like the kid.

On the occasional Sunday when Uncle Weston was in town he would
take me but usually Dad would drive me to the entrance of the then-modest
Central Saskatchewan branch of the LDS Church and head off to PRL to do
some more work. Dad would never set foot in the Church.

About four or sixteen hours later, Dad would be waiting for me in the car.
Listening to the *Rod and Charles Show* or *Gillmore's Albums* on CBC Regina.
That was about as much fun as Dad would allow himself to have.

Aside from the fact that I had to navigate my own way through the c series of meetings and rooms on my own, the absolute worst thing ⅎ the drop-off arrangement was that we never got there on time. About 75% the time I arrived after Junior Sunday School services started and it seeme that about 90% of those times, the other kids were singing this one hymn:

"Never be late for your Sunday School Class! Always be prompt, bright and cheeeerfulllll… "

While they were singing I would slink to some seat at the back of the room. Unfortunately the metal folding chairs seemed to be designed to generate maximum noise as the weight of your body moved them on the linoleum floor. When the other kids heard this they sang the chorus even louder:

"Never be late! *Never be late!*"

God, if you really are out there, I want you to know that I really hate that hymn.

I was grateful for the times that when Uncle Weston took me there,. We were always on time, even though he would ditch me pretty quickly for Priesthood Meeting and Senior Sunday School. I didn't want to risk future escorts so I didn't push him about what they were talking about in there.

Uncle Weston became a somewhat more prominent figure in my life when I turned twelve and was made a member of the Aaronic Priesthood as most Mormon boys did. Dad didn't actually oppose this because he seemed to think he had to honour the phrase "Your Mother would have wanted… "

At twelve I was only a Deacon and the duties were restricted to passing the bread and water out during Sacrament Meeting and attending some more meetings. Not too challenging but more time taken up with Church meetings.

Meetings bloody meetings.

Somebody had to take me to the extra meetings and my weekday caregiver Mrs. Shevchenko was a devout Ukrainian Catholic, so she was the wrong persuasion and gender. Uncle Weston moved from wherever he was living and moved into our basement. He was a pretty good patriarchal surrogate for the two years I was a deacon—he was always polite to the brothers and sisters at meetings and he never said anything that was too controversial or strange.

This arrangement fell apart when I turned fourteen and was expected to move up to be a Teacher—the next level in the Aaronic Priesthood.

My induction began with the customary interview with the local Bishop.

It started out well enough.

He asked me if I understood everything I was hearing at Priesthood and Sunday School and I replied truthfully that I didn't understand quite everything but I was trying.

seemed to satisfy the Bishop and he let me off the hook by telling me
no one expected me to have a fully developed Testimony at my age but
that I had to be resolved to keep on learning and to have an open mind.

Open mind. About as likely as that signal on Uncle Weston's radio coming
from Montana.

"And you have to be honest with yourself and others," the Bishop said.

I said that I would try my best to do that.

Big mistake.

The interview deteriorated when the subject of sex came up.

"Now I have to talk to you about what it means if you ever have sexual
intercourse… " the Bishop said, looking incredibly uncomfortable. "…
before you are married and with the girls… "

I kind of understood that it was bad to have sex before marriage but I
didn't appreciate why the Bishop was making a qualification about having
sex with girls. Who else would you have sex with? Now I know that it was just
one more trap.

But it didn't seem to be a problem for me. At fourteen the idea of having
sex with another person was about as likely as living on another planet.

Now, sex by myself…

And that was when it all got pretty sticky. The Bishop raised the topic of
masturbation and remembering that I had promised to be honest and open
I admitted that I had indeed tried it. My natural modesty kept me from
explaining masturbation was the closest thing to pure joy that I'd experienced.

But I don't think the Bishop thought there was anything pure about it at all.

"Don't you know?!" His eyes were tearing up. "To throw away all that
life, it's next to murder!"

I wanted to die.

I wish I had because then the Bishop exhorted me to "Put on the full
armour of God" and "Struggle to return to a state of spiritual cleanliness."
He concluded the interview by advising me that he and the rest of the local
Church Executive would have to fast and pray about what to do about my
"perilous situation."

It was about as bad a meeting that a fourteen year-old boy could have.

I didn't say a word about it but the outcome must have gotten back
home because Uncle Weston was severely pissed. My Dad just seemed a little
sadder and even more distant than usual.

Two Sundays later I was sitting in the Bishop's outer office while he and
Uncle Weston were having a discussion.

The idea of these two old guys talking about the religious significance of
me touching my penis was absolutely horrifying. Again, I wanted to die.

I kind of hoped there would be a big Technicolor explosion an[d]
would swallow me up, just like when Charlton Heston threw th[e]
tablets at the unfaithful Israelites in The Ten Commandments.

No such luck. Although, Uncle Weston's voice thundered out thro[ugh]
the walls near the end of meeting:

"The only thing a young man learns from that is how to lie!"

About 20 seconds later, Uncle Weston opened the door. He was red from
his collar to the top of his bald head.

"Time to go," he said.

And that was the last time I set foot in that Church.

Back in his Dodge, we were not taking the usual route home.

"Where are we going?" My voice was only slowly returning.

Uncle Weston's face was still red with anger. "I've got some work to do.
You might as well come."

Eventually we came to a stop at a small hanger near Pike Lake. The
building and runway were deserted.

Uncle Weston rolled up the hangar door and inside was something that
looked a little like the CF-100 fighter that was suspended over the Sutherland
Legion Hall. Except that it had no marking, was painted absolute black and
had rows of over-sized nozzles bolted to the undersides of the wings.

Much later, Uncle Weston would explain to me that those were the "Potash-
Uranium Fusion Propulsion Units". They called them "puffs" for short.

They were the result of my Dad's research.

"Married for time and all eternity."

I didn't remember anything all that detailed about my mother. But I do
remember a very sad woman who seemed to hang around the house a lot.

Dad never talked about how they broke up.

Eventually, on those long journeys between the solar systems, Uncle
Weston told me a few things.

I had kind of thought she had gone to Salt Lake City and re-married but
that wasn't exactly what had happened.

As we spiraled into yet another multiple-planet system, Uncle Weston
confirmed that my parents broke up because of some disagreement
between the universe as explained by science and religion. I had always
thought that it was something really stupid, like Dad accidentally
mentioning in Sunday school that Darwin was probably right and that
human beings really were descended from "lower species".

"No, it wasn't that," Uncle Weston said. "Your Dad doesn't give a hoot
about biology."

Ɪȷeepers, Uncle Weston, I thought. Your language is getting pretty

⏑at was the problem?" I asked.

We've got planet fall."

Landing on a new world. Great way to change the subject.

"Come, come, ye saints! No toil or labour fear!"

My first voyages into space were all with Uncle Weston. Dad didn't like going out any more.

I was more of a passenger than a co-pilot and I didn't have any scientific training so I wasn't much help with the research. But there wasn't much accountability back then so my uncle was free to bring me along just to keep him company. It was like another one of our camp-outs.

Once he landed us on a planet with a wide river of glass and set up our tents in the shadow of a mountain of jade.

Another time we walked among the shattered rectangles of an eons-dead civilization of machine intelligences. Nothing left but little plates of silicon.

"Someday we'll visit an inhabited system," Uncle Weston said. "But you need quite a bit of preparation for that."

Okay, Uncle Weston. This is definitely your turf, so whatever you say.

The night under the jade mountain was one my first trips so I had lots of questions. Like:

Since my Dad and my uncle had discovered the secret of interstellar travel, why weren't they world famous?

Why weren't people doing it all the time?

Why were the Americans still stumbling around on the moon? Why had the Soviets given up even on that?

Note the order of my questions suggesting my personal interests and priorities. It took me five or six trips to even think of asking about how the Potash-Uranium Fusion Propulsion system actually worked.

Under the jade mountain, Uncle Weston chewed slowly on one of his Spam sandwiches and finally started answering:

"We do have a little funding from the National and Saskatchewan research councils. That's how we can pay the other pilots."

Other pilots? He told me that they had about a dozen friends, ex- RCAF, who helped him and my Dad do the modifications on the CF-100s.

"The government knows that we are doing something interesting with Potash… " he said and took a very big bite of Spam and Wonder bread.

I sat there, waiting for him to finish, wishing that there were crickets or owls on this planet so I had something listen to.

Eventually, he swallowed and said:

"But I don't think anyone really understands what we're doing here

Certainly our retrofit spacecraft didn't have much room to take anythr.
back. Particularly if you liked to take your alienated teenage nephew along
on your missions.

But the vagueness of what we were doing out in interstellar space, or
even if we were in space, suited everyone in the Programme just fine. They
got to look around the universe without interference, which was pretty
much ideal.

It was fine for me, too. The voyages (we could do a good portion of the
Milky Way on a long weekend) were a welcome distraction from growing
up as an alien in Saskatoon. The local LDS made a few visits and phone
calls but I could sense that they were pretty relieved not to have me
wandering around their Church anymore. Everybody else in Saskatchewan
wasn't all that involved either. As good social democrats they were nice
enough but they really saw me as just another variation of the Mormon
species—and as everything else from Alberta—to be treated with some
distance and care.

Dad didn't really get too involved. As long as I kept my grades up he
didn't interfere with the voyages.

"… *for time and all eternity.*"

Then came Charlene.

I met her when I was doing my undergraduate work in math and
astrophysics up in Edmonton. It was a little further from the Programme
than I liked but I needed the training. I'd gotten my pilot's license before I
finished High School and with my uncle's advice I was more than qualified
to handle the spacecraft. I just needed to learn some science to be useful.

It's hard to explain how Charlene and I picked each other up.

We met at a cafeteria at the University of Alberta and found that we were
extraordinarily compatible. It's only somewhat more amazing than the
wonders of an exploding star how your ethnic background gets back at you.

Yes, Charlene was a serious Mormon. And yes, she expected me to toe
that line if we were to become a more permanent item.

I liked her so much that I was seriously thinking about it. I guess I thought
I could work out some kind of accommodation between the baggage I'd
inherited and the nature of the universe as I'd actually experienced it. Sort
of like my Uncle Weston seemed to have done.

My uncle took action after Charlene and I had traveled to Saskatoon for
Thanksgiving. We had dinner with him and my Dad at the Golden Dragon.

ere's the coordinates," he said handing me a set of punch cards. "You
ı to take this trip."

"*… all eternity.*"

The coordinates were for the Celestial Kingdom.

For those of you who are not Mormons, the Celestial Kingdom is the highest level of Heaven. Where the faithful and virtuous are reunited with their loved ones and live in eternal happiness with God, Jesus and the Holy Ghost. There are lower levels of Heaven for everybody else.

When I landed in my modified CF-100 with its "Puff" drive, I asked some questions and met my mother.

She'd been there for almost 20 years—after my Dad had me taken there.

In some ways I was just going through what every divorced kid goes through I finally had the opportunity to spend some time with my absent parent.

I'm sure she was my mother and I'm thankful to God (if there is such a thing) for the opportunity to see her. She was loving, happy and supportive.

Pretty much the opposite of what I remembered of her when she was married to my Dad.

But maybe that wasn't his fault either.

What I wasn't sure of was… where the hell I was. Maybe the fountains, the glorious choirs, the fantastic tabernacles, the presence of loving family ancestors, the pervading presence of white everywhere, on everything, within everything… maybe it was just *us.*

Maybe these were just telepathic aliens playing up to the cultural scripts my Mom and Dad brought with them. Maybe this holy place wasn't that at all, maybe this planet wasn't an inhabited place at all. Maybe it was just a place that reflected. Reflected ourselves.

I've always been bad with belief.

That's probably why I had to eventually say goodbye to my mother and return to Earth.

Frankly, I don't know where she's really living but I'm grateful that she's so happy.

"*All is well.*"

Charlene and I broke up. Big surprise. I'd been gone for six months without word.

Years later, I teach math at Evan Hardy Collegiate Institute in Saskatoon and the Programme is winding down. Dad died of cancer about three years ago. I try to convince myself that working with the potash-uranium hybrid materials had nothing to do with it.

Uncle Weston and I sit around his weird old radio and listen to transmission from deepest space from one of the aging pilots talking what strange and wonderful things he sees from the cockpit of his equally aging craft.

When the last of the pilots dies, the Program will be over.

I don't go out anymore but I keep wondering about the truth. What did I experience? My Dad and my uncle had found some way to short-circuit the structure of the universe. Had they found some way to hot-wire the keys to heaven?

Unlike many of the people I went to church with, I don't know with absolute certainness. I don't know the one revealed truth.

Maybe that's my testimony.

Learning the Language

Ron Collins

I ran down a corridor that stretched before me as far as I could see. The walls swirled in a camouflage of green and brown and tan and dun. They collapsed from all sides as I sprinted. The drumming returned—a slow pulse, almost the beat of a heart but drawn so thinly I could barely hear. I wanted to turn back, but my legs drove forward. My heart pounded against my chest. The walls brushed my arms. The air thinned.

Near the end of the tunnel I had to duck as I ran, a position that prevented me from seeing the final goal.

I woke then.

I lay in the darkness. Sweat rolled off my forehead, and a briny dampness lay on the flat of my upper lip. The dream was important—not a random event triggered by a daily happenstance. I can't run *from* something without running *to* something else, can't run from *someone* without running to *someone* else.

Even if that someone else was myself.

ooo   ooo   ooo

Gerald Riggs closed his son's diary.

He sat in the worn recliner he had given Daniel when the boy first moved out of the house. He wore a gray suit ten years out of style, and a thin tie even older. His shoes were black—worn, but comfortable with laces that had seen better days. Daniel's apartment was small: one bedroom, a bath, a kitchen that opened into the living area. Not extravagant, but clean. The furniture was neatly aligned, the bookshelves straight, the kitchen counter orderly. Everything was in its proper place.

Everything except Daniel, that is.

Daniel was gone.

He had nowhere to turn, nowhere to look. He had been to Daniel's work. He had called every friend he knew to call. The police wouldn't consider him missing until sometime tomorrow. So now Gerald sat in Daniel's apartment, reading his son's diary and searching for clues.

Daniel had always been a good boy—always kept his nose out of trouble and made good grades. He worked a series of decent jobs after school but never seemed to find one that fit him quite right, so he always talked about doing something different.

It wasn't like him to run, though.

Gerald rubbed his chin, thinking about Jean and about conversations they used to have about their only son. He made them proud of themselves. Raising him had been their life. They had hoped Daniel would settle down, that he would find a girl and raise a family. Everyone said such wonderful things about their boy.

But Jean had been dead twelve years now, taken by a cancer that grew inside her brain and stole what was going to be the finest years of their lives.

And Daniel...

A thin stream of sunlight spilled through drapery from the sliding door. The beam caught the threaded cover of the diary. Daniel always called it a journal, but Gerald didn't understand the difference and it read like a diary so that's what he called it. He ran his fingertips across the cloth, gently feeling its texture.

It smelled of cardboard and burlap.

ooo   ooo   ooo

I talked to Meredith tonight. She was cordial, as always. But she was humoring me again, talking to me but not really listening. I know better now. I used to think it was my imagination, but I know better. I sense things about people. I recognize their shells. I feel the true meanings behind their words.

When she said she was getting ready to go out, there was tension in her voice. A kernel of understanding grew inside me that said she was planning to stay in and watch television. I didn't tell her I knew she was lying. I don't think she meant any harm, and telling her wouldn't have been proper. But I had to know if I was right so I went to her place. Most of her lights were on and I could see the telltale pattern of a television screen.

When I drove home, the street lights made a corridor that seemed to go on forever. The drumming came again and I flashed to my dream. Back to the running—to the green and brown walls. I pushed it away and concentrated. By the time I got home, my temples throbbed and my muscles ached.

The drumming has never come when I was awake before.

ooo   ooo   ooo

Gerald closed the book and stood up.

Maybe his son was crazy, Gerald thought. After all these years, maybe he's gone insane.

His throat was dry. He walked to a small counter with a set of three self-contained bookshelves. Hardbacks filled two, but the lowest shelf was adorned with pictures and momentos. He focused on a small trophy—four inches tall, a golden cup mounted on a slab of wood.

Daniel had received it after a high school debate.

Gerald gave an involuntary smile. He could see Daniel standing at the podium, speaking with self-assurance, using gestures and language in perfect harmony. Chills ran up his spine as he sat on a hard-backed chair in the third row, watching his son control the audience, watching as Daniel gathered their energy, watching as he found the perfect cadence to his phrasing that would bring the judges to his way of thinking.

After the debate, Gerald asked his son how many times he had practiced his argument. Daniel replied that he hadn't practiced at all.

"I just said what seemed right," he said.

Gerald took a deep breath and opened the diary again.

ooo   ooo   ooo

I was restless all day, couldn't concentrate on anything for more than five minutes. It didn't help that Calvin was on my butt for inventory sheets and that Suzanne had called in sick for the third time this week.

Something is happening. When Suzanne called in I heard the sound of her baby's heartbeat through the line—or maybe it wasn't the heartbeat so much as the sound of blood pooling in her womb. The beating was so strong I had to ask her to speak louder so I could hear what she said. She was planning to go to the doctor so I didn't tell her about the child. I don't think she would have believed me anyway but, just in case, why rob someone of that special moment?

I'm glad for her. They've been trying for so long.

I worked the men's department most of the day. And I somehow managed to compose an inventory that appeased Calvin well enough to get him off my back until next month.

Then I skipped out a half hour early.

I couldn't help it. Everything was closing in on me. I could hear people's thoughts, see through their eyes. A stooped woman yelled at her little boy and I saw her towering over me, screaming obscenities and shaking her finger so close to my face that I thought she would scratch my eyeballs out. Heat from the delivery truck idling outside burned through the walls. We've got a snack bar in the store, and the cook's putrid sweat nearly made me gag as she pulled another rack from the deep fryer. The images were so strong, and the air so thick. I couldn't breathe. So I just got up and left.

Outside wasn't much better.

Rush hour was insane. It was hot. People were mad. There was an accident on Sycamore and Fourth Street. Pain engulfed me as I waited for the cop to wave me through. The cop was sweating and angry, too. He drank too much and did terrible things to his wife when he got home. He hated her, called her every foul name he could think of. But the drumming came through under it all, strong and bold, telling me that he hated himself more than he hated her—hated himself for keeping her from going back to school, hated himself for keeping her from growing beyond him.

As I drove, the city's grief cascaded in on me. Every corner had a story. A seven-year-old boy was shot here. An old woman left her coat there. That same old woman died in her sleep under this lamp post. A thirteen-year-old kid turned his first trick on this park bench. It was the same everywhere, every alley, every boarded-up store front.

By the time I left the city, I was crying. Drained. The drumming was still there but everything else had quieted. I drove on. The land spread before me—a carpet of green sawgrass and golden briar that waved in breezes that whipped around cracked boulders and Joshua trees with the same neverending crescendo of the ocean washing up a flat beach. The mountains were a purple ribbon on the horizon. The sky was a domed rafter of crystalline blue that smelled of timothy, wild onion, and brown earth.

I've been on this road a hundred times, but I never really saw before. I never really felt.

An hour later I was in the mountains. It was dark and I was hungry, so I stopped at a roadside diner.

It was a small place with tiled floors and metal tables. Two of the tables were occupied by locals. A lone truck driver sat at another. I took a stool at the counter. The waitress brought a pot of coffee and poured me a cup without asking if I wanted any. I looked at her and smiled. She was in her early thirties, thin, wearing jeans and an old shirt with the name of the restaurant silk-screened on the left breast. The patch was worn and faded so that I could only read half of it. She had tied the shirt tail into a ball at her side.

I ordered a ham and cheese sandwich and drank my coffee.

For the first time all day, I found I could take a deep breath and hold it. I ate quietly and listened to the jukebox as it played country songs. Not the slick stuff they play today. This was Hank Williams and Bill Munroe and Carl someone. I've never enjoyed country music before, but I did today. Maybe it was me or maybe it was the place, but the music seemed to emanate from the very core of the earth. It seemed right. Decent. True like standing in a field of waist high corn that stretched to the horizon. It made the drumming go away, or maybe I should say that the drumming seemed to fold into the music, knitting itself into the fabric of the sound and disappearing.

∘∘∘   ∘∘∘   ∘∘∘

"Disappearing."

Gerald stared at the word. Disappearing like Daniel had done, wrapped himself in the fabric of the world and disappeared.

∘∘∘   ∘∘∘   ∘∘∘

I woke with a start.

I lifted my head off the counter and looked around. I was still in the restaurant. It was quiet and dark out. No one else was there but the waitress, the cook, and me.

"Morning," the waitress said with a crooked smile as she came back with the pot of coffee. "We close in fifteen minutes. Wasn't sure if you were going to wake up or not."

My cheek was sore and prickly from resting on my arms. I rubbed life into it while she poured my coffee. "Thank you," I said. "What's your name?"

"Loretta." She smiled. "But folks who know me call me Lori."

I saw she was attractive. Not beautiful, but attractive in a way that made me want to sit down and talk to her for the rest of my life. She was a center of warmth and quiet and peace that I could circle around and plunge into, deep enough that if I did take that plunge we would never talk about the same thing twice and we would never run out of things to say. She walked down the aisle to put the coffee away. The drumming returned, growing stronger with each of her steps. It had never really left. It was always there, constant. It was universal language, the beat of a heart, the motion of a shark's spiraling stalk, the language of time. But, when she returned, the beat died down and space grew quiet.

She lit a Marlboro and blew the smoke away from me. The cigarette's tip glowed warm against the evening quiet. The smoke's coarseness bit into my throat.

"Who are you?" she said.

"My name is Daniel."

"No, I mean who are you?"

I sat there for a moment, not knowing what to say. For the first time in days, I was sitting with a person whose thoughts weren't leaking out at me. I almost didn't want to speak, preferring to drink in the quiet. But, something niggled at my mind. I flittered around her, darting left and right, looking for a perspective that brought enlightenment. But none would come.

Then, for the first time, I actually tried to read someone. Suddenly and without reservation I dove into her mind.

She had two kids in school and a husband, John, who treated her fine but rarely worked. Her job paid minimum wage with no benefits, and she had to put up with the owner's constant hounding to do it in the storeroom. Her teeth were bad, but she couldn't afford a dentist. When she got off work, she would go home and make box lunches and put them in the refrigerator for the kids to take to school in the morning. This weekend, her family would go to John's folks' for another cookout where the kids would get bored and John would sit on the back porch with his father and they would drink. Lori would listen to his mother talk about her life and then she would pile the kids and John back into the rusted Chevy and drive them home.

It sounded like a depressing life. But there was no regret in her, just the opposite. If I concentrated, really listened, I could still discern the drumming. But she didn't fight it. She was in step with it, in tune. Perhaps she had found true inner peace.

Yet, she was the one who had asked me who I was.

"I'm just me."

"No, you're different."

"Why do you say that?"

She dragged on her cigarette and blew again. A smile touched her lips. "I can't really say. You're just different." She put her hand in front of her, thumb up. "Where everyone else is in-line, you're off the other way." With the hand that held her cigarette, she pointed off in a perpendicular direction.

I looked at her closely, stared her straight in the eyes and saw honesty in them. I've never heard it put any cleaner than that. I'm off the other way. I took another swig of my coffee, slid off the stool, and threw a wad of bills on the counter.

"Thanks," I said. And I walked out the door into the cool mountain evening.

For the first time I realized I knew exactly where I was going. My headlights cut the night as I wound my way over the twisted, two-lane highway. I turned onto a gravel road and drove up into the mountains. My tires ground stones into the earth, crunching as they rolled. I stopped at an overlook, got out of the car, and gazed at the city below. Its borders were etched in yellow street lights that blazed like small suns. Traffic moved, passing under those suns like lifeblood slipping through veins and arteries.

I squinted and strained then. Try as I might, though, I could not find the city's heart.

I walked across the road, making my way around a large boulder before coming to an open space. It was familiar to me. My mom and dad used to bring me here when I was a kid. I remember eating lunch and playing games of tag and leap frog. I remember riding on my dad's shoulders and picking leaves off the trees.

The mountainside here was huge. It was solid, perfect, the smoothest piece of granite bedrock I've ever seen. The rock's sheer face stretched high into the sky so that, standing there at its base, I felt like I looked upon an infinite plane—like I could reach out and know any piece of the universe just by touching it. There was something deep about this place. Something important. The night air was filled with a buzz, a pleasant hum. I drew the deepest breath I could hold and let it out as slowly as I could.

This is the place.

This is where the drumming converges, where harmonics intertwine, their amplitudes merging and cancelling to create pure silence.

∘∘∘   ∘∘∘   ∘∘∘

Gerald knew the place Daniel wrote of.

He remembered Daniel's weight on his back, Jean's smile as they ate lunch. He remembered these moments—and he remembered others. Gerald and Jean used to picnic there while they were dating. Things were different then. Easier. They would spread their blanket, covering it with their meal and drinking in each other's presence. It was where he had proposed. It was where they went on their first anniversary.

But those days were gone. Gerald hadn't been to the mountain since Daniel was a boy.

His watch read 1:30.

If he hurried, he could make it there by three o'clock.

He tucked the book into a big pocket in his suit coat and walked toward the door. The floorboards creaked under his feet, an eerie, rhythmic cadence that made Gerald contemplate the drumming that had apparently driven his boy away. He got in his car. The engine started easily. Daniel said he could hear people's thoughts while he drove. Daniel said he could feel things other people couldn't. It all sounded crazy. But maybe it wasn't. Maybe Daniel wasn't really crazy at all. Maybe his son was special.

Against all hope, Gerald tried to open his mind, tried to hear the beat of a drum.

But he felt nothing.

Daniel's diary was heavy and awkward in his coat pocket. He pulled it out at the next stop light and laid it on the seat beside him. Now that the book was in plain sight, Gerald felt it mocking him, proclaiming his failure as a father, taunting him, daring him to read further.

The light turned green.

Gerald guided the car down the street, the diary still playing at the corner of his mind, weaving itself through his thoughts. At one point he thought to throw the thing out the window, release it into the world and free himself of it. But it was all he had left of Daniel, all that remained of his family. He would never let it go.

At the next traffic light, he opened the book and read.

ooo   ooo   ooo

I'm not as afraid.

The drumming isn't as scary as it was. No longer schizophrenic. It is a song, hypnotic like a mother's lullaby. It heals. It calls me, demanding an answer.

I know I will respond.

ooo   ooo   ooo

A horn blared from the car behind him. The light had turned green.

Gerald put the diary between his legs before pulling away.

ooo   ooo   ooo

He parked the car on a gravel turnoff facing the open sky. Daniel's car was there—empty. He got out and shut the door. Standing in his suit, tie slightly askew, sweat pooling at his armpits, Gerald felt uncomfortably out-of-place.

He crossed the road without looking for traffic, walking along the base of the mountain, rounding the large boulder.

Gerald stopped there, stunned.

"Daniel?"

His son was at the base of the huge wall of stone, embedded in the mountain, eyes closed and arms outstretched, as if he had merely laid back for a nap and been absorbed. Gerald rushed forward, leaping over smaller stones and scrambling to keep his balance amid loose gravel that scritched and clattered against each other.

Daniel's face remained uncovered, as well as portions of his fingers. Gerald clawed at the rock, trying to reclaim his son, prying at it with his bare fingers, scratching and tearing at the stone until his nails ripped and his fingertips bled. He cursed and screamed. His breathing became heavy, the thinness of the mountain air making it harder and harder to struggle against the very Earth itself.

Tears streaked his eyes. Sweat flowed from his brow down his cheeks and nose, down his back and arms, cooling in the mountain air and bringing him shivers.

"Daniel!" he called with a thick voice.

There was no answer.

Gerald rested his forehead against Daniel's temple and whispered through tears into his son's ear of stone. "Daniel…. Don't leave me, Daniel."

The wind blew through the clearing, moaning softly against the smoothness of the wall.

Slowly, Daniel's eyes flickered open.

Gerald cupped the curve of Daniel's temples and stared into those eyes. They were calm and rested, clear blue, reflecting clouds that hung high in the sky. They were the eyes of a sage, wise beyond Daniel's years. They stared back at Gerald, telling him that his boy was fine, telling him everything was okay.

But still Daniel sank. The rock crept over him, swallowing his body, covering him feature by feature until he was a raised form embossed on the mountain. Gerald caressed the stone's surface, feeling its warmth and granularity. His fingers traced the shape of his son's face, his lips and nose, the gentle taper of his cheekbones.

There was peace there, contentment. His fingertips, the only part of Daniel that remained flesh, still curled out from the mountain, pointing to the sky as if beckoning it closer.

Gerald ran his hand along his son's arms, stopping to pat the shoulder. It was an unconscious gesture, one that he had made a million times— patting his son on the shoulder and smiling, patting his shoulder and saying they would talk later, patting his shoulder and telling him how the two of them would get through life without his mother. A familiar sensation eased its way into his consciousness, an attraction, the link that every father feels for his son. He hooked his forefinger around Daniel's, rubbing his thumb gently over an exposed knuckle. Standing there, holding Daniel's hand, Gerald looked upon his surroundings, truly scrutinized them for the first time.

The mid-afternoon sun washed over the clearing, lifting out details and dazzling his eyes with vivid colors—brown bark around sturdy trees, white rock running with blood-colored veins, green grass anchored in cracks and clinging to the stone wall like a child suckling its mother's breast. Leaves blanketed the trees, scarlet with the autumn turn, some drifting on the wind, floating downward to gentle landings.

As if through a fog, the beating came to him then. The drumming. It was clean and rich, pure—a beat that throbbed inside his head. Gerald cried again. He cried for Jean; he cried for Daniel. But most of all he cried for himself, for his wasted years, for letting his life pass him by.

Daniel's finger grew rigid. Heat seeped away and the finger slipped deeper into the stone.

Gerald stood alone at the base of the mountain, running his hands along the smooth surface of the flat rock, whispering to a son who would not be coming home again.

The drumming slipped away, leaving mountain noises to fill the silence and a void inside Gerald's life that was as big as his heart.

ooo　　　ooo　　　ooo

I am a very lucky man, for I can hear.

ooo   ooo   ooo

The rest of the pages were empty.

Gerald sat in the driver's seat and fingered through them, seeing their whiteness against the shadow of the afternoon.

He closed the book and got out of the car. There was no energy to his gaze, no focus. The city sprawled below him. A stiff breeze blew grit into his eyes. He hadn't noticed the wind until now and its presence surprised him. The musty odor of the mountain was everywhere—damp, with the sweet tint of pine needles. He stepped forward until his toes played at the edge of the cliff that tumbled downward at a sheer angle. A few pebbles slipped over the edge, plummeting into the creek that hissed and gurgled somewhere below. Gerald looked down and shook his head. He raised Daniel's diary to his lips and lightly kissed it. With a gentle fling, he tossed the book into the mountain air. It seemed to float for a moment, then tumbled downward, its pages fluttering like a moth's wings as it fell to the water.

He returned to his car, started the engine, and began the trip back home. He turned on the radio and found the only station he could receive that played country music.

He let it play, and he listened for the drumming.

Fear of Widths

David D. Levine

When they got off the plane at Mitchell Field, there was nobody there to meet them. That's when it really sank in.

He had to sit down in the waiting area until the sobs stopped coming. His wife held him, awkward in the hard airport chairs; passing strangers looked concerned but did not stop, intent on their own business. After only a little while of this he blew his nose and joined the crowd. He was already pretty much cried out. But his heart sat in the hollow of his chest like a lonely farmhouse on the vast prairie.

So many times I've flown to this airport, he thought as they walked to the baggage carousel, and now I barely recognize it. Every time before, his parents had met him at the gate. Smaller and smaller, grayer and grayer. After the heart attack Dad lost weight (finally, after years of nagging) but it didn't make him look healthy; instead he looked shriveled, like all the juice had been squeezed out of him. Mom just got smaller and rounder every year, and moved more and more slowly.

And now they were gone. Run down in a crosswalk by a drunk who ran a red light. The funeral was tomorrow.

The rent-a-car place wanted to give him some American tuna boat instead of the Japanese compact he'd reserved. When he received the news, he felt for a brief unreal moment that he stood on a vast whistling plain, cold and alone—but the feeling passed as his wife began to protest. He touched her arm to quiet her and said to the agent "We'll take it."

He didn't realize until later that the car was a Plymouth, like the one his folks had when he was in sixth grade.

The airport interchange was under construction. The Billy Mitchell bomber that had once stood triumphantly at the entrance to the airport was now stuck on a pedestal like some drab and awkward butterfly, tiny and barely visible to the speeding traffic. Nothing was familiar. But when the car pulled onto the freeway, he saw the hotel where he'd attended a high school job fair. The gas station where he'd tanked up on the way out of town, returning to college after Christmas break. Billboards for a bank whose logo had changed, but whose name brought a thirty-year-old jingle ringing into his head.

And the horizon.

How could he have forgotten the horizon?

In Portland there was no horizon. Not like this. In Portland there was always something between you and the edge of the planet: trees, or mountains, or clouds. Even in those places where there was a bit of horizon, there was something to draw the eye away from it. Something important and grandiose, like Mount Hood.

Here there was nothing bigger than the horizon itself. Oh, there were stands of trees here and there, but they were funny little round things, just beginning to bud—a bare wisp of greenery like a teenager's underfunded beard. They didn't have a chance against the line that went all the way around.

The horizon was a lariat whirling around his head at eye level. A shimmering, dangerous line. But who was twirling it?

The blare of a horn and his wife's gasp brought his attention back to the road, and he braked hard. The red lights ahead got much too close much too fast, but the squeal of tires did not end in a crunch, and a few minutes later he was back up to highway speed.

He gripped the steering wheel harder to still the trembling in his hands, to maintain his focus.

It was difficult to watch the road when the infinite horizon sucked at his attention. It was so very flat here. Even the tiny rise of a freeway overpass was enough to give a view for miles. A panorama of factories and churches, standing out from a background of boxy little houses: tiny square things, brick and clapboard, with pointed roofs against the snows. So simple, like a child's drawing of a house. Each with a little concrete stoop, just two or three steps high, and a simple, flat lawn of green grass. Perhaps a bush or two. Not like the overhanging roofs, deep porches, and sprawling rhododendrons of his neighborhood in Portland.

How could a cartoon of a house keep you safe from the vast open spaces? Portland houses had solidity; those overhanging Craftsman roofs enclosed, protected, defended. Just in case Mount Hood decided to blow off its lid like Mount St. Helens, revealing the horizon beyond, they were ready. Milwaukee houses were naive, defenseless. They clung to the flat landscape like lumps of chewed gum; their only strategy was to be too inoffensive to bother with.

The houses were tidy here, but the cars were in bad shape. The one passing him right now was nothing but a lace of rust, its bumpers held on by bungee cords. Back home—back in Portland—a car that age might have five more years in it if you kept the oil changed. But here they salted the roads.

Or was it the salt, really? That was what his father had told him. But now he felt it was the great widths of this flat landscape that sucked the life out of cars. Storms swept hard across the prairies, with no mountains to block their effect; maybe the North Pole, its effects also undamped by terrain, pulled molecules of metal out of cars, leaving them riddled and weakened. Then the weather finished them off.

They got off the freeway and headed west on Capitol. Parks and fast-food places that might have been anywhere; suburbs whose names he'd forgotten. Seen from street level, the houses weren't really so tidy: paint was peeling, shingles loose. Midwestern winters were hard on houses. Or maybe it was the neighborhood; he had not lived here in so long, he didn't know if this was one of the bad ones. Probably that was it. There were too many boarded-up storefronts here for a "good" neighborhood.

But something in him believed those stores were not closed, just boarded up against the pull of the prairie—the infinite widths of horizon that kept drawing his eyes from the road ahead of him. Like a hurricane, he thought. He imagined cautious Milwaukee shopkeepers boarding their windows against the horizon: grim Germanic faces, starched white aprons, pencils tucked behind ears… and ten-penny nails clamped between white lips, eyes glancing over shoulders as the shopkeepers nailed up another sheet of plywood.

Unlike a hurricane, though, the horizon never went away.

He turned right on Brookfield. Though closer to home, this area was less familiar. It had been farm country while he was growing up; now it was all strip malls and condominiums. Square boxes bolted to the land, with parking lots like scabs.

He gripped the wheel so hard his knuckles whitened, but his hands still trembled. He was sure his wife could feel the car shimmy. She touched the back of his hand, an offer of comfort. He held her hand briefly, then clutched the wheel again. Not speaking.

His father had always gone very quiet at times of high emotion. His silences burned like pure hydrogen, a hot invisible flame.

Left on Bluebird. Lots of new houses, but there was the Johanssens' place. Someone had stuck a cedar deck onto it and given it a hideous sky-blue paint job.

And now his house. This tiny, cartoon thing, with its faded yellow paint, had been his home for sixteen years? That gable, that black window, had been his bedroom? He had often wished for a tree outside his window, like the trees down which boys in adventure stories climbed, but he had had nothing but a sheer drop to the concrete patio. That drop didn't look like so much from here.

It wasn't his bedroom now. It was his mother's sewing room. Had been. Empty now. Empty of people; full of possessions, of memories. All had to be sorted, cleared, sold off. His wife had told him about clearing out her grandmother's trailer after the funeral. But there had been sisters and cousins to help there; it had been a family event. He was an only child.

"Are you sure you don't want to stay in a hotel?" He realized he'd been sitting in the driveway with the ignition off for some time. Still gripping the wheel. Staring up at the bedroom window.

"No. Waste of good money, when there's a whole house sitting here empty." It was exactly what his mother would have said.

"Well, we should go inside then." She opened her door, and a polite repeated chime sounded from under the dashboard. A cold March wind tugged at her hair. "Are you OK?"

"I'm… good enough. Just leave me here for a moment." He pulled the keys from the ignition, silencing the chime, and handed them to his wife. "The key with the yellow thing on it opens the front door. I'll be along in a minute." She kissed him on the cheek and closed the door behind herself. He heard the trunk open and close.

The horizon was tremendous. Terrifying. Three hundred and sixty degrees across. He was glad of the car's roof pillars, glad of the tiny house and the garage, glad of anything that could hide a little of it.

The sun was beginning to set, that enormous sky shading orange to purple, brushed with trails of cloud like finger paints. Lights came on in the house.

Finally he could delay no longer. He unbuckled his seat belt. He opened the door.

He clung to the armrest as he climbed unsteadily out of the car. Gravel crunched under his shoes.

He stood next to the car, holding onto the door with both hands.

Then, knowing what awaited him, he swallowed and let go of the door.

Slowly at first, he fell away from the car. Gravel sliding under his shoes, then under his knees. When he hit the black plastic edging at the edge of the driveway he began to tumble, rolling over and over across the flat, green lawn. It was like all the times he'd rolled down grassy hillsides as a child, the dirt and grass thudding against his shoulders and elbows. But as he tumbled faster and faster he began to panic. Clawed at the grass, pulling up clumps of sod and earth with his fingernails. No use. The tidy little house with the glowing windows, clinging like a limpet to the flat, flat prairie, dwindled each time it came into view. Then he was no longer tumbling, but falling.

Falling free.

He fell all the way to the horizon.

THE LONG SKY

John H. Baillie

The land without walls made him nervous,
all that blue pouring down and flowing out.
He felt threatened, whisked away, a speck insignificant
against an expanse too broad
to fit anywhere but the prairie.

So he tied cruel steel hooks to his hands, to his feet,
and he lay spread-eagled, full-bodied across the sod,
digging in; for fear the clouds envied him his gravity.
But he forgot to tie down his forehead.

The sky yanked his eyes back
filling his vision with too much light.
As the sun rose, hooks or no hooks,
he was away.

The little boy sighed,
too late to tie his string
to that disappearing foot—
the man made such a beautiful kite.

Fox in the Wind

Renée Bennett

Uncle Daro was telling her all about the space station and how important Jays was in the building of it, and waving his cane so she could tell how big everything was going to be. Then he stopped walking and lifted his head, sniffing, aged nostrils flaring to the touch of the wind. Little Rabbit scuffled a few paces further through the dust of the road before noticing. She watched him over one shoulder, then the other, as he shuffled to face north, then west, then south, each time craning his neck, nose leading his face, with his big ears sticking out to each side like bucket handles. Finally he faced east.

His eyes grew wide and he took a step forward. Little Rabbit frowned and sniffed at the breeze, but there was only dry grass and dust and cowshit and somebody's tractor. She crossed her arms and scowled. "What do you smell, Uncle?"

Uncle Daro took another step forward. "Fox," he said, his voice so low it wove into the sound of the wind through the grass and the buzz of the grasshoppers, dragging her up on tiptoe to hear it. "I smell Fox." He shuffled forward and put a hand on her shoulder; she came down off her toes with a thump.

"But the foxes all died," she said, wriggling under the weight of his hand. "Ages ago! Before I was born. Teacher said so."

Uncle Daro sniffed the wind again. "Only ten years since the sickness," he said. "What's ten years, to Fox?"

"Forever," said Little Rabbit, who wouldn't be ten years old for another year and a half. "Ten years is forever!"

"Fox is clever," Uncle Daro murmured. "Fox is lucky." He smiled down at her. "They say Fox is about to play a trick on someone, if he lets you smell him. Have I ever told you how Fox got his black feet?"

Little Rabbit shook her head until her braids whipped. Uncle Daro chuckled and started talking, walking again, leaning on her shoulder.

That was all right. Even if he was old and weird, Uncle Daro always told good stories. Little Rabbit hoped Jays hadn't heard this one yet, so she could tell it to him tonight when she called him on the comlink.

000   000   000

He hadn't. «It's 'cause Bear caught him looking through his tent, and he had to go through the campfire,» Little Rabbit said. «He was running away, see? He knew no one would expect him to go that way.»

Jays smiled and ran his gaze over his monitors. Pusher One and Pusher Two were on schedule, moving the third boom into place on the station spindle. He could see them out the port headed toward him, a string of lights against the starry black of space. His headset speakers relayed the chatter of the construction crew. He spoke into his throat mike. "Didn't his feet burn, cousin? Didn't that hurt?"

He could hear her sigh of exasperation over the main speaker. «Of course his feet burned! That's why they're black. And it did hurt—lots. But Bear would have beat him up and that would have hurt more, and it was only a little campfire, and he wasn't in it for long. It couldn't burn all of him.»

He had to laugh. Pusher One asked for a position confirmation; he switched channels and gave it, switched again and said, "How could he run away from his enemies, with burned feet?"

«He jumped in the river and swam all the way home. Wouldn't you?»

Jays laughed again. "If I could find a river. No running water in space, cousin."

«Not even taps?» Little Rabbit sounded appalled.

"Not yet." Two more weeks before the station skeleton was complete and they could spin the ring for artificial gravity and at least another two after that before they'd be able to trust the plumbing. Jays could hardly wait.

«Then what do you do when you're all icky and sweaty from work? How do you take a shower?»

Jays winced and wondered how he could explain the bath bag to his young cousin. "Well, there's this big plastic bag, and we pump it full of mist…."

«Like the sweat lodge?»

"Um. Something like that."

«Ick,» said Little Rabbit. «I'm glad I'm not in space.» Then, «Guess what Teacher asked us to do in school today!»

Pusher Two wanted a confirmation; Jays switched channels and gave it before replying, "What? She asked you to do your homework twice? In purple pencil?"

She giggled on the line. «No! But maybe I'll do that next time, that sounds pretty. No, she asked us to bring fox things to school, so the government men could pick them up.»

"Government? What fox things?" Jays double-checked all his screens with a sweep of his gaze. All clear. "Foxes are extinct."

«I know that! But the government wants stuff like furs and dried paws and stuff. So they can de-con-struct them and make new little foxes out of them. That's what she said, anyway. They're asking everybody to bring stuff, us and zoos and museums and everybody, so they can have lots of var-i-ation. Gene stuff, I think. But Uncle Daro says they don't have to—he says he smelled foxes today. While we were walking home down the road.»

Jays snorted and didn't say what he thought about Daryl Morning Cloud's sense of smell. "Well, that may be so, but… " he dropped his voice to a whisper. "Can you keep a secret?"

He heard her gasp; there was delight in the return whisper. «Yes!»

He grinned. "I have fox toenails in my medicine pouch."

Another gasp. «Really?»

"Really. You can take them to school for the government men tomorrow, if you like."

The position lights for Pusher One and Pusher Two both went red; they were starting final approach with the boom. The voice of the construction boss was tense as he joked with his crew. Jays looked out his window and saw the pusher lights poised on either side of the station spindle, where the smaller glitters of individual work pods swarmed. He tapped out the code for the laser guidance; the position updates came back true to the centimeter. Little Rabbit was saying, «But I can't go into your medicine pouch! That's sacred!»

"I say it's okay, so don't worry. Besides—they're to make more foxes, right? I think the ones Daro smelled might be lonely for cousins." He shot the all clears over to the pusher crews.

He could almost hear her thinking. «You mean, like us?»

He grinned. "I get lonely for you, cousin. Don't you get lonely for me?"

«Well, yes… .»

Pusher Two's light was blinking. Jays tapped out a new position update; Pusher Two was accelerating. He cut to Pusher Two's channel before Little Rabbit could go on. "Pusher Two, this is Guide One. Throttle down, Pusher Two. Harley, you're coming in too fast."

There was a grunt over the link. «Uh… negative, Guide One. No can do. Got a stuck valve… Pusher One, this is Pusher Two. Am releasing the boom, Pusher One. She's all yours.»

«Negative, Pusher Two! Am at wrong angle… .»

«Whoops,» said someone over the construction team link.

Jays hit the all-points alert and looked out his window. He could see the lights of Pusher Two veering away from the spindle. Pusher One's nose was skewing inward. The construction pods were scattering in all directions. His fingers pulled the positions out of his screens; the situation was there when he looked down.

Disaster. "Pusher One! Feeding coordinates! Shove her hard, Greg!"

«Roger,» was the reply, and a lot of heavy breathing. «Engaging burn.»

Jays watched his display numbers change too slowly. "Pusher Two, this is Guide One. We need help with the boom here—she's got too much inertia."

«Guide One, Pusher Two. Taking ventral jet off-line. Be there in seventy seconds, sooner by miracle.»

"Miracle's what we need… ." Jays tapped in more codes, thinking fast and hard. "Pusher One, this is Guide One. I read the back end of the boom accelerating faster than the front end—she's tumbling, Greg." He set the guide computer to calculating possibilities. "Feeding coordinates. Burn for two."

«Roger.» Jays' fingers clattered over the keys. Then, «Burn for two,» said Pusher One, and Jays looked out the port. He could see the back end of the boom rising beside the spindle, the green light on the end glowing like an emerald firefly. He looked down at his boards.

Why wasn't the boom slowing down? That burn should have chopped its forward momentum to almost nothing. And why was Pusher One accelerating sideways? "Pusher One, this is Guide One. I'm reading a veer on that burn, Pusher One."

A pause. Then, «Affirmative, Guide One.» Another pause. «Mia says we lost the service arm to the boom when Pusher Two let go. Best guess: it bent the vent baffles on the way done.»

Jays grimaced and looked out the port; the green light was even with the spindle apex. A quick check told him that the construction pods were all out of the danger zone, at least. He keyed his link. "Pusher Two, where are you?"

«Fifty-five seconds, Guide One.»

He looked down at his boards at scrolling numbers. "Too late, Harley. I read that boom as headed right for me." Like a baseball bat coming down on an egg. He noted Guide Two coming on-line on his board. "Guide Two, this is Guide One. We have a problem."

He traded numbers with Guide Two for ten, fifteen, twenty seconds, aware each moment that hundreds of tons of cross-braced aluminum and ceramic construction boom was headed for an intersection with Guide One, his fragile steel bubble of a habitat module, strung on a cable between booms one and two for positional stability. A construction pod sat at the other end of the module, his ride out—if he could get to it in time.

«Done,» said Stephanie in Guide Two. «Get out of there, Jays!»

He was already getting, snatching for his helmet, shoving off his seat and soaring out the open door in one motion, bouncing off a bulkhead and arrowing through the habitat beyond. He could hear the pushers talking through his headset still; Pusher One was going to try to shove the boom one last time, maybe miss Guide One and hit the cable instead, which might let Jays live.

Or at least present a better salvage situation. "Is this what I get for telling Little Rabbit to go into my medicine pouch?" he asked the air, and grabbed a strut to correct his aim for the last bounce to the pod.

The boom hit. It sheared away the pod and crumpled the doors to the lock. Decompression tore the helmet from his hand, almost tore him from the strut, but animal instinct made him hold on. He was battered from all sides as the fittings to the habitat sucked past him, as the heat whipped away and cold gnawed at him like jaws, like fire…

… And then it stopped. There was still air. Barely.

Jays held his breath and blinked. His nose itched in the lower pressure, drier than the coldest prairie wind, smells attenuated, even his own, rank and terrified. Air hissed, like that same wind through winter grass. He had the absurd impression that something rough and furry had dragged its tail under his nose.

He looked toward the lock. Bunks, a chair, loose panels from cabinets stoppered the opening, all covered, at the moment, with a translucent film in an unstable seal. He could see the film suckling outward in at least two places.

"Bath bag," he murmured, and looked around wildly. Another was flopped over a panel within arms reach; he grabbed it and scooted back into Guide One and slammed the door. Beyond that thin protection, he heard all hell cut loose in the module again… and vanish with the air.

There was no heat left in Guide One; he could feel cold nibbling at his face and hands. Soon it would gnaw and snap. Air pressure was going down as well, slow but sure. Emergency air was under the main panel; he stuffed the hose into the neck of bath bag and dragged it over his head, got the air going and took a deep, badly needed breath before keying his headset into the chatter on the main channel. Guide Two was snarling directions for search efforts into the debris field left in the wake of the boom.

He felt like Fox must have, after Bear, after the campfire, after the river, popping up in the last place anyone would expect to find him. "Negative, Guide Two. This is Guide One. I'm back at the board… ."

Stephanie squealed. There were cheers from the pushers, and he could hear the construction team yelling, too. He grinned.

«Roger that, Guide One. Pusher Two, this is Guide Two. Jays needs a cab ride, Harley. You're catching.»

«Roger, Guide Two. Hey, Jays! You owe us a beer!»

Jays laughed. "You get me out of here before I choke or freeze, you can have two beers, Harley."

«Bribery. Great working with you, Guide One. There in one hundred.»

Jays checked his monitors. He'd barely have room pressure in one hundred seconds, but the bag should hold at least that long. He checked the main boards.

He could see Pusher Two headed toward him; the angle seemed wrong until he realized the boom had broken the cable Guide One was strung on, and he was now swinging nadir to where he'd been. Pusher One was easing sideways toward the boom; he watched the runaway slow down as the ship made contact and commenced a burn. Construction pods were swarming after the ends of the cable and into the debris field. For the moment, he had nothing to do but wait for his ride.

Little Rabbit's comm-link was still active. He keyed it. "Hello?"

«You're back! I got your medicine pouch and the toenails. They're black.»

He had a moment of vertigo; it seemed like years—forever—since he'd had this conversation. It almost had been. "Right. They are."

«I'd show you, but you aren't here. When are you coming home?»

Home. He felt tears prickling at the corners of his eyes, could almost smell home, dust and grass and sunlight and even the herbs in his medicine pouch, the leather wrapped around them. He took a careful breath. "Not for a long time, sorry. Got a lot of work to do up here, before the station is done. Say, cousin… could you do something for me?"

He could almost hear her wrinkle her nose. «Me? What can I do? You're way up in the sky! »

Jays could feel an itch ignite along his soles as cold tickled at them. He winced and pedaled his feet. "You can do one thing, better than anyone else I know." He grinned. "You can tell Uncle Daro he tells good stories."

All the Room in the World
Holly Phillips

Welcome to Canada, the sign said. And underneath, *Bienvenue*.

In the blank space between English and French someone had written in unofficial paint, *The Final Frontier*. Peter eyed the amended sign from the middle of the arrivals hall crowd. He was starting to sweat under his raincoat and wished he dared put his cases down long enough to take it off. The blank, watching helmets of the security guards dissuaded him.

It was always hard, coming home again. Too long in New York dealing with the chaos of the UN enclave and he got to thinking of Canada as the great white North of his grandparents, a silent haven, somewhere to escape to. You and a few billion other people, he thought.

The public address system chimed, then spoke in a woman's voice, barely audible over the crowd. "Would all Canadian passport holders please proceed to the green customs corridor. Canadian passport holders only, please, to the green corridor. Thank you and enjoy your stay in Winnipe—" The announcer clicked off her mike before she finished the word.

The hall hissed with a stifled surge of complaint. Peter avoided the eyes of his fellow travelers as he crossed the hall, he didn't want to see either the envy or the hostility he knew would be there. No-one dared to create a disturbance under the threat of the machine pistols of the security guards—the international news was still full of the Pearson Airport massacre—but the silence that followed the Canadians was sullen.

The line under the green banner in the corner of the hall was short. There were two officers behind the counter there, a blond woman with Slavic cheekbones checking documents, and a man of Asian descent who ran bags through the tunnel of the x-ray machine. The woman took Peter's passport out of its plastic case and slid the card into her computer terminal's reader. Her eyes flickered between the screen and Peter's face, judging the differences between the digitized version and the original. His black hair had gotten a little grayer since the photo was taken, but his brown eyes and blunt features looked the same as they had for years.

"Date of birth, Mister Joseph?"

"June 14, 2022."

"And where are you coming from today, sir?"

"New York."

"Purpose of your trip?"

"I work there. At the UN. I'm just here on holiday."

The customs officer flicked another glance at him, scrolled down to the occupation line where the diplomatic emblem flashed. Her face stiffened. "Sorry." The card snicked free from the reader's slot and she slapped it into its case, slid it across the counter without looking at him. "Next," she said.

"Anything to declare?" her partner asked.

"No." Peter put his carry-on bag and battered computer case side by side on the counter, opened them for the routine search. The man next in line handed his passport to the first officer.

"This isn't a Canadian passport."

Peter looked over, his attention caught by the hostility in the woman's voice. The object of her anger was a small, dark-skinned man wearing a duffel coat several sizes too big for him, so that the soiled hem of his flowered sarong barely showed.

"Yes. Canada." The man bobbed his head a little for emphasis. He pushed the pale blue card across the counter, furrowed his brow in puzzlement when the woman pushed it back.

"No," she said loudly. "This is a UN travel permit. You have to go through regular customs. Over there." She pointed over his shoulder to the crowded, stationary lines. "This," with a thump on the counter between them, "is for Canadian passport holders only."

"Yes," the man firmly replied. "Canada." He pointed in his turn at the sign on the wall. *Bienvenue* could be read above the lowered heads of the crowd. He flipped his pale blue card over so the dove emblem could be seen. "Travel permit, yes? For Canada." In exasperation he ran his finger back and forth over the coded strip, as if he could access the information stored there, display it somehow for this obtuse woman to read and comprehend. "For to be living in Canada."

The customs official flushed and snatched the card from under the dark man's hand. "This," shaking it in his face, "gets you to Canada. It is not—*not*—Canadian. You take *this*," she slapped it back on the counter, "over *there*." She pointed once more into the arrivals hall, where another hundred people were trying to fit themselves in. Something like despair passed over the dark man's face.

"You're free to go, sir."

Peter turned, startled, to find his bags closed and ready for him at the bottom of the x-ray chute. "Ah," he said. "Yes. Thank you."

The customs official nodded without taking his eyes off his partner, his hand on the butt of his holstered gun.

"Welcome home, sir," he said.

ooo   ooo   ooo

Peter took a cab from the airport to his sister's house. It was near the end of a typical February day, cold, with a steel-gray rain pounding the piles of dirty snow into slush. The cab driver was unhappy with the weather, with the traffic, with the cost of the new government-approved solar rechargers and how hard it was to get a means-of-livelihood rebate for one if you were self-employed, especially if your car was a piece of shit that needed a five hundred dollar adapter before you could even use the new recharger… Peter stared out the window, grunting into the pauses, his mind still caught on the scene at the airport. Would the woman have been as hostile to the refugee man if he hadn't followed Peter, a diplomat of the generation that had helped establish the Refuge Zones in the North? Would she have been less hostile if she knew the plans that were being proposed among the Refuge nations? Hard to say, when even he couldn't make up his mind. He found himself sitting with his jaw clenched, his fists tight on his knees, and spent the rest of the trip persuading himself that the need to decide, to choose, just wasn't that urgent. Yet.

His sister Suzanne lived with her wife Patrice in the ground floor of a big frame house near the flood zone. The front garden was full of Patrice's antique roses. On his summer visits, the three of them would sit on the screened-in porch, laughing, drunk on the scent of the damask rose climbing the wall. Now, the pruned canes made stiff black streaks against the disintegrating snow. Peter rang the doorbell again and waited, shivering, until he realized no-one was home. He slithered his way around to the back of the house, the slush on the walk soaking his city shoes, found the spare key and opened the back door onto the cold, dim kitchen.

There was nothing unusual in the chill, what with the late spring and the energy moratorium, but there was also the smell of dust and old grease, the pile of dishes by the sink, the hard-edged echoes when he shut the door. Suzanne and Patrice were proud of their big flat, they tended it like a revered and aging relative, spent most of their combined incomes on it: Peter had never been here when it wasn't warmly lit and smelling of good food and beeswax. This emptiness reminded him of his Ottawa apartment in the days after Mathilde had left. The sound of the rain seemed to seep in with the cold.

There was a note for him in Suzanne's writing on the table by the front door: *Sorry I'm not here, I'm working afternoon shift this week. Booze in the cupboard, I'll bring Thai home for dinner by eight. Love, S.* Nothing about Patrice. Peter went back to the kitchen and dug out a dusty bottle of amber malt, poured himself a slug and drank a fierce mouthful. He turned on the furnace for a guilty blast of heat, then, in penance, ran a sink full of lukewarm water and washed Suzanne's dishes. When they were drying in the rack he took the rest of his whiskey into the living room and stretched out on the couch.

∘∘∘   ∘∘∘   ∘∘∘

He woke when Suzanne came home laden with a net bag full of battered plastic containers. He staggered to his feet and met her in the hall.

"Oh, it is you," she said.

"Sure." He took the bag from her hand. "Who else would it be?"

She closed the door without answering, shrugged out of her gray raincoat and hung it on the rack. She was two years older than Peter, but her long, black braid was scarcely touched with silver. She and Patrice had a running joke about how Suzanne was staying young, waiting for Patrice to catch up the ten years' difference in age, but today Suzanne's face looked lined and weary, dark circles around her eyes.

"Come on," she said. "Let's eat before it gets cold. I'm starving."

"Sure," he said again, and followed her into the kitchen.

When she saw the clean counters, the dishes in the drainer, she said wonderingly, "Did you do that?"

"Yes. Five minutes rental on your furnace."

"Oh, Peter, you didn't have to do that," she said, and burst into tears.

∘∘∘   ∘∘∘   ∘∘∘

They talked over pad thai and spicy prawns, with the background hush of rain audible over their quiet voices.

"There's no story, really," Suzanne said, sighing. "Patrice finally found a job in her field. In Quebec."

"And that's it? She's gone?"

"She's with a freelance software designer in Montreal, a woman with a government contract who's working in exactly Pat's area. It's not an opportunity she could pass up. If everything works out, she could have enough to bring me in as a dependent spouse as soon from now as a year."

"Well," said Peter cautiously, "a year's not so long."

Suzanne made a face. "Assuming they don't change the residency requirements again. It's going to be hard enough proving employability as it is. Nursing is too low tech for immigration, especially to Quebec." She swallowed wine and added, eyes on her glass, "Unless you have microgravity training. Six years since the last lunar mine closed for lack of profit, and suddenly everyone's hiring astronauts."

Peter set his glass down, disguising a wince. "Rumor has it the UN's drafting a new Space Development Incentives Program—"

"Rumor?" Suzanne broke in. "Rumor has it the SDIP's moved in next door to you at Population Relocation."

The rain fell hard against the window. "That's a new one on me. Who's your source?"

"Mathilde."

Peter couldn't stop the automatic stiffening of his face, the clenching of his gut. Even to himself he couldn't pretend it was this minuscule threat to security and not his ex-wife's name. Before he could scrounge up something to say, his sister said, "Come on into the living room. I have something to show you."

They left the dishes, brought the whiskey bottle, and lit candles to save on power. The wavering shadows helped to fill the spaces Peter had missed seeing before, where Patrice's favorite pottery and pictures had been. Suzanne left him to find whatever it was.

The room was designed to feel warm, even when the thermostat was in the teens. There was a red rug on the polished wood floor, the drapes were brown and gold. But it seemed empty without Patrice, the fire of the marriage; sturdy Suzanne had been the iron and bricks that contained the heat. He was like her that way, he thought, nursing a mouthful of liquor. Only she had held on to her flame longer than he had managed to do. The familiar sadness that he thought of as his Canadian melancholy settled in, not entirely unwelcome.

And then Suzanne came back with what she had to show him: a letter, not a hardcopy but an actual letter, handwritten on the back of a torn up map of the North of a hundred years ago, when it was still tundra, and still Canadian. "It's from Mathilde," she said, and handed it to him without meeting his eyes.

He'd already recognized the uneven blue scrawl. "When . . ."

"I got it about a month ago, but it was written in October, you know what paper post is like."

"Why didn't you tell me?" He smoothed the papers on his knee. "Or maybe I should ask, why are you showing me now? I didn't even know you were in touch with her."

"Maybe now I know how you feel."

He flinched from the memory, not of the scenes, the fights, the apartment trashed and empty, but of that feeling when it was all over and Mathilde was gone. All he'd been then was a shell hopelessly waiting for someone who would never come. He drank whiskey, and then picked up the letter and read.

Dear Sue

How are you? I hope you and Patrice are well. I hear the drought in the South is letting up a little. I wish we could trade weather! Its like living in a damn swamp up here, just one big mud puddle with almost more flies than people. Yes, I finally came up North! Every night I go to bed thinking I will go back in the morning, and every morning I wake up knowing I can't be anywhere else but the Zone. In some ways the protest camp is even worse than the refuge townships (we have more dogs!) but the people here are amazing. No damn sleepwalkers like the South (well, okay, maybe one, but he's a poet so it's okay). The UNits are bastards, but sometimes I think true freedom can come about only under true oppression. And sometimes I catch a glimpse of the True North, and know anything is worth this fight. God, Sue, what a mess they've made! Anyway, I'm running out of paper (I stole it from the latrine!). Love to Pat.

Mathilde.

And then a postscript in a miniature scribble up one narrow margin:

ps: is Peter still with UNPRO? Is it true they're making a move on the space exploitation assholes? What goddamn world are they living on? If they'd only come and see my world, it would open their eyes for damn sure! M.

Peter took a slow breath before he spoke. "You've known she has been in the UN Refuge Zone since October, and you are only telling me now?"

"I only got the letter a couple of weeks ago."

"You said a month."

"Okay, a few weeks."

"And you are only telling me now."

"Christ, you sound like dad!"

He put the letter and his glass on the coffee table, pinched the bridge of his nose between his fingers. "Sue, for God's sake—"

"I don't think she writes me because she hopes I'll show you her letters. I'm her friend, Peter, not your spy."

"Then why the *hell*—" he caught himself shouting and lowered his voice "—are you telling me now?"

Suzanne eyed the letter. "Because I wanted to know if what they're saying is true."

"What, that someone from Relocation had coffee with someone from Space Exploitation?"

Her round face hardened, showing muscle at the jaw. "That the new push into space is going to be based on slave labor. That the rich bastards are going to get even richer on moon mines run by the expendables. That Canada and Australia and the other Refuge countries are pushing for profit shares in return for processing the refugees—"

"Oh, for Christ's sake, Suzanne! You sound like Mathilde!"

"Meaning?"

"Meaning hysterical and paranoid." Not wanting to say it, and saying it anyway.

"Yeah? How about right, Peter? Isn't that why she left? Because you never could admit it when she was right and you were wrong?"

"Wrong about what?" he demanded, a decade's worth of anger hot in his throat. "Wrong about saving millions of people's lives?"

"You go up North like Mathilde did and see just what exactly you were saving them for," she said, looking frighteningly like their mother, "before you get all self-righteous with me."

"Why the hell," Peter replied, voice breaking rough, "why the hell do you think I'm here?"

ooo   ooo   ooo

That had silenced her that night, but the next morning, as he was getting ready to leave, the argument had broken out all over again.

"But Suzanne," he had said through his hangover, "if it's so bad, why don't the protesters just leave? Nobody's keeping them there. The reverse, if anything."

"Because they believe in what they are doing. I know how hard you tried to reach a compromise we can live with, Peter, but the fact is that most Canadians are sick of compromising with the rest of the world. The North was ours, it still is ours, and sooner or later the UN will have to recognize that."

It was the first time she had ever spoken so bluntly. Patrice would have turned her aside with a joke long before now. But Patrice wasn't there.

He gave an angry laugh. "And to hell with the eighteen million people in the world who have nowhere else to go."

To which Suzanne had replied, "Peter, the townships *are* hell. The only question is, how much longer until we're all living in one too. Pretty damn soon, I guess, if you start up with the space program again. Too many resources, Peter, too much pollution… "

The same argument, always the same, as if he'd never heard it before. As if he didn't lie awake nights thinking it over, and over. And over.

∘∘∘   ∘∘∘   ∘∘∘

He reached the border two days later at noon.

∘∘∘   ∘∘∘   ∘∘∘

The town of Manitoba Crossing was barely more than a point of intersection between the UN military compound and the Canadian bureaucracy that struggled to impose some sort of civilization on the Refuge Zone. There were a couple of motels, a few restaurants and bars, a department store, and the train depot surrounded by bus bays, customs sheds, the hospital and the jail. Rowhouses curled around the edges on three sides, east, south and west, housing for bureaucrats and officers.

Peter had been to the Crossing on a UN tour shortly after it opened. He would have expected it to have grown, as the Zone had become more populated, but something else had changed as well, something that made him slow long before he came to the first speed bump and peer through the rain-spotted windshield.

They had built a wall around the town.

Massive cement blocks topped with razor wire, the Wall squatted on a base of raw mud and filthy snow as if it had been torn up whole from the earth. No-one had ever seriously considered building a barrier along the thousands of kilometers of moraine and muskeg that was the Northern border: it was rightly assumed that even the few refugees willing to risk the penalties of leaving the Refuge Zone would think twice when faced with the vast, empty wetlands between North and South. But perhaps there are other reasons for walls: some distinction must be made between inside and out. So they put a wall around the crossing, and a police guard even on the Canadian side of the gate.

"May I see your identification, sir?"

The constable wore a stiff black mustache and a yellow slicker with RCMP stenciled across the back. He took Peter's passport, ran it through the reader on his belt.

"What is the purpose of your visit?"

"Mostly personal. I'm on holiday, I came up to visit an old friend." No need to mention the friend was squatting in a protester's camp.

The constable nodded, his eyes on the narrow data screen. Peter's passport card in hand, he glanced over the battered rental, hesitated at the Rent-a-Wreck sticker on the windshield. "Is this your vehicle, sir?"

Peter had put his hand out to take back his passport. Now he slowly put it back on the steering wheel. "No. I rented it in Winnipeg for the drive up."

"We're going to have to take a look, sir. If you could just pull over to the right by the guardhouse there, and park on the yellow square."

It was automatic, the tightening belly, the sweat on the palms. "Can I ask what this is about?"

The constable considered, while the rain ran down the folds of his slicker to drip on the plow-scarred cement. "We had a rental explode in Alberta Crossing a couple of days ago, killed some people including the driver. It looks like someone at the rental agency may have engineered the device."

Peter stared. "I didn't hear anything about that."

A couple more men came out of the guardhouse and stood in the rain, watching. The constable waved in their direction with Peter's passport. "If you could pull over, sir, just a routine check."

"Of course," Peter said, and pulled over to park the car on the yellow square.

He sat in the guardhouse and watched two constables, a corporal and a German shepherd take almost an hour to perform the "routine check." The sergeant in command of the post gave him a cup of bitter coffee and, once she got off the phone with headquarters, his passport as well. She also told him, he supposed on the strength of the diplomatic tag on the card, more than he wanted to know about security threats at the Crossings, most of which, it seemed, came from the Canadian side of the border. She was in the middle of a description of a three-sided shoot-out between Wild Northerners, the First Nations Alliance and the RCMP in Saskatchewan in the fall (and about which he had heard nothing In New York—*nothing*) when the corporal with the dog came in to say his car was clean. They gave him a sticker, signed and dated, to put on the dashboard, and sent him on his way. He got in his car with a headache starting behind his right eye.

There were only a couple of hours before dark, and Peter had intended to get a room in town, go on into the Zone in the morning, but an urgency had come upon him, a feeling of risk, even of danger. Mathilde and bombs and guns had become fused together by the pain in his head. He was afraid to wait, afraid some limit might be reached. So he drove the empty length of Gate Street, wet pavement flanked by stubborn ridges of snow, until he reached the border itself, lit by floodlights even in daytime.

The blue-helmeted Egyptian Peacekeepers were indifferent to the RCMP sticker on the dash. They all but dismantled the car, working with a slow, dispirited diligence that gave Peter plenty of time to read all the notices informing him of what they were searching for and the penalties he faced if they found it. It seemed absurd, the idea of smuggling anything through the Crossing when all anyone needed to get over the border was a canoe and a compass, but he supposed they had to check. A bright blue bus roared past in a cloud of illegal exhaust and the Egyptian lieutenant took a gloomy pleasure in announcing the arrival of another train-load of refugees.

"Pretty soon the North is all full up, hey? Then maybe they set up a Zone in the Sahara, fill up the desert with people. Then Canada sell us some water, hey? Trade some of this damn rain away for something useful."

Peter grunted sympathetically. He had been to Cairo last year for a meeting with the very new African Space Corporation, and just as the North was swimming in water the ex-tundra could not absorb, so Africa was drowning in waves of sand. If only they could trade sun for rain, water for sand: give some of the new lakes decent beaches—not that anyone but the black flies would enjoy them. He said as much to the lieutenant, but the man only shrugged and spat. He had been transferred here in the fall, he knew only the winter miseries of dark and snow and rain. He would welcome the summer heat, he said, whatever the humidity, however vicious the flies. Peter shook his head, but said nothing. No-one could imagine the Northern insect plagues until they had experienced them.

And then this search, too, was over, and he was crossing into the Refuge Zone. Huge steel sign boards lined the road: International Refuge Zone patrolled by UN Peacekeepers. ALL vehicles subject to search. All persons must be prepared to show VALID ID to UN personnel upon request. ALL visitors must register at township HQs. And finally, roughly stenciled on a sheet of whitewashed plywood: *The Final Frontier.*

ooo   ooo   ooo

There were no signs pointing the way to the protest camps, but Peter had a rough map scribbled by the lieutenant, along with an indifferent warning about the protesters' attitude towards the UN. There didn't seem to be much point in explaining the difference between a Canadian diplomat and a UN official. As far as that went, Canadian diplomats weren't likely to be any more popular than the "UNits" were.

The invisible sun settled towards the south-western horizon and the rain grew heavier, pocking the surfaces of the cold-weather rice paddies that flanked the road. In a few weeks they would be full of bare-legged people stooped over bright green seedlings, ringed by children throwing stones at the hungry water fowl that flourished across the expanding wetlands, but now they were as empty and lifeless as flood waters.

The gravel road to the protest camp skirted close by the sprawl of Singapore Township, at one point edging to within a hundred meters of a living compound. Bunkers of gray cinderblock on sandbagged dikes leaked tatters of steam from tar papered roofs. Three men in down jackets and muddy sarongs patrolled the outer wall, clearing the melting snow away to check the dike for erosion. They stared up at Peter's car as he jounced down the track, and they did not look angry or resentful, despite the length of sharpened rebar each man carried. Merely tired and cold, weighted down as the Egyptians had been under the February rain. Peter thought again of the patient crowd in the Winnipeg airport and wondered if they, too, would build a huddled warren of buildings under the vast Northern sky. Did none of them step off the bus and look around them, sighing at the relief, saying, Thank God, at last some room to breathe?

The road wound on, past more paddies, past the generator station and the crow-infested garbage dump almost as wide as the township; on and, eventually, up a low rise clad in young spruce so uniform in size and spacing they had to have been planted. Dusk closed in around the car. Below the rise a yellow light blinked on in the window of a house, and somewhere nearby a dog began to bark. Peter bumped down the hill in low gear and pulled up in front of the house. The rain falling through his headlights obscured the buildings beyond, all but the glow from the neighbors' windows. He sat for a moment in the car, head throbbing, listening to the rain on the roof and the dogs. When none one appeared at his window, he opened the door and stepped out into the mud. The smells of wood smoke, wet dirt and dog shit were strong. He slogged up the piled cement blocks that did duty for front steps and knocked on the plywood door. The rain was cold and hard on his head.

The door opened a crack and a scrawny man with a beard and a bright red sweater stared out at him. "Yeah? What do you want, UNit?"

"I'm not a UNit. I'm a friend of Mathilde Gaston. Do you know if she's anywhere around here?"

The man just looked at him, eyes narrowed in disbelief. A woman in the room behind him yelled, "'Oo the 'ell is it?"

He turned his head to shout back, "A UNit. Says he's a friend of Mathilde." The door opened wider, spilling a wedge of light across Peter and revealing the round, wrinkled face of a native woman.

She looked at Peter a moment, mouth pursed, before asking, "What nation?"

He almost said *Canadian* before he took her meaning. "Cree. Well, my mother was."

"Huh. What you want wit' Mathilde?"

"She's an old friend. She wrote my sister a letter saying she was up here, but then my sister didn't hear from her again. She started hearing rumors, you know, and got worried, and since I was coming up anyway I thought I'd check and see how Mathilde was doing. Is she around, do you know?"

The woman pursed her lips again. The bearded man beside her hawked loudly and spat into the rain.

"Wait 'ere," the woman said, and left the man to guard the door. Peter's hair and shoulders were wet with rain; the air that drifted through the door smelled of wet wool and burnt grease. He stood patiently, trying to look bland and trustworthy under Bearded Man's suspicious stare, half-hoping they'd tell him Mathilde was gone.

But then a familiar face looked out at him over Bearded Man's shoulder and Mathilde said in a voice that made it clear she was less than delighted to see him, "Peter? What the hell are you doing here?"

∘∘∘   ∘∘∘   ∘∘∘

She took him to her "cabin," a one-room shed built of cinder block scavenged from a township construction site. She had a narrow bed in one corner, an ancient orange couch with broken springs in another, an oil drum stove in the third and a table in the fourth, leaving just enough space in the middle of the room for two people to stand and argue.

"What," Mathilde asked for the third time, "are you doing here?"

Peter rubbed his temple, which only seemed to make the pain worse. "As I said. I came up, at Suzanne's insistence, to make sure you were all right. Now that I know you are in prime fighting condition, as I told her you would be, I can go home."

"Fine. So go."

He shrugged, zipped up his jacket, and turned to leave.

"Oh, for fuck's sake, Peter, don't be so damn childish!"

He gave an angry laugh. "I just can't win with you, can I?"

She folded her arms and frowned at him, a stocky woman in a brown cardigan and jeans. She had changed in the two years since he'd seen her last, gained a pound or two, a few wrinkles, a few gray hairs among the brown. But no, he thought as she tipped her head back to look down her nose, she hadn't changed a bit. She was still the most judgmental woman he knew. And she still swore too much.

"There's no damn way you came all the way up here from New York just to see if I'm okay."

"Not New York. Winnipeg. I'm on vacation."

She gave a short laugh, an echo of his, and spread her arms wide. "Welcome to the vacation paradise of the North. You're lucky you came up early and beat the rush, we're getting real popular with the Californians."

He sighed and jerked the zipper on his jacket open. The heat from the peat fire in the stove was stifling. His head started to pound.

"Come on, Peter, you're not here for the scenery, and you're sure as hell not here to see me. So what? Don't tell me you've finally come up to see the consequence of all the deals you've made with the devil?"

"All right."

She went on staring at him. He put both hands to his temples and pushed.

"What's the matter with you? Still getting those headaches?"

"Yes."

"Huh." A pause. "I probably have some aspirin somewhere."

"Thanks."

She didn't move for a moment, then sighed and bent to pull a tin box with a red crescent on the lid from under the bed. She did indeed have a bottle of aspirin, also what looked like antibiotics, and no doubt other things Peter didn't want to know about. She gave him two crumbling white pills and a plastic mug of sour water.

"So where were you going to sleep tonight? The Crossing closes at six, you know."

"Yes, thank you Mathilde, I do know. I will sleep at the Singapore visitor's center."

She gave him that who-let-this-idiot-loose-on-the-world look he had come to hate passionately in the months before she left him. "The visitor's center is full of refugees, Peter. Singapore is eight months behind their building schedule. They had sixteen people freeze to death in tents this winter. I doubt they could give you two square feet of floor right now."

"Fine. I'll sleep in the car."

"Don't be stupid," she snapped. "You can sleep on the couch."

What was he supposed to say, thank you? Judging by her look, yes. He gritted it out through clenched teeth: "Thanks."

"I don't have any extra blankets."

"Fine."

She nodded. "I guess you'd better sit down. You want something to eat?"

Between the peat fumes and the headache, the thought of food made him nauseous. "No, thank you."

She shrugged, pulled another tin box from under the bed and thumped it on the table. "So, how's Suzanne?"

He sat on the only kitchen chair and told her about Suzanne and Patrice while she set a pot of couscous on the stove to cook, and it made her angry. But then, as she went on talking, it became clear that she was angry about everything: the weather, the UNit harassment, the townships. The townships especially: both the conditions of overcrowding there, and the expansion of building and agriculture over formerly "pristine" country.

"But Mathilde," he said, caught once more in the rut they'd dug between them years ago, "you can't have it both ways: either they're crowded or they have to expand. One or the other."

"Not if you'd stop pumping people in by the busload."

"Mathilde." He put his head in his hands. The aspirin didn't seem to have done a thing. "Indonesia is a smoking volcanic ruin. Half of Asia is under water or getting washed out to sea. Half of Africa's sand. Where, exactly, are those people going to go?"

She slapped a lid on the pot and planted her fists on her hips. "All I know is, you can't save the world by destroying what's left of the wild. We should be planting forests, not townships. We need *more* green, not less. *Less* towns, not more."

A bubble of rage swelled in his breast, and popped. "I know that, Mathilde. I've gone to damn near every environmental summit since I was posted to the diplomatic corps. Don't you think we all know?"

"Then *why*—"

"Where do we put the people? Just tell me that one thing. You can save all the wilderness you like, Mathilde. Make the planet green again, clean the air and the seas—God, I wish you could. But you have to put the people somewhere, Mathilde, and you have to feed them something, or else you have to kill them all. And who's going to do that, Mathilde? You? Me? The Wild Northerners?" He waved a hand at the glossy propaganda posters that papered her walls, then shook his head, weary and sore. "You have to put them somewhere."

She opened her mouth, and slowly closed it again. Said, finally, "But not here. There isn't enough room here anymore." And turned silently back to her dinner.

∘∘∘   ∘∘∘   ∘∘∘

Much later that night, lying awake on the back-breaking couch, Peter listened to the wide Northern silence. The rain had stopped sometime earlier. Now there was just the pop of the cooling stove, his breathing, and Mathilde's.

Then Mathilde, knowing he was awake as she had always known, said what he had been expecting her to say all evening. "Is it true, Peter, what they're saying? About Relocation sending refugees into space?"

He sighed into the dark, not sure of what he was going to say until he said it: "Yes, it's true."

"And that's why you came up."

"Yes." More silence. Then: "They've asked me to chair the commission. I wanted to see… "

"It's bad here, Peter."

"I know."

"I know you tried, but it's no good. It isn't ever going to work."

"I know."

Silence. Breath. A soft wind touched the roof of the shack.

"If they send anyone," Mathilde said, "they should send us all. We've been here too long. We've outstayed our welcome."

The wind blew harder, clearing away the clouds that veiled the stars.

Peter said, "I know."

MIR

Mark Anthony Jarman

Outwardly, the Soviet Union and the Communist states (except China) are remarkable for fixity and stability.

—*Robert Wesson (1980)*

Our perfect Moldavian cottage so far below with the desolate neighbours too close to us, too close with their sooty garbage fires and narrow-faced acquaintances slamming doors of stolen German cars. Their rainbow collection of mongrel cars and the sun over the route of the new emigrés. The neighbours' pure white cat hides in our stricken apple tree; this luminous ghost of a cat, in love with my husband, crosses our fence everyday.

For 147 days I have worked in Mir, a woman, a scientist working inside this government skull and sculpture while dragging the drugged southern stars.

Take your vitamins, the peaceful voice from earth says. Ride the bike. Mir means peace. There is no peace. There is too much noise up here, too much machinery. From the Baikonur Cosmodrome (which is actually not near Baikonur) I flew up in a cramped Soyuz on the back of a Proton booster. An American was going to come but he was too tall for the Soyuz. We zigzag the earth. I have special shoes that attach to the floor. I am growing taller but losing weight. I am a cuckold.

Forget the arrogant occurring light that settles itself on your little town at dusk, the low sun opening the molecules of blood in each brick. That last yellow minute bathes us, illumines us, ruining us for work or decency or alcohol. Wait a few minutes more and when the neighbourhood air no longer smells of the day's lost bets and congealed meals and memos, then gaze up at me crossing the plank fence every night, up in the swirling milk eddies. Wave because I can see you. I'm winking. I'm zero at the bone, I'm deciding which port to go out when the time comes.

°°°   °°°   °°°

My province is science since they've put a hood of stars over my head, put the horns on me. They have housed me inside the sky's glittering Chinese alphabet of lights, soured me inside the perishing dialects of spy satellites. Solar panels spread out like lustrous angel wings, feeding us our diet of kilowatts.

Romanenko has a cheap Spanish guitar up here and we sing along. We pin up family photos, faces under the duct pipes. A little chocolate would be nice, perhaps some of my mother's gingerbread. Once we ate sturgeon, caviar, pate. Now the Birulevsky Experimental Plant is out of money. My space station is a clean white bone tossed by a starving dog.

I am conducting experiments on ovulation and reproduction in weightless environs. We're growing crystals, seeds, potato eyes. There are eight computers; so many switches on every wall and nowhere to hide. I'm always bumping into things, like our little lost monkey who squeezed from his harness. The monkey had fun pulling everything out of the walls and floors. He escaped his harness; can I escape mine?

When you float there is no up or down. They painted the floor darker so we can know which way is down.

One of my daily jobs is to examine everyone's tongues, *aaah*, make sure we are going to live long and prosper. This is like being stuck in a rather lively bathroom for months, a small lit tunnel, but we are young; we won't die. Yuri doesn't want to go back, wants to set a record. We smell but at least there's a small shower now. We smile for the photos. We won't be the same though. We struggled to get here, to be heroes. Now we stare out the pocked window, drifting, an eye moving but not moving, homesick, cranky, with no particular place to go, daydreaming about our families. Are they lighting a candle now? 147 days.

My husband is petting that pure white cat. The apple tree has been attacked by caterpillars. It tempts them. They spin webs and lay eggs.

My mother is making black tea and thinking of the war. I can tell these things. Their last evenings and foggy dawns before the counter-offensive, two wedding bands, then trains funneling to the Kletsaya assembly point, moving at night toward the icy Volga, long trains full of excited doomed Mongols moving up to the front in the dark. Their high cheekbones, their new weapons and banners, their fur boots and parkas and the fury of artillery and the locomotive's iron wheels crashing on the single track that leads to the frozen burning enemy.

000   000   000

My mother's first husband died near the end of the Great Patriotic War; died at Memel, on the Baltic Sea, just inside the border of what used to be Prussia. At the edge, at Prussia's eastern edge. The edge of space. Swords and horses and katyusha rockets. How much blood has sluiced down those fluid borders between Muscovy and Poland and Lithuania and Prussia?

Later my mother had another husband. I feel both men are my father, a live father and a dead one. In the Great Patriotic War my mother worked in a half-ruined tractor factory converted hastily to manufacture tanks. Her first husband drove a tank from Stalingrad to Memel, perhaps a tank she worked on. He followed the river and finally hit the sea. The Great Patriotic War would be over soon.

The last of the living Germans were surrounded, shitting their drawers in frenzied pockets on the shore. They were staggering ghosts with dysentery, typhus, their heads emptied of the words to *Horst Wessel*, their eyes black and burning. How many pieces of smoking metal had they left strewn over Eurasia; how many skulls and brains; how many grey horses had they eaten? Memel was just one of their many hells since the Thousand Year Reich had started walking backward from us across the steppes. People forget that it took years for them to fall back, years of losing a few yards everyday. They tried but they couldn't kill us all. We had no help, except for the Mongols.

I wonder if the Mongols still talk about the war, I wonder if they miss their enemy. With an enemy you exist. Maybe they started killing each other after they ran out of Germans and Rumanians.

Someday I'll visit Memel. I could jump out of here if I timed it right. I want to see Memel, Klaipeda, where the Neiman River, coming all the way from Belorussia, pours into the Kurland Gulf.

My mother's first husband was advancing in a T-34 and a German destroyer out on the water hit his tank with a lucky shell. That skull had a tongue in it. My first father did not find the exit. He found shrapnel and pale fire. My first father was excited to smell the sea and then a ship got him. Nothing is what you expect. What do you expect? Not to burn. They all burned. The small groups of howling Germans were saved for a moment. Perhaps they could float down to Danzig.

In Mir I pee into a vacuum tube. Down below my feet is a brightly lit stadium where the Hail Mary pass rises like a rainbow and is picked off by the Cleveland back. The wars are over now, they say. We have screens to show us the world, the grass stains, the lines on the lit field, the rows of zeroes. Greetings comrades. Thanks, the black man jokes in his tight football pants. He taunts the despondent white man who threw the ball. Well why did he throw it to him if he regrets it now? The lost yards, lost face. Thanks, the man now possessing the ball says. *Spasibo.*

　　ooo　　ooo　　ooo

I am starting to see things. Pilgrim ghosts have shied away from the smoking cities, the new wars, the launchpad fires; citizens are searching for a new saviour, searching for a sturdy Slavic lineman on steroids. Monsters of the Midway. Gus Grissom burnt up before they got off the ground; Patsayev celebrated his birthday in orbit but all of his crew suffocated on the way back down to earth. It's so quick. The valve failed and their few cups of air flicked out into space to find a new home. I'd like to do that. Like an old horse knowing the way home, the craft landed on automatic and the ground crew opened the doors to greet the CCCP's new heroes. Patsayev and his crew didn't say hi. Gone such a long time and nothing to report. This counsellor is now most grave. Starstruck and out of luck. My mother had me late in life. I was gone a long time. Someday the Hail Mary pass will work: they have such faith in it. Toss it up and see what happens.

I see Our Lady of Infidelity is a wife, an eye, an eve. She's in a white deck chair, a green apple shining like a globe in her lap. My husband approaches Our Lady of Infidelity with two glasses of something unhealthy. E.V.A: this means to actually get out of the space station: Extra Vehicular Activity. Eva, Eve, even, evening, eventually. Cudgel thy brains no more about it. Floating up here I see them, see it all. Bodies burning like a dust-red rodeo. Their doomed ice cubes clapped to their tongues; their happy hands and quick lands where they travel.

If I wish to sleep they strap my blue sleeping bag to a wall. A monkey's harness. I can't sleep. Polyakov said women are too hysterical for orbit. Romanenko's cheap Spanish guitar: I'd like to bash him over the head with it. I think of my cottage, the fig tree and its charmless long-tailed birds hammering at my two crops of fruit, and my husband whispering with his lady friend, thinking I don't hear them. I let them all feed. The planet doesn't seem like my planet anymore. Too many luminous ghosts and glands crawling the apple tree, the neighbourhood.

The masses cherish simplicity. I'm tied up in my work. I'm tied up trying to sleep in the evening's white stars, their bleached hair shooting out over the day's stuttering apple blossoms, blackberries, and earth's intimate clouds breaking my brain. The stars become backward blossoms, sucking you in; become my backyard, flaming like Quebec sugar. The men's ugly vacuum suits with the zipper down the front. And such obvious obscure love unfolding below me. Such gravity, such attraction between.

000   000   000

Then to place my gloved hand on the steel handles, on the six possible doors that open to it all, allow you to go drifting out where it is so beautiful, where you become a paid ghost with no province.

Poyekhali! I say, Let's go! No fuller earth or exit, no fuller reach. Quiet as sex. Not like my mother's first husband brewing up in a burning T-34. He was not quiet. My mother's first husband roared in his shell, his hell, roared in his chains. My real father. Am I becoming a class enemy? In his burning tank he had no exit. I have six. The airlock's simple bargain. Liberty. I will escape where he did not. I will sneak from the shell made for me to meet him in his. I'll go skateboarding on the moon, ride right up the curved side of a crater, get some air.

ooo   ooo   ooo

Over Canada I spy three blonde children on a night lawn; they clutch their grandfather's Japanese binoculars; their father allows them to stay up late to watch me pass over the mountain. They can watch me tumble out the hatch.

Look Dada! The space station!

And there's the cow jumping over the moon. Or is it a Rhesus monkey? I really need to take a stroll. It looks so serene out there, unnerving. There's Uncle Joe, he's moving kind of slow. Uncle Joe saved us at Stalingrad, didn't he? Our smirking Georgian peasant, our king of shreds and patches. The monkeys in the electrodes make such sorrowful noises. I will come way out, farther than Cho Fu Sa, than Memel. A willow there grows aslant the brook. My sky is full of buzzing freezer burn voices. Look up at me! I tremble like an automobile because you have let me down.

I lack travel, lack trouble, lack nothing really, except a country, a drink, a Hail Mary pass. I'm in orbit, a woman moving but in a circular river. We go round and round, lugging the guts into the neighbour's room. I want out of this circular river. I want to smell the sea, the Baltic, the atoms of autumn. The Berlin Wall is being rebuilt; they got a grant from Exxon. Maybe they can sell it again. *Dosvidanya*: until we meet again. There are no maps; I create new heavens.

I am not mad. I am the new improved post-cold war siren, a little low on currency, standing beside the shifting glittering shore. My fingers on the door that divorces you.

OUT OF SYNC

Ven Begamudre

They were at it again. I listened closely, and I knew. It was more than just the wind.

I must be the only adult in Andaman Bay who falls asleep unaided. Sometimes, though, when the wind rises in pitch and windows shudder, or when it slides down the scale and walls rumble, I flick on the white noise. Its soothing hiss can block out everything, even thoughts of the Ah-Devasi, out there in the aurora. No one wants to believe the aurora is alive. That's only a tale, we claim, invented long ago to keep children from wandering too far. Especially north, where the mountains rise so high an entire search party can lose its way in the canyons. I sighed, got out of bed, and pulled on my robe. From the doorway of the children's room I listened to the twins' breathing, the rise and fall of their breath out of sync. I'm sure they dream of birthdays. They're hoping for a Khond magic show at their upcoming party, and how can I refuse? But, oh, that Cora! She must have been teasing during all that talk about the Khond murdering us in our beds. Teasing even when I asked her point-blank:

"Could you really kill me and the twins?"

"Oh no, Miss," Cora said. "I could never kill the family I work for." She put breakfast in the oven. "But someone else's children—"

"That's enough!" I ordered.

"Yes, Miss."

Now I closed the door to the children's room and slipped their breathing monitor into my pocket. Like me, they rarely need white noise to sleep. I double-checked the alarms before leaving the flat, and the lift arrived at once. Inside I pressed the button for the dome lounge. Even through the whine of the motor, I could distinguish two sets of breathing. It comforted me, as it does even now.

Leaving the lights off in the lounge, I sank into the padded observation chair and strapped myself in. I raised it until the lights on the arm shone dimly in the top of the dome. Around us rise the domes of other buildings, forty-seven in all. More are under construction. In another ten years, the population of Andaman Bay will double. Architects call this planetary sprawl. A hundred kilometers to the east, the lights of Tonkin Bay twinkled in the night. I turned the chair south. Here I could see a faint glow. A cloud of ammonia crystals reflected the lights of Corinth Bay. I turned the chair west and saw nothing. There's no bay out there. Not yet. Then something flickered in a corner of my eye, so I turned the chair north. I was right. It was more than just the wind. The Ah-Devasi were at it again.

The aurora hangs in the sky like a drape spanning the spectrum from yellow to blue. Its shimmer hides the stars in the whole quadrant from northwest past north into northeast. The aurora begins fifty kilometers up and falls in strands. They weave in and out, sometimes even braid, but only for a moment before waving free again, reaching out, curling up, crossing yellow on green. I watched the blue. Sometimes, where the aurora dips below the Pyrrhic Range, I'm sure I can see a strand pull away: one that glimmers in blue shading to indigo. Violet. I wait for shades of violet. I think I saw a violet last month, there at the end of Bight Pass. A violet so faint it verged on ultraviolet. I couldn't be sure, though, since earlier that day we had cremated Cassie Papandreou. We were all upset.

°°°   °°°   °°°

Cassie's husband, Spiro, pleaded with the coroner to rule her death an accident. Anything but a suicide. The coroner did, for her children's sake. Everyone understood. For who could deny Cassie had been troubled? We'd seen it each time she'd said, just as she had the week before:

"I'm telling you we don't belong here. *They* don't want us here."

"Then there's no argument," Zhou Feng said. "We don't want to be here either." Most of the guests laughed with him because he sits on the bay council. Other guests laughed at him. He doesn't care. The main thing is to make people laugh since he has his eye on the governor's suite.

"Don't patronize me," Cassie snapped. "You know what I mean." Spiro looked past her at an empty crystal goblet on the sideboard. The goblet reflected light from the chandelier. I wasn't the only one who sensed his unease.

Still, Zhou Feng couldn't let things rest. He called down the table to our chief of maintenance, the lone Demi on the bay council. "Harun al-Rashid," Zhou Feng called, "do *you* want us to leave?"

When Harun smiled, everyone looking directly at him protected his or her eyes. "Sorry," he said. The glow faded with his smile. "Cassandra, dear lady," he insisted, "it is not a question of leaving or staying. Your people have been here for nearly a century. Your parents were born here, no?" He made his voice a pleasant bass to reinforce his gravity. Most times it's difficult to know when he's being serious because his natural tenor carries the strong, laughing lilt of his people. The Demi are famous for their sense of humour.

"That's just what I'm talking about," she cried. "Every time I have to deal with a Khond it looks right through me as if I'm not even there. I know exactly what it's thinking. 'Why don't you people leave?' Not you, Harun. You're not really one of them. I mean… "

"I know exactly what you mean," he crooned. "These same Khonds call me a diamond when—"

"A what?" Spiro asked.

Oh, that Spiro! Sometimes I wonder whether he takes his eyes from his spectrometer long enough to notice the colour of the sun. I told him this once, when he asked for advice about Cassie, but he didn't want to hear he might be neglecting her. "Sometimes I wish you'd keep your eyes on the spectrometer more," he said. "But I suppose you're too busy trying to guess what colour the sun will be."

It's been some time since people coddled me for being a widow.

"Like the gem itself," Harun was saying, "though I am one of the few privileged to savour its beauty." He nodded at Zhou Feng's wife, Zhou Li.

She was fingering her necklace. She basks in knowing she's the only woman in Andaman Bay wealthy enough to own such a necklace. Small things keep her happy.

"They call me a diamond," Harun continued. "Dull on the outside like a human, blindingly bright inside like—"

"Like your Khonds?" It was Zhou Feng again, trying to be humorous. The Khond are Harun's only on his father's side.

Everyone except Cassie and I laughed. She was staring at her hands, clasping and unclasping them on the damask tablecloth. I was raising mine to my ears. I wanted to be ready for what might follow. It did, and I was. The moment Harun opened his mouth to laugh, a dazzling light flooded the room. The moment he did laugh, china rattled and the chandelier swung in the shock waves. The empty crystal goblet burst. After he stopped laughing, all of us lowered our hands and blinked to clear our vision. He shrugged an apology to Zhou Li for breaking the goblet.

"It's nothing," she said.

"I can tell you," Harun said at last, "what I tell the others. Humans gave us form." Raising his left hand, he tilted it to display its translucence. "You gave us time, even if most Khonds are rarely on time for anything. But then it is not always easy for a Khond to synchronize its existence with yours. Unlike we Demi, the Khond are born out of sync."

Again, everyone except Cassie and I laughed. He can be such a show off sometimes.

"We were spoiled," he said, meaning those on his father's side. "We thought time did not exist the way it does in the rest of the galaxy. We thought we were immortal."

"Aren't you?" Spiro asked. "I mean, aren't *they*?"

"In some ways, yes," Harun said. "In other ways, we are created and destroyed just as humans are born and die. Or in your case," he said, addressing me, "reborn. You are still a practicing Hindu, I believe?" Everyone knows I am, to some extent. Harun continued: "By bringing us the concept of time, you brought us the realization we were not the only beings in the galaxy. It was a hard lesson to learn but with it we also learned—" He wiped his lips with a serviette, then studied its brocade. "—to love."

"Come again?" Zhou Li asked. It's her duty at these gatherings to ask questions no one else can ask unless they want to look gauche.

"I simply meant," Harun said, "that when there is no urgency of time, there is no urgency to love. Your long-dead Bard of Avon put it so well." Harun's voice dropped lower in pitch so there was no mistaking the gravity of his words:

∘∘∘　　∘∘∘　　∘∘∘

This thou perceiv'st, which makes thy love more strong,
To love that well which thou must leave ere long.
Zhou Feng applauded softly.

Spiro complimented Harun on his gift for recalling obscure literature.

Harun reminded Spiro that, as everyone knows, the Demi are famous for their inability to forget. "It comes from having to live so long," Harun said.

When Cassie slammed her fists on the table, her place setting rattled as violently as when Harun had laughed. "You're not listening!" she cried. "Damn you," she said, looking at the rest of us. "Damn you most of all!" she added, glaring at him. "We have to do something before the Ah-Devasi help the Khond destroy us! We have to leave while there's still a—"

Spiro tried to uncoil her fists. "You're just tired," he said. "The aurora beings—" He paused. "The Ah-Devasi just want their land back."

She began to laugh, a laughter others joined nervously until hers became a cackle. "You fool," she hissed, "they don't need land. They don't even have *bodies*."

"That's enough," Zhou Li said. Her necklace glinted when she turned. "Cassie, dear, you've been up in the dome again. Spiro, you're still listening to fairy tales. The beings you're both talking about don't exist. The aurora is not made up of the spirits of this planet's ancestral—"

"No?" Cassie demanded. "Haven't you ever listened to the wind? I have. Haven't you ever watched the way the strands dip down behind the mountains and the blue breaks away into indigo? I'm telling you people, one day that glow is going to roll down Bight Pass and the whole of the plain will be red. With our blood!"

No one dared to laugh then, just as no one laughed a week later at the cremation. Cassie had driven her Morris up into the Pyrrhic Range. The search party had found her two days later, halfway through Bight Pass, with the Morris on its side and her life support system drained. No one wanted to believe what really might have happened: that she'd gone out there to speak with the aurora. Only I believe it, just as I'm the only one who knows the fatal error she made. She hadn't been driven by a desire to make contact. She'd been driven by fear.

ooo   ooo   ooo

I unstrapped myself even as the observation chair lowered me from the dome. The vinyl creaked uneasily. What was I doing, staying up so late again? If I'm not careful I'll end up as obsessed as Cassie, whose ashes Spiro scattered to the wind. Now he's trying to raise the children with help from his new domestic. Cora's sister. Is that how they'll do it? Will Cora kill the Papandreou children and her sister kill the twins? I found myself wishing the lift could go faster. Downstairs, even as I entered the flat and reset the alarms, I heard the wind rising. I pocketed the monitor and checked on the twins. No one will hurt them. The plain will never be red with blood. Not theirs.

I decided to make some Horlicks. But halfway to the kitchen, I stopped. I'd left my bedroom door ajar and the blackness around it glowed. I crossed to it and eased the door fully open.

Harun floated near the ceiling. He lay on his side with his head propped on a hand, his elbow casually propped on thin air. Not thin to him. When my eyes met his, he trilled on a make-believe flute. He does this when I look annoyed. I told him once about my favourite incarnation of Lord Vishnu: Krishna Gopala, the cowherd who played his flute for gopis, those cowgirls of Ancient Indian Earth. I closed the door behind me and locked it. Then I switched on the white noise.

Harun grimaced, but no one could hear us now.

"How did you get in?" I demanded.

He tapped the ventilation grille.

"And what do you think you're up to?" I asked.

"Tsk, tsk," he replied, shaking his head. "Don't you know?"

It's a game with us, a re-enactment of the first time he appeared like this, unannounced. As he did then, he floated down to offer his hands. This time, though, I threw off my robe and flung myself onto him. We rolled across the bed, and I clung to him so I wouldn't fall off the edge. Then he pulled me back, over him. While I pressed his left hand onto my face, the hand grew even more translucent, and I breathed deeply. I tried to breathe particles of his very fabric into myself. He smells like jaggery, the palm sugar I loved to eat as a child. When I raised his hand to kiss his fingers, they grew opaque.

Everyone knows what the Demi are famous for: their sense of humour and inability to forget. But few humans have discovered what the Demi should be famous for. I like to think I'm the only woman, perhaps the only human, who has ever made love to a being of another species. I know this isn't true. Where did the Demi come from, after all, if not from the union of early settlers and Khonds? Now humans love only humans. Most of them. The Khond reproduce as only they can. And the Demi? They claim they have little use for others. Not my Harun. When I'm alone with him, no white noise can shut out the wind as well as he can. He can shut out the world.

He wrapped his arms around me and lifted me off the bed. He always does this. Provided he doesn't let go, and he never has even in jest, he can slip my nightgown up and over my head more easily in midair. More easily than when my elbow or thigh pins the fabric beneath me. The nightgown felt suddenly heavy. I pulled it away and tossed it into a corner. We floated down onto the bed. I nudged him onto his back and felt him grow opaque to support me. Then he rolled me onto my back and grew translucent so I could breathe. Translucent everywhere except on top of my thighs, where I like to pull the weight of him down. His clothing always seems to evaporate. One moment it's there, the next moment his flesh quivers on mine. I clamped my legs over the small of his back and pretended to draw him in. I still need to pretend he can enter me there first. He began to glow. The more he glowed, the warmer he felt. The warmer he grew, the farther I could draw him in. And not just there. He filled my body. His flesh pushed up under the surface of my skin. Finally, when every particle of our bodies mingled, he laughed. The room filled with blinding, violet light. I squeezed my eyes shut, I clasped my hands over my ears, and I shrieked.

When he tried to draw out of me, I said, "Not yet." This is the best part: lying together afterward with his body in mine. Knowing that nothing which happens outside this room or this building or this bay matters.

He drew himself out slowly, one particle at a time, one part at a time. First a finger, then a toe. He pulled out his arms and his chest and his trunk and legs until I could feel only his head inside mine. I stifled a moan when he pulled out completely. He slid his arm under my shoulder and his arm grew opaque. My head rose and he cradled it on his chest so he could toy with my hair.

At last he said, "I watched one of your old dramas. This is where they smoke."

I laughed, and so did he. When light poured from his mouth, I kissed him to block the light. To stifle the sound in his throat while his chest quaked. The light also tasted like jaggery. I drew away and pressed his lips together. Trying to flex them, he made soft, protesting sounds.

"Shh," I warned, "you'll wake the children."

He became serious then. He pulled away and said, "Can't have that, can we?" His voice was a grave bass.

"That's not what I meant," I said. I rose and found my nightgown inside out. I fumbled it outside in. Even as I pulled it over me, I said through the now comforting fabric, "No one should know, that's all. Not yet."

"No one does know," he said. His clothing reappeared, and he sat up. "How've you been?"

"Same," I replied.

"Is it your friend?" he asked. "The one the others could never call Cassandra because of that prophet of the Ancient Mediterranean?"

"She wasn't my friend," I said. I lay down beside him and urged him to lie close. Once again, I rested my head on his chest. "Cassie was going mad. No one can be real friends with someone like that."

"Because you couldn't help her," he asked, "or because you were afraid you might become like her?"

"I read a book once," I said. "It was about the first law of space travel. It's not really a law because it can't be proven empirically."

"And it's not like you to change the subject," he said.

"No matter how far the human race leaves Earth behind," I told him, "we can never be completely at home anywhere else. I'm paraphrasing, of course." I sighed. "Maybe that's what Zhou Feng was trying to say the other night, at dinner, when he said we'd all like to leave."

"You can't go back," Harun said.

"Are you trying to tell me something?" I teased.

He pretended he hadn't heard, and I should have known better. He talks glibly about love except when we're alone. "Physically you can go back," he was saying, "but you were all born here."

"Try telling that to the Khond," I said.

He snorted, then smiled at allowing himself to become annoyed. It's all humorous to him, even annoyance.

Everyone knows the last thing a Khond or a Demi does before dying is to laugh. A loud, long laugh which empties its body of its spirit in the form of a light. The light begins with the red of destruction, races through the spectrum into the violet of creation, and fuses into a blinding, white light.

So people say. No human has ever seen a Khond or a Demi die. When the time for this comes, they flee into the Pyrrhic Range.

"The Khond," Harun said, "dream of an age that never existed. It's true your coming brought them the notion of time but now they're weaving a fantasy of their past. 'Time without time,'" he scoffed, repeating the Khond chant. "'Form without form. Life without death.'"

I pulled away from him and sat up. "I wish you wouldn't mock your own people like that," I said. "I mean not your own people but—"

"I know what you meant," he said.

I turned with my jaw set and found a weak smile lighting his face. I kissed the spot where his navel should be. He grew translucent, and I moved my hand down.

He clasped my hand to stop it from sliding between his thighs. It still bothers him. He can make love to me as no man ever could, yet he's still not completely human. He moved my hand up to his chest, which rippled from translucence into transparence. My hand sank until I could feel his heart, there below his breastbone. His heart beat under my palm. He likes doing this to show his heart beats only for me. It's part of the wedding ritual of the Demi: to clutch one another's hearts for the only time in the presence of others. During those long nights when I still grieved, when I couldn't allow myself to make love to him, he would say, "Touch my heart." The night I could finally bring myself to do this was the night we finally made love.

"Once long ago," he now said, "before you were even born, I went up into the mountains. I forced myself to endure a ritual my father told me about. 'Spread yourself thinly,' he said, 'and when the sun eclipses, your ancestors will sing to you.' I don't think he ever dreamt I'd do it." Harun's face hardened. The light between his lips faded into a grey that might have been either sadness or anger. It must be sadness, I thought. He's incapable of anger.

"Then what happened?" I asked.

"The aurora appeared," he said. "The Ah-Devasi—"

"They do exist!"

"Of course they do," he said, "only not the way you think. And not the way the Khond think either. That's what galls them. I've heard of Khonds who go into trances and see the world through the eyes of the Ah-Devasi. And these same Khonds don't like what they learn about themselves because they've become, well, unworthy of their ancestors. Don't ask me if it's true."

"The ritual?" I prodded.

"The ritual," he said. "It was the middle of the day and the sun was eclipsed. It was cold. So cold. Then the aurora appeared and its beings really did sing to me." He reached for my hair.

"Well?" I asked.

"They cast me all the way to the other side of the world," he said. "'We are the spirits of the aurora,' they sang. 'The aurora of the spirits.' They? It was many voices. It was one voice. Maybe the Khond never did speak with one voice the way some of them like to believe. Just as some of them like to think humans speak with one voice. When a Khond looks at you, all it sees is a human. Not an individual, distinctive being. When they look at me, all they see is a Demi."

I shuddered even as his lips drew back. He was capable of anger, after all, if compassion failed him. If he saw the Khond exactly as he claimed they saw humans. The light from his mouth glowed red. Even his eyes glowed faintly red. He closed his mouth and his eyes. When he opened them once more, they looked normal, the irises a pale violet. He opened his mouth to speak, and the light from within looked normal, too. "I'm sorry," he said. He clutched my hand to his heart and it beat rapidly beneath my palm. "You see, I still have vestiges of the Khond in me. Too much for my own good. If only they could find a way to lose their anger, then their own eyes wouldn't glow so much. Do you know what happens to a Khond if it's consumed by anger? It goes blind." Harun smiled, and light flickered between his lips.

I couldn't decide whether to believe him. "Did the Ah-Devasi say anything else?" I asked.

"Oh yes," he replied. "'You are not of us,' they or it said. 'Nor are you of the humans,' they-it said. They-it sound like I do when I'm in public, like a character from one of your old dramas." He shrugged. "I went through all that to learn what I must've known all along?"

He smiled again, so brightly I kissed him to stop the light from flooding the room. The light no longer tasted like jaggery now. It tasted bittersweet. We made love again, less playfully than before, but I made him remain inside me a long, long time.

ooo   ooo   ooo

As soon as Harun left, through the ventilation grille as always, I glanced at the clock. It was the middle of the night and I still wasn't sleepy. I barely sleep on the nights he visits me and yet I never feel tired. It's as though he leaves a residue of his energy in me.

I left the flat once more and, this time, found the Khond at work. Silently. Few of them looked me in the eye. In the eyes of those who did, I saw a surly glow. When I reached the lift I found it out of order. I still punched the up button, then waited with my arms crossed. Through the large window, I watched the twinkling lights of Tonkin Bay far to the east.

A voice startled me: "May I be of service?"

I knew even as I turned that I would find a Khond. A faint smell of ammonia was filling the air. The Khond's head poked out through the closed lift doors.

This is why the Khond are so good at maintenance: they can go anywhere. Up to a point. The very oxygen we humans breathe gives them their form and they like this. They like feeling useful. But too long among humans and a Khond can never venture into the ammonia rich atmosphere. It's trapped inside and lives out a life shortened by oxygen. The Khond sneer at the Demi, who move so fluidly between our two worlds, and yet Khonds who are no longer useful slouch through walls if they can. Slouch against them if not. No Demi would ever slouch. I watched this Khond closely and waited for it to speak.

"I believe the stairs work," it said at last.

"No kidding," I said. I turned toward the flat. I wasn't about to walk twenty floors up to the dome.

"I believe kidding is for goats," the Khond said, "though I have never set eyes on such a creature." The Khond pulled itself farther out from the lift. "Might you have on your esteemed person a modicum of divine tobacco? It refreshes the weary and makes one sleep as soundly as a babe. Oh, if—"

"I'm sorry," I said, as politely as I could. "I don't smoke."

The light in its eyes barely flickered when it smiled. "Do not concern yourself," it said. "Tobacco affords a truly fetid and diabolical smell. It chokes the air…

I let the Khond continue. I should say I let this particular being continue. It was an individual, distinctive being, not the representative of an entire species. But I knew exactly what it was doing: entertaining me with servitude. Ingratiating itself. Any other time, late in the day when I'm tired, I would have let my annoyance show. I do care, but I resent having my politeness used against me.

"Look," I finally said. The Khond stopped in mid-soliloquy. "I'll make you a deal. Let me up to the lounge, and you can come by later and help yourself to anything in my pantry." I raised my index finger. "Any one thing."

The Khond snorted. I expected the smell of smoke yet smelled only more ammonia. "A test," it said. "Nothing more." After it looked left and right, up and down to ensure there were no Khonds within hearing, it said, "If any of my kind inquires, however, pray insist you exchanged a gram of tobacco in return for my humble service. Irreparable would be the harm to my reputation, such as it is, should rumours begin to the effect that I bestowed my favour on a human." The Khond's right hand emerged from the lift door. "Okey dokey, liddle schmokey? Shake."

I reached forward but we never made contact. The hand pulled back through the door. Chortling, the Khond stepped completely out of the lift, then pressed a button on its work belt. The lift lights came on.

When I touched the up button, the doors slid open. I stepped inside and turned in the doorway so the doors couldn't close. "What's your name?" I asked.

Startled, it said, "Pray, why do you inquire?"

"So I'll know what to call you next time."

"I have long believed," it said, "that no member of your species could distinguish any member of mine from another. Except domestics, but familiarity also breeds—"

"Okay," I said. "Fine." I stepped back.

"A moment," the Khond cried. "I beg you!" It stepped forward and the doors slid back. "You require my human appellation or my original appellation?"

"I wouldn't be able to pronounce your original name," I said.

"This is true." It chortled until a faint light glowed in its eyes. "My human appellation is Henry—short for Henry the Fourth, Part One. My sibling, as you may surmise, was Part Two. Alas my sibling is, to all purposes, no more, having stiffened in a living death somewhere in Corinth Bay. My original appellation, however, might roughly translate as—" The light in its eyes dulled, and its shoulders sagged. "Even my comrades, my kith and kin, address me as Henry. Why is this?"

Before I could try to answer, it backed away and the lift doors closed.

I consoled myself with what I now knew. What most others, even Zhou Feng and Zhou Li, don't know. The Ah-Devasi didn't drive Cassie mad. It's avoiding contact that drives a human mad, and not simply contact with those we love. Or once loved. If we can't make contact with the aurora beings, we can at least make contact with Khonds. They're all around us and yet, just as most humans pretend the Ah-Devasi don't exist, so most humans treat the Khond as if they, too, barely exist.

Spiro, for one, but then he's so caught up in his precious work… No, that's not fair. It is precious. We're trying to find a way to oxygenate the entire planet without killing off the Khond. As for the Ah-Devasi, Spiro cares about his children as much as I care about the twins, but I wonder if he could defend anyone with his life. If it came to this, if the violet glow ever rolled out of Bight Pass onto the plain, I would protect the twins with my life. I would even kill to protect them. What am I thinking of, though? There are likelier ways of dying than being murdered in our beds: meteor showers, quakes, vehicle crashes. Especially crashes. Life is full of danger even for the Khond. They simply have less to lose, or so people say.

The lift doors opened and I hurried to the observation chair. I strapped myself in and raised it. I turned the chair through north toward the northwest. Toward the aurora.

The strands hung down, even braided, then waved free and curled blue on green. Where the aurora dipped behind the Pyrrhic Range, a strand glimmered in blue shading into indigo. The aurora was resisting the rising of the sun. Before long, though, the aurora lost its battle. It retreats by day and surges back at night. Now it has faded, drawing into itself while the sun keeps rising. While its harsh, harsh rays wash out the lights of Tonkin Bay. The sodium content of the atmosphere has increased since yesterday morning, when the sun looked more blue. Today the sun will be a warm, yellow-orange.

I should go downstairs now to let Cora in. I should be there when the children wake. I think they will like Harun.

A Good Day

D.K. Latta

He dragged on his boots, the mud grey and caked on like paint. Then he leaned back against the white porch pillar and stared at the field spread away before him. Yellow stalks undulated in the late summer breeze, the wind cool and warm all at the same time. The sky was blue and endless, dwarfing the field, the farm—everything seemed to bow before it in obsequiousness, as though it were a monstrous tidal wave hovering over all, ready to crash down at the first sign of insurrection.

The golden sun was still newly born, low in the east.

How could anything so insubstantial as the sky seem so concrete? he wondered idly. Still, he wouldn't live anywhere else. The sky put a man in touch with infinity, reminding him how small he and everything he knew was, how transitory. Everything came and went in the blink of a cosmic eye. Except the sky. The sky and the endless prairie.

Two halves of an equation that added up to eternity.

He chuckled, deep in his throat. He had a long journey ahead of him and it was making him oddly contemplative, he realized. Even pensive. He had known that when the crop came due, he'd have to begin the journey—it's not like it should come as any surprise, he chastised himself good-naturedly.

"Hiram."

He craned his neck as Marion came out onto the porch, the screen door creaking a mournful wail. He'd meant to get around to oiling that. Well, he supposed, it would have to wait until he got home, assuming he wasn't too tuckered out from his travels. He smiled at her. She was the most beautiful woman in the district, with chestnut hair you could bury your face in, a wide, happy mouth, a high bosom, narrow waist, full hips.

"Do you paint those jeans on, my dear?" he asked with a mischievous grin. Though it was her hands that struck him as the prettiest thing about her. It wasn't easy to maintain soft, pretty hands on a farm. Self-consciously he folded his powerful, callused mitts over each other.

Marion grinned at him as he rose to meet her. Her kiss was long and deep and promised so many things that he actually blushed a little. Then they parted, reluctantly. "I have to go, eh?" he said sadly. "If I don't get an early start…"

She nodded, and for a moment the humour left her eyes. Then she looked away, as if not wanting to meet his gaze. "The thresher-andy needs a new flow tube," she said.

He followed her gaze to the big machine lumbering lazily across the field now that the main crop was in. The silver android up in the driver seat glinted cheerily in the morning sunlight. He nodded. "I'll try and pick it up first, so's I remember it."

She looked at him again, smiling weakly. "And salt."

He nodded, securing his cap on his head. He pulled her close, kissing her again, wanting to remember the taste of her, to keep him warm while he was away. He hugged her, then stepped quickly from the porch. There was no sense in dragging it out, he knew. The sooner he was off, the sooner he was back. He clambered up onto the wagon, glanced back to make sure the flatbed trailer was firmly attached at the back, the bales of wheat latched securely. Then he twitched the reins and the big, hairy barggas snorted and lurched forward. The wagon jerked under him, but he steadied himself and steered the beasts toward the west.

Stay west, he knew, and that was all that was needed. The route of the sun.

"Hiram!"

He glanced back. Marion was on the porch growing smaller and smaller. "Hurry back," she called. Then she pulled aside the front of her shirt, flirtatiously flashing a beautiful, pale breast.

He grinned and blew her a kiss, then turned and tried not to think about his warm loving wife waiting for him. Instead, he focused on the endless flatness before him and the sky looming over all.

A couple of miles out he passed his nearest neighbour, Ted Morton, who was laying a new fence.

"Off to market, eh?" called Ted. "Lord, how time flies."

Hiram waved and the barggas lumbered on.

ooo   ooo   ooo

Sometime later, the first people he came to after leaving his familiar district were a little group of Krat'chkoo camped by the side of the dirt road. The little ones, still swathed in the soft blue fur of pre-pubescence, danced around the wagon, making odd chortling sounds. The barggas snorted belligerently and the children jumped away, giving the great beasts more room. The leader of the family approached the wagon, his skin a pale blue, hairless, his four legs carrying him forward as though walking on air.

"I am Chofo. You looking to trade?" the Krat'chkoo asked, breathing out through the funnel on top of his head.

Hiram glanced at the little cluster of tents and the dozen or so adults. It didn't look too promising, but it wouldn't hurt to see, he realized. "Could use a flow tube for a model F-1600 farm andy, eh?" he said, squinting at the blue creature.

Chofo glanced back at his companions and muttered something that sounded halfway between a burp and a chuckle. One of the other adults ducked into a tent. While they waited, Hiram showed off some of the other things he had. The wheat wasn't much good to the Krat'chkoo since it needed to be processed, but he had brought other things. On the seemingly endless prairie, where farms and communities and nomads like the Krat'chkoo lived in utter isolation, with ages passing between encounters, it was never wise to pass up a chance to do a little trading.

Who knew when the chance would come again?

Hiram had in his wagon some fruits, some old tools that were still good but he didn't really use anymore, some wood carvings he'd whittle from time to time, a crystal generator set that would be good, if only he had some fresh crystals to power it, and other odds and ends.

While Chofo picked through the items, trying not to let his interest show too much in case there was bargaining ahead, the other one re-emerged from the tent, brandishing an old tube. He handed it to Chofo who handed it to Hiram. It was dirty and frayed, and still warm. He pursed his lips, realizing they must have an andy in the tent.

One of the children screamed. He glanced over, seeing it pointing at the tube as one of the females went to quiet him. Hiram frowned. Krat'chkoos had little need for a farm andy. Presumably the one in question had been reprogrammed as a playmate for the kids. Hiram felt like a jerk, but life was hard. He knew that, Chofo knew that. To the kids it was a playmate, but his andies kept the farm going, and no doubt the Krat'chkoo needed things more important than a kid's toy. Then he saw the numbering on the tube. It was with a mixture of disappointment and relief that he handed it back. "This is for a C-1500," he said. "That's no good to me, eh?"

The wailing child stopped crying once one of its older siblings muttered to it, presumably explaining that they wouldn't be losing the andy after all. At least, not today.

Chofo tried to hide his disappointment as he glanced at the treasures in Hiram's wagon. Hiram chewed on his cheek for a moment, looking at the bedraggled little family. Finally, he said, "So what else've you got, eh?" It wasn't just charity that made him ask. He could pick up a few things that maybe he didn't need, but he could trade somewhere down the road for stuff he did need.

Eventually he left the Krat-chkoo with two sacks of dried grubs, which he figured he could trade, and a handmade Krat'chkoo shawl he figured on keeping as a gift for Marion. Chofo happily displayed to his kin the hacksaw and magno-locks he had gained in the deal. The children raced after the wagon for a short ways, shrieking gleefully. The braggas bellowed good-naturedly, all being forgiven.

Once more, Hiram faced the level horizon.

∘∘∘　　∘∘∘　　∘∘∘

It grew cold, but Hiram had known it would and had a heavy coat and blankets to wrap over himself. The braggas, thickly coated to begin with, muddled through without complaint.

Snow commenced shortly, and Hiram muttered curses to himself, as if such utterances would keep him warm. It was at times like this that he wished he did have some crystals for his old generator.

Through the haze of the falling snow he could make out another wagon trundling along in the distance, too far away to call to. He watched it for a time, until it dwindled to nothing, like a half-remembered dream.

He woke with a start, having dozed—well, he was not sure for how long. When had he seen the Krat'chkoo? When had he said good-bye to Marion?

A while ago.

One of the braggas made a coughing sound, a warning. He blinked and looked around blurrily, shivering slightly from the lingering cold. There wasn't anything that actually threatened a bragga, but they could be annoyed. However, he couldn't see any field rovers or anything that might be encouraging this distemper.

∘∘∘　　∘∘∘　　∘∘∘

He heard a rustling at his back.

Hiram turned and squinted at the trailer piled high with stokes of wheat. For a moment he saw nothing, then one of the stokes seemed to shiver, just a little.

"Damnation," he hissed, leaping to his feet. He stumbled over the back of the wagon, grabbing up his galvin-stick as he went. He leapt on to the trailer and stabbed the galvin-stick into the bale of wheat, releasing a hefty electrical shock. There was a squeal and a couple of hartifares leapt from the bundle, the palm sized parasites bounding to the ground. He stabbed into the bundle again and again, sending more of them scattering, electricity the only sure way to discourage them.

He crouched and tugged out a handful of stalks. They were spotted black, mouldering from the effects of the hartifares' saliva. He cursed again, using language Marion wouldn't tolerate at home. A quick survey of the rest of his load provided one plus, though. The creatures had only ruined the one bundle. Bitterly, he heaved the infected batch off the trailer, onto the side of the road.

As he started the braggas lumbering forward again, he glanced back to see the discarded stoke nestled in the melting snow, quickly disappearing beneath a black sheaf of hardifares, hundreds of the loathsome creatures emerging as if from nowhere to devour it.

He cursed them and he cursed himself. If he wasn't careful and didn't stay alert, he could lose half his load to the little monsters.

ooo   ooo   ooo

In the distance he made out the vague angles of a town. It was not the main market, but still it was worth checking out. On a flat prairie beneath the big sky, though, distances were impossible to gauge. He did not hurry the braggas, nor allow himself to fixate on the little community with anything approaching anticipation.

He would come to it when he came to it, not before. Quietly, he and his beasts trundled along under the big sky.

ooo   ooo   ooo

"Some hair dye maybe?" asked the freckled travelling saleswoman who had parked her rickety covered wagon at the main road leading into the tiny community. The only road as a matter of fact. "Take ten years off, mister. The missus will love you for it."

Hiram frowned and glanced at his reflection in the glass display case the saleswoman had laid out showing a series of handsome all-purpose laser-knives. He hadn't realized he was developing a touch of gray here and there. He looked at the woman sullenly, damning the messenger for the message. "Got any salt?"

"Got salt," she agreed.

"Need a bag of dried grubs?"

"Not particularly," said she, but her eyes momentarily betrayed her. "Could go for one of your bales, though."

Hiram glanced back at his load. He knew she didn't need it personally, but no doubt she knew where she could trade it for something. "Already lost one to hardifares, eh? Don't suppose I can whittle it down much more. Got a crystal generator, though. Good condition."

"Need a wheel."

"Nope."

"No, it wasn't a question. You need a wheel, mister."

Hiram looked at his wagon and cursed under his breath. He had not noticed the hairline crack that had formed around the rim. The wheel wouldn't take him much farther before it would come apart like a husked corn. He looked back at the saleswoman, then at her covered wagon. "You don't have a wheel in there," he said suspiciously.

"I can get one."

Hiram scowled. If she could procure one, it wouldn't be hard for him to do so, either. It had to be either someone in town, or in a nearby farm. But the saleswoman knew where to go, while Hiram would have to hunt a wheel up. He glanced over at the wide horizon.

"Storm's coming," observed the saleswoman quietly.

Hiram wasn't sure if it was just an observation, or a bargaining device, pointing out that Hiram didn't want to stick around too long. The open sky had become dark and foreboding. Hiram looked back at the freckle faced woman. "All right. A bale for a wheel and a sack of salt and throw in one of those sonic cleaning brushes," he nodded at another display case.

"A bale and a sack of dried grubs."

Hiram frowned, then glanced at the horizon. A storm was coming, and he still had a long way to go. She had him in a bind and she knew it. He shouldn't begrudge her, he admitted to himself. After all, her observation about his wheel might have saved his life. If it had come apart in the middle of nowhere… Still, he didn't want to leave feeling he had come out the loser in their negotiations. "Throw in the hair dye, then," he muttered.

∘∘∘   ∘∘∘   ∘∘∘

The braggas howled mournfully, unwilling to move from their spot as the fluttas whined all around them. The sky was dark with the tiny insects. The big sky vista, which, when blue had seemed majestic and intimidating, was now a frightening dirty brown of whirling, whining bodies as far as the eye could see. Up, up, up, left or right, it was the same. The world had become nothing but fluttas, and the fluttas had become the world. He pulled his blanket closer over himself, grateful for his goggles that kept them out of his eyes. He had encountered a fellow traveller sometime before, going the opposite direction, and traded the sonic cleaning brush for the goggles.

The braggas' thick fur kept the fluttas out of their eyes, their pathetic howls notwithstanding.

He shivered uncontrollably, the incessant whine driving him almost mad. The current plague had been going on for… Well, he could no longer be sure for how long. He tried to think of Marion, as if her memory would keep him anchored, but it was hard.

At his back, laser-snaps erected at each of the four corners of the trailer whipped and hissed as they incinerated fluttas by the millions around the wheat. A plasti-tarp covered over the bales as best it could, hopefully discouraging the fluttas that got past the lazer-snaps. He knew he would lose a few bales, though—he had to be realistic about that.

He clenched at his blanket and felt an arthritic twinge in his hand. Somewhere at his feet was a long-empty bottle of hair dye.

o o o   o o o   o o o

He was tired. He was bone weary. He had lost bales to hardifares and to fluttas, he had traded some for needed goods on the road and lost some to the weather. Attacking Chiters had stolen two. The shawl he had bought for Marion from the Krat'chkoo he had had to tear into strips to knot over cuts from Chiter lasers.

Looking back at his dwindling load, he felt his throat burn. So much work, so much effort, and now he had but half a flatbed trailer to show for it. Still, that was life. Can't complain, he thought resignedly—and it wouldn't do any good if he did, he added.

o o o   o o o   o o o

He had been on the road a long time. So long certain events blurred into others and some had vanished entirely from his mind. But as he pulled up before the grainery depot, he knew the main leg was almost over. He still had enough of a crop—just barely—to make a respectable sale. Tucked in his breast pocket was Marion's list of needed items.

He climbed down from his wagon, wheezing a little with the effort and slowly, stiffly, walked up the steps to the main doors.

o o o   o o o   o o o

When he was done, and had got the best deals he could negotiate, he took the reins in his bony hands and started the braggas home. Still west, of course. No point in heading east. East was just backward. Always westward, aways forward, like the sun.

o o o   o o o   o o o

The endless sky was black with night over the featureless horizon. If the blue was majestic, the stormy clouds ominous, the flutta plague frightening, then the awesome spectacle of unending blackness left him just… empty. Alone. Sad.

Sad as he saw the lights from his farm house twinkle like earthbound stars just ahead of him.

He had been gone all day. He had driven through storm and fluttas and Chiters attacks, watching warily as the day rolled over head on its great cosmic wheel, taking with it everything, all his hopes, his dreams. Even his passions.

The wagon creaked to a halt before the front porch. He breathed out, too tired for a moment to move. He heard footsteps, the familiar creak of the screen door, still not oiled. He lumbered down from his seat and mounted the steps.

She was there. White haired and plump, tiny eyes behind spectacles. He took her face in his liver-spotted hands and smiled, barely making out the memory of the young woman he had left behind in the morning. He smiled and kissed her lips. A cool, dry kiss. Affectionate more than anything.

"You've gone grey," she said, touching his snow-white hair.

He shrugged. He had tried dying it, he recalled, but that was a long time ago. Morning, possibly early afternoon.

"Come on," she said, "I'll heat up stew."

∘∘∘   ∘∘∘   ∘∘∘

Later he lay in bed, staring up at his familiar ceiling, glad to be in bed, glad to be home. Over re-heated stew she had told him about the daughter she had had while he was gone, and of their grandchildren. He would see them in the morning.

"Hiram, you awake?" came her voice from the darkness, soft and sleepy.

"Yeah," he said.

"Did you have a good day?"

He did not answer right away, thinking things over, his journey, the trades he made, the goods he brought back that would benefit the children and grandchildren he would see for the first time in the morning. Of course, there was so much he had missed, but that was the life they lived, the life they had both accepted long, long ago. Life under the big sky.

"Yes," he said at long last, after Marion had probably drifted off to sleep. He didn't have any more days like that in him, he knew, but all in all, he nodded to himself. "Yes, it was a good day."

Horsepower

Judy Berlyne McCrosky

Arabella watched as the two Securipooches delicately sniffed beneath each other's metal tail. Behind them stood three identical workbenches with matte grey work surfaces and shiny grey sinks. *Everything is always the same*, Arabella thought. *The ad men all in black and the scientists all in white. Outside, the same flat prairie landscape and me in here, as I always am, looking for a story.*

"They're a resounding success." Mr. Emmanuel, CEO of the Trumpeter Swan ad agency, smoothed his droopy mustache and then rested his hands on the platform conveniently presented by his bulging stomach. "Securipooches provide safety to home owners the world over." He stood in the center of the biochem lab like a king surveying his realm. Arabella tapped her pen on her screen, imagining headlines: "Home Security Going To The Dogs?" "Dog Genes Outsmart Criminal Genes." But the most important words would come after the headline: 'By Arabella Esther.'

Her boss thought he could run the science beat by waiting for scientists to call him. He never went out after a story. Well, if this product was as big as its mouthpieces implied, the story could be enough for the Editor to name a new senior science reporter. As she glanced at Clive, the photographer, his face twisted into an embarrassed grimace. Looking down, she saw that one of the Securipooches had buried its nose in his crotch. She hid a smile behind her hand.

Emmanuel pulled the creature away and shooed it towards the workbenches. Clive aimed his holocam at it to hide his blush. "So sorry," the ad man said jovially. "Sometimes genes code for more than one trait. It appears that this sniffing," he wrinkled his nose until he looked like a cherub who'd just eaten a lemon, "is connected to territory defense or loyalty to owners."

"Love and protection," Arabella said to her screen. Everything she'd learned showed that people grew to love the dogs with metal bodies and beating hearts. But the real story was the biogrid, and it hadn't been easy finding even the little information she had. Last year's Nobel Prize in Artificial Intelligence had been expected to go to the biogrid's inventor, Dr. Javed Syed. A woman who'd created an intelligent hairdryer received the prize. Arabella heard later that Dr. Syed had withdrawn his invention from public use, saying it needed more work. "Tell me about the biogrid," she said, pointing to the Securipooches who were now trying to dig through the linominium floor.

"The biogrid," Emmanuel said, "will do more to change the way humans interact with their world than has any other invention."

"The biogrid," said Arabella, hoping he'd get on with it, "has enabled genetic components to interact with machines."

"Exactly." He beamed. "For years we've added machine parts to living beings. Now we can add human, animal, or even plant traits to machines."

Plant genes? Arabella pictured a mechanical Venus Fly-trap. Would it be used to help people fishing? Maybe she could get a mechanical implant in her skull and use plant genes to replace her dark wiry hair with a golden flow of corn silk. "Have human genes been used— ?" Arabella asked.

Emmanuel continued as if he hadn't heard her. "Securipooches are an engineering marvel, but they're only— "

"Have human genes been used in this way?"

Emmanuel sighed. "Would you build a ship to carry you to the stars before anyone had yet walked on the moon?"

"I would," she stuck out her chin, "if I thought I could. Nothing's accomplished until someone tries."

He was all smiles again. "And just look what we've accomplished by trying. The Securipooch encompasses the strengths of both dog and machine. They're faster and stronger than dogs, they can bite through a two inch steel bar, and yet they play with little children and lick their owner's hands."

"What kind of saliva do they have? Motor oil?" Emmanuel opened his mouth to reply, but she held up a hand. "Never mind. Bad joke. Weren't mice the donors of the first mammal genes used with the biogrid?"

Emmanuel rubbed one shoe on the material of his gaitered trousers."The biogrid," Arabella told Clive, "was placed in a computer mouse."

"You said it yourself," Emmanuel said. "Nothing's accomplished until something is tried. The biogrid enables genes to become part of the machine, to produce muscles and other proteins, and use the machine's metal frame as skeletal support. There's even a brain of sort created, or a neuro-command center, as we prefer to call it. Our bio-machines are a most impressive accomplishment."

Arabella grinned. "The mouse was a joke. It had a tendency to hide in shadowy corners, scuttle around the edges of the room, and it also, as I recall, squeaked quite becomingly."

Clive laughed. "Good thing it didn't have teeth."

Emmanuel glared at them both. "Just how, may I ask, did you learn about that?"

"I'm good at research." Arabella smiled.

"Well," Emmanuel smoothed his belted jacket. "All your research hasn't netted you the real story."

"And what might that be?"

"Horsepower."

Clive filmed the Securipooches, one of whom turned around three times and lay down. Arabella shoved her notescreen into her bag. "Horsepower has been around forever."

"Not like this, it hasn't." Emmanuel seemed unfazed by her preparations to leave. "Imagine this: a car that will fill your mind with images of muscle and grace, of wind streaming through a silken mane. A car with a personality, a car you will love, and that will love you back."

Arabella paused in the act of inflating her coat's insulation layer.

"Cars have been around a long time." Emmanuel's voice was as silken as any mane. "They're so familiar we don't think about them. They're just there. We get in, tell it where we want to go, and turn on the morning paper. But, there was a time when people loved to drive. That time is with us once again."

"Okay." Arabella shrugged, but inside her chest a spark leapt into life. Maybe this was the story that would get her noticed. "Good hook. You've got me listening."

"Driving is no fun, because we aren't involved with our vehicle."

"It's safer, now. With road sensors for guidance and to control speed, traffic accidents are down to almost zero."

"But," Emmanuel lifted a finger and waved it under her nose, "is safety all people want from life? I don't think so. Near the end of the 20th century, the speed limit in the USA was lowered to 55 mph. Fatalities decreased, but a few years later those speed limits were back up. Why?"

"I'm sure you're going to tell me."

"Because people wanted to drive, that's why. They wanted power and speed. They wanted to feel the car, be part of something greater than they could be alone. Driving now is like sitting at home on a sofa. Horsepower will change that, will return us to the days when driving was fun. And just think of what an increase in car sales will do for our economy."

"Are you telling me," Arabella asked slowly, "that someone has used horse genes on a biogrid, and put it into a car?"

Emmanuel just smiled.

○○○   ○○○   ○○○

Kitsy lovingly ran her hand down the hood of her pale cream car. Its front end was longer and narrower than those of modern cars and the back end was rounded, the fenders giving the impression of bunched muscles ready to spring. Solar strips ringed the roof, but there was also an intake valve for hydrogen fuel centered at the back. The car nickered and butted Kitsy, gently, with its bumper. Its body shone in the sunlight, but not with the hard gleam of metal. A fine coat of hairs contributed to the colour. The front headlights, Arabella knew, held cameras so the car could see.

"Can you tell me," she asked, notescreen held ready, "about your relationship with your car?"

The car's side mirrors flicked forward, as if listening to this unfamiliar voice.

"Get in," Kitsy said. "I'll show you."

Eying the side mirrors nervously, Arabella slid into the passenger seat. The upholstery was also pale cream, but unlike the exterior skin, the seat appeared to be made of a durable fabric, not of anything that could move on its own.

"I love my car." Kitsy leaned forward for the retinal scan that started the engine. "I've named her Shining Sands Rani Princess in honor of her Arabian roots."

"Isn't Rani an Indian term?" Arabella asked, but the car started moving and Kitsy didn't seem to have heard.

The car sounded like every other car, a muted machine purr, as it merged with the suburban traffic. "Are horses and cars a good mix?"

"The best," Kitsy gushed. Arabella knew the woman was twenty-eight, but she seemed much younger. "Only three of us got Arabians."

Arabella searched her mind for a question that would elicit a useful, or even intelligent, answer. She knew each Horsepower had been created with genes from its own individual horse, but discussing the pros and cons of various horse breeds didn't seem promising. "How were you chosen to be an owner in this pilot project?"

"I guess it's because I just love horses so much." Kitsy clasped her hands together in ecstasy. "I can't think why else. Can you?" Her blue eyes were wide.

Arabella masterfully ignored this opening as Kitsy prattled on about written tests, "Only multiple choice. Isn't that lucky?", and games she had to play with the testers. "One was where we had to pretend we were driving back in the days before guidance and sensors. They thought I'd be scared, but I wasn't. I loved it. And I only hit two traffic cones!"

"All the owners were tested?" Arabella asked. The car was leaving Kitsy's neighborhood, an area of houses that all looked alike, even though they were different colors, and some had a big double door on the garage, while others had two single doors.

"Yes." Kitsy stroked the dashboard above the GPS display. "This is her favorite place to be scratched."

"Have you met the others?"

"Not yet. I look forward to seeing what color they all are."

"The owners?"

Kitsy, busily at work with her nails, each carefully filed into minute serrations, looked over, her thin face puzzled. The car slowed for an intersection. Kitsy's face cleared, and she laughed. "No, I meant the other Horsepowers. Mr. Emmanuel and Dr. Syed felt it would be best if each owner and Horsepower developed a personal bond before we get together as a group."

"Dr. Syed?" The biogrid inventor refused all requests for interviews.

"He sent a message." Kitsy's eyes, heavily shadowed with orange, turned dreamy. Little gold horseshoes flashed on and off within the makeup. "He told us our vehicles were a new breed, and that they'd teach us about being alive. And I do feel more alive now. I do. I knew we were soulmates the moment we met." The car moved into an intersection, stopping at the embedded turn line until the road system gave it permission to turn left.

"You've met Dr. Syed?"

"No, silly," Kitsy giggled. "When Shining Sands Rani Princess and I first met."

Arabella gritted her teeth. "In your experience, how do the horse traits affect your car's performance?" The car turned and moved into place exactly ten feet behind the car ahead.

"The horse and machine traits mesh perfectly." Despite Kitsy's earnest voice, Arabella was sure she was repeating something Mr. Emmanuel had said. "After all," Kitsy continued, "horses have worked with people for thousands of years, providing transportation, muscle, and companionship. There is no other animal so well suited for—"

Something huge and noisy crashed beside them. A construction crane had dropped a crate filled with steel beams. That's all Arabella had time to see, for the world tipped, and she fell heavily against the seat back. She thought fleetingly that perhaps seat belts should still be mandatory, as her feet rose above her head.

The world became level again, the switch just as sudden, and Arabella found herself in a heap on her seat, one leg twisted painfully under her hips, only to be hurled against the seat back as the car accelerated fast. The guidance system quickly caught it and the vehicle slowed to the speed of the others around it.

Arabella gasped for air. Kitsy pouted. "That nasty construction site," she said. "It scared my poor Shining Sands Rani Princess."

Arabella blinked. "Scared? You mean… the car reared up?"

"Of course. And then she ran. It's what horses do when they're scared. But the mean old guidance system didn't let you run." She stroked the dashboard. "There there, sweetie, it's okay. I won't let anything hurt you."

This is nuts, Arabella thought. But the car gave a soft rumble and the dashboard curved so as to better fit Kitsy's caress, and Arabella wondered.

∘∘∘   ∘∘∘   ∘∘∘

She interviewed three other Horsepower owners. The cars all behaved just like cars, and the owners spoke passionately about the need to disable the guidance systems and sensors. One owner, a retired policeman who wore a cowboy hat and a big-buckled belt, said, "They need to be free. It's a crime, keeping these cars penned up like this. They've got to be true to their nature."

But they aren't natural. Arabella travelled, in her own car, to the newsroom. All around her cars moved at the same speed, equidistant from each other. The newsroom was chaos, as usual. People sat in tiny cubicles, or crammed together at desks. They talked into phones, into screens, to people on vids, even to people physically near them. Chairs rolled, squeaking and scraping, pens tapped screens, footsteps rapped the old lino floor.

Arabella wove her way through the maze of equipment and people. Her boss had asked to see her. What could Maximum Maximilian want? Did Max Max, so known because he always made sure he got maximum credit for any story, even if it was researched and written by someone else, have his eye on the biogrid? Her byline had appeared on each of her stories so far. That didn't mean, though, that Max hadn't been talking up his contribution, even though it was nil, to the Editor.

"Arabella." He greeted her jovially, his small eyes gleaming, and her unease grew. He was actually a rather minimal person, thin and gangly, hair sparse although she could see from the reddish tufts that sprouted all over his head that he was trying yet another of the frequently advertised baldness cures. She supposed this was an improvement, as the last attempt had turned the little hair he had a lurid green.

"I wanted to congratulate you," he said, waving her into the only other seat in his small office. "You're doing good work."

Arabella forced her lips into a smile, but the longer he spoke, the worse she knew it was going to be.

"I've been talking to the Editor about you, in fact." He leaned forward, his hands rubbing together. "Told him how well you're coming along under my supervision. He's very proud of you, said you've done a superb job with the biogrid. But now that it's drawing international attention…"

Arabella fought the urge to close her eyes in preparation for the blow. "Yes?"

Max beamed, his thin lips revealing perfectly capped teeth. "Trumpeter Swan called today. Mr. Emmanuel insisted on speaking to the Senior Science writer. He told me that since the pilot project with the Horsepowers has gone so well, he's ready to introduce the cars to the world. There's going to be a rally, with all twenty Horsepowers showing their stuff. Isn't that exciting?"

Emannuel, Arabella thought. I dug him up as a contact. Disloyal bastard.

Max put a serious expression on and leaned forward in a fatherly way. "I want you to attend the event. You seem to like participating in the outside world." He shuddered. "But I'll write it up. The Editor felt it was too important to trust to anyone other than me. Keep in mind every paper in the world will be covering this event. See if you can dig up something new. You'll get research credit, of course."

"Something new?" Arabella said through clenched teeth. "For a research credit?"

Max nodded. "Go for it. Something like an interview with the biogrid's inventor." He laughed. "Hell, pull that off and I'll share the byline with you. That guy's been as slippery as— "

Arabella shot to her feet. "So I'll do all the work, and you'll reap the glory."

"Since I know you love to be busy," Max Max continued quickly, "I've got a new assignment for you. Multisound Labs called, they've got a new vinyl record in production. It's an important story, I'm counting on you."

"This is so like you." Arabella kept talking. "Well, it's not going to happen. Not this time. Not again."

"I don't know what you're on about." He pouted. "It's not like you to be so feisty, Arabella."

"It's exactly like me." She kept her tone even only with a great effort. "My feistiness is the reason I find so many stories. Stories that you steal, because you're too busy sucking up to the Editor to do your job."

"I'd be careful if I were you," he said, stroking his chin. "We have to follow protocol. I am senior to you. The Editor knows best." He pointed to the door of his office, and Arabella spun around. Standing there, sporting a flinty little smile, was the Editor.

"I don't like being careful." She stared into Max's eyes and then the Editor's. "You never find stories, Max, because your whole life is spent in your home, your car, or here in your office. What are you so afraid of? Good journalism doesn't come from being careful. A new angle won't appear while you're one of the crowd. You have to get out there and take risks." *And if this is the sort of newspaper where careful people are encouraged, then I don't want to be part of it.* She heard the words in her head, felt them pushing to come out, but she pressed her lips together, and left.

People clustered around the edge of the newsroom that held the department offices, all trying to look busy, listening for all they were worth. As she pushed her way through them, she realized her anger was now directed at herself.

∘∘∘   ∘∘∘   ∘∘∘

A wide street downtown had been closed to all traffic but Horsepowers. A boulevard with trees and tubs of flowers slit the road down the middle, and tall faceless buildings lined either side. The Horsepowers were parked along the street, each with its owner sitting inside, door open so as to be better able to show off the vehicle and answer questions from the admiring people clustered thickly around. Clive headed into one of the buildings for overhead shots, leaving Arabella to look about.

Some sort of signal must have passed between the twenty owners, because they began driving down one side of the boulevard and up the other, a triumphant circle of cars.

They didn't look like normal traffic, though. The distances between them weren't equal, and the cars changed speed. A roan pulled up behind a grey and passed. Arabella blinked. Could the owners have disabled the guidance system and distance sensors in their vehicles?

A sorrel car moved behind a white one until its bumper was scant inches from the car in front. The white turned and the two faced each other, side mirrors pinned back.

The standoff blocked the road, and the other Horsepowers clustered behind. Clive reappeared beside Arabella as Mr. Emmanuel, wearing a top hat, ran across the boulevard, ducking so branches wouldn't knock his hat off. "What have you done?" he cried. "How is this possible?"

Arabella wondered the same thing. No one had ever been able to disable safety features. Encryption, locks, and multiple redundancy made sure of that.

A slight man with coffee-colored skin stood not far from Arabella, his dark eyes intent on the cars. A small smile curved his mouth beneath his plaited mustache.

Arabella nudged Clive, excitement tightening her chest. "That's Dr. Syed." Clive lifted his holocam.

Mr. Emmanuel had reached the cars and was waving his arms and yelling. An owner, a small elderly man, got out and began yelling back. He was joined by other owners, including Kitsy dressed all in yellow satin, the latest rebel clothes.

"Yes," the old man cried, and his voice rang triumphantly. "We have disabled all that kept our Horsepowers enslaved."

"Other cars may be happy with a life of safe speeds and obedience to rules," someone else yelled, and Arabella saw it was the cowboy she'd interviewed. "Our Horsepowers will never submit."

"Cars aren't capable of happiness or unhappi—" Mr. Emmanuel tried, but he was drowned out by the owners, all of whom had left their vehicles. Kitsy jumped onto the hood of a chestnut car, but was quickly pulled down by the elderly man, who seemed concerned that her clogs would hurt the vehicle.

Mr. Emmanuel, joined by other ad men, yelled. The owners yelled. The smile on Dr. Syed's face grew. The two cars with pinned-back mirrors put their back ends toward each other, and one suddenly kicked with its back tires, the roof arching to enable the move. The other cars moved about, some snapping with their hoods, others using their radiator fans to blow into each other's grilles.

Arabella was glad she'd come. This was fun. But now it was time to get Dr. Syed to talk to her. "Horses," she said loudly to Clive, "get to know each other by blowing into nostrils."

Dr. Syed glanced over. "You know horses?" His accent rounded vowels and turned his words into music.

Arabella shook her head ruefully. "Based on what I've seen of the Horsepowers, I wish I did. But no, I'm merely thorough in my research."

He nodded in understanding. Arabella fumbled in her bag for her notescreen. No way she'd share a byline for this interview. But Dr. Syed was turning his attention back to the cars. Arabella, desperate to keep him talking, said the first words she could think of. "Do you like horses?"

He turned back. "I admire horses. I like all living things."

"You mean animals?"

"Living means being true to one's nature. Thinking, but not as we now define it. A tree doesn't accept what other trees tell it to think. A worm has worm thoughts, and no amount of people trying to tell it otherwise will prevent it from burrowing into dirt. A horse," he gestured to the Horsepowers, "has horse thoughts. Trees, worms, and horses are alive."

"You create machines that think?"

He swept an arm out, taking in the identical facades on the buildings, the perfectly timed stream of traffic that could be seen in the distance. "That depends on how you define thinking." His brows came together. "They wanted to use my biogrid to make even more beings who think as they are instructed."

"You mean," Arabella said slowly, "you create beings that think for themselves? And that makes them alive?"

He looked away, his eyes now distant. "Do you have the freedom to be who you are?"

"How can I?" she asked, but he was once again intent on his creations. Arabella, following his gaze, saw the owners pushing the ad people away from the cars, Kitsy in front, pounding on Mr. Emmanuel's chest. His top hat was gone, probably crushed underfoot.

Despite the barrage, Mr. Emmanuel stood his ground, his voice ringing above the angry owners'. "We can't have a car that isn't obeying the rules of the road. Think of the increase in accidents. You don't want your nice new car hurt, do you?"

Arabella couldn't make out individual words amid the swell of anger from the owners. A thought struck her. "Are Horsepower owners alive?" she asked Dr. Syed. He said nothing, only smoothed his mustache and smiled, and she knew who'd disabled the safety features.

The cars had become a tight group, and they moved within the cluster uneasily, side mirrors flicking. A few of them lifted and stamped their tires.

A siren blared from the end of the block. "I've called the police," Emmanuel shouted. "What you've done to these vehicles is illegal and now you'll be arrested." The police cars, sirens in full wail, pulled up beside him, and one officer jumped out and shot a stun sound wave over the crowd.

The Horsepowers panicked. The increasing tension in the air, the sirens, and now this sudden loud noise sent them into chaos. Some reared, some bumped others, but they all ran, at first in many directions, some crashing through the trees on the boulevard, or knocking over the tubs of flowers. Soon, though, as if they felt greater safety in numbers, they regrouped and raced together down the road, past people hurling themselves out of the way, until they vanished into the haze of traffic at the end of the blocked-off street.

The owners stood in a forlorn clump. "Come back," the cowboy yelled. "We wanted you free, but not like this."

Dr. Syed still stood beside Arabella. He spoke now, maybe to himself, maybe to the owners, Arabella couldn't tell. "Free?" he asked. "Free to follow your commands?" With that, he vanished into the crowd.

∘∘∘   ∘∘∘   ∘∘∘

Arabella sat at her desk in the newsroom, watching the latest edition of the paper. 'No trace has been found of any of the runaway vehicles,' her screen told her. A holo of a brown Horsepower floated beside the projected words. ' "Amazingly, they avoided accidents and made their way through traffic to the edge of the city," said Mr. Emmanuel, responsible for promoting the new form of transportation. "This is a very new technology. We still have high hopes for a car with which an owner can have a fulfilling relationship. Dr. Syed will no doubt have learned much from this experience, and he'll perfect his design very soon." ' There was no other mention of Syed in the article.

"You did the right thing," a voice beside Arabella said. Looking up, she saw Clive.

She sighed. "I guess so."

"He doesn't want people to know this design turned out exactly as he'd planned. He added a little chaos to a world that's too predictable. And he wouldn't have spoken to you if he'd known you were a journalist."

Arabella looked back at the screen, at the byline above the article, that said, 'By Maximilian Thurston.' "Most of my successes as a journalist have come from listening to people who don't want to talk to me."

"But they do want to talk." He smiled at her, his brown eyes warm. "It's one of your gifts, Arabella, letting then know you want to listen." He turned to leave.

"Do we," she asked, grabbing his elbow, "only think what we're told to think?"

He squeezed her shoulder. "Let me know when you want me to take pictures again."

She stared back at the screen. The holo now showed the cars racing away en masse. Across the room, Max Max sat in his windowed office, accepting congratulations on his dynamite story.

Arabella wished she had told the Editor what he could do with her job. Was security really more important than being true to oneself? For many people it was, but the thought brought a wetness to her eyes, which she impatiently brushed away. "I am feisty," she whispered. "Does that mean I'm a little bit alive?" As she switched off her computer, it comforted her to know that somewhere a herd of cars raced free across the prairie, the wind streaming cool and fresh over their windshields.

BACK HOME

Bev Brenna

Easy again
to walk and watch
the sun's first glance
against soft could

I walk alone;
I know this place
where shy defines
a space for words

Fields I had forgotten
Scratch their backs
against my step
as voices curved in travel
straighten—
memory adjusts itself

PRESERVES

Bev Brenna

This morning she counts the jars.
Still eleven, hidden under pillows,
behind doors, inside the closet

She has breakfast—dry toast and tea,
then sits at the television
With the sound turned off.
In case someone comes.

It is her responsibility to protect them—
the sealers of carrots, radishes, beets.
The last of their kind,
she keeps them a secret.

There used to be twelve.
But last week one disappeared
while she was sleeping.
Later she found the jar, empty
under the sink.

Baruch, the Man-Faced Dog

Steven Michael Berzensky

*Prop. XXIV. The more we understand particular
things, the more we will understand God.*

Spinoza, The Ethics, Part V.

*I believe that a triangle, if it could speak, would
say that God is eminently triangular, and a circle
would say that the divine nature is eminently
circular; and so it is that everyone would ascribe
his own attributes to God… and everything else would
be seen as ill-suited [to be like God].*

Correspondence, Spinoza to Boxel, 1674

I.

I stood in front of the cage with my friends. We were passing a large bag of popcorn back and forth. One of my friends threw some popcorn into the cage. I watched the kernels bounce on the floor before they settled there among the peanut shells and food scraps.

On a paint-blistered sign outside the cage the black-lettered words read:

Dog with Human Face—
One of the World's Wonders
9 am - 12 noon
2 pm - 4 pm
7 pm - 9 pm
Closed on Holidays

At the back of the cage the creature napped. I could not see his face, but he looked like a dark, long-haired sheepdog. One of my friends was trying to coax him to get up, to show his face. "Come on, boy! Come on! We wanna get a good look at you! Here, boy! Here!" My friend tossed in some more popcorn.

The dog raised his head. Every one of us responded in surprise and shock. No question about it: this dog had the eyes and nose and mouth of a man. His ears were covered by his long black hair, so I couldn't tell if they were human ears or dog ears.

He stared at my vocal friend. The expression on the dog's face seemed to be one of disgust. He shook his hairy head as if to say, "No matter how hard you try, you won't bring me down to your level. I may be a dog but I'm more intelligent than you."

His thoughts seemed to register in my mind through his very expressive eyes and from the way he turned his head. Yet everything else about him was totally doglike. Large paws that sprawled before him, a curled tail that occasionally flapped against the concrete floor, and a slow breathing, hair-covered body that was unmistakably canine. I thought of him then as "the man-faced dog." "Dog with human face" seemed softer, less blunt, less accurate—wrong, somehow.

It pleased me to see the man-faced dog not eating any of the stuff tossed onto his cage floor. He stood and stretched his front legs the way all dogs do, but yawned like a man as his body quivered. Now he had an almost arrogant or defiant look in his eyes, as if he refused to stoop so low, to even pretend to notice us. At this point I was staring at him, trying to understand him, trying to figure out how a dog ended up having a man's face and a man's eyes. Usually dogs have the saddest eyes, but this one had the eyes of an insolent human being.

I made eye contact with the dog. I knelt by the cage, so I would not have to stand above him. He must have noticed this gesture for he scooted towards me. My friends jumped back. It was an amazing moment. In that instant I could sense that both of us wanted to assess the intelligence and the empathy of the other. I saw the insolence leave his eyes, replaced by something that seemed closer to openness and amiability. Now I couldn't help myself; I began talking to him:

"You don't like popcorn, do you? And you certainly don't like being treated this way." It was a statement of fact as far as I was concerned.

But one of my friends, his mouth stuffed with popcorn, looked down at me and elbowed another friend: "Hey, Gerald is trying to communicate with the pooch. He thinks it will talk to him."

I glanced up, feeling perturbed at my companions, even embarrassed by their friendship. "Listen, I'll see you guys later. OK?" I wanted to talk to the creature, to at least make the effort. This whole scene in which I had been taking part was making me feel dispirited and alienated. Was I the kind of human being who likes to cage other not-so-human beings?

My friends grumbled and cursed but walked away; now no one else was standing outside the man-faced dog's cage. At least I wouldn't feel so self-conscious trying to talk to him.

"Please forgive my friends," I said. "They don't know what they're saying. They—"

A voice interrupted me. "Oh, but Gerald, they know what they're saying. You know it and I know it. So it does no good to cover up for them. I see through them just as much as you do."

My god, it was the man-faced dog. I jerked my head back. "You're talking. You're actually talking. And you know my name."

"See, not only can I speak, but I can hear too. And do you notice, I'm speaking English, not Italian or Portuguese. Quite a shock, eh?'

"God," I said, "this is fantastic. You're not only a man-faced dog, you're actually… partly… human."

"I'm fully human, my friend."

I glanced around to see if anyone else was witnessing this unbelievable encounter. "Fully human?"

"I'll prove it to you," he said. "Just squeeze between these bars, Gerald. You're thin enough."

Suddenly, I was wary. I didn't respond, just stared at the man-faced dog now conversing so easily with me from his cage.

"Don't worry," he said. "You'll be safe. I guarantee it. I won't bite you, Gerald. See, I don't bark either. I talk. I told you, I'm fully human."

I was shaking my head. "How can I be sure it's all right? What will happen to me once I get into the cage?"

"My friend, I'm going to take you behind the cage—to my real home. I want you to meet my family and see how I live. That's all. I'm really a friendly sort of person. And I don't eat human beings either. In fact, I've become a vegetarian. Now how do you like that?"

For a talking dog, he was certainly persuasive. I glanced around, then squeezed myself between the bars. They were cold and rusted and it was difficult maneuvering my body between them; they hurt my shoulder blades and scraped my head, but I did manage to end up inside the cage instead of out.

The dog was restless, circling in front of me. "Follow me, quickly." Some people were approaching the cage, so I figured he wanted me out of sight. I watched him crawl into a large circular hole in the back wall of the cage. I had to get down on my hands and knees to follow him inside that hole. I couldn't move as fast as he did, but I was amazed at how promptly, without any more hesitation, I followed the dog's commands.

I remained in my crawling position in a narrow passageway, lit by one electric bulb in the far wall. I could see another circular hole just ahead, to the dog's left. I could hear the hollow, amplified sounds of a television game show, with the host and the audience cheering on some screaming contestants. Then I heard a man and a woman laughing inside a room beyond the hole.

"This is where I live, my friend," he said, nodding his head toward the hole. "The cage is just for show."

Wagging his tail, the man-faced dog bounded through the hole. The only way I could follow was on my hands and knees.

II.

As I crawled through the second hole, all I could think about was an endless stream of questions: What will his family be like? Will it be his mother who is also a dog? Or his father? Will one parent be human? Where do his parents sleep? In a bed or on the floor like the man-faced dog in his cage? Does he talk to his parents? Do they talk to him? How do they treat him? How do they live? Are they a happy or an unhappy family?

As my brain overflowed with these questions, I realized I was crawling on the carpeted floor of a trailer home. Should I stand up or stay on all fours?

The man-faced dog stopped in the middle of the largest room. "This is Gerald, a friend of mine."

He nodded towards me. I had remained hunched over, eye to eye with my host. I looked up.

A man and a woman were lounging before a television set, the woman leaning back in a drab green armchair and the man sprawled out before her, his head in her lap, his feet propped on the coffee table in front of the chair. Red and white beer cans glittered on the coffee table and on the floor. The man was thin and the woman was plump. She wore a skirt and blouse and white bobby sox, he wore tattered Levis and a white T-shirt. He was wiggling his bare toes. She was massaging his scalp.

"Yeah, another friend," the woman said. "We've got eyes, Bayruch, we can see." She was not even glancing at me.

The man burped. "This is one hell of a show, son."

"*Wheel of Fortune*," the woman said.

"Hey, guys," the man said, "don't just stand there. You and your pal, come and join us. This show's a million laughs. Drag your tail over here."

"Yeah, don't be a party pooper," the woman added.

"No thanks," the man-faced dog said. He said it with politeness. Then he turned towards me and lowered his voice.

"I didn't invite you in here to sit with my mother and father and watch a bunch of greedy human beings making fools of themselves. I want to show you my library."

I was flabbergasted. These two people were his mother and father? And his name was Baruch? And he read books? And this is where he lived—here, in a trailer home behind a cage in a traveling exhibition? How could this be?

Someone as intelligent as he was, someone who could talk as clearly and distinctly as any human being I had ever met?

He scampered into the kitchen. In a corner near an aluminum sink he placed one of his paws on a small stack of hardbound books. The covers looked old and worn, like library discards. I could make out some of the titles. *Thus Spake Zarathustra* by Nietzsche. Plato's *The Republic*. Spinoza's *The Ethics*.

"My god," I said, crawling after him, "you're a philosopher!"

"A philosophy student," he said. "There's a difference. I haven't written anything yet."

"Do you plan to?"

"Maybe. One day."

I hoped we were out of earshot of his parents, but I knew we weren't out of their sight.

"You don't have any privacy here," I said. "How do you manage to stay sane? Do they watch TV all night? And drink beer?"

"Unfortunately, my mother and father are a pair of souses." He said this the way someone might inform you it's starting to rain outside. "They like to do their thing, I like to do mine. We don't always understand one another."

Delicately, with his paw, he opened the top volume on the stack, Spinoza's *The Ethics*. "This is my favourite book," he said. "I've read it at least forty times."

He didn't gaze at me to see if I was impressed. He kept right on talking, with intense enthusiasm.

"After my third reading of this book, I knew I didn't want to be called Benny anymore. So I told my mother and father, 'Stop calling me Benny. From now on, my name's Baruch.' After Baruch Spinoza, the Dutch-Jewish philosopher. I told them how he changed his name from Baruch to Benedict--and now I was doing the opposite. That's what I announced, quietly but firmly. They just laughed at me and refused to call me anything but Benny, the name they gave me the day I was born. But I insisted they call me Baruch. For a day or two they kept calling me Benny, out of sheer habit. But I didn't respond. 'Benny, wash the dishes. Benny, scrub the floor. Benny, vacuum the rugs. Benny, clean the toilet.' Finally, in exasperation, my mother started calling me Baruch. It was only then that I responded.

Then it was official. Baruch, Baruch. Such a noble name. You notice that my mother doesn't pronounce my name correctly. But I use the correct intonation. My name. Baruch. That's Hebrew for Blessed."

I was feeling dazed, rapt in admiration. But I still couldn't think of the dog as fully human. I put my hand on his back and stroked his fur.

He let me pet him for a few seconds, then pointed to a page in The Ethics. "This is my favourite passage. It's actually from one of Spinoza's letters. His analogy of the triangles. Are you familiar with it?"

"No, I'm afraid not."

Baruch, the man-faced dog, was one up on me. He knew more about philosophy than I knew about English and History.

"These were the words that made me accept myself just as I am. I no longer felt ashamed of myself. I no longer believed I was ugly or abnormal. That's what my mother and father had taught me: I was special but unnatural. They still believe that. But after reading Spinoza I knew who God was and who I was." His eyes glistened with tears. "For me, God has a human face… and the body of a dog."

"Pardon me?"

"It's simply a logical extension of Spinoza's analogy on triangles. And it's like everything else he wrote. Cold and clear and carefully thought out. His mind was mathematical. He structured his universe according to a system of geometric definitions, axioms, propositions, proofs, and corollaries. He wrote his entire Ethics this way. Baruch Spinoza, my 17th century freelance rabbi. My rational teacher. My spiritual father."

"I can see you're a fan of Spinoza's, but what did he say about triangles?"

He grinned. "Spinoza proved to me: If men were triangles and worshipped God, then God would be a triangle."

That did it. It felt like my head was being twisted out of shape. My body was cold and feverish at the same time. "This is all too much for me," I said. "I'm feeling dizzy. I'm feeling faint."

"Spiritual vertigo, my friend. Spiritual vertigo! I experience it every day. It's the internal proof—eternity's testimony—that I have an immortal soul. And so do you. And so do my father and mother, although they don't know it." Here he started chuckling; this human being in a dog's body was chuckling. "For all we know, even triangles have immortal souls. How do you like that?"

I sat down on my haunches on the cold kitchen linoleum. I was trying to recover from this stimulation overload: the television set blaring too loudly in the trailer, especially during the commercial breaks; the laughing and burping of his drunken parents; the astounding revelations of how the man-faced dog really lived; the concrete evidence of how extremely intelligent he was. All this was more than I or any human being could handle.

"Don't you ever want to leave this place?" I finally said. "I mean, this way of life. It seems so demeaning, surviving here like this. Someone who's a genius like you should be teaching at a university—and not be displayed in a cage like a freak."

Then I added: "And how much housework do your parents make you do? While they're sitting back and guzzling beer and watching TV? I'm telling you, it's inhuman and unjust."

Baruch wasn't chuckling now. But he wasn't crying either. He was laughing—laughing with all the heartiness of an easy-going soul, a contented man.

"Forgive me, my friend. But what you say is hilarious. I can see you're feeling sorry for me. But you're not asking me if I'm feeling sorry for me.

"You need to understand something. My life is not perfect, but it is a good life. Now, how can that be?

"The world will never accept a dog with a human face to teach an introductory course in philosophy. But the world will accept a man with a dog's body in a sideshow."

He lifted his head toward the window above the kitchen sink.

"At least I can say, the world out there is leaving me alone. And, my friend, most of the time, I want to be left alone. I need my solitude. I need my books. I need my time for serious studies.

"Do you realize what would happen to me if I went to university—not as a professor but as a student?

"I'd end up on TV. I'd be interviewed on all the late night talk shows; I'd even become a contestant on some of those game shows—*Wheel of Fortune, Let's Make a Deal, Jeopardy*. My parents would walk into taverns and order rounds of beer and poke complete strangers in the ribs and say, 'That's our boy! That's our Benny! Have another beer—it's on us!'

"No, I'm better off just like this. I'm safe. This cage and this trailer, they're my world, my cocoon."

I could not look him in the eyes. "Baruch, can I ask you a very personal question?"

"Ah," he said. "I know, I know. It's the one question everyone asks. Or wants to ask. I can read your mind, my friend. Yes, that's really my mother and that's really my father. So how is it possible I was born with a human face and a dog's body? That's what you want to know, right?'

I nodded.

He grinned.

"My friend, this can no more be explained than the virgin birth of Jesus."

"Aw, don't listen to him!" his mother said. "That son of mine is full of more cock and bull than a field of cows. He reads too much. He doesn't watch enough television. He doesn't live in the real world. He's not like the rest of us."

"Hey, Marlene, that's telling him," his father said. "It's nothing but the God-awful truth that leaves her precious lips." As if to punctuate his statement, the man burped. "Come on, son, come on over here. You and your pal, you're missing out on all the fun."

"I think I'd better take you back outside," my host said. "They'll be entering their belligerent phase in just a few minutes. No sense putting you through that."

He padded towards the door to the trailer. "You should leave this way," he said. "No sense crawling back into the cage." But when he pushed on the door with his front paws, it wouldn't budge.

"Locked," he said. "I apologize. They've done it again. Sometimes my mother and father are afraid I'm going to try to escape. I'm their livelihood, after all. Their ticket to the good life."

He led me away from the door. "My friend, you'll have to leave the way you came in. Through the hole. Sorry."

"Oh, that's all right," I said. But I was feeling sad and depressed.

At the circular hole he looked contemplative, solemn.

"This is as far as I go. I've got to make supper now." He glanced back at his parents. "Tonight it's spaghetti and meatballs for them, spaghetti in butter sauce for me."

Then Baruch, the man-faced dog, wagged his tail. "I know this isn't heaven, but I don't believe it's hell either."

He winked one eye. "Purgatory, perhaps. But that's not so unusual, is it?"

I shook his paw. "Goodbye," I said.

"Goodbye," he said.

ooo   ooo   ooo

As I entered the cage, a cluster of people stood outside the bars. When they saw me crawling on my hands and knees, they nudged one another and pointed at me and began laughing.

"Look," they said, "the dog is wearing a suit!"

I could see it would do no good to tell them I was a human being with a human face. I'd have to stand up and squeeze through the bars to prove that.

For now, I felt ashamed of my own humanity. As a form of penance, I remained on all fours and began to bark.

WEAK IS (FIERCE IN COMPENSATION)

Gillian Harding-Russell

weak is (fierce
in compensation)

If all we are is
molecule against molecule, bumping in the night
aminos effervescing in blood black stream, activating,
neutralizing. jelly fish brain...

... if all you are is chromosome
locked into chromosome (twenty-three askew
or disfigured so you are
who you are, will succumb to messages
written in the blood, Joan of Arc wieldings
to take effect at exactly eighteen;

or chromosome thirty-three ever-so-slightly
out of shape, you are to be
found deficient), *who is*
to blame?

If it is written in the blood that
in your forty-seventh year you will suffer
brain haemorrhaging (to be averted until
your fifty-seventh, except for your lifestyle, the untidiness
of the dreams littering your day : despair, a sagging cloud
with happiness, you are sure of it
on the other side
of yourself : a mirage—

...if all you are is chemical soup, substances
in balance
or out of it, amoebic desires mapping
ahead your life (divotally knocking off
my clod of dirt) dream, your life
in stencil, with something unawares
bulldozing your brain to the appropriate
topography: bridges/synapses, mental /blocks
set up by old reluctance, fears, doubt—a roadside ditch
rankly, inescapably, to be breathed
on either side of you—

Say at high noon, you shout
at me—
invisible words riding the perfect air,
(slicing to the quick) spermazzoic scarring
with jet-like spume through azure nonchalance
subsiding, on the outside, changing me,
on the inside , endometrically (your version
of me, my version of you) translating
us both into our undiscardable
other selves—

When the moon is a sack on the Devil's shoulders,
and I shout back, transforming myself
into the werewolf I need
to become to blaze my way
through the dark (remembered untidiness of the day
interfering with my conception
of myself, leaving me grappling
in a windy skein of the mind's clouded
tanglings—excessive tidiness
of certain other dreams, etched on that blackness
engraving themselves, allowing for
no substitute
satisfaction, less than
themselves) —
… but, you say, you did
not choose those obsessions?

Through another chemical change
thought (brain's high ball)—lubricated by desire's
two-facedness—through chemically-charged passages into
words, words. Actions, yours, and
mine, sporadic cutting—

Afterwards, just these hieroglyphs
on the trampled landscape of ourselves: rumpled sheets of the bed
left unmade, your car keys, the lost ones,
after you've gone off with the spares in the upper drawer
this holographic memory: your face, unsmiling
(when I notice a lonely tree still standing, which is
yourself—)

THOSE WHO REMEMBER

Martha Bayless

I.

On an afternoon in early fall, 1887, a day of gray skies and horsetail clouds, Frank Kelly, itinerant trapper, ranch hand, and sometime buffalo skinner, came across a cave in a bluff overlooking the Fox River. It is not clear why he ventured inside the cave, nor what he was doing on the vast loneliness of the plains after so many years of loss and bad fortune there. The Bismark *Tribune* reported that he was looking for Indian grave goods, but he told a journalist from the Fargo *Democrat* that he chanced upon the crevice while looking for his dog, the only living thing left to him after sixteen years on the frontier.

Kelly was out on the plains, where landmarks are scarce, and he never did say for certain where that bluff was. The Democrat reported that it was on the boundary of the Spotted Tail Agency, but the Chicago Sun put it on the Great Wallow ranch, a spread which had just been fenced the previous year, when the last of the buffalo had been killed. It could have been either of those places, or another one altogether: the bluffs of the Northern Plains are riddled with caves.

The bluff which contained the cave, said Frank Kelly, had been called Niyapelayi by the local Indians. In fact, the word Niyapelayi does not appear in the local Lakota tongue; it is one of few words surviving from the Pelayi Indians, who had perished under the force of the movement westward in the earlier part of the century. The word "Pelayi" means "Those Who Remember."

Kelly had climbed up to the opening of the cave, a scramble of about four feet, and found that it led deeper into the bluff, at a gentle downward slope. The air was cool and still: "moist," he said, "like something breathing." The passage opened out until it was wide enough for a man to walk along with his arms outspread, higher than he could touch. The earth floor was packed tight. As he moved away from the entrance, venturing carefully along a corridor of hard-packed clay, the tunnel darkened, Kelly proceeded in the gloom until he could scarcely see his hand in front of his face. "I was hoping I finally got lucky," he told the Fargo Democrat. "Thought I was going to find some Indian ruins, maybe treasure. I seen some hard times since they closed the frontier. Lost my wife because I couldn't pay for a doctor. My oldest boy got killed, looking for gold over at Tomahawk Creek, not eighteen years old, and then my other boy drowned over at Sawmill. I was thinking maybe something in my life was going to turn happy, for once." He wondered if he should go back for a lantern, but decided to press on. "Was hoping I found my fortune at last," he said. Instead of Indian treasure, however, he found a vast chamber, "bigger than a church," he said. "But there wasn't no echo. Like that chamber was packed full of something."

The truth is, what Kelly really did see in that chamber has never been clear. What he said can hardly be believed. He told some tall tales, Frank Kelly, after he came out of that cave in the bluff. The fact is, he was half crazy when he came out.

II.

Jack Finch laid his mother to rest in Baltimore, the first day of March, the first year of the new century, nineteen-hundred. First Roscoe had been taken with diphtheria, then little Mary, and finally their mother, leaving Finch alone, fifteen, with no home and no trace of his father but a watch and an extra pair of shoes. He sold the contents of the tenement: the iron bedstead, the tin basin, his mama's worn calico dresses and her buffalo robe, the last of the wedding presents, which had served as quilt and comforter in the dead of winter. This bought him a ticket to Chicago and from Chicago on to the Dakotas.

On the train he took up with a man who'd been a skinner in the boom days of the West. His jacket was buttoned very tight, as the fashion had been some years before, and he had patches on his boots.

"I done it all," said the man. "Traded with the Cheyenne, the Nez Perce and the Pend d'Oreilles, before most of them got killed. Spent a winter trapping in the Yellowstone, came back and did the medicine shows, and now I'm heading up to Blackfeet territory." The train swept them into a landscape of grasses tinged with purple. The man eyed Finch's shoes and traded him a skinning knife for his extra pair. As they crossed the plains he told a lot of stories about hidden valleys teeming with elk and trapping martens as big as mountain cats.

Finch said later that it was this man and his rumors that sent him off in search of Niyapelayi.

At Cut Bank he pawned his father's watch and hired a horse and a mule from a man at the Western Prairie livery stable. He set out just at sunrise, a bright cold day in April. Reached the Sheyenne River the evening of the first day, made camp. Frost on the ground the morning of the second day. Two more days through wild country and he saw the bluff on the horizon. It was cold out there on the plains; he was wishing he was back feeding the tenement fire with coal, watching over the children; wishing he had the buffalo robe with him, the robe that always made him think of his mother. Wishing he weren't alone in the wilderness, and all his family in the world cold and dead.

He got to the bluff just at dinnertime, the third day, hobbled the horse and mule, noticing their long shadows stretching over the pale ground. He went in the cave straightaway, carrying his only weapon, the skinning knife he'd gotten in trade from the man on the train. Somewhere along the way he dropped it. His photograph shows him to be a pale man, as if the blood had drained clean from his face. The legends say he got that paleness at Niyapelayi.

Finch didn't have a living relative in the world, so when he got a little unsteady, got to raving to people about everything he'd lost, it was the North Shore Asylum, back in Chicago, that finally took him in. The Asylum has kept detailed records, but none of those records say what Finch saw at Niyapelayi.

Seems understandable one man might go a little crazy, being underground, maybe seeing something strange and old. But must be mighty strange and old to haunt two men to their graves, and those two never able to tell a story a sensible man might believe.

III.

Joseph Porter and his new bride Louisa, both from Pittsburgh, went out to the West young. It was 1927, and the spirit of progress was accelerating through the country like a locomotive. With the autos and aeroplanes so cheap and fast, a man could get out to the West in a matter of days, to see it all the way it used to be.

Porter worked for the Carnegie Museum, American Collections: he was twenty-six, raised in the Allegheny Mountains, a tall man, lean and hard-muscled, with spectacles. He often rambled the countryside looking for Indian relics. That was how he met Louisa. She was out on a sketching expedition at the edge of town; he tipped his hat; they had pleasant conversation. He collected everything he could lay his hands on: quartz and gypsum, tiny arrowheads, stone axes, birds' eggs, trilobites, seed pods. He hankered to see the West. In July 1927 he and Louisa, married ten months, closed up their house and set out for North Dakota.

Porter, an antiquarian by nature as well as by trade, kept field notes of every expedition, and the journals he left the museum describe their trip in detail. He had meant to make the journey in autumn, when the days would be cooler, but Louisa was still much affected by the death of her younger sister, Margaret ("Meggie," they called her) some six months before. "I hope the unfamiliar landscapes of the West will distract her mind from the loss," Porter wrote. "Her grief is still quite severe." He thought it would be helpful to visit a different countryside, one Meggie had never seen. With the museum sponsoring him, Porter planned a trip to the northern plains to chart the ruins of Indian camps and ghost towns. He noted as he plotted their itinerary that he particularly wanted to visit Niyapelayi.

On the eighth of July they loaded two suitcases, a trunk and a collecting chest aboard the Super Chief to Chicago; after a night at the Drake Hotel, they continued on the Nor'wester to Fargo. Even before they left Minnesota Porter found the sky larger and deeper than he had ever imagined, the land more vast and varied with draws and hollows.

They arrived in Fargo in early evening and were met by Mr. Adamson from the Northern Plains Historical Museum; he was an elderly man with a dusty suit. The station was surrounded by cars: LaSalles, Reos, Model A's. Adamson led them to a buckboard with two horses tied to the railing amidst the cars. "You're wondering, why's this man still keeping horses?" he said. "Well, I hang on to the old ways long as I can. They were good ways for a thousand years, no need to throw 'em away so sudden." It was the first time in many months, Porter noted, that he had seen Louisa smile.

In the morning, before they set out on the long drive to Fox River, they took a tour of the Northern Plains Historical Museum itself. "It's all things we chanced across here and there," said Adamson, unlocking the door of the museum, a small brick house three blocks from the main street. "We don't go in for digging the way you Carnegie folks do. Poking around Indian caverns and such - they say there's no end of riches out there, when you know how to get to 'em. But it's all dead men's riches, and I want no truck with the dead. Leave 'em sleep, I say. We don't go fetching things up; they come up soon enough by themselves."

They entered a dark anteroom lined with glass cases, and Adamson pulled up the shades. The strong morning sun illuminated a wall of arrowheads. "All Indian things in this room," said Adamson. Porter leaned over a case and studied the array of objects with their hand-written labels. There were painted rawhide bags, moccasins with green and white beading, and a yellowed buffalo skull labelled "Prey of Former Times." Along the side of the case were two story-sticks etched with figures and pictographs.

"Dead men's things," said Adamson. "You might say I'm the keeper of the dead, and this is the land of the lost and gone."

ooo   ooo   ooo

By the time they had toured the museum it was mid-morning. They rented a station wagon at Fargo Livery & Autos and set out for the Ingermans' ranch house, six miles from Fox River, where they had arranged to take a cabin for a fortnight. Soon after one o'clock they reached the Sheyenne River, shaded by cottonwoods, where Louisa spread out a linen cloth and they picnicked on plums and sandwiches with chicken paste. When they had finished Louisa shook the cloth into the long grass. "This is buffalo grass," said Porter. "Look at it all. Peppergrass, wolfberry, saltgrass. They grow along the river still, where the sod hasn't been broken. See where it ends?" The grass fringed the water; across the river they could see a strip of prairie grasses moving in the wind like the swell of the sea, and beyond the narrow strip a plain of ripening English wheat.

They reached the Ingermans' ranch just after sundown, the edge of the sky still glowing, the prairie grasses cast into darkness. After they had stowed their satchels in the cabin, Mr. Ingerman, a widower, presided at a late dinner of salad and cold beef. The dining room in which they sat was small but elegant, with oil portraits of elderly gentlemen, a candelabra and a marble-topped sideboard of golden oak.

"This house has been here forty-three years," said Ingerman. "A family name of Hanson homesteaded this piece in 1884. The Indians had hardly been gone when they moved on the land. There was considerable blood shed here in times gone by, but those days are over. I bought the place when my boys were in short pants—now they're helping me out on the north range. Of course you've got the run of the whole spread, but I can't give you much advice. Don't hold much store by digging up the past, myself."

Porter reached for another slice of cold beef. "We were hoping to find Frank Kelly's cave. My wife and I are both very curious—we've read the old stories."

"Well, good luck to you," said Ingerman. "I went looking for that cave myself once, and never found a thing. I have a hunch it's all crazy tales. People get out on the plains, out by themselves, sometimes they think too much. We had a woman out here from the Spiritualist Society, wanted to speak to the ghosts of the early pioneers, brought her whole seance group from Fargo. They were rapping tables and I don't know what all. Then she had a dizzy spell, we had the doctor out—turned out she had sunstroke from riding out to the ranch in the heat of the day." He raised an eyebrow. "Be sure you keep your hats on when you're out."

"So you don't believe in ghosts, Mr. Ingerman?" said Louisa. "You believe the dead are gone forever?"

"Now that's what I mean about thinking too much," said Ingerman. "You know, we got so much to do on this ranch, with fencing and coyotes, blizzards, calving—the living are plenty trouble. We just let the dead be." He took the platter of beef and offered it to Louisa.

Louisa took the platter. "But where *are* the dead?" she asked. "Where do they go when we forget them? I've been thinking about these things, Mr. Ingerman. Do you think if we looked inside our minds, we might find them living there?"

"For goodness' sakes, Mrs. Porter," said Ingerman. "We try our best to be sensible folk around here. Have some horseradish."

∘∘∘　　∘∘∘　　∘∘∘

They woke before the sun rose; the breeze, already warm, sent the muslin curtains of their cabin playing about the windows like spectres. Porter checked his leather satchel for his small linen bags, ready for artifacts, his collecting boxes, his magnifying glasses and his botany presses. He poured kerosene into the lantern. They ate a small breakfast of bread, apples and cold coffee, and hefted the canteens to be certain they were filled. When they set out the fields were cast in a brilliant light the color of brass.

They drove for an hour at a mule's pace, bumping over the rocky ground of the southwest range, before they came to the tea-colored water of the Fox River. There was a stand of ash along the banks and then the river dipped into a hollow. Above the river stood a dark bluff, steep, sending the water into shadow.

"It's larger than I imagined," said Louisa, "if that's it. Are we here?"

"If I calculated right," said Porter. He turned off the engine and got out of the car. The sun was almost blinding. He leaned against the hood and studied the ordinance map, Louisa beside him. "There's the river," he said, looking up to check the landscape. "The bend, the bluff. This could be it. Frank Kelly described it just like this."

Louisa bent over the map. "Why isn't the name Niyapelayi marked on the map?" she asked. "Why isn't there any name at all?"

Porter looked at the brown water, the bluff and down to the map. "I don't know," he said.

They got their satchels out of the car and slung them over their shoulders, and Porter took the lantern. They made their way around the bluff, pushing between thickets and sage. There was a stand of juniper and clusters of mountain mahogany. The sides of the bluff were a dark clay, the color of old blood. They scrambled up between the bushes and tore away leaves and grass, searching for an entrance to the cave. The bare face of the bluff stood before them.

Louisa stooped down to pull at some weeds, peered closely, and then drew back. "Oh, Joseph!" she said. She had her hand around a small plant with slender leaves and a blue flower like a nodding trumpet. "It's a bellflower," she said. "Do you remember Meggie loved bellflowers so much?"

She reached up to pick another bellflower from the steep face of the bluff and started back.

"Joseph," she said, "This is the cave."

He came up next to her and drew her to him; she kept the bellflower clutched in her hand. The entrance was just above them, a dark crevice partially obscured by a thicket of sage, some four feet from the bottom of the bluff.

"It doesn't seem hidden at all," said Louisa.

Porter scrambled up the slope, catching at the soil with his left hand, until he came to the mouth of the crevice. He set the lantern down, turned and stretched out his hand to Louisa, who climbed up after him, guarding the flower, her walking shoes sliding on the stony clay. Inside the crevice it was cool and dim; when they turned back to look at the plains, the light was dazzling. They could see the fields stretching out behind the river, acres of grass, the stand of ash along the water. Porter knelt to light the lantern and fiddled with the knob to adjust the flow of kerosene.

They turned their backs on the sunlight and began to follow the path into the heart of the bluff. As Frank Kelly had said, it began to slope downward and widened until the lantern-light barely reached the dark rocky walls. Porter reached up: he couldn't touch the ceiling. As they walked the light behind them dwindled until their path was darker than a starless night, the lantern-light barely penetrating the immense blackness.

"It's so dark," said Louisa. "It's like a grave."

They felt their way forward.

"Joseph," said Louisa, stopping all of a sudden.

"What is it?" he said, turning at the sound of her voice, catching sight of her face, dim in the wavering light of the lantern. He reached his hand out to steady her. Her voice was unsteady, as if she were trying not to cry.

"I'm as close to the past here," she said, "as I am back home."

"Lou," said Porter, worried, "are you all right? Shall we go back?"

She looked up at him, as pale as a ghost, and he had an uncanny feeling that he would always remember this moment and the way she looked, clutching the bellflower, small and white in the enormous darkness. It made him shiver to think of it.

"I'm having awful feelings," she said. She was almost whispering. "I can't stop thinking of Meggie. Wherever I go, the same thoughts are with me. It's as if I'm always heading toward them." She shook herself and straightened up. "I'm sorry," she said. "I'm all right. Really. Let's go on."

After a moment they continued to move forward, slowly, studying the ground ahead of them, their small circle of lantern-light framed by the darkness.

ooo ooo ooo

"I try not to think this way," said Louisa. "Do you suppose the dead know when we think about them, Joseph?"

Porter stopped and touched her shoulder. "I don't know, Louisa." The cave was so dark that he could hardly see her, even with the lantern in his hand, and yet the air was not close, but cool and moist. For some reason he himself was thinking about his grandfather, who had shown him all the flowers and mosses along the streams, many years before, and who gave him the first arrowhead for his collection. He hadn't really thought about his grandfather in years.

"Let's go a little farther," he said.

They felt their way deeper into the heart of the cave. "We must be deep underground by now," Porter whispered. He couldn't have said why he was whispering.

The walls widened out further and they felt a breeze on their faces, as if they had come to an open cavern. It was then that they began to hear things: small sounds, as if something very old and sleepy was breathing and shifting in the dark.

"Joseph!" said Louisa, clutching at his arm. "Joseph, I want to go back. Here in the dark, there's nothing else to think about. I'm being overwhelmed by all the thoughts. It's more than I can stand, Joseph. Let's go back."

"You're right," said Porter. "We'll go back."

And before they turned, he raised the lantern.

ooo ooo ooo

Later, he attempted to describe what they saw in his characteristic precise detail, but even so the account is confused. It is not the recollection of a composed man.

"Everything is there," Porter wrote. "All at once. The caverns must be vast, but even so I can't see how it all fits in, just as I can't see how all my thoughts fit in my mind. It's as if the cave, like the mind, stretches on forever.

My grandfather was there—I can hardly write it—holding the arrowhead in his hand, and yet he was asleep, and I couldn't speak to him. He was sitting in the rocking chair from the old house, the one with the embroidered back. I haven't thought of that chair in years. My great-aunt was there, with her lace collar, who died when I was quite young. She never comes into my mind these days, and yet I loved her very much once. And Pouncer, my mother's cat, and Dusty, my old dog, curled up, asleep. And of course Meggie was there, and she was alive, sleeping in her old rocker, but we couldn't wake her. Louisa was beside me, weeping as if her heart was broken. 'Meggie, can't you wake up?" she said. "Can't you answer me?" They couldn't speak—they were all asleep in a sleep as deep as death, and yet they were all living there, all vital, with the color, the intensity of life, just the way we remember them. And the other things: in the side-caverns are the pioneers, asleep on rough blankets, and the Indians who owned the rawhide bags on buffalo robes. Somehow there are whole forests in there, ancient creatures, all the old things sleeping down there, the half-forgotten things. There was a musky smell of saber-tooths and a damp-fur smell of mammoths. Prairie cougar, bobcat, dire wolf. Buffalo. Hundreds of them, maybe thousands of them, in caverns that go back and back, packed close, heads low, asleep, steam rising from their nostrils. All of these things were there in full intensity and detail, and the more we studied them the more they came into focus, and yet it was hard to look at so many things that have passed away, that have been left behind. So many lost and gone things.

"There's no telling how far back the caverns go. I had to take Louisa away. I couldn't have stood to go any farther. But I think the caverns may go on forever. I imagine there may be entrances all over the world. You can get to the place where the lost things sleep from anywhere. I think we came at them from the plains, just like Frank Kelly and Jack Finch, because loss is so raw out there. It wasn't forty years ago that the plains were full of buffalo, pronghorn, prairie dog; Lakota and Kansaw, Blackfeet and Cheyenne. There's so much new sorrow out there, the land can scarcely hold it. People rarely speak of it, but the remembrance of it is just below the surface.

"But then often I think I must be raving. Perhaps we were overcome by sunlight and grief, and it was all in our heads. If it was in our heads, then it can't have any real existence, can it? It would be a hard thing to bear all the lost and gone things so clearly in mind."

Porter and Louisa left the west earlier than they had planned. Porter wrote about their venture into Niyapelayi in his journal and then never opened his journal again. He abandoned excavating and collecting, and instead travelled throughout the Alleghenies recording the mountain ways: songs, weaving, mountain medicine. The only thing he wouldn't listen to was ghost stories.

Louisa never spoke about their experience in the cave on the bluff. To the end of her days she was a woman with a tinge of melancholy. She had two daughters, and she kept them tight by her. She helped the poor, brought food to the hungry and was the first at the door when there was trouble in someone's family. She baked pies, held the hands of sick folk and laboring mothers, and helped watch over the dead.

LITTLE SISTER

Donna Bowman

As soon as I saw the way he stood, I knew him. His head was thrown slightly back as if tossing long hair, although his waist-length black hair was shaved down to a prison buzz, like the rest of ours was. His broad shoulders were characteristically thrown back, hands on his hips. He's not tall, but he makes you think he is. He looked around the eating hall, as if searching for somebody. My heart started thumping. Instinctively, in that way that I'd always known what he was thinking, I knew he was searching for me.

Then he turned around and saw me. His teeth flashed in a huge, white grin against his dark skin. I grinned hugely, helplessly back. He poked the man standing beside him, who turned, and I saw it was his older brother, Norman. Norman frowned, but Wendell still grinned like an idiot. I sat staring at him, the smile fading from my face, Why the hell had Wendell never gotten the band to come for Angela and me? Part of me instantly leapt to his defense. It would be very hard to get someone out of here, and besides, I'd broken with the band to take care of Angela.

Finally, I turned away from him and Norman, slowly and deliberately. They were, after all, the reason Angela and I were here—Wendell, especially. We'd been in prison for three years because of the whole Acoose band, but especially because of Wendell. And PrisonCorp knew that I'd been connected to the Acooses; best to be careful.

"Nicola," my little sister whispered beside me. "What's wrong?"

"Nothing," I lied. "Finish eating your breakfast before they yank us out of here."

For a long moment, she just looked at me, a slight frown between her dark brows. Her eyes flicked from me to the Acooses. "It's not nothing," she contradicted, uncharacteristically. Then she shrugged and went back to concentrating on her food, serious business in this place.

She'd only seen Wendell once before, when she was thirteen. I hoped she hadn't recognized him. Ignoring him would be easier if she hadn't. An ache in my chest told me how hard it would be to ignore him at all.

I glanced up at the long line of barred windows that, in the darkness of early morning, reflected our images. In that makeshift mirror, I could see that Wendell's head was turned towards me. I looked down quickly, face flaming as it had when I'd first met him six years ago.

"All right! That's it! You've had enough to eat," one of the PrisonCorp guards yelled. "Time to get to work."

We stood up in our two sex-segregated groups of a hundred or so each, and began fastening our clothes, putting goggles and dust masks over our faces and broad-brimmed hats on our heads. Though I didn't look at him, I could feel on my skin exactly where Wendell was, and knew his eyes were on me. I hoped he'd stay away from me. I would have to push him away myself, otherwise.

The guards herded us out through the big wooden doors of what used to be the library and was now our mess hall. Our boots echoed in the high, despoiled hallway outside. As we all trooped into the huge entry hall, I stared at anything, the green marble columns, the walls with their facing marble ripped off, the darkness up under the dome, to keep from looking at Wendell. Dad had told me that, when Saskatchewan was still a part of Canada and this area was still prairie, the old Legislature had been the province's glory. It had been faced in marbles from all over the world. Now it was gutted, everything of value removed. The only reason the green marble columns were still there was that they were solid marble, and structural. I wondered as I always did, what all the long-dead politicians would have thought if they'd known that their building would be used as a prison for their descendants. But then they could never have guessed that Canada as a whole would die after Quebec separated, and the corporations and weather shifts took over.

Outside, it was still cool with the chill of the desert night. The eastern sky was just beginning to grey with the dawn of late spring, and we'd be out working until sundown. The guards herded us in groups of roughly fifty into the four wheeled transports. I was glad for the enforced segregation of the mess hall, the transports, and the cells. Wendell'd find it hard to talk to me, at least.

They assigned him to an entirely different section of the dig. Part of me was absurdly disappointed. Don't be an idiot, I told myself.

Angela and I worked on our section with a couple of the other women and three men, the wind carrying dirt relentlessly into the metre-deep pit we'd dug into the garbage, the sun lightening the sky above us. Grit seeped into our clothes and itched ferociously. The sky was brown with dust. The land was brown, too, and flat, other than the drifts of dirt, the piles of garbage, and the dig pits. There were only a few trees left, and they were mostly dead. The ruined skyscrapers of old Regina were stark against the horizon. I wished, as always, for the trees and green of the north.

The day progressed. The sun, an orange disk, the way it looked during a forest fire at home, was directly overhead. Sweat ran down my sides and between my breasts. We were finally getting through the last layer of the previous century's garbage with our trowels and hands and brushes and hitting the old twentieth century landfill underneath. We knew this because of the sudden appearance of plastic bags full of those old disposable diapers. Pampers, Dad had said they'd been called. Good name. Nobody'd waste trees on such a stupid thing now. A hundred and fifty-two years after the end of the wasteful twentieth century, we were still cleaning up their mess.

Once you got to the pampers in an old landfill, you never knew what you might find. And the government, that'd leased our labour from PrisonCorp, wanted to get the most for its money. I sometimes found it almost unbearably ironic that the government had to buy a permit from one corporation, and lease prisoners from another, just to dig up the garbage of the good ol' days because some rich guys out in the Republics of BC or Ontario would pay good money for it. Of course, that's why I was here in the first place—because I'd been part of an Old Canadian antique piracy ring with the Acooses.

With the sun going down in the west, we started crowding to the transports. Some people pushed, but many just stood in dazed exhaustion and had to be moved on by others. I was so tired I was practically sagging. Then somebody grabbed my arm. I whirled, and even through his goggles and dust-mask, I recognized Wendell.

"Let go!" I said, yanking my arm away, and hoping no guard would see me with him.

He pulled his dust mask off over his head. "What's the matter with you, Nicky?" he hissed. "Don't you know your friends when you see 'em?"

I took off my mask, too, in order to be heard better without talking too loudly. A couple of male prisoners stared at us, and I dragged Wendell away from them. "Friends! Some friends you were to me! You let me take the fall for that find we made! You didn't even get your lawyer to try to clear me or anything!" I deliberately didn't say "or nothing," like he would have. I used to imitate the way the Acooses talked, to make Wendell happy. Making him happy now would be stupid, so no more uneducated hick for me.

Someone pushed into me from behind; Wendell and I both moved further down the line-up by several places.

"D'you think I agreed with that? It was Norm convinced the others to let you take the fall!" Wendell said. "You shouldn'ta broke with the band, Nicky.

You know what happens then—you're on your own. Did you really think that auntie of yours could get you and your sister on with her corp out there in BC? Jesus, Nicky, what a daydream!"

"Better than getting Ange in with your lot. Especially after the way you lured me in."

He looked like I'd hit him. "I didn't lure you in, not for the band, not for nobody. I love you, Nicky, just like you love me. It was Norman who used us both!"

"You don't love me!" I said, curling my lip. Again his face scrunched with pain. I forced myself to go on, but more quietly; a woman was looking at us from behind her dusty goggles. I turned away from her, hunching my shoulders. Wendell moved to face me. "You wanted me for my Dad's knowledge, just like the rest of your family!" I continued. "Don't lie to me, Acoose."

He reached out and lightly touched my arm. "Nicky, you know that's not true!" He lowered his voice until it was hard to hear him above the talking around me and the wind's noise. "I wanted the band to bust you an' your sister out, but they wouldn't listen to me. Really!" he said, seeing my hard, disbelieving stare. "You could come with us, when they bust me an' Norm out. Norm doesn't want 'em to do it; too dangerous, he says. But they'll come." This last was said so quietly that I almost had to read his lips to understand. You never talk about breakouts above that tone; it's too dangerous. The guards would be on to you like mosquitoes to blood. I looked around nervously, and saw Angela watching from a few metres away.

"I wouldn't come with you to Heaven!" I said in the same extremely low tone. "Man, you are such a liar! You just told me that the band wouldn't help before, and now you tell me they will. Get your damn story straight, Acoose. And leave me the hell alone!"

My voice got louder on the last sentence. Hopefully, if they heard anything, a guard or informer would hear that. I turned abruptly away from Wendell. Unfortunately, I slammed into somebody else, who hit out in return; soon there was a milling, restless, angry knot of brawlers around us, with others too tired to join in standing and watching. I looked for Angela. I saw her slight form with the 117 on the jacket inside the area of the disturbance. She was hitting out savagely at someone quite a bit bigger. My stomach clenched, and I started pushing through the crowd to help her. She usually managed to get clear of trouble, fading away without people even noticing. She hated fights. So why did she join in this one?

An elbow thunked into my solar plexus. I doubled over, gasping for breath.

"Stop it!" a guard yelled. He shot in the air.

I tried to twist my way towards Angela, but someone pushed me so that I ended up close to Wendell again. He stood in front of me, shielding me from one of the bigger guys, who looked murderous.

Then my ears started ringing. Oh, shit, I thought, and blacked out.

ooo   ooo   ooo

With the usual head-splitting shock, I jolted back to consciousness, face down in the dust. My arm ached from the implant which allowed the guards to knock us out and bring us to again with their remotes. Someone was on top of me. He groaned; even that little sound was enough for me to identify Wendell.

Shit. That was all I needed—to be found with Wendell. I tried to scramble out from under him, but it was too late. I emerged only to see a guard staring down at me. He looked from my face to Wendell's, and grinned. "It's the warden's office for you and your sister, Bourassa." He pushed a button on his remote, and, ears ringing, I faded out again.

ooo   ooo   ooo

I came to sitting slumped in a chair, head hanging, pain throbbing in it from the after-effects of the two implant-induced blackouts. Where the implant was, my left upper arm, hurt like hell. I rubbed it and lifted my head.

And looked straight into the eyes of the warden, sitting at his desk across from me.

He smiled widely. "Don't rub too hard, Bourassa," he said. "You've just had surgery."

My stomach twisted. Bile rose to my throat. That could only mean one thing. They'd changed the implant to the deadly kind. It'd still knock you out and bring you back. But now it'd also trigger a fatal heart attack if you left the perimeter of the Legislature or the dig site.

From beside me came a gasp. I turned and saw Angela sitting in another chair to my right. She stared at the warden, eyes wide, rubbing her own arm. Then she turned to me and her eyes narrowed into such a look of accusation that this time I almost did throw up.

"Couldn't wait to rejoin your old comrades, eh, Bourassa?" the warden said. "Judging from how you and Wendell Acoose were found, we know you and your sister have joined up with his lot again."

Bastard warden. It was guilt by association all over again, and even without that, he was always ready to make your life miserable. Some things never changed. I shook my head. "No, I haven't rejoined, I swear. He was trying to get me to, but I refused. And my sister never had anything to do with it, ever."

The warden snorted. "That's always your story, isn't it? I don't believe it now any more than the judge did when she sent you here. You two can go back to your cell, but we'll be watching you. You and the Acooses try anything, we'll know."

∘∘∘　　∘∘∘　　∘∘∘

I lay on my back on my cot in the night-time cell. Tears leaked from my open eyes. I'd done it to Angela again.

Six years ago, when I was sixteen, Norman had used my and Wendell's love to the Acoose band's advantage. They'd needed someone like me, or rather, like my dad. There was no way they'd subvert Dad into giving them historical information, but lucky them, they didn't have to. Dad, being a history teacher, loved giving me and Ange lectures about what it was like in Saskatchewan when we were still a province of a unified Canada, instead of part of the Northwest Federation. It was easy to pump him about sites where good antiques might be found, like schools and stuff in the abandoned towns in the south.

That's where we'd found the stash of Pentium IVs in the basement of just such a school, buried under a whole lot of boxes. Of course, the electronics didn't work anymore, but the band had connections with people who could fix that. Just the bodies of those old computers brought a mint on the B.C. collectors' market. We'd found twenty. That was the find that finally got the corp's police on our trail, though, and, again, lucky Acooses—the corp found me first.

Our parents died of the Red Flu when I was nineteen and Angela fifteen. It happened practically right after the band found the Pentium IVs. Our parents' death made me responsible for Angela; Dad's will even stated that, though I would have taken it on without the will. By the time we were teenagers, Angela and I were really good friends. I couldn't leave my little sister, and I couldn't stay with the band and get her involved in crime. Though I hadn't wanted to leave the band, especially not Wendell. The thought of the anger and yelling when I broke with them, of Wendell's dark eyes staring after me as Norman kept him from following me, still made me flinch. But I'd done it. Angela and I had been on a train bound for BC and Dad's sister when the corp's police caught up with me. They'd charged Angela, too, not giving a damn that they had it all wrong. They couldn't even legitimately charge her with being an accessory after the fact, since we were using the money Mom and Dad left us to get to B.C., not some of my profits from the band. But the assumption of guilt by association meant she hadn't stood a chance.

I'd had to live with the responsibility of landing Angela in jail ever since then; she hardly ever said anything about it, but I knew she thought about it a lot. Dad would've killed me—this was how I took care of my baby sister after he died? And all because I'd fallen in love with Wendell.

I couldn't help worrying about Wendell, though. He might get killed in the escape attempt. The implants were the main danger, since PrisonCorp relied on them so heavily that they only sent fourteen guards out with us, one in each of the transports, and two each in five little open all-terrainers. But the kill signal for the deadly implants came from a satellite, not the guards' remotes, and Wendell and Norman had automatically gotten the deadly implants for being likely prison breaks. How could the Acooses co-opt a satellite? They'd have to jam the signals from the guards' remotes, too, or Wendell and Norman would be nothing but unconscious dead weights. And they'd have to bring a medtech with them, with an imager, to get the implants out. The damn things were located right next to the major artery in your arm, so that you'd bleed to death if you tried to get one out yourself. I rubbed my arm, mouth drying at the thought.

The implants not only could kill you, but they sent PrisonCorp a homing signal, too. The Acooses had their work cut out for them. But I knew as surely as the corp would protect its assets—us prisoners—that the Acooses would fight to get their people back. They were family, after all.

Well, I wasn't letting the remainder of my family down again. I wasn't going anywhere near Wendell and Norman Acoose. My stupid teenage romantic notions of the Acooses as a band of Robin Hoods fighting the evil corps had been shattered by reality. I'd been too wild then, too much the rebellious teenager.

The problem was, Angela, the good one, had paid the price for that wildness.

ooo   ooo   ooo

The next night, I woke suddenly to a pressure on my arm. It was our signal that one of us had to talk to the other without being overheard. I eased carefully over to the edge of my narrow cot; Angela, on her belly, was already leaning towards me. She put her mouth against my ear.

"The warden was right, wasn't he? The Acooses are going to try something."

A jolt went through me at the sound of her talking about a breakout. "Shh!" I breathed.

"Don't treat me like a kid, Nicola. You always treat me like a kid." The spotlight outside our cell shone through the barred upper-storey window and half-lit Angela's face. One eye gleamed; the other was in darkness. But even in that low light I could make out the frown, the narrowed eyes, and the twisted, bitter lips. Ange had never looked at me like that before.

My stomach sank. "I was just trying to protect you," I said.

"Yeah—you, our parents, everybody. Everybody was always trying to protect me. Well, I'm not a kid anymore. I know what you and Acoose were talking about." I could barely hear her, even with her mouth right against my ear. "They're going to try to get him out, aren't they?"

I lay on my belly listening for the breathing of the other two women in our cell. It sounded even and regular, but you could always fake that. One of them could easily be an informer.

"Jesus, Ange, shut up about that!" I said, my hand cupped around her ear like a little kid telling a secret. "That wasn't what we were talking about. We were talking about us, about him and me. About how he lured me into the band in the first place, and ruined my life, and yours." It was only a partial lie.

Her glinting eye narrowed. "You're lying, Nicola," she said. "I can always tell, even though you think I can't. He asked you to go along, didn't he? Any idiot could see by the way you two were grinning at each other that you're still in love. Why don't we go along? What do we have to go to when we get out, in seven fucking years? We can't go to Aunt Isobel anymore; B.C. doesn't let ex-felons in. We can't go to work for any corps here—same thing. What's that leave us? You know damn well that about all we could do is be whores. I've had enough of that here."

I gasped.

"Oh, yeah, you thought you protected me, didn't you? But guess what—a few got through. So why not join up with the Acooses?"

My breath huffed out of me. "Who? Who raped you?"

"Never mind that. That's not what we're discussing. Why not join the Acooses?"

I clenched my teeth at the thought of anyone even touching my little sister, but I wrenched my mind back to her question. Everything she'd said made me feel that she'd just taken the floor out from under me—this was the first time she'd ever challenged me. She's a very quiet kid. Not to mention that she's always been the good one, the more sensible one. "Are you crazy? The Acooses could die."

"Yeah, but they're trying. And they'd be striking back at goddamn PrisonCorp, too," she said.

"No! It's too risky. Forget about it." I grabbed her wrist. Even barely whispering, my voice took on the tone that I'd used with her since we were both kids, when I gave her an order and meant it. She'd hardly ever gone against that voice. She frowned now, grimacing at the tightness of my hold. I didn't let go. She seemed to deflate, and finally nodded.

"Yeah. You're right," she muttered.

ooo   ooo   ooo

I drank a mouthful of precious water and continued gently brushing the dirt off my latest find, an ancient television set. The thing couldn't possibly work anymore, but that didn't matter. People in the Republics and further abroad liked them for expensive end tables.

It was over three months since Angela and I'd had the implants in our arms changed, and still the Acooses had done nothing. The guards were less watchful, the idiots. Half kept up a cursory patrol of the dump's periphery, while the other seven were dispersed, bored, as usual, amid the dig pits. But I was still fully alert, to see that Angela came to no more harm when the Acooses finally did make their break for it.

At the rumble of thunder, I looked up. The sky was changing. Through the dust haze, piled thunderheads drew closer. Lightning flickered. Maybe the guards would take us in.

But they didn't. The storm swept nearer. The thunder boomed, and the ever-present wind picked up. Dust devils whirled everywhere. A huge black mass of approaching dirt and cloud darkened half the sky over the lumpy, pitted landscape.

The hair on the back of my neck rose from more than just the electricity in the air. I'd grown tense at every storm during the past three months; this being the south, there'd been a lot of them. Storms would provide the perfect distraction for a prison break. If I were the Acooses, I'd strike during a storm.

Everyone was staring at the sky now. A guard several pits away spoke into her comm. Maybe they would take us in. Thunder rolled and cracked, right overhead, practically at the same time as the lightning struck. The dust cloud was on us, making it hard to see beyond a few metres. Grit pinged on my goggles and scoured my hands.

Adrenaline shot through me. With rock-solid certainty, I knew that this was it. This was when the Acooses would finally act. I moved closer to Angela. My breathing quickened and my heart pounded.

I saw the first muzzle-flare of a gun, but I could scarcely hear the shot for the wind and thunder. I grabbed Angela and pushed her down, holding her there with a hand on her back. Kneeling, I peered over the edge of our shallow pit. More muzzle flares. Lightning struck not far away. The guard screamed into her comm, hardly audible. A few prisoners realized what was going on and flung themselves to the ground. Angela rose to her knees beside me. "Keep down!" I yelled.

Vague through the dust, two bent forms ran towards the attackers' position. Wendell and Norman.

Faster than I could react, Angela leapt up beside me and ran after them. In a flash of lightning, the 117 on the back of her jacket showed starkly black on white.

"Ange! What the hell?" I yelled. I got up and ran after her, stumbling over the rough ground. I just managed to avoid one of the dig pits; two prisoners crouched in it like soldiers in a foxhole.

"Ange!" I yelled again. "You idiot! What the hell are you doing? Get down!" I could scarcely see her through the dust. I knew that she couldn't possibly hear me, and probably wouldn't have listened anyway.

"Angela!"

It started to rain, sudden, hard, pelting drops. Because of the dust, it rained mud. My goggles got half-covered, blinding me even further. I tripped and went down flat. "Fuck!" I said, sprang up, and ripped my goggles off. A guard shot at me. The bullet whistled past my head.

"Angela!" I could hardly hear myself against the wind. Lightning flashed and thunder gave a stentorian crash. The smells of rain and electricity were overwhelming.

Now I couldn't see Angela at all. My jaw clenched. The blazing idiot! She was going to get herself killed. She'd lied to me when she'd said she'd do nothing. She'd lied. The last time she'd done that, she'd been twelve or so. I ran in the direction she'd been going, head bent against the downpour. I passed a pit with prisoners crouching in it—crouching, not sprawling. It occurred to me then that I wasn't knocked out, either. The Acooses must've gotten into PrisonCorp's computer system and disabled the knockout signal. But what about the death signal from the satellite? The skin on my left upper arm crawled.

I ran on, slipping and falling repeatedly. The indistinct bulk of a hovervan passed me. Gunshots came from it and towards it. I threw myself down to be out of their way. My breath came in painful gasps. I didn't want to think about the fact that everyone I still loved could be dead.

The indistinct bulk loomed ahead through the pelting mud. "Nicky!" Wendell's voice yelled from it.

Despite myself, my face broke into a huge grin. "Is Angela there?" I yelled. "Yes!"

I could just make out the open door. I sprang up and ran for it, lungs burning, dust from before the rain crunching in my gritted teeth.

My left leg collapsed. I plunged face-down into the muck. When I tried to get up, my leg wouldn't hold me. Pain seared through it. I screamed, clamping my hand on my thigh. Blood ran through my fingers. Some son-of-a-bitch guard had shot me.

"Nicola!" Angela's voice barely got to me through the wind. But it was her, thank God.

The hovervan kicked up mud and dirt and made towards me. More muzzle flares came from it. More bullets whistled over me. I clutched my wounded leg and stayed where I was, flattened in the mud and garbage. The hovervan swept around me; through the pounding rain, a mud bath half-covered me and soaked the dust mask. I yanked it off so I could breathe. The van stopped between me and the guards.

"Get up!" Wendell said.

The door swung further open and hands reached down to me. I struggled to my good leg, crying out involuntarily at the pain in the other. The hands pulled me in. Angela slammed the door shut.

"North, before they get through the armour! But don't cross the periphery—Nicky's still got her implant!" Wendell yelled at the driver.

The hovervan lurched. The implant. Any moment now, we could cross the periphery. My heart faltered, as if it had already received the fatal signal.

The driver bent over the holo-map that showed her where she was going despite the muddy rain that slathered the windshield. An Acoose I recognized vaguely as a second cousin of Wendell's pointed an automatic rifle out of a small opening in the right side window and shot. Wendell sat next to him, with me on the left. Angela and an unknown Acoose with a medical imager sat on the bench behind us.

"Remember, shoot to miss!" Norman yelled from the back of the van, where he glared through another small opening in the rear window, holding but not using another automatic rifle. "Coming for me an' Wendell at all was stupid; don't make it any worse. We kill a guard, and the whole band's had it! That's why you idiots shoulda left us in prison!"

Wendell squeezed around me to the left middle window, rifle in hand. He set it on "one shot," to avoid the greater risk of hitting someone if it was on "multi." His shirt was ripped, showing a cauterized wound on the inside of his upper left arm where the implant had been. I swallowed. The implant in my arm seemed to burn me. The hovervan lurched right, then left, then ran on in that direction. Where was the periphery? Did the driver even know?

Wendell looked carefully through the computerized scope on his gun, aimed a little higher to make sure to shoot over someone's head, and pulled the trigger. "There's an all-terrainer flanking us, with three guards in it!" he yelled above the drumming of rain on the roof. It was just water now, making it easier to see.

A bullet ripped through the opening in Wendell's window and out the opposite one. "Shit!" Wendell said, and returned fire.

"Faster!" Norman yelled. "We'd've been outa here if you hadn'ta stopped for those two! Pass the periphery if you have to!"

"No!" Wendell and I screamed. However, maybe Norman was right. If it saved the others, especially Angela, my death would be worth it. But my heart raced and my stomach clenched.

Then Wendell's window exploded. More bullets flew through it, over our ducking heads. Glass rained on us.

Angela climbed over our bench's back. Her left sleeve was ripped, like Wendell's. She shoved Wendell out of the way, grabbed the gun, and hit the "multi" button. She shot a spray of bullets out the broken window, moving the rifle from side to side several times.

"That'll do it," she said, not yelling, but as if she were holding a casual conversation. "They're dead."

"They are," Wendell said, swallowing hard. His voice broke. "Their all-terrainer flipped, but she shot 'em anyways. She nearly took one guy's head off."

"You killed them?" I asked, voice small. I couldn't breathe. I felt like Angela had hit me in the gut. This was worse than crossing the periphery with the implant still in me. This meant a slower death than that.

"Yes," she said, looking at me with that terrible matter-of-fact calm. She even had a slight smile. "Well, we couldn't get the implant out of you with all that jerking around they were making us do to evade them."

"Yeah, but their all-terrainer had flipped. Good God!" Norman said. He whirled on her. "You bitch! They were already harmless! You didn't have to kill 'em! Now we're all dead!"

"The others can't chase us too far," she said steadily. Her nostrils flared, though, and her eyes glittered. That little half-smile was still on her face. "They haven't got enough people or vehicles, and they'll have to deal with the other prisoners, too."

"They'll hunt us later, though!" Norman yelled. "They'll find us, the whole band. They'll take the kids, too! My daughter's only three. You just fucked up her entire life!"

"Mark, get that goddamn implant out of Nicky's arm and let's get the hell out of here!" Wendell yelled.

More jostling around. I must've lost a bit too much blood. I knew when the hovervan speeded up; my heart did, too—the periphery couldn't be far. But people's voices faded in and out and my head felt fuzzy. The medtech ripped my left jacket and shirt sleeves up to my shoulder. He couldn't seem to stop glancing at Angela, eyes wide.

Even through my growing haziness, my thoughts kept coming back to this: my little sister had just slaughtered three people. My little sister, the good one, the sensible one. My little sister, the innocent one. I shook my head helplessly, mouth open. Tears started in my eyes.

The medtech looked through his imager and cut, hand shaking. "Shit!" he said. Blood spurted from my arm onto both of us. A stab of fear went through me. The world spun crazily. I blacked out.

○○○   ○○○   ○○○

Two people shouted. No rain drummed on the roof to interfere with their yelling.

There was something wrong with me, because I couldn't quite make out what they were saying, and surely I should be able to with all that noise. I just lay there, eyes still closed, listening until it started making sense. And then I wished it would go back to being just noise.

"What the hell did you think you were doing?" Norman's voice. "Why'd you have to kill 'em? Everybody'll be on the whole band now, corp police, Federation police, everybody. They'll never stop 'til they get us all. What'd those guards ever done to you, that you had to kill 'em, knowing all that?"

"What's anyone ever done to me? They kept me in jail with the likes of you, when I'd done nothing! They ruined my life!" Angela. The new Angela who scared me silly.

I opened my eyes. I was lying in the back of the van, leg and arm heavily bandaged. Wendell sat on the floor beside me. I saw the backs of Angela's and Norman's heads. "Ange," I said. Hardly anything came out. "Ange," I tried, louder, and sat up, head spinning.

"Nicky's come to!" Wendell said. His eyes closed for a moment, and he cupped my face in one of his big hands.

"You!" Angela said, twisting around to see me. "You're the worst of the lot!" Her tone was venomous. I stared at her. This was worse than the warden's office; I'd always been afraid she hated me like this, but she'd never shown any sign. I swallowed, trying to keep down the sickness. Tears ran down my face. Everybody in the van listened.

"It wasn't my fault you were so goddamn wild," she continued, her voice breathless, words tumbling out of her. "Why didn't you just send me out to Aunt Isobel and let me get on with my life? Well, now we're on the path that you started us down; there's no going back. And this time it was my choice."

"You did all this just because you hate me?" I said, drawing in a gasping breath.

"I hate you, I hate everybody! The corps, the courts, the guards. Nobody gave a damn that I wasn't guilty at all!" She breathed rapidly, eyes shining feverishly, cheeks flushed.

"I don't blame you," I said. "But why did you have to—we would've gotten out, in time. And if you really wanted to join a band, we could've then."

"Living like that for seven more years, never knowing when I'd be raped again?" she demanded.

"Well, but at least then you wouldn't have— "

"Killed somebody? You're all a bunch of hypocrites! You say you'll only go so far, never stoop to murder. You, you Acooses, you carry high-powered guns—why, just to shoot over people's heads? You had to know someone'd get killed someday!"

"Not in cold blood. No Acoose ever murdered nobody," Norman said coldly. "We don't have much choice in robbing, but we do in killing. You did, too. Now the law'll never stop chasing us; they might've given up if you didn't kill a guard. You go on about everybody ruining your life. What about the ones you just ruined? Our kids'll be marked forever as the children of murderers—you did to them what you say we did to you. They'll have no chance at all. Was your revenge worth it?"

"Yes!" she said.

"Ange!" I said, stomach dropping. What had happened to my little sister? I put my hand on her shoulder. She threw it off.

Norman looked around the van. "Well?" he said to the other Acooses. "You wouldn't let me dump 'er near a town, but we're in forest now. You seen how crazy she is. You know what she's done to you an' your kids. Can you live with her? I can't."

"We're north o' La Ronge," the driver said. Jesus, I'd been out for hours, then. "She'll have a bit of a chance, in the forest." She looked at me, her eyes softening; it was Sandra, Wendell's sister. "Sorry, Nicky."

"Dump 'er," the medtech and the Acoose second cousin said, almost simultaneously.

"Wendell?" Norman said.

I grabbed Wendell's hand. "No. Please. It'd be murder, too. They'll execute her if they catch her."

Wendell looked from me to Norman, agonized. "No," he said at last.

"You're outvoted," Norman said. "She goes."

"Then I go, too," I said.

"Fine," Norman said.

Wendell glared at Norman. "You can't, Nicky. You're too weak."

Angela, who'd been sitting silently through all this, chin up, looked at me, lip curled. "See all your fine friends now."

"Stop the van," Norman said.

Sandra obeyed. Angela stood proudly. I made to stand, too, but found that my legs wouldn't hold me, so I tried crawling. Wendell grabbed my shoulder and held me in place. I tried desperately to pull away.

"Don't be stupid, Nicky; I said you were too weak."

"I don't need you anyway, Nicola. You've never been any good to me all along." Angela said.

I flinched. It was true. Everything I'd ever done to help or protect her had only made things worse. And now I couldn't even stand, let alone try to protect her. "At least give her a gun!"

"So she can murder more people?" Norman demanded. "No. Now get out," he said to Angela. He opened the door on his side.

Angela squeezed past him and stepped out into the forest. "No food, even?" she said mockingly, but I thought I heard a faint tremor in her voice.

"Ange, I'm sorry!" I said, pulling against Wendell's hold.

"Nicky, don't," he said, trying to make me sit up and look at him. His eyes looked like they had when I'd broken with the band—bruised, lost; part of me wanted desperately to stay.

But if I'd been able to, I'd have followed Angela, even with the knowledge that I could never make things right with her. Ever.

She stalked away into the trees, not looking back.

OF BONE AND HIDE AND DUST

Carole Nomarhas

Golden baked clay, sandstone outcroppings, filmy red dust, trees shedding their skins in long tangles of bark, pewter spikes of grass which might never have been green and growing...

The Jeep Cherokee battered its way down the rut of a road, and Joanna craned her head to look back, again and again. There was precious little to see, the glimpse through the dust-blurred rear window was wavering and indistinct. But *different*. Somehow. Through the haze the light and dust were curiously liquid, shimmering and distorted with heat.

She shifted on her seat, hot despite the air conditioning. Panic, undefined, bleeding from her pores.

"Is something following us?"

She caught one of *those* looks from Paul. The quirky lift of his eyebrow, the tiny tease of a smile that tugged at the corner of his mouth. Anger stabbed her, and for a moment she hated his gentle amusement, layered with patience. Another man might have reminded her that this holiday had been her idea. Another husband might have harped and complained. Not Paul, oh, never him.

Joanna wanted to answer his question with one brief, pungent phrase. Her anger, her unreasoning panic, his patience - his damn self-satisfied cope-with-everything attitude melded into an uncomfortable mix.

"Yes," she said, "always. Our past." A sharp as glass, bitch answer.

A real frown then. Patience thinning. She waited for him to say something; he merely began a soft whistling. She was totally out of her depth here, in these surroundings. *Let's see something of the country —* God, she'd been mindless to even suggest it. *A real adventure, a road trip... just the two of us.* Oh, they had seen something of the country. But it was not a country she recognized.

She'd glanced out of the window, stomach tightening. A dead camel lay by the side of the road, reduced to tattered hide and bone, dusty. There were always dead things here, never fresh with blood and guts, the blue buzz of flies. Always the bodies were already dried and leeched to papery hide and ivory bones. A dead camel… long ago she had seen live camels, roos, wallabies, birds, and mobs of sheep. People. How long since there had been a living thing save her and Paul anywhere in this landscape? Idiotic fear kept gnawing at her.

She ignored the reproach in his look. "Have you noticed there's only feral things here? And they're all dead? Camels… goats… wild donkeys."

"Hmm?" Paul spared her a brief moment's attention, the road badly pitted and eroded was demanding most of his concentration. "No road sense, probably. Here they don't need much, it's hardly Sydney."

He'd missed her point, but then she childishly didn't want to say it aloud, and make it true. *The only things here are things that don't belong… like us. And they all die, just turn to dust and bone.* Like the rusting carcass of a 4WD, turning the color of old blood, miles back, by the side of the road. There must have been people in that vehicle, once, where did they go? What swallowed them? What dissolved them into dust and heat and little else? The thought was irrational, the reasoning illogical. The jeep had been abandoned, the people had walked away from it, perhaps been given a lift… oh, yes?

"No," she said dully, "it's not Sydney."

"There's a town, 'bout another hour. Kadjiump. They'll have a pub, or at least a cold beer. We'll spend the night there. Solid walls, Jo, not a tent again. A real bed."

Pride wouldn't let her admit how much the thought of solid walls appealed, how close she was to screaming from the not-emptiness of the land around her. It wasn't barren, it wasn't empty, *something* always out of sight followed them. The heat was smothering, the air too dry to breathe and scratchy with dust, spiced with the smell of… something. 'Fresh air?' Paul had joked when she mentioned the strange tang in the air. No, it wasn't that, it was like some *hot* scent, ashy, burning, scarce of oxygen.

"Kadjiump. Sounds great." She forced a thin smile. "The beer and the bed sounds even better."

It was such a long way from home, from her *country*. Her country was one of Sydney's North Shore suburbs, of leafy streets and gardens full of English plants, of green lawns and swimming pools, of timetables and seething city roads, of crowds and trains, of beaches and cafes, of dinner parties and restaurants, of shopping malls where nothing more wild and feral lurked than small lost tribes of teenagers. The outback was *foreign*, totally alien, and nobody had ever explained that to her. Not the newspapers, not the television, not books—nobody had warned her about this other land.

No borders, no language barriers, breezy, happy indifference—all lies. There were borders, but they were invisible ones, and she had crossed them, unknowing. *We don't belong here, I know we don't.* Joanna wanted to scream the words. *We've crossed over to somewhere else, somewhere dangerous.*

Kadjiump. Jo counted five buildings when they arrived in the township, white, dun, red, and all dusty. Bessa brick and tin roofs. A motel sign hand-lettered, a couple of planks of wood and faded. Good God, civilization. Paul pulled up in front of the 'motel', a sometime white-painted brick building, with a railing made of pipes in front of the verandah. A sagging wire door hung from the front of the 'office.'

"Not exactly five star." Paul shook his head. "But we can get something to eat at the pub over there, and *maybe* the air conditioning works."

"I don't think so," Joanna said softly. "No people."

"They're inside, do you think they stand around and gape at the tourists? They'll have their fun, believe me, just don't believe a damn thing anyone in the pub says, okay?" There was an edge in Paul's voice, a faint unease.

There were battered trucks and an old Jeep, parked in front of the pub, and all indistinguishable in color from the red dirt of the main street. If the vehicles had moved once, it had been long ago, Jo thought. Still, she refused to totally acknowledge the stabbing fear. Of course, she was being ridiculous—there would be people in the pub.

The heat hit her as she opened the car door and climbed out. She drew a breath as dry as talc, coughed, couldn't breathe. Her legs wouldn't support her for a moment, and everything swam.

"Jo?"

"The heat, sorry. Let's get that beer." Please God let there be people here.

Paul took her arm as they crossed the street, a gentle gallantry, or perhaps a fear much like her own, and the need to hold onto something living.

The door to the pub was open, thick malt and hop scents wafted, there was even the buzz of an electronic voice, a radio or television.

"Hi! Hello?" They stood close together in the hot dark and dust of the pub. A very old radio murmured to itself on the bar. Snatches of static-filled voices that could not be understood. Otherwise the room was empty.

"Well, must be a town meeting on." Paul said lightly. He pointed to a pile of change and notes on the bar. "Definitely the bush - they operate on the honor system. So, what will madam have?"

"Paul, let's go… this is… eerie."

"Jo, it's okay. And I'll be damned if I'm going to leave without a beer. I wouldn't mind something to eat too. Anyway, I can manage the bar stuff, worked my way through university pulling beers and mixing drinks. And if you think this place is strange, you should have seen that leather bar in Oxford street... "

She'd heard all his stories, of course, and couldn't smile. "This will be stranger," she said in a half whisper.

Paul lifted down a bottle from the shelf. Opened it. Empty. Another. Tried the beer-tap. Dust layered everything, thin and fine.

"No wonder they don't get any customers—this must be the original pub with no beer, and nothing else to boot."

"And no people. Can we go now?" Joanna was already edging for the door.

Paul hesitated, then came around from behind the bar, and stopped.

"Paul? What is it?"

"The money. I know the bush is supposed to be twenty years behind— but this is crazy." He held up one of the notes. "How long since you've seen a dollar note?"

"Let's just go. Damn it, Paul, *now.*"

"Maybe we wandered into a real ghost town."

He was worried; she knew that, and he was making jokes simply to mask his fear.

"I don't think this is Kadjiump." Paul said low-voiced, as he joined her. "Crazy as it sounds, I think we made a wrong turn."

"On a road that didn't have any... " Jo felt hysterical laughter bubbling up through her. "Oh, it must have been a *really* wrong turn."

He took her arm again, and they walked out of the pub, but moving faster this time. Paul wasn't that much of a fool, time to go, time to get out and not look back.

The wind had picked up, fluting between the buildings with a faint nerve scratching resonance. But that was not what caught Jo and held her beside the Cherokee. The dust was slowly drifting out of the walls of the motel, she would have sworn that beneath the dust the walls were pocked and hollow, eroded. Oh, no. Paul hadn't noticed and she wasn't about to point this out to him.

Joanna's first thought was that the Jeep wouldn't start, she held herself stiff with tension, and with that strange laughter that was almost a scream still trying to escape. But the engine didn't miss a beat, it positively purred.

Once, Jo looked back at the township, but only once. It was blurred by the rising dust and she imagined the buildings falling away, nothing but dust. She concentrated on the road ahead, and the thick, liquid heat shimmer that waited for them.

"There'll be another town." Paul said. "We might even find the real Kadjiump."

"I hope so." Jo said, mechanically, not believing it, then frowned as he said: "The aircon's packing up— "

There it was—that *hot* scent again, but now the heat and the scent leaked through the car. The road ahead was straight, the landscape flat, grass spiky and lifeless, trees shedding their bark like flesh, a dry creek bed, crazed clay and barren of water ran beside them.

There was something dead by the side of the road, a donkey this time, dried hide and yellowed bone. They passed it, driving too fast, not looking back.

Joanna gave a gasp, there, the same rusting hulk of a jeep they had passed before… it couldn't be…

"Kadjiump soon." Paul promised, or maybe it was a prayer. The jeep bounced, hard, jarring Joanna to her teeth. The track was getting rougher. She saw Paul's gaze flicker, then jump to the rear-vision mirror, his eyes going wide.

"Did you see something?" She asked.

"Not anymore. I thought I saw… oh, it's damn stupid." He suddenly punched the steering wheel. "This whole thing is stupid, this whole trip. Dammit, I don't want to do this anymore. I want air conditioning, and a shower, and a bloody ice-cold beer. I want to go home."

Joanna stared at him, momentarily amazed; Paul *never* lost his temper, not in that fashion. It was fear, she realized, not anger. Stark, mindless fear. He'd seen it too, or rather hadn't seen it—and that had scared him.

"We can't go home… " *The road disappears, Jo thought, it disappears behind us. It melts back into a landscape that didn't ever wish for roads. Or for trespass of any kind.* The wind sang thinly, ghost notes through hollow bones. The shimmering heat haze, swirling with red dust, was now a wall behind them. Strangely liquid, golden, glimmering… closer.

"Pull over, damnit! Pull over!" This was real, a dust storm. It was upon them before Paul had quite managed to stop the jeep, they bounced, blind, with the red dust falling thick and instantly coating the windows. They must have jarred to a halt somehow. Joanna knew she had screamed, once, briefly. They sat there, in the eerie silence, with the dust falling and falling.

"Just a dust storm." Paul managed to mutter, slowly taking his hands from the wheel, and flexing them. "We're okay, we just stay inside."

"For how long?" Joanna demanded, unreasonably. The dust-dimmed light cast them in reddish shadow. The wind truly did howl as if it was a creature let loose to batter the car and devour the occupants. "What if it doesn't stop?"

Paul gave an irritated sigh, and unbuckled his seat belt. "Of course it will stop. Don't be ridiculous. It always stops."

"*It always stops…* " Joanna echoed, with a sick numbness. "It always stops… " Those words were familiar. Too familiar.

The wind was dropping, losing its ferocity. Paul tried the windscreen wipers. Nothing. "Damn. Engine's dead." He tried it again. "I'll have a look, see if there's any damage."

Before Joanna could say anything he had the door open, dust falling on him as he jumped out, swearing and shaking himself like a dog. He made an odd sound, a sort of choked cry. "Joanna… "

She didn't want to get out, but she forced herself to open the door and to climb out. The windstorm had died, the jeep was coated with dust—a thick, filthy layer of it… but the road. Red dust had peeled layers from the road and now it was peppered with white.

"Joanna… " Paul said again, sounding strange. "Look… "

"What?" But she knew when she took a step and something brittle broke under her boot. "God."

Bones, the road was red dust and bones… as far as the eye could see. Skulls and arm bones, hands, all partially buried. In front of Paul there was a skull staring up at him, embedded in the dust.

"What happened here?" Joanna wanted some logical explanation, desperately "An aboriginal massacre?" Yet, there was so many bones… the road was really nothing but bone and dust. So many other half-buried things she saw when she looked closer, the skulls of horses and goats and tattered pieces of hide. Human remains, grinning, dusty skulls. "Oh, my God. This can't be real."

"It must be… prehistoric, or something." Paul said, trying to keep his voice steady. "Amazing isn't it?"

"Jesus Christ! Prehistoric? Does it look prehistoric to you?" Joanna shouted. "Does it look *natural* to you?"

"Jo, don't panic." He was close to snapping himself, she saw. "Okay, it's weird. But there has to be an explanation. Anyway Kadijump's not far. We'll walk out of here."

"Walk?" Then she turned and saw the jeep… the rusting, dust covered wreck. "No… Oh, dear God, no… "

Paul's eyes pleaded with her, even more terrified than she was. "Jo, please. Let's just start walking. Let's just *leave*."

She didn't want to walk on the road, on the bones, but walking beside the road the silky dust buried each step to her ankles. She took Paul's hand, not daring to look back at the jeep. The dust storm, that was it, it had scoured the metal, had clogged the engine, had turned the jeep the color of rust. It wasn't really as *old* as it looked. It couldn't be…

Paul squeezed her hand. "It's okay, Jo. Really it is. Kadjiump's not far… "

No, it never was, Joanna realised, but we never reach it, Paul. *Never.* We'll just walk until we're part of this road, part of the landscape. Until we're dust and bone and nothing more.

Onto the Next Dead Planet

John Grey

There are freak storms.

Its welcome mat is one massive fluid
   inorganic cloud.
Below that, it's like exhumed bone,
with maybe a little cartilage here and there.
If there ever was skin,
it's been burned down to a cosmic sheen
or hacked away by the wind.
Its rock props it up,
its sky pushes down on it
and out of the grinding melange
slips the end game between gravity
   and light.
Now, like all death, it's a history
   vulture's delight.
I peck at its sedimentary sequences.
I greedily gather up its past's leftovers.
It's the Natural History Museum of itself.
In fact, it's so well organized
in its fire-storms, clock-work earthquakes,
   it's more like the living
   than they are.
As its moons dissolve in the
   magenta twilight,
I've even seen faces emerge
   from the aurora-dust
to inform me that creation
most distinguishes itself from chaos
in the flies it attracts to its corpses.

Flatlander pro tem

Geoff Hart

Ivar Jonsson raised his head from the couch with considerable effort, his eyes focusing only slowly on the panel before him, and reached shakily to reboot the con and figure out where he'd actually landed. Now that his brain was coming back online, bodily sensations returned; moving took more effort than he'd expected, and his long damp hair pulled stickily away from where it had clung to the back of his neck. He hoped fervently that the planet was heavier than it'd looked from orbit, for if not, the weight on his chest and sluggishness in his limbs probably represented the beginning of the MI he'd assured his doctor would happen "any day now". He shuddered. Best just to assume he'd made planetfall and had more serious problems than figuring out how to jury-rig a defibrillator.

Could Hansen's Fortune have somehow managed to hold orbit? No, the Captain would never have sounded the sauve qui peut if he hadn't been certain the liner was going down. Jonsson was alone, and no harsh voice poured over com to accuse him of jumping the gun. The viewscreen flickered briefly, darkness morphing into grey noise, then faded to black as the power-conservation modules kicked in: "essentials only" until he chose to override the con. The main status readouts remained lit, so he let his head settle leadenly back against the crash couch, the evacsuit's neck ring digging into his neck, his thoughts slowly clearing enough to make sense of the data. The pod had grown uncomfortably warm, and greasy sweat oozed down the back of his neck—well, he hoped it was sweat, leastwise; it could well have been blood, since he'd obviously whacked his head against something during the descent. Sweat, then, and the waning chest pain reassured him slightly that it wasn't pre-MI diaphoresis. He scrubbed at his his eyes with his index fingers, clearing away something that intermittently blurred his vision and resolutely not looking at his moistened hands to find out what that something was. Instead, he focused owlishly on the readouts.

His heart pounded, heavy and fast, until he'd confirmed the hull's integrity, and that the airlock had neither been sprung by the impact nor jammed forever in place when the hull crumpled. The gravitics had kept him from liberally redecorating the pod's insides with his insides, but were out for the duration; planetary gee sat at about one Terran gravity, so the odds were good his heart really was simply responding to that unpleasantly unfamiliar strain.

Reserve power read just short of half, and he fought down a moment of panic; even that small a reserve would last several days if he used it judiciously—which the computer was doing its efficient best to ensure. He continued his post-flight checks. Ambient temperature: high, but falling as he watched. Probably whatever he'd landed in had ignited when the pod came to rest. Relative humidity: drier than ship-standard. Atmosphere: standard oxy-nitrogen, but high in noble gases, denser than normal, and windy—though perhaps that was natural for an uncontrolled environment. He'd sound like a clown at a children's party, but at least he could breathe— assuming the native bacteria hadn't been patiently waiting several score millennia solely so they could spring upon Ivar Jonsson with shrill microbial cries of delight. Shuddering, he instructed the computer to sample the atmosphere for bugs, and as the pumps whined quietly in the background, he forced himself to continue his status check.

The main water reservoir, sandwiched between the inner and outer hulls, had been holed during the landing. So… The emergency supplies inside the pod were the only water he'd have available until he found more somewhere. All at once, his throat felt dry, and he hit the quick-release on his harness and tried to sit up. The harness slammed him back into his seat, and his heart raced again for a moment until he realized he was still buckled in. The higher gee hadn't helped; he'd briefly tolerated Terran gee on-station, and the Captain had insisted on regular high-gee exercise for all hands, but that didn't mean he'd liked it enough to do more than the bare minimum. He relaxed a bit, tried the quick-release again, and this time the straps fell away, the buckles clanking heavily against the tough sides of the couch. Grabbing his knees, he pulled himself into a sitting position using both his biceps and his abdominals, sweat beading on his forehead and dripping onto the increasingly stained evacsuit.

Now upright, lungs moving a bit more easily, he took his first full breath since he'd landed and felt the weight on his chest relax further. Yes, he could survive here—he'd be missing standard gee even more than during an enforced sojourn station-side, but he'd survive. Gritting his teeth, he braced himself and swung his legs over the edge of the crash couch. It was difficult, but not nearly as difficult as he'd feared.

A thought occurred to him belatedly, and he sniffed the air with trepidation. In the confusion of abandoning ship, he'd missed his usual dose of decongestant, so his nose remained stuffy, but his narrowed nasal passages let pass no scent of burning insulation—in fact, no scents more unpleasant than his own acrid sweat. So the readouts were working fine, and he breathed deeply and slowly as his therapist had taught him, fighting both gravity and his nerves, until he began to relax. Avoiding looking directly at the power indicator, which had faded from a reassuring green to a distinctly ominous yellow, he glanced again at the temperature indicators. It would be some hours yet before things cooled off enough for him to even consider leaving the pod—a horrifying thought best postponed for now. Forever, one could hope. Joints creaking, he got to his feet and moved slowly about the narrow confines of the pod.

A quick inventory confirmed his worst suspicions. The Captain of the freighter that was probably now an astrobleme somewhere west of his own position had been a rulebook fanatic, but that discipline had finally paid off. Jonsson had at least a month of food—with discipline and more time spent sleeping than moving around—and ample reserve air, even if the planet's atmosphere didn't prove, against hope, to be safe. His reader would last longer still on its current charge, and he'd just downloaded a new library last time Fortune was in port, so he wouldn't lack for reading material. But water was going to be a problem, for without the hull tank, he had enough for only a few days, no matter how carefully he rationed it. And rationing would be easy, given that he could barely force himself to swallow the captain's preferred brand of spring water; snob appeal aside, he much preferred vacuum-distilled, radiation-sterilized water for the safety its taste promised. He wiped his brow again, hesitated for a moment, then reluctantly examined his hand—no blood. He shook his hand, scattering sweat around the cabin. No need to start recycling sweat just yet; the environmental controls would recover that from the air well enough, and the still would harvest his urine too when that became necessary.

He shuddered. If it came to that, going EVA to replenish his water supply might not be so bad after all. EVA'd always looked easy enough in the endless sims he'd endured onboard Fortune, and even though he'd have to do this first real EVA in a crisis, at least he'd be on solid ground. Hundreds of generations of ancestors had thrived in that very environment, free of the risk of flying off into the endless depths of space, so surely he could succeed too. Still, a guy had to plan for the worst.

Fortunately, he didn't need to leave the ship for a while yet, and that left him time to prepare for the ordeal that lay ahead. Taking a sedative from the medkit, and an antacid tab from the supply in his evacsuit's breast pocket, he swallowed both dry, the meds sliding chalky and bitter down the back of his throat. Then he sat back down on the crash couch, butt thumping hard into the cushioning. The con hummed quietly on standby, the readouts and beacon glowing sedately in the pod's dim light. He lay back, banging his head harder than he'd intended, and strapped himself in again. As the drug took hold and erased the world, he briefly worried over— and only reluctantly discarded—the image of waking to hostile aliens pounding on the airlock.

ooo   ooo   ooo

When Jonsson woke a day later, with neither aliens nor a Navy patrol pounding on the hatch, the planet's greedy gravitation still oppressed him, but at least he found himself breathing more easily. The pod's air had cooled to a tolerable level, and though its hull temperature was on the thoroughly unpleasant side of standard, it would be survivable, and the surrounding air would be at least ten degrees cooler. He booted nav briefly, just long enough to confirm that he'd indeed landed within a reasonable distance of free water.

"Ivar, my boy," he muttered to himself, "the time's come to seek an excuse to stay inside." The distress beacon pulsed quietly, with no companion light to indicate anyone had heard his cries for help. He scowled. "Next stop: quarantine." He released the straps that pressed down so reassuringly upon his chest, and pulled himself back into a sitting position. That done, he took a deep breath, ignored his suddenly racing pulse, and pivoted to face the panel behind him. At his touch, the thick plass screen grew translucent, revealing rows of flasks, each filled with different culture media. Not a one showed the slightest sign of growth. Jonsson chewed his lower lip. "Strike three?" He inspected the water-level readout, tapping it with a well-chewed fingernail and finding, as he'd feared, that it still read zero. He sighed loudly.

"Damn." Doggedly, he made his way to the chemical toilet on the far side of the four crash couches and relieved himself, wincing at the smell's strength in the enclosed space. With a last hopeful, fruitless glance back at the beacon, he steeled himself and tugged a collapsible headpiece free from where it lay velcroed to the nearest couch. Focusing on the practiced motions of his fingers to distract himself from what he was actually doing, he clipped its neck ring to his evacsuit, the self-contained oxygen supply triggering automatically. Air hissed in his ears as the headpiece inflated gently into a rigid helmet, the cuffs around his boots and wrists tightening until the ballooning of the suit confirmed its integrity; at least he'd be sealed away from whatever unpleasant surprises the outer atmosphere had in store for him. Though he'd grown somewhat accustomed to the gravity, it suddenly took an effort to get himself moving.

Sealing the heavy work gloves to his sleeves took some of his attention away from what lay ahead, but he still walked like an old man heading for his annual prostate exam as he made his way to the airlock. The inner door cycled open silently to admit him, and he stepped firmly within, but as the door slid shut against his back, he shuddered; the dim light making it through the sooty smear that covered the viewport didn't really make it feel much like a coffin, he comforted himself. Wishing that the Captain had trusted the crew enough to permit sidearms on the crash pods distracted him enough that he could ignore the darkness and the vibration from the pumps throbbing dully against his feet. He braced himself, but still gave a start when outside air rushed into the airlock with a force that fluttered his suit's thick fabric.

With the pressure equalized, the safety light turned green. Taking a long, slow breath, he released the failsafes and wrenched the handle downwards. The door swung suddenly outward, pulling him halfway from the airlock before he could release the handle, and for an adrenaline-charged moment, he was certain something had seized the outer handle and tried to pull him into its grasp. But the door slipped free of his grasp, coming to rest far enough open for him to see out. No tentacles. No claws. No large, furry chelicerae—yet.

It was still day, and probably midafternoon judging by the angle of the pale yellowish sunlight slanting in past the curved door. Nothing animate had as yet come into view, so he took hold of his courage, and with a nervous dart of his arm, pushed the door wider. The soot that had coated the airlock's viewport had prepared him for the powdery grey, wind-ruffled ash that covered the earth before him, and feeling a bit bolder, he pushed the door fully open.

A shallow trench dug by the pod's landing extended a few score metres across a reassuringly flat stretch of char. Occasional shoulder-high clumps of something greenish that had escaped the fire reminded him vaguely of the bulrushes Mother had once brought back from her vacation on Earth. She'd undoubtedly figured he'd enjoy a souvenir of his planet of origin, but by the time the rushes had cleared quarantine, they'd been too dry and brittle to be worth much. He'd attached them to his wall to please her, but he'd always been secretly worried that one of the heavy brown seed heads would fall on him. And the lengthy quarantine had confirmed beyond any doubt that he'd never voluntarily spend any time planetside, a decision he'd never regretted until today.

Though it'd been less than a day since he'd landed, small, thin, lime-green shoots were already emerging from the char that had been the original vegetation. Peering cautiously around the edge of the airlock, he scanned the ground immediately to his left and right to confirm that nothing lurked just out of sight. Nothing moved, not even the pitiful vegetation that remained. If he'd read nav correctly, the water lay a few hundred metres off to his left. He resisted the urge to return inside to confirm the reading.

Reluctantly, he grasped the handhold that stretched the full length of the open door, and hesitantly lowered his left leg to the ground. "One small step for man," he muttered grimly, surrendering his will to gravity and letting it tug him downwards. The earth gave way alarmingly beneath his feet, and he was on the point of withdrawing his foot in a panic when it firmed up again. His boot had sunk a good 3 centimetres into the black soil that lay beneath the layer of ash. "Fool!" he berated himself. "It's not a ship's deck; of course it's going to compress!" But until he was certain he'd sink no further, he kept his other foot in the pod and clutched the handhold tightly with both hands. He looked left, past the curve of the pod, but only a smudge of green in the distance gave any sign of the supposed water. He smiled, cautiously at first and then wildly. "Damned if I'm not a Flatlander after all!" he shouted into his helmet, relinquishing his grasp on the handhold in a sudden surge of optimism and taking a long, confident step away from the pod.

He'd taken no more than a dozen steps, reeling nervously as the ground gave way repeatedly beneath his feet, before he made a terrible mistake. Thus far, he'd kept his gaze focused mostly on his destination, across land that swept away on all sides as flat as the space between the stars, and had seen no signs of anything untoward. But having grown overconfident, he gave in to his curiosity and looked up—and froze, gazing into infinity.

Above, a clear expanse of featureless blue spread in a seamless expanse of cold, featureless color, spanning his universe from horizon to horizon. It was like stepping out onto the hull of Fortune in a sim and suddenly seeing the warm, familiar stars vanish, robbing him of any sense of depth and perspective. He felt a sudden vertigo, as if that expanse of sky were sucking at him, trying to tug him away from the planet beneath him, and his knees went weak with the thought, feeling himself briefly in free fall as he fell, mind going blank in terror. He had time for only one thought: This can't happen on a planet!

But the part of him that had always resolutely shied away from actually walking on Fortune's hull was in command now, and it sought refuge in unconsciousness.

ooo   ooo   ooo

Consciousness returned in the form of a sudden, stabbing pain in his right thigh. He sat up with a muffled shriek, adrenaline clearing his mind instantly, his eyes focusing in on the source of his pain.

Something from a spacer's worst nightmare stood on his leg. A full two centimetres long, its iridescent wings glittering in the fading light, the alien had many more legs than any decent life form should have: six at least, and perhaps as many as eight, though they moved with such menacing rapidity that any estimate was a mere guess. Stubby, independently mounted compound eyes swiveled on jointed stalks to meet his wide-eyed gaze, but the rapier-like proboscis kept biting into his leg through shielding that would have stopped a slow micrometeorite. That galvanized him into swinging wildly at his tormentor, the downward arc of his hand accelerating gratifyingly fast under the heavy gravity.

He struck his leg with a sharp thwak!, reinforcing the pain, but the alien escaped skyward in a shrill, mocking whine of wings, unscathed, pursued by a puff of air escaping his suit. Even as he fell backwards, scrabbling again for the comparative security of the charred earth, the alien stiffened into immobility then fell, rigid. Despite the adrenaline slowness of his senses, he clearly saw the corpse accelerating swiftly downwards, landing with an audible thud! by his feet. But Jonsson had more urgent things to think of.

Spacer reflexes warred with the primate fear of falling, and compromised. One hand clutched desperately at a stalk of the thick, burned vegetation, grasped it, and held tight; the other slapped the meteor patch he'd not remembered grabbing over the hole in his suit. The deflation stopped, but for a moment, until the scrubbers kicked in, his suit was full of a miasma of charred vegetation, acrid fear-sweat, and—he felt himself growing faint— his own blood. Belatedly, he pressed on his wound, expecting—but not feeling—a stab of pain, hoping that despite the awkward angle, he could press hard enough to keep himself from bleeding out. A moment passed, and when no blood had begun pooling in the leg of his suit, he released his grip, wincing at the cramp in his hand, and took stock of his desperate situation.

He lay pressed flat to the ground, covered in black, sooty dirt. The plant he clung to remained firmly in place, though how long it would support his weight was anyone's guess. Cautiously, he seized its neighbor with his free hand, and only once he had attained that comparative security did he dare to look down past his feet. His former assailant lay flat on its back, still as the pod. But beyond the alien—the abyss!

Jonsson hung spread-eagled on a cliff wall that stretched as far into infinity beneath him as the sky above him, though much more fearsomely so; the sheerness of the cliff provided benchmarks and a vanishing point that clearly defined the scale of his predicament. Though the pod's gaping airlock door beckoned a scant two metres below his dangling feet, promising an escape from this nightmare, it might as well have been in orbit. The rational part of his mind reassured him quietly that gravity would keep him pressed to the cliff face, but the voice that shouted in his head prophesied centrifugal force plucking him from this unstable surface, the planet's rotation accelerating him downwards past the pod until, at last, it propelled him off the planet and into that terrible blue void. That he would then have returned to the relative safety of space provided scant reassurance, given that an evacsuit wasn't designed to preserve its wearer for more than half an hour in hard vacuum.

He closed his eyes and tightened his grip on the bulrushes, fully prepared to cling here until his rescuers arrived, but the aliens gave him no time. Again, a lancing pain seared into him, this time in the middle of his back, where he had no hope of reaching it even if he could safely free a hand to defend himself. The pain grew, crested, then all at once, vanished. Again, air hissed from the suit, but he could do nothing about it. Grimly, he pressed his faceplate into the char, smearing it and dulling his vision, if not his hearing. There came a faint, familiar-sounding thud, and he forced his eyes open.

There, within easy reach should he choose to grab for it—and he most emphatically didn't—lay the second alien, dead as the pod. A strangely musty aroma entered through the hole in the suit, briefly overpowering the charred smell, and he began breathing shallowly, hoping to limit the contagion that would even now be entering his lungs. He'd probably have noticed the suit's sealant automatically closing the tiny hole, like the first one too small to merit a meteor patch, but his wildly sweeping gaze fell blurrily upon the pod's still-beckoning airlock, promising refuge from these vicious alien predators. Before he could consider how to reach it, lancing pain stabbed into his forearm.

Wrenching his head upwards, his helmet gouging a furrow in the earth, he spotted a third alien digging viciously into his arm; as he watched, a fourth tormentor landed, and entirely disregarding his frantic writhing, began probing at the suit's tough fabric. Torn between clinging to his lifeline and defending himself, he hesitated too long, and yet another fiery needle sank into him. Shouting incoherently, enraged now beyond thought, he released his grip and slapped dementedly at his two tormentors, smashing one flat and smearing his suit with sticky and undoubtedly toxic alien viscera. But the other one had already fallen from his arm, dead before he could even take aim.

A fifth alien alit on the victorious arm, and before he could stop himself, he'd released his remaining grip on the vegetation and swatted at it, missing cleanly as the flying thing evaded his grasp with a shrilly evil whine of wings. His triumph abruptly vanished, swept away by the sick realization that he'd just let go with the only hand that had been holding him to the cliff. He felt the familiar vertiginous queasiness in his groin as he anticipated the long plunge past the pod, and braced himself to lunge desperately for the door as he hurtled past—only to discover that somehow, unaccountably, he still hung suspended on the cliff face.

The rational part of him, having waited patiently in the background all this time, now mocked him openly. "Ivar, you boob. You're pressed flat against the soft ground of a planet with far more gravity than's decent. You won't be falling anytime soon, which even someone as dim as those voracious aliens predators should have figured out by now. But if you don't get to your feet and get moving—soon!—they're going to suck you dry, and the fact that you'll take the entire local population with you will be of scant comfort."

Taking firm hold of his sudden courage, Ivar Jonsson rose slowly and reluctantly to all fours, still half-expecting to be flung off into that awful blue void. Eyes locked resolutely on the airlock, he crawled cautiously downhill past the small alien corpses, crushing the small green shoots that were now poking everywhere above the char, and made his long, slow progress back to the pod. He stopped counting the alien predators that died en route, the pain of their attacks goading him onwards past his waning emotional and physical reserves, into the airlock.

ooo   ooo   ooo

Ruefully naked in the safety of the pod, he surveyed his damaged suit in disbelief. It was speckled with dots of blood and sealant, and coated with undoubtedly pestilential mud and crushed vegetation. He shook his head at the holes, disbelieving; they were impossibly tiny for what they'd felt like during their creation and the size of the welts the bites had raised. Unable to reach several of those welts, he'd smeared steroid cream over the ones he could reach, and painted the soft edge of the crash couch with enough of the lotion that he could rub the unreachable parts of his body against it. The imprecision of the process had numbed his entire back by the time he'd finished, but he was beyond caring. A large shot of broad-spectrum antibiotic had improved his morale, though repeated visits to the culture media had continued to reveal no trace of alien life, suggesting his blood was as toxic to the local microorganisms as it had been to the winged predators. A dose of antihistamines strong enough to leave his ears buzzing had also helped, since he was now reasonably confident that no anaphylactic reaction would kill him.

He'd drained a goodly quantity of the bottled water after his brief yet disastrous adventure before he'd realized what he was doing and stopped himself, hating the aftertaste in his mouth. To add insult to the injuries already inflicted on him, he'd bruised his right thigh badly re-entering the pod, and had been too preoccupied to notice the damage until more pressing concerns were addressed. Now he winced, both from the aches and pains that oppressed him and from the growing realization that he'd have to dare the planet's surface again to find water. It was one thing to understand logically that he'd be safe from falling; it was quite another to accept that emotionally, and the alien assassins didn't help.

"Well," he mused, "you could delay a bit longer. When the water runs out, thirst will provide all the motivation you need." Roughly, he kicked the battered suit off the couch, then froze before he could kick it again. Just maybe there was a way to make at least part of the challenge easier! He crossed the pod as fast as his shaky legs permitted, and wrenched open the medical cabinet. Then he smiled a cold, vindictive smile. There was a way he could escape further injury! If only there were a way to keep himself from thinking of the sky too! Then his smile grew even wider. That too could be solved.

ooo   ooo   ooo

With cardboard ration containers sealant-glued perpendicular to his helmet's faceplate and gravity tugging his increasingly heavy head towards the ground, he could easily prevent his gaze from straying upwards towards that terrible sky and away from the approaching patch of green that marked the vegetation around the water. Even so, the trip away from the pod on his hands and knees was a slow, tedious nightmare, and if the ground hadn't been so mercifully free of obstructions, he'd never have made it. Filling the water bags had required him to half-enter the shallow pond, water oozing into his suit through its many holes and making his skin crawl with revulsion. But he'd focused on his task with an intensity born of desperation, and eventually, the bags were full.

He returned quicker than he'd left, despite dragging half again his weight in murky water. He'd pay for those exertions later, but now, with the pod almost within reach, all he felt was elation. Elation that became a strong sense of anticlimax as he squinted through his ash-spattered, sap-smeared, condensation-fogged faceplate at the Navy scout emerging from the pod. The man was barely visible in the gap that lay between the decimetre-high new vegetation and his blinders. The shocked look on the other man's unhelmeted face proved almost worth the disappointment at having made his epic journey to the river and back, hide and pride both intact, for nothing.

"My God, man, don't move!" shouted the scout in a high, squeaky voice, short-sleeved and face naked to the hostile atmosphere. Seeming to not notice the oppressive gravity, he approached at a run, swinging his backpack around to the front on one brawny forearm and rummaging frantically through its innards with the other, emerging, triumphant, with an emergency first aid kit. "Where are you hurt?" he cried, falsetto, as he flung himself to his knees by the exhausted spacer, too concerned at saving Jonsson's life to hide the horror contorting his face.

"Hurt?" Jonsson's voice emerged faintly, muffled by his headgear and his exhaustion, and he had to repeat himself, his lungs hurting at the effort, before the man heard him. "I'm not hurt. Half-eaten, yes. Exhausted, yes. Hurt? No, I'm not really hurt." His neck muscles screamed their rebuttal, but he overruled them.

"But the blood… "

When understanding dawned, Jonsson collapsed, chuckling helplessly, his mirth interrupted only briefly as the soft ground drove the air from his lungs. Prone, he kept his eyes downcast as the chuckling became outright, bellyaching laughter, and the Navy man sat back on his heels, alarmed. Jonsson finally ran out of breath, waving his hand feebly in denial. "It's not mine." He gestured at the last of his blood bags, now nearly empty on his hip. "Alien repellent. Damned local creatures'll drain you dry if you haven't got something to keep them off."

The scout winced suddenly and slapped at the back of his neck, confirming Jonsson's prediction. "I see what you mean. But—"

"We're toxic to them. See?" He nudged the corpse of an alien that had just taken its last meal. "I figured, if I spread enough warpaint on me, they'd be dead by the time they chewed their way through the suit and reached my hide. Want some?"

The scout shook his head no, getting to his feet and smashing another alien with commendable skill.

Jonsson smiled. "Not to seem too ungrateful, but do you think you could carry me inside until we're rescued?"

SUMMER CEREMONY

John H. Baillie

The stranger appeared the last day of threshing - the same day Mr. Smith in Toronto bought a controlling interest in Estragonics, the company that bought horse urine produced by the grain grown in Oaken. That particular diet produced the particular quality of equine urine so useful to menopausal women. As the sun was setting, Buri Samuelsson, at 73 the oldest farmer in Oaken still working the fields, found a clump of grain growing tall that the combine had missed. The last sheaf.

He stared at it, perturbed. "Bloody machines," he muttered, taking his knife from his belt. At the same moment, the woman wandered into the threshing house. When Buri arrived, some minutes later, she was already a topic for discussion.

"Could be from Rosehorn," Tom Snidal commented to Jim Burke.

"No," Jim disagreed. "They're all Swedes or Uker-rainians up at Rosehorn. Her name sounds European. More central, like."

Buri stopped at the door of the threshing house, staring at the woman.

She looked thirty, very tan, and had golden brown hair tightly tied back. She wore a long, thin, flower patterned dress. No shoes. She stood quietly smiling.

"Where'd she come from?" Bill Yaworski, the town constable wondered aloud to no one in particular.

She wasn't saying. She had no luggage - no pack. The only item she carried was a single wild rose.

"Your name's too hard," Jackie Thorleifson, the team leader laughed, addressing the intruder. "We'll just call you Rose." The woman nodded, still smiling.

Buri solemnly walked up to the woman. He held out the last sheaf of grain. She took it, without show of surprise.

"All of you," Buri ordered, in a tone not to be disobeyed. "Give her some grain."

Ingo Wagner, local boy appointed by Estragonics as company representative, frowned. "What the hell?" Everyone looked uncomfortable, perplexed. No one moved. Then Bill, the constable, laughed and picked up some loose grain stalks from the floor and handed them to the woman. Each of the men followed suit, one by one. At the end of the ceremony, the woman's arms were full.

She turned to Buri, and with difficulty, burdened as she was, presented him with her rose.

Buri took a moment, then smiled faintly. His whole body relaxed.

"She'll stay with me, this winter … "

∘∘∘   ∘∘∘   ∘∘∘

Rose came to Buri's bedroom, late that night. She lay down beside him like a young lioness. He felt happier than he had in years - since before Greta died. But he laughed at her. "I'm too old."

"When did your wife die?"

"Young." His mood darkened. "In childbirth. The baby died too."

"Why didn't you ever marry again?"

" … There were no women. There are even less women now, for the young men. They all go away, one by one. The town is dying. All we farm now is horse piss. Urine from pregnant mares. And we don't talk about what we do with the babies. There's no call for anything else. We do not feed anyone with what we grow, except the horses."

"What do you do with the horses?"

"We save every golden drop. They do not run anymore. They just stand in their stalls, and eat, and pee into a machine. God forbid a single drop of liquid gold falls anywhere but into one of Ingo Wagner's machines. This is not a life, for the horses. This is not a life for the men. But if the horses don't pee, the town dies. Everyone leaves. Everything dies."

"Why?"

"People don't farm for people anymore."

Rose was already bored with the subject. She ran a hand down Buri's massive chest. He took the hand gently in one of his. "Wait," he told her. "Just sleep. I will find you someone."

∘∘∘   ∘∘∘   ∘∘∘

The frost came the first night Rose spent in town, followed by the snow a day later.

"Christ," Ingo Wagner complained to his mother, looking out the window. "We just got the crop in in time."

"You must kill the girl, and throw her in the Broken Red River," Anna Wagner muttered from her rocking chair, fiercely stabbing her embroidery needle through the cloth she held in her lap.

Ingo was nonplused. "What girl?"

"The stranger."

Ingo sighed heavily. He often wished the pregnant horse urine had more of the effect it was supposed to on his own mother.

"Mark my word," Anna jabbed the air at her son with her needle. "When the new year comes, it will not snow. It will not rain. You will plant the seed and it will not grow. Nothing will grow and it will not rain until you kill the stranger and throw her body into the Broken Red River."

"It's time for your medicine, Mama," Ingo suggested wearily.

000   000   000

Rose settled comfortably into Oaken town life, as Buri's housekeeper. At the Town Halloween Feast, Buri brought her to Jackie Thorleifson. Jackie, six foot four, two hundred pounds, was dressed as a jockey. Rose wore a long clean white gown, with a wreath of grain wound through her hair. Jackie didn't know what to make of it. He slipped away from her and confronted Buri at the bar where he had stalked off to order his beer.

"What's up here?" Jackie demanded. He was bristling with anxiety. His muscles were taut, and ready to spring. He looked more like a horse in the starting block, ready to run, than its rider.

"You're young, what've you got to complain about?" Buri tipped back his stein.

"Yeah but she—she's pretty—she already—she—she— You know what I mean?"

Buri smiled slyly. "You have a problem with this?"

"What are you trying to do to me?"

"You going to meet a lot of other beautiful women around here tonight?"

"Not bloody likely. But… " Jackie set down his glass and leaned close to Buri's ear. "Me and Ingo and Jim and Tom are heading for Winnipeg next week, to settle the yellow gold shipment. We were going to - you know - have a pretty good time. Even if we have to pay for it."

"You can't have a pretty good time in Oaken? Without having to pay for it?"

"I can't get involved with someone and then just - just - "

Buri put a hand on Jackie's shoulder. "Relax. Don't worry about Winnipeg. Worry about Oaken, for once in your life. See what happens. And don't forget to enjoy yourself."

Jackie stared at the old man, completely stunned. He blew out a loud breath. "You crazy old bugger."

He tore away, back to Rose.

000   000   000

Ed Jonsson went with Ingo, Jim and Tom to Winnipeg, instead of Jackie.

Rose announced she was pregnant on Christmas Day. Jackie said they would marry in June. Buri told him not to wait, they should marry in May, or late April even, but Jackie refused.

He and Ingo had to go on a long trip to Toronto in May to buy new machines for the horses. Don't worry about the goddamn machines, Buri shouted, but Jackie insisted.

Buri gave up. And he knew it would have done no good to argue with Rose.

It didn't snow again that winter, after December 25th.

∘∘∘   ∘∘∘   ∘∘∘

What snow there was melted by mid-March. The spring came hot, and sooner than it should have. But it did not rain. The men were able to seed the fields early. And in May, Jackie left town with Ingo to go to Toronto to buy the new machines. When they came back, Jackie was a changed man for a few days, until Rose settled him down again. He was filled with an uncontainable force, and looked as if he was about to explode. Rose gradually released his energies.

The grain did not grow. The fields remained barren of life, despite the seed within them. The ground grew hard, and cracked. The wind began to blow the fields away.

The sun was relentless. Every day, the temperature crept up a degree or two higher than it had the day before, and dropped one or two degrees less each night.

Jackie no longer took Rose out into the streets of Oaken. Everyone stared too accusingly at the stranger, and at the man whom they had thought they could trust. The man who had chosen the stranger over them.

In their stalls, the horses ran low on feed, and did not micturate the proper amount of liquid gold into Ingo Wagner's new machines from Toronto. The company heard of this, and began to phone Ingo daily. Water was being rationed in Oaken. Ingo couldn't even give the horses more to drink to increase the quantity of the product, although diluting its quality. He grew more and more frustrated and anxious.

His mother relentlessly told Ingo what he should do to remedy the situation.

∘∘∘   ∘∘∘   ∘∘∘

The day of their wedding, Buri Samuelsson carefully prepared his gift card for Jackie and Rose. It was June now. Estragonics daily threatened to abandon Oaken. It still had not rained. The seed still did not grow.

Buri checked the contents of his card very carefully, before sealing it. Two bus tickets to Winnipeg. A cheque, in the amount of Buri's life savings.

A note, telling the couple to remove themselves as far as the money would take them from Oaken. To somewhere where farming was still for people to do, not for machines. Buri wasn't certain where such a place could be found, but he was certain there still must be such places. The events of the last nine months would not have unfolded as they had, if not. He also knew this wedding gift to Rose was wrong. But Oaken was wrong - the reason they still farmed there was wrong. The way they treated the horses was wrong. Buri knew it. Jackie knew it, certainly regarding the horses. So this was logical, then. Jackie would understand. Buri would give them the card that night, after the ceremony. They would leave Oaken tomorrow.

Buri went to dress in his black woolen three-piece suit for the wedding, despite the 37 degree heat.

The entire town came to the wedding, and for the day, forgave Rose her strangeness. They needed a release. By late in the evening, everyone was drunk, and the party in the town hall was growing completely out of hand. The heat made the crowd drink more beer, made them grow wilder and louder in their dares to each other and in their responses to the dares. At the height of the chaos, Buri physically dragged Jackie away from Rose and pressed the card upon him. Jackie was too drunk to realize what was happening. Buri securely deposited the card in Jackie's inside suit pocket, to make certain he would not lose it. When they returned to the madness, they could not find Rose. Tom Snidal said he'd seen her walk out of the hall with Ingo Wagner.

But they found Ingo almost immediately, still in the hall. Rose was not with him.

Yes, he'd gone out, Ingo angrily snarled at them. But not with Rose. He'd taken his mother home, to get her away from this debauchery. What were they doing anyway, putting on a show like this with all their jobs on the line, and the future of the town and all.

They left him and ran from the building, to search for Rose.

There was a loud rumble in the west. By the moment, the clear night grew darker.

When it started, the rain broke like a scythe, cutting down from the heavens. It didn't stop until an hour before dawn. In the morning, the new growth of grain pushed upward to the sun. They found Rose's body in the Broken Red River, swept half a mile downstream. Her throat had been cut, apparently with an old fashioned sickle. Bill Yaworski swore to Buri and Jackie that there was no real evidence against Ingo Wagner, but Jackie didn't hear him. Buri argued who else could it be, in the circumstances? Bill argued back the entire town, including himself and Buri, were drunk at the time, and bad feeling had been raging at Rose for months. Who knew for certain who it could have been?

And anyway, Bill added in an undertone, why go after Ingo or anyone else now? With what had happened.

Estragonics had phoned Ingo first thing that morning. Mr. Smith, in Toronto, was closing operations in Oaken. Estragonics had found a new source for liquid gold, in Mexico.

Buri stared at Bill silently.

Jackie ran from the room, unable to bear the tension. He still wore his wedding jacket, with Buri's card in the inside pocket.

"There is no evidence?" Buri pleaded angrily with Bill.

"The rain washed everything away … Besides. Ingo couldn't have killed anyone. He hasn't got the balls for it. You know it, I know it."

"He could have carried her to the river. The old woman - "

"Never mind, Buri. Go home and try to figure out what you're going to do with the rest of your life."

The grain grew higher and fuller than in any time in living memory. And before they all left, the people realized practically every female in town over the age of fifteen was pregnant. An inconvenient consequence of the wedding feast.

∘∘∘   ∘∘∘   ∘∘∘

Jackie had continued running right out of Oaken when he left Bill Yaworski's office the day after his wedding. They stopped searching for his body a month later. As the townsfolk began their departure, they soon ran out of people to look. By the end of August, every person had left. Every building, every farm, stood empty of human existence. The buildings began to fall in on themselves, one by one. The machines began to rust.

Buri was the only farm owner who did not sell his horses for dog food. He waited until all the other people left - then he freed his horses, most of whom had never seen the sunlight except filtered through glass. The animals walked out hesitantly, into the fields of waving grain. Then Buri left Oaken as well. He walked slowly out to the highway, and waited for the last bus that would ever stop near this land.

The horses adapted quickly. They ate well, and remembered how to run. Everything around them was green and sunlit, and the water in the Broken Red River was fresh and clean. Quickly, the horses grew strong, and they grew fast. And no one cared where the horses pissed.

HERE BE DRAGONS

Sophie Masson

Eighteen—nineteen—twenty red crosses on the calendar; how many more would there have to be? Twenty days since Michael had left with the sheep and his taciturn offsider Craig; twenty days since Gillian and the child had stood at the gate and waved them off; twenty days since, no longer able to see even the most remote cloud of dust churned up by the heavy wheels of the truck and the trailer for the bikes, Gillian had turned to the child and said, with a determined attempt at levity, 'Well, then, we two will have to entertain each other till Daddy gets back, won't we!' Twenty days since the child had given her back look for look, and nodded, silently, challengingly. Twenty days. Twenty long, long days.

Practically all the neighbours' sheep had already gone to the greener pastures of southern Queensland by the time Michael decided he could not wait for a rain-miracle any longer. There must be a great gathering of western districts graziers out there in the Queensland stock routes and reserves, Gillian thought; quite some party it must be, all those sheep out on the road, and motorists cursing as yet another mob drifted and jostled across the tar. Michael had wanted to be up there with the sheep for a fair while now; he had left it as long as he possibly could, for pregnant Gillian's sake. But it was she who had said to him, one morning, 'Please, darling, take them out on the road, I don't think I can bear it any longer.'

She meant, I can't bear listening to the sheep bleating, their pathetic rushing for the last bit of hay thrown out from the ute, your worried face, drawing down into the same harsh lines as the steadily skeletonising landscape under the merciless, beautiful pale blue sky. When she'd first come here, two years ago—could it really be only that long ago?—the whole place was a mass of knee-deep pale green and yellow grass, thick, waving in all directions like an endless, shimmering sea to the very edges of the horizon. On the edges of the horizon, the earth curved, noticeably, enclosing the farm, and it was as if this place was all the world there was. Sometimes, you could see cars or trucks moving along the road on the horizon's outer edge, and in the pure, refracting light, it was as though they were ships, perhaps those of the Argonauts seeking the Golden Fleece, sailing the limits of the known sea. She watched them as if she was a remote goddess watching the far off, strange commerce of human beings, their bustling meaningless busyness.

The farm had been named Grasmere, by Michael's great-grandparents, who'd come out from the Lake District in Britain, but the signwriter had never heard of that far away place and assumed it to be 'Grass Mere', taking it to be a some kind of daft joke on the farm's most dominant feature: mere grass perhaps? There were a few short wilga trees dotted here and there in the paddocks, and rich deep brown soil, and thousands of little native flowers in amongst the lush mixed native and exotic grasses. The kangaroos and emus that jostled the sheep for a living in this rich land were not too much resented, in times of plenty; and the land's fragility was not apparent, at least not to Gillian. Born and bred in the city, and used to hills and plunging bays and steep slopes, the flat grassland had charmed and delighted her. Its strange, deceptive horizons and enormous skies and secretive animal pathways in among the prairie grasses seemed to promise endless freedom, recalled to her mind childhood dreamings of nomadic horsemen ranging over immense steppes, and herself as a Scythian princess in armour, carrying a bow, the equal of her brothers and father. She had pestered her parents to let her learn to ride, back in the city, and to everyone's surprise but her own, had done rather well at it. When she married Michael, she had assumed that at last she'd have a horse of her own and go out on musters and long droves. But here, in sheep country, few people used horses any more; it was all motorbikes, two wheelers and three wheelers and four-wheelers, and she hated them with a passion that Michael found amusing.

'You needed to marry a cattleman if you wanted horses, love,' he'd say, smiling at her when she complained how the bikes stank of oil and grease and hot metal, all the industrial smells she hated and thought she'd put behind her when she came to live in the country. She gave up on the idea of horses, but refused to ride a bike, and instead walked out to the sheepyards to help with dipping, or bumped along in the ute to the far paddocks to help dose the young ewes with flystrike powder, or go round the lambing ewes to check all was well. She went on long walks, too, and sketched and sketched. She was still selling her drawings and paintings to her agent in the city, though he was complaining that her work was getting more and more realistic, that she didn't have the fantasy edge anymore that she used to have. Soon, she thought, he'll tell me not to bother. Yet, the first year, she'd painted possibly the best thing she'd ever done, a massive picture, fantastically detailed, like a three-dimensional map, really, of the farm as a kind of fantasy realm, the Mere of Grass, with every paddock name—Long Mile, Shortfall, Wilga, and so on—functioning as the name of a village, or manor, whatever. At the edge of the Mere of Grass, there was an inner sea, with a black-sailed ship and a white-sailed ship sailing towards the far horizon and the outer sea, where, just as in medieval maps, dragons and sea serpents writhed and waited. In the centre of the picture, where the house stood in mundanity, there was a castle, with flying turrets and drawbridge; and she'd drawn two tiny figures, a blond-haired man and a dark-eyed woman, standing at the door in welcome, hands outstretched. She had intended selling the picture, but somehow could not bear to part with it, though she knew her agent would have raved over it. It stayed there on the wall of the room Michael called her studio but which more and more in recent times had become the child's bolthole.

The child... no, not the child wriggling and diving in Gillian's distended belly, but Michael's daughter by his first marriage, living with them since only a few months ago, because of the death of her mother in a road accident. Gillian had been more than ready to welcome the child, horrified by the trauma the poor little thing must have suffered, full of a certain expectation that she would soon grow to love Michael's child, no matter what. And Michael had assured her Bianca was just like her—bookish, clever, prone to dreaming and imagination. It would be easy for them to get on, she'd thought. But alas, Michael's child—the child Bianca, flaxen-haired and blue-eyed and graceful as some orphaned mite in a fairytale—did not respond to Gillian's advances and did not seem interested in anything at all. At least not anything that Gillian wanted to do, or suggested, or spoke about. She spent the days and hours when she was not at school, or rattling along in the school bus, aimlessly wandering about in the top paddock, near the gate, or reading, or playing the rather dull computer games Michael had installed for her on his office machine. She changed as soon as she heard her father's step in the hall, as soon as she heard the sound of his ute drawing up in the dust of the drive. Then she would be bright, lively, chattering, when only a couple of minutes before, in Gillian's company, she had been silent, uncommunicative—not sullen, exactly, just blank, as if Gillian were not human, but, say, a tree, or worse, a wall, or a table: something that you could not expect to interact with at all. At first, Gillian had taken little notice, telling herself that poor little Bianca was bound to feel some very complicated emotions indeed; her mother had not taken at all well to Michael's remarrying, though it had been her who had left him, and no doubt the child had heard all kinds of things about her. She was patient and kind and gentle with Bianca, and never told Michael that there was anything wrong, and so of course he saw nothing wrong. For when Bianca was around him, it was as if she were a different person; and even Gillian was included then in her reflected glory.

The only thing of Gillian's that Bianca was remotely interested in was the picture in the studio, the fantasy-map of the farm. She spent hours just looking at it, and Gillian had found her once with her nose pressed up close against it, as if she were physically trying to get into the picture. She was murmuring something as she did so, jerky little words that seemed to be in no language Gillian had ever heard. That did not concern her; as a child she, too, had made up all kinds of 'languages'; as a Tolkien-worshipping adolescent, she'd started writing some down and devising grammars for them, but gave up soon enough, bored by linguistic formulae that seemed altogether too close to mathematics for her liking. But Bianca had started when she'd become aware that Gillian was in the room too; a strange look had come into her eyes, a look that even now Gillian could not interpret properly.

Perhaps it was from then that Gillian's feelings towards Bianca began to change. Or perhaps it was as her pregnancy advanced. She began to feel there was something of a calculated malice in the child's rejection of her, and a superstitious dread fell on her whenever Bianca's eyes fell on her round belly. In his innocence, Michael assumed that Bianca was as thrilled as he was by the coming arrival of a new brother or sister; Gillian thought she knew better. The child's blue eyes, it seemed to her, were as mercilessly, blankly hostile as the drought-sky; her slender, pale little hands seemed to become claw-like at any mention of the new baby. The child hated her, she thought breathlessly; hated her and the new life growing inside her, and the hatred was growing, becoming a thing that could literally endanger Gillian and her child…

Stop it, she would tell herself sternly. You are just falling into the archetypal wicked stepmother trap. Bianca's just a child; you're an adult. She's lost her mother, trying to share her father; of course she hates you, or thinks she does. When the baby's born, everything will change. You'll see. We'll be one happy family. But who knows if all those wicked stepmothers, the ones that wanted to poison and kill and destroy their stepchildren, what if it was just a matter of survival, a fight to the death? What if the children really, really hated them and just wanted to destroy everything between their father and this usurping new woman? What if children, especially daughters, have a much greater power than people will admit? Oh. Stop it. Stop it.

Michael noticed something was wrong between them; you'd have had to blind and deaf not to. But either he didn't want to, or couldn't, imagine the depth of antipathy that existed between his daughter and his wife. But the obscure unease that was obviously in him kept him at the farm for much longer than he should have stayed, for the sheep's sake, and that was highly unusual, for Michael was a born sheepman and loved his charges, though he would never have admitted to it. But he was relieved when Gillian told him he must go, for he knew it was crunch time for the sheep if he'd stayed even a day longer. He must have thought, too, that if she urged him to go, then things must be all right. Indeed, Gillian managed to persuade him that this would be a 'good opportunity' for herself and Bianca to 'get to know each other better'. She did not try to persuade him to take her with him, for that would have meant taking Bianca too, anyway; and though she knew that some women went on droving camps these days, she honestly did not fancy it. At least, not tagging along, with Bianca, and the stockman Craig. Alone with Michael, that would have been different. At least for a while. She knew enough about farming life by now to know that if you did not have an instinctive feel for land and animals and things agricultural in general, you could soon become very bored indeed, when there were not even other things to distract you, just keeping an eye on sheep grazing on the roadside. No; she would be fine here, she assured Michael; she'd do lots of sketching; though it was school holidays, she'd try and do things with Bianca, take her to the cinema in the town an hour and a half away, organise school friends to come and play or sleepover with the child, whatever. They'd find lots to do. Won't we, Bianca? she had appealed to the child, who, because her father was there, anxiously awaiting her confirmation, smiled in a regal way.

But now, it was twenty days since he'd gone. At least fifteen since Gillian had run out of ideas and patience with the child. At least six since she'd begun to lose hope that it would start to rain, and Michael would return soon. Two days since he'd last rung. He'd taken the mobile phone with him, but it did not always work, out on the road, and he wasn't always close by a public phone to ring her every day. He'd promised to ring at least every three days and had more than fulfilled that promise. She clung to the idea that she'd hear his voice soon; because he was a reminder that there was another world, beyond the house, the garden, the paddocks that stretched dry and flat and dead in every direction, and the endless, merciless sky.

For Bianca refused to leave the farm. In the last three or four days, she had pointblank refused to come on any shopping expedition or to visit any friends; she hung out in the top paddock, by the gate, waiting by the big wilga tree for hours on end, so that Gillian was forced to trudge out to her every so often to check she was OK and to bring her little snacks and drinks, things that Bianca accepted without comment, as her due, but without apparent hostility, either. Once, she had even unbent so far as to say to her stepmother, 'I saw the ships again today... they're closer, now..they're coming to help me... ' but clammed up when Gillian tried to reply in kind, about how she'd seen them too, one with white sails, one with black, which was why she'd put them on her picture. The funny thing was that though it was deeply annoying, it also made Gillian feel a little more sympathetic towards the child again, to make her remember that it was a child she was dealing with, and not a fledgling witch.

∘∘∘   ∘∘∘   ∘∘∘

Twenty days... Gillian put down the red pen with which she'd marked the calendar, and sighed deeply. She'd listened to the weather report last night, and heard the weatherman claiming that a big low was on its way. But she'd heard those things before; big lows which blew up over the ocean, steamed in over the coast, hit the dividing range with a big splat and evaporated over the western plains. To see distant clouds and know that somewhere, somewhere that didn't need it, it was raining fit to burst dams and flood already sodden paddocks, was to add insult to injury. She'd thought of doing a rain dance, but knew no steps, no words.

Now, she got up, and driven by some aimless impulse, came into her studio and stood in front of her painting, staring absently at it for the first time in many weeks. A funny twisted gaiety rose in her. She was the queen of this painted place, the chatelaine, the Morgana le Fay of this particular Avalon. She could do anything in this realm. Perhaps she should take up her brush, paint in a big low or something, skimming lightly in on big gusty gales and driving rain, saturating the entire realm? Why not?

She picked up a brush, and stood back to look carefully at how she would do it. Then she gave an exclamation, so sharp that it actually felt to her like a physical pain. For the tiny figures in the castle door—they were no longer a man and woman, but a man..and a child. A child with flaxen hair, confident, relaxed, the man's hand on her shoulder. Of the woman, there was no sign..not a trace..except yes..there, in the barred window at the bottom, the dungeon window, there was a face, a woman's face, staring hopelessly, the dark eyes sunken. And under the window, in the soil just below, a tiny cross...

Some deep detached part of Gillian stood and gazed in admiration, knowing that the hand that had made these changes was an artist's hand; a little awkward, perhaps, a little immature, but remarkably vivid, for all that, quick, almost cruel brushstrokes giving somehow an unforgettable picture of calm triumph on the one hand and wild desperation on the other. Yet the greater part of Gillian rose up in horror and revolt at what she was seeing. Her breath whistled in her throat, burnt in her chest. The child's malice seemed truly without bounds…

Without stopping to think, she flung out of the house, and instead of walking, started up the ute, throwing it into gear with such force that it kangaroo-hopped down the drive for an instant. Bianca heard the roar of the engine; Gillian saw her raise her head. But then she turned away, again, indifferent, and somehow it was that turning away, as if nothing her stepmother could do would ever be of any interest or connection or anxiety to her, that filled Gillian with a terrifying fury. She threw the vehicle up the road, straight towards the slight figure waiting at the gate, her mind and heart roaring with fire, her veins full of what seemed like the most virulent poison in the world, corrosive and powerful and deadly as dragon's blood.

At the last moment, the child looked up and saw her. Saw her face, her real face, not the kind-but-irritating-stepmother-who-understands-and-tries, but the wild and wicked witch, the poisoner, the killer, the she-dragon, fiercer by far than the male, bearing down, unstoppable and inconsolable. Bianca gave a shriek; threw herself sideways in a desperate attempt to get away; tripped over a wilga root; went sprawling, flung her arms up over her head, and fell, and was still. But there was the sound of breaking glass, and the roar of waves, and Gillian, braking so hard that the tyres smelt burnt, and the car spinning, sliding, the steering wheel in her hands like a loose, crazed, determined thing, the horizon whirling, throwing her to the limits, the limits of everything, of love, of truth, of life itself. She saw the ship, then, tacking swiftly towards her, flying black sails, for mourning, for sorrow, for endless night, coming not to help her, but to avenge, to destroy… She saw the captain, standing on the deck, fierce dark face alight with savage glee, knowing that the castle would be sacked, the crops burnt, the land put to the torch, everyone and everything slaughtered as the brass-faced goddess of war and destruction rampaged over all. She heard the bang as the world ended; and then silence.

ooo   ooo   ooo

Nothing to be seen from the one barred window but endless harsh blue sky, stretching on and on and on. Nothing to be heard in this dungeon deep below the castle, but endless, thick silence. The prisoner groaned, and stumbled back to her pallet, her head in her hands.

This was her last morning on earth. Last night had been her own last night. And she'd not rested, but had the dream again, the tormenting dream of another life, a life strange in its details, yet close to her own heart-knowledge. For there was a child in that dream, too, a child just like her own stepdaughter Blanche. But in the dream, the child was called Bianca; and her own dream-self was called Gillian, and not Julian. Only Michael had the same name. And that was perhaps the hardest thing of all..

The door rattled. She heard a key turn in the rusty lock. Her flesh crept. They had come. There was nothing left for her now. She could not even die with honour, for she must expiate her crime, the crime of attempting to murder her own husband's daughter, while the girl's father was away. It was Michael, Prince Michael of the Mere of Grass, admiral of the fleet and lord justice of the court, who had judged her, condemned her, and would now wait, black-robed, straight-backed, stony-faced and hollow-eyed, for the sentence to be carried out. And by his side, there would be his daughter, blond and frail and calculating, lately returned from the dead, and twice as vindictive. There would be no mercy, the Lady Julian knew that, no mercy, not even in times to come. Her memory would forever be tainted, her story always told by the child, the victorious child. There would be no telling of how she'd tried to win Blanche's love; no recounting of her doomed attempts at understanding. Instead, there would always be her, the wicked stepmother, whose one wild attack would be made into many, as if by evil magic: and the child, innocent, suffering, frail, always lovely. An old story: that of the dragon, and the dragon-slayer. And everyone knew how such stories ended.

VERY LARGE ARRAY

Carolyn Clink

I am alone here,
if you ignore the herd of cattle grazing
amongst the radio dishes gazing upward
listening, listening,
while I could shout
and not be detected
on the flat plain crisscrossed
by rail lines, positioning
the large white ears
pointing straight up
unlike the many hares
whose long ears fold back
against their tawny fur
as they sit between the rails
silent, silent,
while the setting sun silhouettes
antennae against
the big empty sky
waiting, waiting,
tracking my loneliness
as it echoes outward
at the speed of sound.

Please Keep Off The Grass

James A. Hartley

The first touch of their minds against mine made me shiver. I was alone then—I am still alone—but now I know why. I almost knew that first night, when Susan flew away.

That first day, our ship descended on Aurora, floating through the ruddy clouds, the attitude jets making the craft shudder and roar around us. Six of us sat in the descent vessel, the first base camp team. I was there as mission historian, to record and annotate for posterity, and I sat and watched the faces as I recorded. They glowed with excitement. Andy, Laura, Susan, Max, Ivan—all trained mission personnel. Then there was me. I was the outsider in the group, but then that was nothing new. I'd always been an outsider in one way or other.

The initial survey teams had decided the planet was safe. Things were different down there, but I'd been assured they would do me no harm and I believed them. The virgin world below beckoned with the promise of dreams to be fulfilled. For me, it was history in the making and that was enough. And almost being a part of it.

"So, Andy," I said. "How does it feel to be a pioneer?"

Andy grinned back at the camera lens and struggled for something to say.

"Well, I guess it's better than sex," he said. "Oh, hell. Can you cut that, Phil? I reckon I ought to say something meaningful, right?"

"Sure. Take your time."

Andy ran his palm back across his stubbled head, adjusted his seat then looked into the camera again. Square jawed and deeply tanned, he looked the part. His clear blue eyes fixed the lens with intensity.

"I feel proud," he said. "Proud to be among the first to take our dreams to the stars."

That brought a slow handclap from the rest of the crew.

"A bit thick isn't it, Andy?" said Laura. "Hey, guys, I think he might be after the Academy Award."

"And playing Andy Johansen is … himself," said Max.

The others laughed and I joined in. The good-natured banter continued to the ground, Andy looking sheepish.

I planned to pipe the images up to the main ship at the end of every day, after I'd finished editing them. I thought perhaps I'd leave Andy's bit in.

As the ship touched down, the others were busy with their instruments and readings. I let them get on with it and sat back, slightly envious, recording it all. I'd often dreamed of being in their position, but hadn't made the grade. I'd done the tests and the company physicals, but failed on the first attempt. Historian was the next best thing. Being there with them was the next best thing.

Our landing vessel was big—big enough to accommodate all of us for an extended duration if we needed it—and as strong as a rock. It had been designed to withstand anything the planet could throw at us, but as we were there to set up the first real base on Aurora, secretly all of us hoped it wouldn't come to that.

It took an hour or so for them to finish the final checks before they were ready to open the doors and then, one by one, the crew stepped down to Aurora's surface. I followed, camera on my shoulder, capturing it all for the records. Together we looked out over hills and fields touched with crimson and breathed in the moment. Max whistled softly.

"Will you look at that," he said.

Susan knelt down and fingered the tightly clumped knobs of vegetation packed hard against the ground.

"It's like a miniature gorse or heather," she said, more to herself than anyone else. "You wouldn't want to walk barefoot on this stuff."

She got to her feet, brushed off her gloves and like the others, stood staring at the alien landscape stretched out before us.

"All right, all of you," said Andy finally. "We could stand here looking at this all day, but we've got work to do. Max, Ivan, you start breaking out the prefabs. The rest of us can start lugging. We've got a lot of stuff to shift. You too, Phil."

Ivan stood looking at Andy with his hands on his hips. His thin face held a slight quirky grin. "Well, as official team driver, I say we ought to take a bit of a spin first," he said. "It'd be a shame to waste this light, now wouldn't it?"

Andy shook his head, all seriousness. "We don't break out the vehicle until we've got the camp set. You know the drill as well as I do, Ivan," he said.

"Yeah, okay," said Ivan reluctantly, then gave a shrug. He headed back inside the ship to start shifting the equipment.

The crew all got on pretty well, and technically had the same ranking, but when it came down to it, Andy was the one in charge.

"And you too, Phil. You waiting for anything in particular?" he said.

"Um, no… sorry," I said and tore my gaze away from the gently rolling fields. I could have stood there for hours drinking in the strangeness, but I shook my head, took a deep breath of the slightly fragrant air and went inside to help.

It took us about five hours to get the makeshift camp into some sort of order. The prefab bubbles slotted into place perfectly and looked like strange, silver golf balls scattered around the ship. I captured it all for posterity—or at least company archives and promotion clips—during the short breaks between shifting.

As the Auroran evening drew in, we cracked a couple of bottles reserved just for the occasion, staking our claim to the planet; we were going to make this new world our own. Andy finally relaxed, satisfied that we had done enough for the day. He'd been in touch with the mother ship from inside the lander while the rest of us stared out of the communal dome at the purple sunset.

"Okay, guys," he said as he joined us. "Hey, save me some of that."

"Well, I don't know whether we should," said Laura, her pale round face showing mock disapproval.

"Yeah, mission leader and all that," said Max, swinging the bottle out of Andy's reach. "Have to be in full command of your faculties."

"I'm surprised he's deigned to join us," said Susan, only half-joking.

"Come on, guys. Mission hat off. Sure we can have a good time, but the company's paying us to do a job too. Be fair. We've got to be prepared for any eventuality, not that anything's likely to happen." He made an ineffectual grab for the bottle.

"So what do you say?" said Max, dancing his stocky form out of reach. "Should I let him have some?" He held the bottle at arm's length, away from him.

Andy gave up trying to grab for the bottle and stood with his hands outstretched, pleadingly. Max finally relented and passed it over. Andy poured a cup and joined us over at the main window. The dome light spilled out into darkness; the only illumination on the vast undulating plane, but far above, flickers of lightning or something else showed within the clouds.

"A toast," said Andy. "To the first base team on Aurora."

"To us," we said and raised our glasses. We stood and watched the deepening night in silence after that. Over the rim of my glass, I thought I saw vague shapes shimmering in the distance, but I couldn't be sure. I dismissed it as the result of staring through my lens on and off most of the day. Then it came again, something swooping up toward the clouds above the distant fields.

"What the hell was that?" I muttered to myself.

"What is it, Phil?" asked Laura.

I peered into the darkness, but I couldn't see anything. The shape had gone.

"Oh nothing. Just tired I guess," I said.

I didn't want to say anything. I wasn't trained mission personnel after all, and I wanted to be sure I'd seen something. It was probably just my eyes, or perhaps the wine playing tricks on me. I stared at the clouds for a long time, but saw nothing more. Finally, we drifted to our individual bubbles.

I slept like a baby. The exercise of setting up the camp had worn me out. My sleep inside the bubble was painted with images and color. The vague shapes that had shimmered in the distance tiptoed through my dreams sprite-like. Every time I reached for them to give them shape, they retreated into the background. When I woke, they scurried away, almost forgotten, but they stayed lurking as a half memory in the back of my thoughts.

Normally, I wasn't much of a morning person, and I'd stagger around until I'd had my first caffeine shot, but this time it was different. I woke feeling light and airy, full of energy and eager to get on with the day's tasks. I bounced around the bubble in the slightly lighter gravity, dressing, collecting my gear, eager to join the others.

Most were already in the mess bubble by the time I arrived. I could feel the energy infusing the group as I entered. They seemed to have caught whatever was coursing through my own veins. I nodded to each of them and grabbed a ration pack for myself.

"Morning, Phil," Ivan said and grinned. "Almost the last. We're just waiting for Susan. What a great day, eh?"

And we kept waiting. After a time, Andy's expression darkened.

"Has anyone seen her?" he asked. "Laura? You want to go see what's happened to her?"

Laura nodded and ducked out. I tore open my ration pack and sat chewing, one hand resting on my camera. I wanted them all there so I could record the first breakfast on Aurora.

Laura reappeared a few minutes later. She poked her head around the door and leaned on the frame, her short dark hair framing the worry on her face.

"There's no sign of her. She's not in the bubble. I can't find her anywhere."

"Did you check the lander?" asked Max.

Laura nodded.

"Well, she can't just disappear," said Max. "Maybe she's in one of the other bubbles."

Laura shook her head and hung on the door frame waiting for suggestions.

One by one, we turned to face Andy who cleared his throat.

"Yeah, well, as Max said, she can't just have disappeared. She's probably noticed something and gone off to investigate." He sounded unconvinced. "She knows the routine." He scratched his chin, then sighed. "I'm sorry guys, but we're going to have to find her."

Max groaned.

"Look, can't we finish breakfast first?" said Ivan. "She can't have gone far. And what's out there that could possibly harm her? Nothing."

"Come on, Ivan. You know how it is. By the book. Max, you're almost done. Why don't you go with Laura and see if you can find where she's got to. I don't want to make this official yet. Not unless we have to. Let's see if we can locate her and then we can forget it." He placed his hand flat on the table. "Although she sure as hell won't."

Max nodded, shoved the last of his breakfast ration into his wide mouth and walked out to join Laura.

"Great. Just what I need," said Andy with another sigh.

As I wasn't going to get the shots of breakfast I wanted, I made do with recording the remaining two. The whole thing was more subdued than I would have liked. I decided I could patch in other shots of them all together later.

After about a half-hour, Max and Laura returned.

"No sign of her anywhere," said Max.

"Great," said Andy. "This is cutting into our schedule. How could she do this? She knows the routine. Well, break out the vehicle and try tracking her by the signal chip. I hope to hell she's remembered to take the unit."

"Um, some bad news," said Laura. She held up Susan's unit.

"Wonderful!" said Andy. "What's got into her? Ivan, just do it. Get out the vehicle and find her will you? There'll be hell to pay when she gets back."

Despite the seriousness, Ivan beamed. "Yes. At last!" he breathed and slammed a fist into his hand.

"Listen, Andy," I said, wanting to do something. I didn't know why, but I thought I should be out there. "Can I go along? It'll give me an opportunity to get some good shots of the landscape, and I can at least feel useful."

"Well, I don't know… ," he said, rubbing a hand across his stubble. "Yeah, okay. Why not? Without a signal, two pairs of eyes will be better than one."

"Right," I said to Ivan. "Give me a couple of minutes to get my equipment together, and I'll meet you alongside the lander."

Ivan nodded and went out to prepare. I joined him just as he was rolling the vehicle down from the ramp at the lander's back.

The vehicle was sort of like a four-wheel drive. Fat bubble tires gave it an all-terrain capability; not that it looked like we'd need it on Aurora's gentle fields. It was enclosed with thick roll bars forming a cage around the passenger area. There was room for four, but only the two of us were going. Ivan was grinning like a big kid when I clambered in beside him. All he needed was a helmet and driving gloves to complete the image.

"All set?" he asked.

I nodded. "Any idea which way we should go?"

"Not really. I thought we'd take a wide circular sweep running in a spiral out from the camp. What do you think?"

"Sounds good to me."

Ivan accelerated out of the camp with a jolt that threw me back into my seat and slammed my lens into my eye-socket.

"Hey, take it easy!"

"Sorry," he said. "Just getting used to the controls."

"Yeah, sure," I said, knowing full well he'd spent years training in a vehicle just like this.

The vehicle bounced along and I struggled to keep the camera steady. The smooth rolling plane stretched on, distance blurring the crimson ground cover into tones of mauve. There were no trees, at least not on this part of the planet. There didn't seem to be much in the way of life either— only the unbroken field of gorse, or heather, as Susan had called it. The thick purple clouds hung in a shadow above. I looked behind us and saw the twin tracks from the vehicle circling out from the campsite. I took a few shots of Ivan at the wheel and he obligingly looked enthusiastic for the camera. Not that he needed me there for that.

We found Susan around midday. She was standing staring into the distance, her arms folded around herself. She didn't even notice as we drove up. Ivan idled the vehicle and opened his door. I had the camera going the whole time.

"Susan?" called Ivan.

She didn't respond. It was as if she didn't hear.

"Susan, what are you doing out here? Are you okay?"

Slowly she turned, a dreamy expression on her face. "What?"

"We've been worried about you. How could you just wander off like that?"

She lifted a hand to her brow and traced her fingers over the skin at her forehead. "It's just so… I fee… . "

"Jesus, Susan. I don't know what you're on, but Andy's going to have a piece of you when we get back," said Ivan. She had turned away again and seemed to be watching something in the distance. She lifted her hands and rubbed at her shoulder blades.

"Susan, will you get in? I'm starting to get pissed," said Ivan.

She shook herself, walked over to the vehicle and stood staring up at him as if she didn't quite know who he was.

After a lengthy pause that made Ivan's frown grow deeper, she clambered up behind us. I turned to talk to her, but her eyes were focused somewhere in the middle distance. A slight smile played at the corners of her mouth. I turned back to face front as Ivan gunned the vehicle. Ivan's face was like thunder.

Susan said something, and I turned back to look at her.

"Please keep off the grass," she said softly and giggled. She wasn't looking at us. She was staring up at the clouds.

At first I didn't believe I'd heard right. She was smiling to herself. One hand still massaged her shoulder.

"What?" I asked. "Did you say something, Susan?"

Susan just shrugged and smiled, then turned from the clouds to watch the passing Auroran landscape. I looked at Ivan, but he just shook his head, hard lines etched into his face. Something was weird. Very weird.

We drove into camp and the others were arrayed waiting for us. Susan stepped serenely from the vehicle and walked over to join them as if nothing had happened. Andy's face radiated displeasure. The rest just looked bemused. Andy started in before Susan was ten paces away.

"What the hell do you think you are playing at, Susan? I expected a little more sense from you. What were you trying to do, jeopardize our mission?"

Susan merely shrugged.

At that moment, Ivan caught his foot climbing down from the vehicle and fell heavily to the ground.

"Ow! Dammit, this stuff's sharp," he said, picking himself up and looking down at his hands.

"You, okay?" asked Laura.

"Yeah, fine," said Ivan, picking a few scraps of vegetation from his gloves as he walked toward us. "Just stings a bit. It's gone right through the fabric." He rubbed his hands on his chest and joined the group.

Andy was still going at Susan, but it seemed to wash over her as if it meant nothing at all. The other team members cast concerned glances at each other.

Laura finally raised a placating hand.

"Listen, Andy, let's just cool down for a minute and work out what's happened here." As team medico, the group's welfare was Laura's prime responsibility.

Andy grudgingly stepped back and let Laura move forward to check Susan while the rest of us stood back and watched. She seemed to find nothing untoward. Despite repeated questions, Susan refused to be drawn about what had caused her to go off like that. Laura finally backed off with a concerned expression.

"I want her to get some rest. I'm sending her to bed for the rest of the day. There appears to be nothing physically wrong with her, but … " She shrugged. "And Ivan, you let me take a look at those hands."

That night, Susan flew away.

We were gathered in the mess bubble, all tired from the final set up of survey equipment and the remaining camp prefabs. The lab was in place, and monitoring equipment. I'd got some good shots of the interplay between the team members during the day, and even managed to lend a hand here and there, so felt a little more like a part of the group. The feeling was good. It didn't happen too often.

We were sitting around a table, discussing plans for the next day, when Susan walked into the middle of the bubble. She stood looking at us, saying nothing, a faint smile on her face, her short reddish hair forming a nimbus in the dome light. Then she took off her shirt.

Max choked on his drink and came up spluttering. Laura stood and edged around the table toward her. Andy just sat open mouthed. Ivan snickered, and then stared, grinning from ear to ear. I don't remember exactly what I did, but I think I finally managed to close my mouth.

Before Laura had taken three steps, Susan held up her hand.

"No, Laura," she said. "Don't bother. It's not important. I'm fine. You'll see. You'll all see."

Then she unfurled her wings—vast gossamer wings iridescent with rainbow colors—walked calmly out the door and took off into the night.

A couple of us raced to the window and watched her soar up and out into the purpling sky. Like an idiot, I'd left my camera on the table. The silence dragged on and on. Finally someone spoke. It was Andy.

"What the… ?"

"I don't know," said Laura. "I'm not sure I… You all saw her, right?"

"Uh-huh," said Max, nodding his head and still goggling at the place where she'd stood.

"Did she just—"

"Fly," giggled Ivan.

"Like, she had—"

"Yeah, wings," said Ivan. This time he laughed.

"What the hell's going on here?" Andy slammed his hand down on the table. He looked from Max to Laura and around the other faces, but everyone merely shrugged or shook their heads. Andy stood and walked over to the window. He peered out into the darkness, shaking his head.

"Andy, what are we going to do?" asked Laura. Andy shrugged without turning. He was still shaking his head.

"Please keep off the grass," said Ivan.

Andy spun. "What?" He almost spat the word at Ivan.

Ivan shook his head and looked away. I gave him a hard look.

Ivan was staring down at his hands. He was smiling.

Andy stalked back over to the table. "Well, what the hell is that supposed to mean?"

"It was just something she said," I offered.

Andy growled, turned and strode outside. He started calling Susan's name—shouting at the night sky. Max and Laura went out to join him. Moments later their voices joined his.

I looked out the window, but there was no sign of anything up there in the purple clouds. I turned back and saw Ivan, still staring at his hands and smiling. He turned his face to the window and looked out at the sky. There was an expression like longing on his face. He reached back and rubbed his shoulders. We were alone in the bubble.

I came back to the table and stood looking down at him. After a moment I sat down opposite.

"Ivan," I said. "What did you mean?"

"Hmm?" He dragged his attention back from the window.

I had a suspicion, but I wanted to be sure. "Ivan, about the grass. What did you mean?"

He shook his head and smiled. He turned back to the window. His face bore the same serene expression I'd seen on Susan's face earlier.

"Talk to me, man! Tell me what you know." He kept smiling, a dreamy expression, and shook his head.

It looked like I wasn't going to get any sense out of him, so I went out to join the others. Between calling for Susan, we tried to work out what had happened, but all of us were as lost as each other, barely able to believe what we'd seen, despite the suspicion lurking deep in my mind. We called and searched well into the night, but we saw no further sign.

By morning, Ivan had gone too.

As soon as we found him missing, we fired up the vehicle and went out searching. Though we rumbled around and around the crimson fields in shifts for most of the day, we found nothing. Andy made his report in the afternoon. He locked himself away in the lander, clearly a worried man. He was in there for over an hour. When he returned, his face was grim.

"We're to continue searching, in shifts," he said. "If we've not found them by morning, we're taking off."

Laura looked horrified. "You mean we're just going to—"

"That's right. Leave them here. Those are the orders. What else can we do? Aurora will be put under quarantine until we work out what the hell's going on here."

Max went next. I knew he would when I saw him sitting outside his bubble fiddling with a piece of equipment on the ground. I was still recording, but none of the images would see the light of day. Not yet, anyway. I got the pictures of his transformation later that night. I recorded the way the dreamy smile played over his lips. I smiled myself as he peeled the shirt from his stocky body. Then those massive, beautiful wings unfurled as he stepped outside and soared into the night sky. I tracked him until the speck faded among the clouds. Then I walked in and told the other two. They looked at each other with expressions of disbelief. When they came back in, the disbelief had changed to a sort of fear.

Andy and Laura were out searching. I was sitting in my bubble, playing back the images and getting them into some sort of order. Then Ivan's voice came to me in my silence, filtering through the corners of my perception.

Phil, can you hear me?

"Ivan?" I said to the bare walls.

If only you knew how beautiful it was.

"Ivan, where are you?"

You can join us, be with us. You can be one with us.

"Are the others there with you?"

We are all here, Max, Susan and the… others. It's so beautiful. I always dreamed of flying. Didn't you have those dreams? It's so easy, Phil. Come and join us. You belong here.

"Who are you talking to?" Laura popped her head around the door, a worried expression on her face and Ivan's voice faded.

"No one," I said.

"But I heard voices. Are you all right, Phil?"

"Yeah, I'm fine. You must've just heard the equipment." I waved my hand at the decks. "I was playing back some of the recordings." That seemed to satisfy her. She walked right in to the bubble and sat on the end of my bunk.

"What are we going to do, Phil? We can't just leave them here. I can't talk to Andy. I just can't believe they want us to go without them."

"I don't think we've got any choice."

"Have you got any ideas about what's going on?"

"None at all," I said, comfortable with the lie for the moment. "I wish I did."

Laura bit her lip and nodded slowly. "Well, as long as you're okay," she said.

"Yeah, fine."

She stood and placed a hand upon my shoulder. Just for an instant, I thought about telling her, about sharing with her what I knew. But I pushed back the feeling. I knew now there was too much at stake.

She left and slowly I packed the equipment away.

We spent all night searching. Orders came through that we were to wear extra protection on top of our normal environment gear, so we suited up. The full suits were heavy and clumsy, and though we'd trained in them, I still couldn't get used to the lack of mobility. If only I could be like Ivan and the others. Despite the discomfort, the protective gloves suited my purposes. They gave me the opportunity to do what I needed to.

We spent all the next morning packing what we could get away in the time. The company didn't want to take too much of a loss, so wanted us to salvage whatever we could. Finally, in the late afternoon, all the gear was stowed. Neither Andy nor Laura looked happy about what we were about to do, but it wasn't our job. The company could sort out the rest. Andy did the final checks, then with a roar and a vibrating shudder lifted us off Aurora and to the waiting mother ship above.

I've already worked out how I'm going to do it. I used the hollow spaces inside my cameras and my recording decks. It was an easy matter to collect the seed heads, push them inside, then seal them away from view while the others were busy loading the gear. I think I made it look like I was checking the equipment ready for travel. Hopefully there'll be enough there to seed the planet, a new planet far away from Aurora. Hopefully the seeds will take. Somehow, I know they will.

As soon as I get home, I'll start. First, I'll resign, citing the stress of the mission as the reason. I should have enough funds to last for a few months, to get me from one place to the next. I won't need money after that. All I'll have to do is to reach down and grasp the nettle myself. And when I've joined the rest, all of us, we'll all be together, apart from those few we left behind on Aurora. But I know within that they're happy too.

Finally, at last, I'll be where I belong. We all will.

LOST ROAD

Carolyn Ives Gilman

It was a dry year. By June, the corn that should have been knee-high was stunted and papery in the fields; the pasture grass rustled, stiff as broom straw, in the constant wind. The topsoil had turned powdery, and you could see it blowing off the fields in clouds, making the sunsets red.

To Betty Lindstrom it seemed like her whole world was drying up and blowing away. She and Wayne had had to lease out the last 40 acres that spring to a man from the next county who was farming nearly all the land in their township. He'd taken out the fences and cut down the beech-tree windbreaks Betty's father had planted in the '30s, and now plowed fields came right up to the edge of the farmhouse yard on every side.

After supper one evening Betty took Chipper and walked out to the endless cornfield where her grandfather's original farmstead had been. She stood with the wind blowing strands of gray hair in her eyes, trying to trace the outline of the foundations. But they had been scraped away, planted over. Just like Wayne had been scraped away by the stroke, his wit and cheer dried up, powdered, and scoured in the wind.

Betty drove Wayne into the town of Lost Road every week, inching along in their 1978 Volare with Chipper in the back seat. She didn't like driving. Wayne had always done the driving before the stroke. Whenever she sat down behind the wheel with him to her right, it made her aware that the man she had married was gone and a stranger now shared her life. The county road blurred in front of her, a straight line meeting the horizon in a T. Every now and then another car would come along, and she would veer over onto the shoulder till they were safely by.

Their car was the only thing moving on the main street of Lost Road. The buildings were weathered, colorless, and spaced too far apart. A block off the main street the derelict shells of old grain elevators stood along what had once been a Soo Line feeder track. Around them the prairie had begun to reseed itself.

The gas station stood under an old Pure sign no one had ever bothered to take down. Its garage door always stood open on a cluttered, grease-stained interior. Betty had never been inside the garage; that was a man's world. She had been in the office a few times, and remembered faded packs of gum under a glass counter frosted by a half-century of quarters passing over it. No one was around, so they helped themselves from the single pump, filling the car and the two five-gallon cans in the trunk for the generator. Wayne shuffled into the office, his overalls hanging loose on his stick-thin body, his visored cap saying CENEX. Dan Erickson would soon show up. They'd talk field hands and field goals, forward passes and tillage passes. Wayne would say, in that old-man way he had now, how hard farming used to be and how glad he was to be out of it. And he would fool no one.

Betty drove on down to the corner store. Inside, the dusty windows cast a tired light on half-empty racks of drugstore sundries. Betty picked up some toilet paper, bread, bananas, and milk.

"How you getting through this dry weather?" Dot Meyers said when Betty brought her purchases to the counter.

"Oh, we're okay," Betty said.

"Didn't see you at church last Sunday. We get kind of worried about you, you know, out there all alone in that farmhouse."

"We're doing just fine," Betty said. It was none of Dot's business anyhow. Wayne had always teased Betty about being a deadpan Swede who never let any troubles show. She probably was, and too late to change now.

"We had a big meeting about our Lost Road Days festival," Dot said, taking a hand-printed sheet and sticking it in Betty's grocery bag. "We're looking for people to make things for the bake sale."

Dot was always trying to organize things.

"I'll think about it," Betty said.

As she carried her bag out to the car where Chipper waited, Betty looked over Dot's flyer. On the back it had a typed paragraph about the history of the town.

Lost Road was founded in the 1870s, when New York speculator Jeremiah Parker surveyed a road over his land holdings between the Yellow Medicine and Big Sioux rivers. Returning east, he published a map showing the road studded with towns. He induced several hundred settlers to buy land and move west. But when they arrived they found none of the promised road, traffic, or towns. The hardy pioneers among them who survived the first winter called the fiasco "Parker's Lost Road."

°°°   °°°   °°°

As she started the car, Betty had a strange, reckless idea. What if she just turned east instead of west and drove off out of town? What if she just left Wayne at the gas station and didn't come back? But deep down she knew she didn't really want to get away from Wayne. He was a part of her, like arthritis. No point complaining.

They left town about 4:20, driving west. The sun glared into the windshield from a cloudless sky. Red-winged blackbirds flew up from the unmowed ditches as the car passed. Down the roadside, telephone poles marched in an endless procession. Every few miles they passed the remains of old driveways that used to lead to farmhouses. Every year the land was getting emptier. They said farming was a business now, not a way of life.

"We've got to go back," Wayne said suddenly.

"Why?"

"We didn't get the mail."

"Yes, I did. It's in the bag. Your magazine came."

He didn't turn to get it. Their daughter Alice had sent him the subscription, but he never read it.

"Alice hasn't called for months," Wayne said.

"She called just last Saturday," Betty said.

"How come you didn't tell me?"

"I did. You talked to her. You just don't remember."

Alice was off in the city having a life filled with events. A trip to Hawaii, a job reassignment, her daughter competing in a state tennis tournament. Betty couldn't remember events like that ever happening to her. Her life was more like the paper than the writing—the background you had to have in order to see the ink.

Betty realized she had been driving automatically, not seeing where she was going. "Did I miss the turnoff?" she asked. But Wayne just shrugged. Betty slowed down. She kept expecting to see their house ahead. Though she couldn't place just where they were, she knew they were close.

In all the landscape the only thing moving was a combine far away on the horizon, big as a factory on wheels. Betty's thoughts strayed back to those settlers who'd followed Jeremiah Parker's map out here, imagining towns and communities and finding only prairie and wind. She didn't think they were heroic at all. They'd been duped into believing legends. She could almost feel their bitterness and longing around her, as if their dust was in the air.

At last Betty decided she'd gone too far, and when they came to a dirt township road she turned around.

After half an hour the road ahead still looked exactly the same. Betty was puzzled; she had driven far enough to be all the way back in Lost Road by now. She pulled to the shoulder and stopped.

"What's the problem?" Wayne asked.

"Do you know where we are?" Betty said.

"I thought we were going home."

Betty didn't want to say she couldn't find their house. She'd been driving this stretch all her life. "I guess it's a little farther on," she said, and started up again.

Everything looked familiar, just like deja vu. Before long she had convinced herself she was on Highway 35, driving parallel to the county road. No wonder she couldn't find their house. When she came to a township road she turned south.

"I've got to pee," Wayne said plaintively.

"Why didn't you go at the station?"

"I didn't have to then. We've been driving a long time."

When he had to go, he had to go. Betty pulled over. Wayne got out and shambled over to the grassy ditch. Betty got up to let the dog out, shoes crunching on gravel. Grasshoppers buzzed in the heat.

When she looked over to see if Wayne was done, he was staring fixedly out across the ditch. "What're those?" he said, pointing.

The low hill was dotted with uniform rows of gray cylinders lying on their sides. They were too big for oil drums, and they looked purposefully arranged, like manufactured artifacts. Betty squinted, searching for an explanation to quell her rising sense of the sinister.

Then she laughed. "Hay bales," she said. "They don't make them square any more, you know, Dad. They're all round like that these days."

But as she shooed Chipper back into the car, she felt fear at her own confusion. Why had they looked so strange for a second? They ought to be so familiar.

They drove on. The telephone poles by the road were casting long cross-shadows over the grassy banks, and birds perched on the wires like silent notes of music. "This is the same road," Betty said. "The same road we were on before."

She speeded up, desperate to get somewhere, anywhere. She scanned the fields for the telltale groves of oak and elm, each with a clutch of white buildings nestled underneath. That was the landscape she recognized. But it wasn't here now. No warm, buttery light leaking out past gingham curtains, no dogs in the yard wagging a welcome, no noisy kitchens inviting them in. It was all just legends now.

The sun was on the horizon by the time she came to a deserted crossroad and stopped.

Wayne, who had fallen asleep, roused and looked around. "Where are we?" he asked.

"I don't know," Betty said.

"You mean we're lost?"

He took it very calmly. Matter-of-fact, as if this happened all the time. They sat together on the bumper of the car, eating bread and bananas and watching the sunset. Chipper nosed around in the roadside grass. Eventually he came up to beg, and Betty poured him some milk and gave him bread.

The wind had died down, and the only sound was the crickets. "I know where we are," Wayne said suddenly. "This is Brown's Corner."

Of course. Across the road was the spot where Brown's store had stood, and behind it the pasture where they used to show movies on a sheet strung between two phone poles. She could remember the grass parked full of Model T's, and people from miles around sitting on plaid blankets. It had been a night just like this, with a wide-open sky above, when she and Wayne had shared an ice cream and she'd decided he was the one she wanted to spend her life with.

"I chased you for ten years, you know," she said.

"Yeah, I was Mr. Popularity back then. Remember how we used to go dancing? Glenn Miller. Now that was music." He began humming. "Hey, I bet you still can dance."

"Not me," Betty said, smiling. He hadn't acted like this for ages.

He fell silent, and Betty gradually remembered that Brown's Corner was back in Blue Earth County where they'd grown up, not out here.

Wayne slept on the back seat that night. Betty lay awake in the front, listening to time pass.

She was wakened by the roar of a semi. She sat up in a daze to catch sight of the back of the truck disappearing down the highway. It was broad daylight. She woke Wayne, and they breakfasted on bread and milk. The sight of the semi had put her in good spirits. She was embarrassed to think of her confusion the evening before. Now she knew they would soon find a town, and be home before noon.

And in fact they had only been driving for half an hour when grain elevators appeared on the horizon to the south. As they drew closer, Betty could make out the white steeple of a church and the roofs of houses. She kept expecting the road to veer toward the town, but instead it continued on west, straight as a ruler. Betty looked with fading hope for a crossroad leading south. Somehow she knew there would be none - and even if there were, it would not lead to the town.

She stopped the car and looked out across the fields. It was no more than a mile or two to walk, but Wayne could never make it, and she couldn't leave him alone in the hot car. She willed back the frustrated tears that filled her eyes. She wanted nothing more than to see a Safeway sign or a

xall drug store. She wanted to call out across the fields, "Here I am!" But
her voice was a thin, old-lady voice now. No one would hear her.

The road rolled by, familiar as ever. They crossed an Interstate, but there
was no exit or entrance, and a tall chain-link fence kept them from the
roadside. They stopped on the bridge and tried to signal cars to stop, but
no one understood.

They drove on.

"Maybe we could signal an airplane," Wayne said as they sat resting by
the roadside that afternoon.

Betty poured the last of the milk into Chipper's bowl, and he lapped it up
thirstily. "You mean lay our clothes out on the ground in an SOS?" she asked.

"You want to take off your clothes?" he said. She looked at him in surprise;
there was laughter in his eyes that hadn't been there for a year.

"Not me," she said.

"Then maybe we ought to just flash a mirror at them. You've got a mirror
in your purse, don't you? You've got everything in there."

There was no mirror in her purse, so they decided to break the rear-view
mirror off the car. They stood in the middle of the deserted road, trying to
catch the sun in an SOS pattern. But all the planes they saw were jets so high
they were just specks in the cloudless sky. "They'll never see," Betty said.

That evening they stopped at a place where a railroad embankment
crossed the road. Betty and Wayne strolled arm-in-arm up to the tracks,
Chipper at their heels. Field mice skittered across the cindery railroad bed,
and the smell of old creosote rose from the sun-baked ties. Betty stood
gazing at the tracks curving off into the west. She felt sure these must be the
old Northern Pacific tracks that went out to the coast.

"My brother Lars went away to work on this railroad when I was a kid," she
said to Wayne. She remembered standing just like this as a girl, when the
tracks had been the golden road to Seattle and the Orient. Lars had brought
her back a black enamel jewelry box with Chinese scenes painted on it in gold.
She'd wanted then to follow the tracks off the farm, but never did it. And now
the tracks didn't really gleam any more; in fact, they looked rusty and unused.

"I know what our problem is," she said suddenly. "We're on the lost road.
It's got to be. Those old settlers imagined it so hard it just came to be. No
wonder it doesn't connect to anything."

They drove aimlessly the next day. They put the extra gas into the tank,
but even that gradually dwindled away. Betty felt tired and thirsty. She was
sure there had to be some way off this imaginary road. When they turned on
the radio the Marshall station came through just fine. They were so close.

As twilight fell, they spotted a homey light coming from curtained
windows in a little grove far across the cornfields. It looked so warm and

inviting Betty felt a surge of desperation. She jerked the wheel to the side, and the car jolted over the shoulder and through the ditch. Its wheels spun a moment, then it lurched into the field.

"Whoa! What are you doing?" Wayne said.

"I'm leaving the road. I'm going to drive right over the field. Maybe that's the answer."

The car bounced over the corn rows, its bumper breaking off brittle stalks. Wayne looked aghast at the damage she was doing to the field. They were almost at the top of a rise when the back wheel sank into a deep trap of powdery soil. Betty put the car in reverse and tried to back out, but the wheel spun deeper. They were stuck.

Betty laid her head down against the wheel. The mad drive through the field had taken the last of her energy. She couldn't cope any longer.

At last she said dully, "Well, that was pretty dumb."

"I don't know what there is left to do that's very smart," Wayne said. It was so like something the old Wayne would have said that tears came to her eyes. To hide them, she got out. She let the dog out of the back seat, then walked on to the top of the rise, hugging herself tight. When she got there she stood looking out over the broad, rolling landscape growing dark under the fading sky. There were no lights, no houses as far as the eye could see. So that window she'd seen had been another mirage, another disappointment. Well, she was used to that.

Chipper, sensing her distress, pressed against her leg. She heard the car door slam behind her, and Wayne's footsteps. He stopped a few feet away.

"Don't worry, Betty," he said. "It'll all be okay."

Her throat was aching. He stepped closer and spoke softly, a little joking. "Hey, don't worry, I'm still here. As long as we stick together, we got no problems we can't solve."

It was the old Wayne's voice. The tears she'd been holding back for months suddenly came, rain on parched earth. She turned and hugged him, hugged him tighter than she ever had. "Don't ever leave me again," she said, her face pressed tight against his shoulder. "I've been lonelier than I thought I could be."

"It's okay," he said, then just held her and patted her on the back. It took a long time for all the tears she hadn't cried to come out. At last he gave her a hug and took her hand. "It's okay," he said again.

"Yeah," she said, wiping her face. "I guess it is now."

They walked back down the hill and sat in the dirt with their backs against the car and their arms around each other. Chipper lay down with his head on Betty's ankle.

"Hey, I know what to do," Wayne said.

He got up and switched on the car radio. A sweet old Glenn Miller song was playing. He sat back down beside her.

"I suppose we should have kept on following the road, wherever it went," Betty said.

"Oh, I don't know," said Wayne. "I don't think there was any right or wrong thing to do. You just do your best."

Betty was gazing off toward the west. The horizon looked rumpled, like an unmade bed. "Wayne, look," she said.

"What?"

"Clouds. There's rain coming."

"So there is."

They sat there as night fell, watching the rain clouds sweep slowly toward them over the land.

GRAINS OF WATER, BEADS OF DUST

Alexandra Merry Arruin

Anahita was hungry moments after the bus sped across the Canadian provincial border, en route from misty Vancouver to arid Alberta. She gazed back at darkening fields of cloud scratched from ether, sky gods harrowing blue to harvest rain. Then shuddered and turned to the boy beside her. He was covered in jam from nose-tip to elbows. His fingernails were perfectly trimmed.

"You going to eat that piece of pie?" she said.

ooo   ooo   ooo

Lately, Ana thought the world was dry as grains of dust - lives wound to clock radios, timed to pizza delivery, speeding playground zones, cruising suburbs in search of… well, what? Another tv dinner? Another new toy? The world was wafered with microwave miracles, wine to water, precious little communion.

Yet here she was, following the precepts of fast-forward culture, sacrificing all for a career move as a banker. She stared out the window and watched the sky rush past at high tide.

"No renewal," she whispered.

"Nope," the jammy boy said.

She didn't hear, sniffed hand soap. Under his perfect nails?

Still they sped eastward, into landscapes of snowy cacti and sage. The prairies, Ana thought, riddling herself. Endless, arid, exposed. How long before she fell into the sky?

ooo   ooo   ooo

By the time they reached the outskirts of Lethbridge everyone on the bus seemed emptied and distant. The whole landscape echoed—empty plains, distant cattle on the hillock, distant shore of the horizon.

ooo   ooo   ooo

Ana missed her Granny, missed the sensuous green tangle of Vancouver, the mist and smell of sea salt. The vacant prairie made her feel like dust.

"Is there water here?" she asked the boy.

He pointed. "Old Man River."

Beyond the dip of coulees a silver seam twinkled and splashed sunlight over rocks and ice.

It was laughing at her.

ooo   ooo   ooo

Lethbridge stretched, streets wide as an estuary floating sandstone buildings out to sea. Wind blew in waves. It made Ana sick to the stomach, rehydrated her worst feelings. She hoisted her pack and took the long way to the hotel. For days she left only to go to her new bank. The rest of the time she stayed zoned between hotel walls, getting the real world online through satellite tv. After a week she wanted nothing more than to go home, leave these strange avenues and wind-rinsed coulees to the locals. One night, in desperation, she phoned her grandmother.

"Sounds like you need to get out and create your own reason for being there," Granny said.

"Gran?"

"When you've lost meaning in some sort of vacuum, you need to create it anew."

"What does that mean?"

"You need to wander, girl."

So in the evenings, after work, Ana wandered winter streets, expecting bite and desolation. Her Granny would be wrong. There were no meanings here, only strange omens: broken trees, whispering children, tramps with rumored names—Iceking, Rain Man, Skeleton Tim.

One twilight, when snow swirled like topsoil, Ana stopped at The Onion Pub to watch a group of dryland farmers perform three sets of Celtic folk. After a long nursed pilsner she stepped into the alley and thought about getting food. Something jigged at her visual periphery, something hunched and moonlit. She looked after it, but there was only dark.

She was about to return to the hotel and dial room service. But she stopped, looked again. There, flickering between fence posts—a small boy riding a german shepherd. She sneaked after, stopped at a fork in the alley to peak around the fence. The boy dismounted at a back gate and stood quietly, long dark hair seaweed in the wind.

ooo   ooo   ooo

He's lost, Ana thought. But no, the kid was up to something. He put a hand on the dog's head, then whistled, low and soft. The gate creaked and a girl emerged in a hooded coat, carrying a hockey stick like a staff. They smiled at each other, turned to climb the steep alleyway to the north, dog padding between them.

Ana smiled. Sneaking out, the ancient urban ritual.

When the kids reached the summit of the alley, the boy reached out a hand to stay the girl. They stooped behind a mailbox, as a police car cruised by slowly at the top of the world, searchlight washing streets. When the cruiser rolled on, the kids tip-toed from view.

Ana scrambled up to the sidewalk, just in time to see the kids dip into a thick wood across the street. She followed, then stopped at the wood's edge. Where was she going? She glanced about, found a stone arch carved with the name Galt Gardens.

A green strip, she thought. The trees couldn't be thick enough to get lost in, not in the suburbs. Not on the prairies.

She plunged. As soon as the path turned, all street-noise disappeared. Wind rushed the leaves; at the treetops light bent and refracted, shimmering down from the surface in slants, snow holding the hushed greens and blues. Ana floated through a coral reef of frozen berries, over the sunken hull of a dead birch. The kids were gone, drowned.

No, there they were, up ahead, kneeling at the bole of a giant poplar. The boy was elbow-deep in the tree. Boughs loomed like tentacles; mist drifted from barky tangle to the treetops.

Ana crouched to watch. She felt loneliness again, but it was alright, more like an awareness of each cell thrumming her body. Her stomach grumbled.

At the tree, the girl laughed, leaned on her staff. The boy pulled a silver tin whistle from the bole and blew a note. He was answered with another note, a high clear singing voice. Ana squinted and leaned closer. Nobody's lips had moved.

The boy reached back into the tree, this time pulled a hand, an arm, another boy in a long stocking hat. The hatted boy tumbled out of the tree and stood sleepily, tassels dangling to the ground. The girl laughed again. The dog barked.

The hatted boy snatched the tin whistle and looked about to say something.

"Shhhhh." The girl put a finger to her lips. All three crunched off through the snow, down a sharply dipping path.

Ana waited a few minutes, then rose to follow their footprints. She heard music, wisps at first, then louder—some kind of ambient dub, threads of tin whistle, rattle of tambourine. She crept down the slope and paused beneath a stunted birch.

The woods opened to a small clearing, an island bristling with kids, most in motion, some hanging from trees. A bonfire cracked at the heart, roasted nuts popping and exploding. Beyond the fire, a row of bikes rested against the trees, and a tribe of shaggy-haired feral kids glared out from between spokes. They had stuck a stolen playground zone sign between the frozen roots of a tacamahac.

I hope they're not drinking, Ana thought.

Under a giant black cottonwood, a gang of brightly mittened girls were building a snowman, sticking poplar wands for arms. Ana watched the rest of the crowd jump and dart around the fire, wondered what they were doing. Oh, I see, she thought, it's some kind of dance, takes a bit to understand. Kind of weaves between the beats.

Snowballs whizzed the island. A shriek, and the dance shifted: they were throwing a hot tin foiled potato, steam sizzling its vapor-trail. Then toys— flying Yo-Yos, checker boards, glass-eyed dolls blinking as they somersaulted the air. Ana noticed an open pirate's chest or tickle trunk by the fire, still half-full of puppets and paints. A few kids held sticks to the fire and raised torches to the frosty sky.

I hope they don't burn the place down, Ana thought.

Then a sudden hush. Twigs and leaves drifted down, flotsam, sinking bits of unwound time. At the clearing's end, a leafy gallery rustled and swept open. A pizza delivery boy stepped through the curtains, boxes held high leaking heat.

The feral kids leaped, hooting and spinning bicycle wheels. The music swelled. The dance fragmented. The dog began to bark. The fire roared high, singeing leaves.

Oh dear, Ana thought. She got up and stepped into the clearing. "Hey, you kids be careful—"

Instantly the fire doused. Torches sizzled in the snow. The woods dimmed; the island tipped and sank to the bottom.

Ana stumbled, blind, eyeballs dried with smoke and cold air. "Hey, just a minute... ." She looked down, closed her eyelids, forced her pupils to adjust. Heard a clatter of bicycles, a crunch of footfalls. A tidal wind swished through the woods, leaves bobbing in currents, bits of laughter washing up and trailing under the oldest lunar spell.

Ana reached out and steadied herself against something cold. She opened her eyes, still prickly and dry, saw her hand on the snowman. Somehow she had crossed the length of the clearing. The entire pageant was vanished, leaving only toys and cinders and one uneaten pepperoni pizza, still steaming on the snow.

Her stomach grumbled.

She reached for a slice, bit until the juice trickled her chin, then kneeled in front of the snowman and giggled to tears. All around her, the scattered toys remained still and silent, except for one glass-eyed dolly overhead, caught by its hair at the tip of a long branch, eyes blinking, still swinging.

SNOW SEMAPHORES
Gillian Harding-Russell

I: grey matter

He shovels snow into the night
over his left shoulder,
filling the dark

with stars

hoarfrost trees bending
under a weight of whiteness

before him this sheet of smoothness
he could write his name across
amid shadows, undulations
invisible white lines
he's moving between

shades of grey, semaphoring himself—
silhouette of sharp elbow
shadow, bended
knee

angles of himself against this landscape
generating mind circuits, nuances
inside himself and
the blurry night

small letter of movement, half-expressed,
with blunt-shooting eyes, orbs
travelling the straight fence

rim of sky overflowing
into endless night, periodic
star smudges, abbreviations of understanding
and light's intensity

He tries to find Orion's sweep of arm
in the presence of a fatuous moon,
his own dark pupils bending
into nocturnal slits, making
only partial sense of it.

II: white matter

He heaves snow over
his right shoulder,
lifts it

 into open sky.

 No space between himself
and the sun, a faceless coin
masked as a moon
under cloud

 But the brown fence is a familiar line
to throw himself against, away
from, puff of snow
into the far

 distance in front of him,
standing small
among drifts ;

 his own square house, deck
shipwrecked under white waves,
car parked   driftwood

 swirled up a nebulous driveway,
down an invisible road
heaped high with snow

 Still this white matter, he can
just fill his shovel with

 sift over
his shoulder,

 drop
at his feet.

GREENER GRASS

Anne Louise Waltz

One morning, Minnesota was rudely awakened by a friendly neighbor to the north.

"Good morning, Minnesota! Rise and Shine!"

"Mmrgrumple rumph," went Minnesota.

"Up and at it! The sunflowers are looking east!"

Minnesota opened one eye. "Oh, it's you, Manitoba. Go back to bed."

But Manitoba would not go back to bed. "Up, up! Shall I sing Frère Jacques?"

"You start singing Frère Jacques, I'll have to hurt you."

"Oh, don't worry. I don't even know it; it's just a law, eh? But why you act such a grump? You sleep bad?"

Minnesota thought, how can one sleep while being kicked in the head by a land mass the size of California?

"I've every right to be grumpy," said Minnesota. "I got troubles with my capital you wouldn't believe."

"Why you say that? St. Paul's a beautiful capital."

"You only see it from a distance," said Minnesota. "The streets are full of potholes and the city council is full of bums. Suburban sprawl is out of control, our downtown is practically boarded up and our biggest export is something called 'Pig's Eye.'"

"Oh," said Manitoba, looking perplexed. "I always thought you had it made. I mean, I have to live with Winnipeg."

"Winnipeg's a nice, clean city. You don't even have suburban sprawl. You've got all that fresh air, spacious land and a nice waterfront on two rivers. And best of all, Winnipeg doesn't have to compete with the Mall Of America."

"But I like the Mall Of America."

"Sprawl Of America."

"I wish I could visit it."

"Temple Of Mammon!"

"I wish I could go to Camp Snoopy."

"Camp Sniper!"

"I'd like to try the Mystery Mine Ride," said Manitoba wistfully, "but I'm too big."

"I'd give anything to trade with you," said Minnesota. "If I could have Winnipeg instead of St. Paul, I'd be the happiest land mass in the world."

Manitoba paused. "Really? Our two capitals are roughly the same size. What if we traded?"

"You serious?" Minnesota almost laughed.

"Serious. We can dig the cities out of the ground, file off a few edges so they fit better and switch 'em. I'll take St. Paul off your hands if you promise to take Winnipeg."

"It's a deal!" cried Minnesota.

"You sure?"

"I'm sure."

"Okay, then… no backs."

ooo   ooo   ooo

Julie Roettger locked up her mountain bike and hurried into Middlebrook Hall, which towered over the Mississippi on the West Bank Minneapolis campus. Her pleated skirt was smudged with bicycle grease, her white blouse was soaked with sweat and her chestnut hair was wind-blown. Breathless, she ran up to the suite she shared with her international roommates, Yamni, Ying-Fen and Ya-Ling.

"St. Paul is gone!" cried Julie.

That morning, Julie had left for the St. Paul "farm campus" to see The Klezmatics' noon-time show. But instead, she ran into something tall, dark and shiny called Scotiabank.

The frightened looking people clinging to Scotiabank had never heard of the farm campus. Behind them lay streets and intersections that Julie didn't recognize.

"Did you hear me?" she said to her roommates. "St. Paul is gone!"

Ying-Fen, an educational psychology major, was warming her tea in an electric pot. She was seated at her reading desk, huddled inside her quilted jacket, which had pink poodles and said in appliqué English, "Dancing Girl Loves Rock 'n Roll."

"St. Paul is gone!" repeated Julie. "Vanished! There's another city in its place!"

Ying-Fen glanced up from Statistical Analysis of Dynamic Systems and said, "Oh… uh-huh," with the same polite expression she would've used had Julie informed her they were serving chimichangas instead of cheeseburgers in the cafeteria.

"You don't understand. The city of St. Paul has vanished! I don't know what that is over there, but it's not St. Paul!"

Ya-Ling looked out the window at the new skyline and said, "I don' know. I don' know how they do that."

Yamni's Korean friend, also in the room, had just recently learned the word "wow." She said "wow" like there was a slide whistle stuck in her throat.

"WaaaAHowww! Wow! Wwwaaaowww!"

Yamni said, "Ah, Julie, I have a paper due… could you please read it first?"

Oh no. The last time Julie had agreed to "proofread" one of Yamni's papers, she ended up completely re-writing it. Yamni was apparently one of the interior design department's brightest stars, but her written English was, well… better than Julie's Korean.

Four evenings had been quite enough, slogging through sentences like, "When did the Memphis School, now, that I think was very." Translating the Rosetta Stone couldn't have been harder than turning Yamni English into Standard English.

"Ah, could you read it?" asked Yamni.

How do I get out of this?

"I don't know," said Julie. "With St. Paul gone, I'm sure I'll have to re-schedule my classes, and, uh, I'll have a lot of make-up work."

Good grief, she thought. Was she using the disappearance of St. Paul for a lame excuse? What was going on? The whole metro area must be in turmoil right now!

She grabbed her clock radio and found WCCO, where she always turned for tornado warnings, but there was only static. KQRS was playing *Let It Ride*. In panic, she swept the bands for news, but all she found was:

KDWB - Girl, You Got It by Hopelessly Immature

KQRS - Behind Blue Eyes by The Who

93X - My Life Sucks by some guy with a flat voice

KQRS - The Long Run by The Eagles…

"I gotta get outta here," she said.

∘∘∘   ∘∘∘   ∘∘∘

A few days later, Minnesota was again awakened by being kicked in the head by a friendly neighbor to the North.

"How's Winnipeg doing?" asked Manitoba.

"Fine, I guess. It took Minneapolis two days to notice."

"What? You're kidding!"

"Well," said Minnesota, "nobody in Minneapolis ever has any reason to go to St. Paul. I guess some commuters from Roseville needed to get to

Eagan, but they couldn't because Winnipeg was in the way and now the highways don't match up. When people called the Minnesota Department of Transportation to report that some big stone ruin called Cathédrale De Saint-Boniface was standing in the 94-35E interchange, whoever took the call sent it to another department, and they sent it to another department, and finally, when there were no more untried departments, well, MNDOT just wasn't prepared to handle a situation like that."

"Unmatched roads are a problem here too," said Manitoba. "People in St. Paul can't get out. They can't go to the mall. They've got their little neighborhoods and parochial schools, a downtown nobody wants and an area called 'Frogtown' that nobody wants either, although I don't think Frogtown's so bad; kind of looks like my Logan and Main area, only bigger and with Hmong people. Hey, the Hmong make pretty wall hangings. You ever look at their wall hangings?"

"Forget that! What'll I do about these unmatched highways?"

"Easy," said Manitoba; "let's trade suburbs."

"But you haven't got any suburbs. That's not a fair trade."

"What do you call St. Boniface?"

"That's part of Winnipeg," said Minnesota.

"It's a suburb."

"Winnipeg!"

"Suburb! Listen, St. Paul's not complete without its outlying communities. The people feel trapped and restless. I want Roseville, Eagan, Lauderdale, Maplewood and White Bear Lake."

"Absolutely not!" Minnesota got a sinking feeling in the mine pits of its stomach. What did NAFTA say about this kind of thing?

"What good are they to you?" asked Manitoba. "Without St. Paul, your suburbanites can't get anywhere. You'll just have more problems if you keep 'em."

Minnesota sighed. Manitoba was right. "Fine. Take my suburbs."

"And thanks for the carousel and science museum."

"Yeah, whatever."

ooo   ooo   ooo

Treben TwoBears locked up his bachelor suite above the Main Street MacDonald's and headed for his music lesson, bass slung over his shoulder in a canvas sack. This wasn't the nicest part of Main, by the Logan train bridge, but at this hour on a Sunday morning the drunks were mostly off the street or still sleeping.

A lot of people had opposed the new MacDonald's, saying it spread the infection of homogenized American culture that was consuming Canada.

But these were mostly Winnipeggers who would never live near the corner of Logan and Main. The locals weren't so bothered; some were glad to finally have a restaurant that employed their kids, some thought the Golden Arches were more attractive than the fire hazard that used to stand in that spot, and some kind of liked the food.

In worn-out runners, Treben walked four blocks to Portage then three blocks to Main Street Music. Looking down Portage to what used to be Trans-Canada One, Treben smiled at the Minneapolis skyline. The premier of Manitoba was still waiting to hear from Toronttawa whether it was officially safe for Winnipeggers to cross into the Mini-Apple.

But Treben couldn't wait; he had heard about the neat music stores over there, along with that Prince studio, the First Avenue club, and all kinds of places he would want to play.

Main Street Music—a funny name for a store on Portage—did mostly school business and Suzuki programs. They had every kind of book, from Sissy And The Skidmarks for guitar tab to vocal scores for Handel's Messiah.

Treben bowed to his new teacher and followed meekly to the tiny practice room in back.

The teacher was a rock veteran in his sixties, who had recently left Toronto for a gentler life with his son and grandkids. His glasses were perched on his nose, which was as big as Treben's, and he wore a hand knit yarmulke, stitched with little gold stars and pine trees. Treben thought it was a cute hat, but the guy had never worn a yarmulke back when his band was still touring.

"Good day," was all Treben could stammer as he tuned up his clunky Fender, which he had bought just before graduating from high school. His eye was on a graphite-composite bass-to-MIDI controller, and as soon as he could save enough from his job at the video rental, he would get it. Then look out, Minneapolis!

He knew the teacher had once played a graphite bass, and had screwed around with MIDI. But now the man liked the warm sound of wood against plain electro-mag pickups, and didn't care for all that new techno-cyber stuff.

As the teacher plugged into a Mesa Boogie amp, Treben fidgeted, clasping and unclasping his hands. He was nervous and grateful; three lessons had passed, and he still could hardly talk to the guy. After all, why was this famous legend giving lessons in this tiny room, in this mis-named Mom & Pop store in Winnipeg?

"Treben," said the teacher, smiling at his student's perplexity. "You need to relax and understand something. I'm doing exactly what I want to be doing."

"B-but you could be anywhere!"

"I have children here. I have grandchildren. I hustled on the road for forty years. Why would I want to continue all that?"

Treben nodded and tried to adopt the calm composure of his teacher, who suddenly looked like a natural extension of the store, of Winnipeg, of Canada… except they were no longer in Canada.

"Come to Minneapolis with me today!" said Treben in a burst of eagerness. "We'll check out gear at B-Sharp! Or go to Groth or the Homestead Pickin' Parlor! Heck, I wanna see Schmitt!"

The teacher took a slug of water from a thermos, removed his glasses and rubbed his brow. "You go ahead. You're much more resilient than I am, and I really can't deal with these sudden changes in geography. I'm gonna take my little granddaughter to the zoo today."

"The Minnesota Zoo? I hear it's great."

"No, the Garry Zoo. Now, let's hear your arpeggios. Give me a circle of fifths, starting from G, first position…

000   000   000

Minnesota grieved over 3M, the Pig's Eye Brewery and HB Fuller. There had also been an awful lot of White Castle restaurants lost in this exchange, and for what? Minnesota woke Manitoba with a not so friendly shove.

"Hey, Flatty! I've got a bone to pick with you. Winnipeg's got some maintenance problems you didn't tell me about."

Manitoba wiped the sunflower seeds from its eyes. "What, did I say it was perfect?"

"You sold me a big, flat Duluth! I gave you St. Paul's Cathedral, and what do I get?"

"Le Cathédrale De Saint-Boniface is a historic treasure," said Manitoba.

"It's a big pile of rocks blocking my interchange. It burned down in 1968, and you left it in ruins! Why didn't you ever rebuild it?"

"With what? All the money we got from the fur trade?"

"Except for a new MacDonald's, your Logan and Main area looks like a war-zone. And Winnipeg's other neighborhoods aren't much better. Block after dumpy block of those squalid, two-room houses… haven't your people ever heard of lawn mowers?"

"Winnipeggers aren't into the Little Astroturf On The Prairie look," said Manitoba.

"Well, you could at least give your houses a new coat of paint, say, every thirty years!"

"Winnipeggers are more concerned with important things like food and heat, eh?"

"And you have the nerve to put up gated streets in the rich neighborhoods. That's very un-egalitarian, very un-Minnesota."

"Oh?" Manitoba crossed its tributaries and drummed the tips of its spruce trees. "What about all those Southeast-Asian immigrants you kept trapped in that crummy Frogtown? With the downtown standing all empty? I think it's shameful."

"Sure," sneered Minnesota. "Blame me. I suppose you'd do something about that."

"I did. I gave them the downtown to redecorate."

"What??" Minnesota hadn't considered that Manitoba might take St. Paul and change it.

"They did a good job," said Manitoba, "putting up beautiful wall hangings all over those dreary skywalks."

"They're called 'skyways.' "

"Whatever. Now the skywalks look kinda nice."

"Fine. But what am I gonna do with this pile of rock in the middle of the 94-35E Interchange?"

"You mean Le Cathédrale?" said Manitoba. "Do what you like. I turned St. Paul's into a youth art colony."

"No!" Minnesota almost choked and swallowed Milacs. "That's the city's crowning glory; you can't do that! That's a, a sacrilege!"

"It was so empty during the week. Now it's full of kids. They love it."

"I bet," snarled Minnesota. "How would you like it if I let graffiti artists spray paint murals all over your bland, gray government buildings? How about that?"

"I don't think Winnipeg has any good graffiti artists, but I'd be happy to lend you one of St. Paul's. There's a kid from St. Paul Central named Twana Sheldon who's exceptionally talented. You should see the history museum now. She's got Shaq O'Neil's likeness down cold."

Minnesota tried to bury its face in Le Seur Valley, but the valley was choked with Winnipeggers posing for photos by the Jolly Green Giant. "You can't do this," Minnesota whimpered. "You can't just rearrange my favorite city."

"Hey, it's my city now," said Manitoba.

∘∘∘   ∘∘∘   ∘∘∘

Pao Tou loosened his tie under the warm Manitoba sun, then took Little Foung's hand as they walked beyond the suburban limits of Lauderdale into a ripe, golden Manitoba field. Clumps of wild grass and hay grew right up to the highway; this province didn't waste land on wide shoulders and turf-lawn embankments. To the south, Pao could see endless stretches of sunflowers, past bloom, drooping heavy and brown.

Little Foung dragged his sneakers in the dirt, sighing. "Why are we walking here? I wanna go to the mall! Mom said to take me wherever I want!"

"Mom said to watch you." Pao, a civil-engineering major at the University of Minnesota, had little to do since the Great Exchange, for his classes were on the Minneapolis campus, and Pao had been at home when the switch happened.

He lived in an apartment near the Capitol building, with his mother and uncle and their children. Now he could help out the new Downtown Development Cooperative and babysit Little Foung.

Little Foung groaned. "The mall!"

This land was so flat, Pao couldn't find the horizon, as his eyes adjusted for distance. The fields were broad between hedges and the air was almost too clean…

ooo   ooo   ooo

Little Pao sweated under a morning Laotian sun beside the corrugated sheets of tin surrounding the camp's latrine, while his father held his shirt sleeve in two fists, pulling until the cloth ripped. Then his father rubbed mud on Pao's face and into his hair, trembling with frantic haste. Little Pao saw his father cast quick glances behind him.

Finally, Little Pao asked, "Where are my shoes?"

"You don't have shoes," snapped his father.

Little Pao couldn't understand all this. Of course he had shoes. But he stood without protest as his father made yet another rip in his shirt, and smeared mud over Pao's legs and bare feet. It was hot, but his father moved in quick jerks as if chilled.

"You don't have shoes! And you never went to school, and you cannot read! Understand? And you are not the son of Tou Deng! Your father's name is, is… your father's name is Cho… and you don't know your clan name! Can you remember that? Can you remember that!"

Now Little Pao was shaking, for his father had never spoken so harshly, nor had he ever hurt Little Pao like this, gripping his arm so tightly.

"Listen to me! Stay with your sisters, and don't speak! Don't say a word anywhere, and don't don't look at the men with guns!"

Tears streamed down Pao's muddy face as he ran to the wet-fields to work in the wet-rice, for the sharp stones hurt his tender, bare feet, and he didn't know what he'd done to anger his father to the point of disownership.

Pao never saw his father again.

ooo   ooo   ooo

With a gentle tug, Pao walked Little Foung off the highway and into the field where the spongy ground gave way under their shoes. Yellow autumn blossoms mixed with purple. White butterflies darted in and out of their path. Pao removed his suit jacket.

"I wanna go to the Mall Of America!" cried Little Foung. "I hate this place! There's nothing to do in Manitoba!"

Pao said nothing and walked farther into the field.

"Take me somewhere! I'm gonna tell Dad you're mean to me!"

Pao smiled. "And what will Uncle do then?"

"He'll kick your—" Foung stopped mid sentence as Pao gave his little half brother a stern look.

"Don't tell lies about your Dad. He's a good father."

Little Foung was subdued for about a minute, and then, "I wanna see the new Jackie Chan movie. Jackie Chan kicks—" Little Foung stopped himself again, sighed, and kicked a clump of dirt.

"Hate this, hate this, hate this… this SUCKS!"

°°°   °°°   °°°

Young Pao's mother had explained that the Church of Luther in Minnesota had to take them in because those who worshipped Luther must obey his command to help the refugee. But why did the Luther woman insist he play with her two children, who were almost women?

It was the day of the Hollow Wing, and the Luther woman drove a nervous Young Pao to her house to teach him how to celebrate the Hollow Wing. When he got there, her two daughters had horrible, bleeding gashes across their faces and arms. They ran to him, bloody arms outstretched, shouting, "It's Hollow Wing! Happy Hollow Wing!"

They made Pao wear a long, black robe and plastic skull mask. Young Pao was too frightened and confused to disobey these new playmates, so he followed them through streets crowded with monsters. Pao's mask made his face sweat and sting, but he didn't dare take it off. And he couldn't refuse the sugar treats, which hurt his teeth and stomach.

Young Pao was sent to the school of St. Paul Central, where many children of Hmong immigrants went. Because he'd done well at the special puzzle and symbol games the social worker had given him, St. Paul Central called him "gifted," and placed him in a high-honor class for reading the stories of great elders such as Vonnegut and Tolstoy. Young Pao thought this was strange, for he could barely speak English, let alone read it.

The first day, his teacher, who wore long hair and sandals like a peasant, tossed a chair across the classroom, startling Pao. What had they done to anger this teacher?

The teacher wrote on the board, "Parts of Speech: I threw the chair. I was throwing the chair. I may throw the chair again." Boys and girls started to giggle and said, "He's crazy." Young Pao stared. They would dare to laugh at the teacher?

In Family Development class, Young Pao had to sit alongside women while Mrs. Johnson talked about uncomfortable married subjects and showed drawings of body parts that Young Pao didn't think he needed to see until he was older.

The Cambodian girl beside him had been ridiculed by her classmates for not knowing how children were made, while the woman beside her was already married and had a child on the way.

And once a student rose his hand and hollered, "Teacher! The girls in the back row are sewing!" Young Pao had often seen them discreetly doing needlework behind their textbooks. Would they now be dismissed from school? But Mrs. Johnson said, "Oh, let me see!" and she hurried to the back and studied all the pieces, saying, "Sa-ahdt, sa-ahdt," which was the only mountain word she knew.

ooo   ooo   ooo

"I wanna go home!" whined Little Foung, dragging through the hay stubble by Pao's sleeve. But Pao, straining his eyes at the receding horizon, barely heard him. Land! So much fertile land! Suddenly, Pao's shoes and socks were off. Arms outstretched, he was running in his bare feet, which had not felt real earth in years.

"I'm going to buy this land for a farm!" he sang to no one but the round hay bundles.

But the cut stalks jabbed his tender, bare feet. After a minute of running, he stopped in pain and hobbled, wincing, back to his shoes and to Little Foung.

ooo   ooo   ooo

"Manitoba! Yeah, you!"

"How's it goin', eh?"

"Don't how's-it-goin' me, you metric-embracing, frozen, pinko wasteland. You've been making more changes to St. Paul!"

"But Grand Avenue always should've been a pedestrian mall. I'm surprised you didn't think of it yourself. Gerten's Greenhouse is trucking in the larches and Russian olive trees, Bachman's will provide the woodchips—"

"You stop this right now!" said Minnesota. "I liked St. Paul the way it was, and you're turning it into a little Toronto. Next thing, you'll make Snelling Avenue into a copy of Yonge Street."

"Actually, I thought Rice would be a better choice."

Minnesota screamed.

"It's my city now," said Manitoba.

"I want it back!"

"But I said 'no backs.' Keep Winnipeg and be happy."

Desperate and helpless, Minnesota went crying to America. But America was fussing with foreign affairs in East Europe, West Africa and South Florida.

"Can't you see I'm busy?" said America.

Minnesota pleaded, but America said, "Manitoba can only bother you if you let it."

This advice was never very helpful, so Minnesota turned back to Manitoba and resorted to threats. "I'm gonna scoop up Winnipeg and St. Boniface, and throw the whole mess into Iowa!"

Manitoba's fall colors flared. "You do that, and I'm gonna toss St. Paul into Hudson Bay!"

"You wouldn't dare!" screamed Minnesota, reaching over the border to snatch back St. Paul.

"Get off my side! Canada!"

Canada was not amused.

"Stop it, both of you!" shouted Canada. "I've had enough of your fighting. Province of Manitoba, you will rip that city out of the ground and give it back to Minnesota right this instant."

"But—"

"You're grounded! No casino permits for a month."

As Manitoba reluctantly switched back the capitals, Minnesota stuck its tongue out the Northwest Angle. But Canada saw, and said, "Minnesota, you can't play here anymore. Keep your tourists and your MacDonald's on your own side." Turning to America, Canada scolded, "Can't you watch your states? No wonder they're out of control. Nations like you make me wish we had licensing." And with a "Hrumph!", Canada resumed de-lousing Yonge Street.

ooo   ooo   ooo

Julie's bus was only a block away, but she had to swim through hordes of students racing toward the civil-engineering building.

"Oof! Oh, sorry. Excuse me!"

They swarmed like salmon. One Southeast-Asian student with muddy shoes knocked right into her and spilled his books and jacket.

"What's going on?" said Julie as the boy apologized, helping her to her feet as he gathered the books.

"We're back! St. Paul is back!" He joyously disappeared into the crowd.

What? thought Julie. Not already! She was just on her way to see the new Winnipeg bands at First Ave; but if St. Paul was back, the Winnipeg bands would now be hundreds of miles away.

She slumped against a kiosk, where signs for a student contest read: "Cost Efficiency In Rebuilding Fallen Cathedrals." No point in hurrying to the bus now... unless... maybe First Ave could get The Klezmatics.

Epilogue

That night, while the land masses slept, Minnesota was awakened by a neighbor to the north.

"Pssst, Minnesota."

"Ontario?"

"Shhh!"

"What do you want?" whispered Minnesota.

Ontario shifted its weight back and forth (which had a disturbing effect on the Laurentian Shield, but I'll leave explanations to the geologists). "I, uh, hear you're having problems with that little city of Stillwater. You know— snarled traffic, too many antique shops on Main Street, disputes over the new river bridge."

"Yeah? What about it?"

"Well... I got this little burg called Parry Sound. Nice, little, river town. Very scenic. 'Bout the same size as Stillwater—"

"Oh, no. No."

"Aw, c'mon," said Ontario. "It's in pristine condition. Hardly any antique stores at all. I'm just looking for a change. No one would even notice..."

Sugar Night

Nancy Etchemendy

We gaze into the sky,
A cup so deep and ebon
Balance abandons us
And we must lie longitudinally
Supported by Earth at every point
Or risk freefall
Side-by-side in the desert sand
My young son and I.
Child of the city,
Stars puzzle him.
—What is it? That white place?—
And he points toward the zenith.
I could say it is the scar
Where god's heart broke open
When he unfolded time and saw
The unthinkable mistakes he'd made;
See how it's healed now
Into a band of gentle light,
Evidence that a man,
And you in his image,
Can forgive himself for anything.
Instead I dig in gritty pockets,
Find a nickel, hold it up.
—See? One way a circle, One way a line.
There hangs our galaxy, on edge.—
He laughs, a warm gold in the dark.
—No, that sky looks like sugar.
Can we go for ice cream?—

BLACK DOG

Candas Jane Dorsey

I

Drawn to the last indistinct cravings of day like a beast to the light. What you can expect from sunset: sadness (nostalgia), flame, death of the sun, birth of night.

Night, the tranquil time of blessedness, time when the hard blue bowl is lifted, beneath which by day we labour and scurry and complain of details. Night. Freedom. Infinity. Peace.

All this a way to introduce my favourite darkness. I have learned that savagery is the province of day; daylight a cocoon from which by dark I burst, wings unfurling into the cool moonlight, silver and silk. Night is the gossamer time of reflection; night is the freedom to fly unchecked. Spread your wings, sister/brother, come speak the once-heard language of aspiration with me, search for stars and soaring flights of life.

Out on the darkling plain I stand where the smooth silver expanse of the snowy field begins. No one larger than the black dog has been there this winter; the dog capers dark across the blankness like a cutout into a deeper night.

If I am ready to live alone now, I am not ready for complete solitude. Up there in the stars I read the history of my far-flung travelling friends; they are so far away, and the dog and I stand on this snow-field, freed, watching their gleaming traces in the winter sky.

Are they trapped in their destiny, or set free also, freed from their past or the need to see me, or the love that bound them to me? Who gains, who loses? The eternal and newly-minted question.

The dog's great feet propel it in long leaps across the shining clearing. When I follow, my feet sink into the snow and I sink into a moonlight struggle with my breath. I am older than I want to be and my body tells me at times like these: remember when you were at the beginning, exploding across every new challenge like this young dog?

The dog has crossed to the willows beyond the broken down fence, and is nosing at a deeper shadow beneath the bushes, then leaping back to me with a happy bark: look what I've found!

Is it a child? No, a teenager, huddled back in a downfilled parka, face inside the hood, a smudge broken by the glint of moonlight on eyes and white teeth. A dark face. Hands bare, pulled from pockets to push away the dog's friendly face. Afraid? Yes.

"Back off, dog!" Reluctantly, wagging half its body, the dog retreats a few yards.

"The dog won't hurt you." I reach out my hand. "Neither will I. Would you like to come out of the bushes?"

Silently the youngster takes my hand to pull upright; then lets go and manages without moving to retreat to the furthest corner of the field, the night, the sky. "Are you cold?"

The muffled head nods. The fur on the coat (fur?) now shades the face completely.

"I have tea at my house. Are you hungry?"

Another nod. Whence sprang this silent apparition? Child of the willows. I laugh, the kid is startled.

"Don't tremble like that," I say, irritated, "it makes me nervous. Where did you come from?"

Hand out of pocket to point west, wave across the whole quadrant of sky and scrub prairie. Fine.

"Can you talk?" Only another nod. "Why don't you, then?" The shoulders rise in a bulky, expressive shrug. Ridiculous conversation. I whistle for the dog, who has found a chunk of wood under a bush, is standing flirtatiously attentive with the stick in its mouth, ears alert.

"Might as well get used to the dog. It lives here with me. It's my friend now, it keeps me company."

Small guttural voice. "What's its name?"

"Just the black dog. When it's the only dog around, I don't see the need for a name." Silence. The sound of snow and frozen grasses crunching under well-wrapped feet. Mine are boots. The kid has—leather? Moccasins? Must have come from a far distant west, somewhere beyond even my line of night vision.

"You got a name?"

Good question. By the argument I've applied to the dog, I have no name but the fact of my being. The footsteps I make in the snow were until half an hour ago the only human footsteps; we are following my solitary trail through the birch and poplar and pine, past the stream which beneath ice still offers a muffled susurrus. The single footprints don't define me any more.

"Not any more. Call me what you want."

"Okay." But that's all.

"And you? Willow child?"

"Call me what you want." With a brief hand gesture, the youngster turns to the path.

The circle completed with such abrupt, natural grace. A shadow, I walk through, reflexively looking up to see a skiff of cloud, rainbow-edged and insubstantial, blow across the moon. Orion is brightly walking above the fields, warming my face with his archaic splendour. The youngster is oblivious to the sky. If whatever people lived in the west have gone to the stars as my people have gone, this young one has no tendency to watch their tracks, or maybe avoids now the dangerous heavens.

At the cabin where the dog and I live, we humans stamp snow from our feet and shuck off outer skins. The youngster stands out of the parka as a wiry, slender girl, brownskinned, black hair roughly hacked short and rumpled around a closed, smooth face. Prove it to me, her glance says as from her stance as near the double door as possible she studies my home.

"Do you know where you are going?"

"No."

"Do you want to stay here?"

Shrug. The beginning of this relationship is as tough as chewing twigs. Never mind. The dog isn't verbal either. It slouches with a clicking of claws to its rag mat in front of the heater, drops the piece of wood it has carried all the way home, falls into a heap with a great oof of breath. The girl laughs at the oafish sigh, sees me see her face opening in a smile, turns away slowly with the smile fading.

"I've forgotten how to talk," she says. "Everybody is gone where I come from."

"Here, too."

"If I stay here, what?"

"Whatever you want. There's a place for you if you want it. There's plenty of food for three."

"Okay."

The shyness between us is washed over with the picayunish of providing blankets, pillows, towels, the spare bed, information about chores, hints, tiny shared pieces of personality. Inside the log-built cabin is like inside the day-domed sky; full of detail and lost to the music and the brilliance of space, stars and night. Even though I have kept things as simple as I can.

I look at my hands, which have lost the roughness of country childhood and the smoothness of city youth, have settled down to accumulate wrinkles, scars and experience. The flickering lamp light catches the face of the youngster, projects an unreliable shadow, makes her face older/younger/older in its variable illumination.

"How old are you?" I ask, and she turns until she faces me out of the shadows, her black eyes shadows themselves, and smiles directly at me. "I'm growing up," she says, and her cheek dimples. She takes my hand in her brown hands, draws me to the table where the lamp sits, holds my hands and hers into the light. Hers are roughened by cold and work, long-fingered, with knotted joints. Mine are square capable hands, well formed it's true but not as long as hers. She puts her palm to mine to show how my palm is wider. She twines her fingers among mine.

"You don't know," she says, "how fast this world here is going around. I get dizzy just trying to stay on."

"You didn't have to."

"You didn't either, but you and that dog stayed."

"Well, it seemed like a good idea at the time."

She shrugs, untangles her hand, walks to the curtain door of now her room. Stops with the cotton barricade that passes for a door held half aside, in shadow, her face the same dark mystery I saw among the willows.

"It always does—then," she says, and the curtain falls flat behind her. The dog walks to the curtain, noses around it, stands with hindquarters in this room like half a dog, backs away, comes back to flop beside me, wide chin on my foot.

"That's right," I say, but not sure if I've talked to the dog, the willow girl, the stars or my own uncertain self, bereft of stars in this many-celled shelter (house/body).

And dreams, and day, and dusk, and night. I am learning how to be dizzy at the speed of consciousness. The speed of light, of synaptic response, of space flight, of the earth's rotation. Why couldn't we use this rapidly whirling sphere like a catapult to hurl us toward expanded consciousness?

We've stayed plastered to its surface like desperate lichens, clinging to the rock that has been our only home.

Even if we can learn to be dizzy, it's one step. Toward the same goal sought by those others who swift away from us at damn near the speed of light, those fickle and farsighted travellers.

And for them their journey is no more than a physical catapulting, taking their weak and limited bodies inside shells of metal and polymer and hurling them frail into the mystery. Still the same bodies, still the same human bickering about the way to proceed.

For the first time I realize relief, how glad I am to have heard that bickering fade away beyond the earth's ability to hear. How glad I am that silence has fallen again on the night world.

To celebrate my relief, I've welcomed more noise into my silent house? Well, that's a little too romantic a description—the dog's unsophisticated breathing echoes from the walls, and I bustle through the activities of daily living, with all the clatter they entail. And when I sit and am silent, even if the dog is outside, I can hear my own body ticking away, blood's hushed flow through the vessels (like the sound of the stream flowing under ice), heart's stubborn throb, click of joints and creak of muscles. I make a lot of noise all by myself.

II

My thoughts fall back to that night when I put out my hand to her (as she cowered under a bush hiding from the black dog) and she took it, took my hand and all I offered with it.

Then she was afraid of the dog, now she rough-houses with it under the dapple shade of leafy spring trees. She has the affinity for shadow which she has always had. Her face has grown thinner and more defined, has lost the puffiness of childhood.

Out among the stars, the people of Earth are travelling. Here in a small country made of our perceptions, we too are travelling among stars. Though it is now day, and the stars are invisible, all of us know they are there. Black dog, brown human (still willow-graceful though her face is welcoming the lines of age), and me.

III

So easy to die inside without ever again seeing the night. Wasn't what I chose a way of dying inside? To stay inside the well of gravity, as it is called, to stay beneath the blanket of air, to limit my life to this generation, no continuity, no connection? These are the tired doubts which come back to trouble me as I sit before the safe and comfortable heater, warming my aching body against the constant changeable moods of age.

Or of humanity. I am no different than I was before the ships left, except that for years I have had fewer people to talk with, to surround me. If it weren't the odyssey I had to doubt about, it would have been some other preoccupation robbing me of the serenity I thought to have earned by now. What's getting old for, if not to settle doubts?

Restless, I shrug into my coat and slide my feet into pile-lined boots, wade through the sticky snow of a chinook wind until I am among the trees, the cabin behind me. The willow woman catches up to me and walks beside me through the night, her hood back and her hair blowing behind her. She does not have to say anything, but occasionally our eyes meet. We have become friends, though it took some time for her to trust me with her not-unusual history of decision and loss. I have found in myself a temptation to talk too much. She smiles and listens, but in her turn she too can tell long stories from her own and other lives and mythologies. She tells them in formal, patterned sentences, which like the orderly beading on her winter moccasins are from the tradition to which she was born and from which she has come a long, long distance.

She helps me across the stream unselfconsciously, such a change from the teenaged child who trembled as I hauled her out from among bushes in mid-winter. Yet for all her words, and smiles, and stories, to me she is still the mysterious country in the west.

At the fence we sit on a fallen log and watch the sky. Orion, skywalker, is low though the night is young. By now I hardly remember to wonder what the other starwalkers are doing. I put out my hands and one at a time she takes them and warms them between hers. My hands are stiffening with arthritic ache, one of the remembered signs of spring.

Time is a ponderous mysterious engine. I cannot imagine how to think properly of it—as a force, a wonder, an absolute? The night's progress to the final night without change or comprehension of how we live like insects clinging to the inexorable path, the blade of grass or flower stem or pine branch that is our immutable span of existence.

The dog has lost the playfulness of puppyhood, comes like a shadow through the midnight to lie down beside me with its massive head against my thigh. I am growing tired, and the willow woman (I still think of her that way, though long since we traded our social, daylight names) pulls me up and indicates the homeward path.

"You go," I say, and in the full moonlight see her face, with the lined signatures of laughter and the rest of the score life composes. Her face I have always thought was beautiful and mysterious but in the moonlight it seems to open to me like night itself opens out into infinity.

"You always want to be alone with it," she says.

"It isn't that," I say. "But how can I remember the lost human race and be lonely when you're distracting me here?"

She grins. "Manufacture of melancholy?" But she walks back into the forest and I hear her leap across the stream.

The black dog looks after her, but chooses me, turns again and settles with that rush of spent breath. It can change and grow old, and still be the same through all its changes. And from within I can see myself in the same pattern, learning slowly and living so fast along the time line.

The days, the seasons seem to go by so quickly now. As if now that Earth is almost deserted, there is no drag, no friction of billions to hold it from spinning.

IV

After all, the sky is full of something, be it refracted light of day or direct and uncomplicated starlight. Only the stars themselves are uncomplicated, I mean, for we make so much of them, running after them like the most opaque of lovers, or most of us did—

Except the few stubborn ones who wouldn't play sycophant to the universe. I'm sorry, the naked sky will have to get along without me; I like mine cluttered with atmosphere and obscured with diurnal rhythms.

Oh, what does it matter? Here at the place where I buried the old black dog when it finally loosed its tenacious hold on the years—that's how long ago I came across a snowy field and found the one other human in my part of the world, hiding in the willows, in the snow-field, in the middle of a brilliant night.

Nothing is different. That's the curse of the ones left behind, but also the blessing. They'll see light bend in that Einsteinian grace, they'll see something new every time the ship rolls. The stars will truly wheel and dance, new patterns, new myths and fantasies. We will live something like we always did, or always wanted to, but more solitary.

If loneliness was my concern, why couldn't I go with them? Not just that I was too set in my ways to want that much change, for I knew my life would never be the same whatever I decided. No, I think I was too much in love with the night of the world. Not the pure vacuum packed darkness of the void, but the lovely imperfect blue-black of Earth, the wavering stars' light bursting through like a revelation of mortality.

And the other one? She was in love with the Earth itself. Its sweet spinning was fast enough for her. She wanted to watch the moon come up forever over the playground of rabbits and wolverines and bears and bright water. She loved the way the contents of the earth roiled and moiled around her. She wouldn't give that up for relentless foraging through a vacuum. So here she is.

That's the matter with some of us. We can't exist in a vacuum. Aware of gravity, we stand spellbound before the stars, but we don't want to get any closer. We love another force, the one that holds us together, to each other, to the ground.

Don't ask me to name that force, I was unable even to give a name to the black dog, nor can I now remember that of the woman who is sharing my old years. They exist, that is all. I have no name myself, I have only got the place where I am. It has been enough.

In the end, like the black dog, we will dissolve into gravity, we will dream dark earth dreams or dream no more.

A River Garden

Ursula Pflug

I'd grown up having a summer garden and knew I'd miss the homegrown flavour of organic vine-ripened tomatoes. I knew River Garden, who lived not far away, had seven acres so I drove over one Saturday morning in early May to see if he'd let me plant at his place. River had inherited his little white frame bungalow from an aunt when he was just nineteen, and had lived there ever since.

"Go ahead and plant, Mel," he said, "I couldn't grow a garden if I tried."

"Why's that?" I asked, because from what I knew River's family was good at everything they laid a hand to.

"It's stuck in my hand," he said, "I can't get it out."

I left that alone. Both River and his mother Gifted spoke cryptically on occasion, a kind of metaphoric Life Poetry. Sometimes I knew what they meant; sometimes I didn't; sometimes I felt stupid for not knowing and sometimes I was irritated.

"Whatever," I said and River started the tiller and motioned for me to get to work so I did.

The machine was hard to control as are so many tillers but what didn't help was I'd incurred a bad cut the winter before and my hand wasn't quite back to normal. River told me to get a beer out of his cooler for my break; he was busy under his truck. I told him about my accident and asked if he could help me till the last few rows.

"No," he said, "other people's gardens make me too sad."

I didn't know what that meant either and I didn't want to say something dumb so I finished my beer and got on with the work. At last I was done and could plant my seeds; I put in a little of all the usual: beans, corn, tomatoes, lettuce, peas, beets and carrots, cucumbers, cabbages; I had lots of cabbage seeds. At sunset I thanked him for the beer and the use of his land; he grunted "You're welcome," from underneath his GMC half ton and I drove home.

Everything grew even though I didn't get up there much. River told me so when I passed him on the road coming home from work; we'd both stop, roll our windows down and have a little chat. I was teaching a pottery class in town for children, and what with one thing and another there hardly ever seemed the time to get to River's even to gather greens for salad. I told River to eat what he wanted and he said he would.

By the time I set aside a full day to weed it was already the beginning of August: tomatoes turning orange before red. We'd had a lot of June and July rain, which was unusual but the only thing that had saved my garden from neglect; the cabbages were huge, Findhornian. River pulled a carrot, brushed the dirt off and began munching. They're never sweeter than when you have them that way. He was staring moodily at my faerie cabbages, as though they meant something other than good soil, lots of rain, and his three black hens having the run of the garden, picking the cabbage butterfly larvae off.

But between the cabbages the weeds grew even taller: pigweed, lamb's quarters, mallow, purslane. Actually the purslane wasn't tall but it was rugged, a dense succulent rug. Of course you can eat all those too but it's a little pointless when they're crowding out the things you actually planted.

There I was, weeding, when River came out of the house to chat. "Why don't you have a garden at your dad's instead of here?" he asked, watching me. "Peter's tiller is big and new; the soil's got years of compost you've been adding. It's closer and you'll get to it."

My father had hundreds of acres of land, but I didn't live there anymore. "He doesn't want me gardening there, now I've left," I said, "and where I live they don't want me to plant either." I didn't add that I'd never grown giant pumpkin sized cabbages at my father's house.

"Where do you live?" River asked.

"I thought everyone knew by now. I squat in that house in the county forest."

"Oh, I know that house; it's cool," River said.

"I love it," I agreed, "except the floorboards are rotting out. I know I shouldn't but at night I worry rabid skunks or rats will scramble through the holes and bite my feet while I'm asleep."

River smiled indulgently. "That's a pretty house, though," he said. "Tell you what, let's drive over and I'll help you fix the floor."

"That's nice of you but I haven't got any wood."

"I've got lots; I've been collecting planks other people have been throwing away for years," River said. We went around to his shed, filled up the back of his pick-up with floorboards, a saw, a bag of screws, a hammer and nails and a drill; I made sure he brought a cordless as we didn't have hydro.

He was following me in the truck; I was in my little red Mazda with rust in the floor I'm always hoping the cops won't notice. He stuck his head out the window when he pulled up beside me at the intersection and we talked about how wonderful summer was in our part of the country, made up as it was of fishing, swimming, road trips, playing with turtles, watching herons and eating out of the garden. "Still, everything's not quite right," I said.

"So what's the matter?" River asked.

"The matter is I'm having accidents," I said.

"What kind of accidents?"

"I cut an artery in my hand," I said. "I told you before. I was sorting cans for recycling, believe it or not."

"I guess you did tell me. So how'd you fix it?" he asked and I rattled off the list: ambulance, emergency ward, Demerol, anaesthesia, microsurgery. But the sadness and terror my accident had left me with still hadn't faded, and I told River how I felt; he somehow made me feel I could.

We drove, our windows still rolled down, still pulling up side by side at intersections. It was nice to be getting to know him better, in a different way from him being that guy three lines over it seemed I'd always known. He rolled two smokes and passed me one, explaining it was tobacco he'd grown and cured himself. Lighting up, River said, "I can't grow a garden at all, except for the tobacco."

I said, "So you keep saying, River, but why not? I mean with a last name like Garden? By the way, I've always wondered what your first name was before you decided to call yourself River."

River said: "My mother gave me this name. You should know; we've known each other forever."

"What does she do now? Software?" I said snidely. The truth was, people often said unkind things about River's mother. She lived alone, had lovers, and was more than a little eccentric.

"She lives in the woods," River said mildly, ignoring my insult. "She home-schooled me. You're a bit of a dryad yourself, why I like you I suppose."

"I did go to school but it was the Waldorf; it hardly counts, although I learned enough pottery to get a job teaching it, straight away after graduating."

"Beats working behind the counter at KFC, like most kids your age," River said.

"I wouldn't know," I replied. "But you must have gone to school eventually?"

"Home-schooled, like I said, and by the time I left home I knew how to study on my own."

"You've turned out quite well," I said, thinking what a wit I was, "considering you were raised by a nut case."

"Look who's talking," River said amiably, nonetheless giving me a level stare so I'd know I'd crossed the line. It was true my father was known as a little on the prickly side. Peter The Porcupine, people called him behind his back and sometimes in front, not without reason; I'd run into his prickles more than a few times. Probably it was where I got my famous sarcasm. "But you're right," he added, to make me feel better for having put my foot in my mouth, "Gifted is a nut case."

"What's she do?" I asked again.

"Grows a garden, goes deer hunting in November, sells a few pigs in the fall and eggs throughout the year."

"I mean aside from that," I said, "She must have one little job or another, if only to pay for gas and repairs on her van."

"She tells people when their cats have been taken over by aliens," River replied, totally deadpan.

I snickered. It sounded exactly as fruity as I'd always heard. "She gets paid for this?" But with the Gardens you just never knew; anything was possible. Maybe exorcising cats actually was software; maybe his mother was one of those back woods types who was always building new neural pathways, had no fear or mental blocks whatsoever about learning. It was quite possible she'd taught herself graphics and programming at the age of forty-two, had a dedicated work station running on solar panels with a satellite linkup. Or maybe she had hydro after all; maybe I was the only one who didn't. Maybe "Alien Felines" was a computer game written by a nut case for other nut cases, cashing in on the current media-generated fad for fringe kookiness and River's mother was actually a Gatesian billionaire.

Stranger things had happened, and, I figured, would again, maybe very soon.

"No," River said, "but people give her stuff to make her go away."

"Yeah—stuff like what?"

"Oh, usually the stuff she wants. She'll come and hang around for a couple of days and harp on about their cats and the aliens and then she'll finger their best Guatemalan shawl or their beautiful hand-blown glass bowl with the fish designs in it and they'll say, "Here's a present for you, a trade for exorcising my cats," and she'll take it away.

I wasn't sure if he was pulling my leg or not, feeding into all those rumours. Perhaps he was defensive about having a kook for a mother, just as I was sensitive about having a porcupine for a father.

"Gifted?" I said snidely, as though I'd never heard that was her name before. "What was she called before that? Sandy?" It's been said before that sarcasm is harder than cigarettes to kick and it sure seemed true for me that day and dumb to boot, considering how cute and companionable I was finding River.

"No; Gifted Dreamer is what her mother called her," he said, still maddeningly, stubbornly sincere, still ignoring my mean streak.

"Wow," I said, still unable to help myself, "You're a third generation squatter nut case." It occurred to me he was so sexy and nice it made me nervous and my acerbic wit leapt up as an instinctive smoke-screen. Worse yet, he could probably see right through me.

"As you know I don't squat, I own," he said, and then added, just to prove he wasn't completely bereft of snideness himself: "You're the one who squats, Melneeda."

Melneeda, that's my name. Sorry, but it's the unfortunate truth.

River went on, "Hard cases. We're not nut cases exactly but hard cases. Hard seeds. You need to soak 'em to make 'em grow."

Hard seed cases? It was a gardening metaphor too dense for me, and I was tempted to make another prickly aside but figured even River might have a limit to his tolerance, so I let it go.

My place is where the river crosses under a bridge. When we pulled up the owner was standing there with a crabby look on her face. She started screaming at me, having suddenly decided I owed her four months rent even though she'd said several times it was okay for me to stay there, and what with the house's condition she couldn't have charged a normal tenant anyway. It didn't seem fair but what could I say? I didn't have it on paper. But River strode forward and gave her six hundred dollars in cash, crisp fifties pulled off a roll, said, "I think that's quite enough for four months at this place."

"Three hundred a month," she growled, looking wonderingly at all that hard currency.

"For three-fifty you can still get a rundown farmhouse with hydro, flush toilets indoors. Who'd pay three for this place?"

She growled some more. River started to reach for his money then, asking politely whether she needed any exorcism on her cats. Looking just a tad alarmed, she put the money away, got in her van and left in a hurry.

I looked at him in stunned awe, meaning to thank him profusely, instead saying, "Seems like all those rumours about Gifted stand you in good stead."

"What rumours are those?" he asked archly.

I sighed; he was on to me in too many ways.

"Well, I'll pay you back," I said.

"Of course you will."

"So who's your dad? For some reason I don't know." It occurred to me belatedly I sounded like I was prying.

"Stuart Garden," River replied. "A good guy; they're still friends, even though he lives in Nova Scotia now. We talk on the phone a lot, him and me."

"So that's where you got your last name," I said.

"Well, Gifted had a dream when she was pregnant that my true name was River and she thought River Garden sounded better than River Dreamer."

"River Dreamer's nice too, though."

"Yes, but perhaps a bit too drownable," he said.

Not knowing what he meant like half the time I just ignored it, asked "What about my floor?"

"Okay, let's get to it."

We worked: high speed, butt busting work till I hammered my thumb in August's last light. In any case the drill was out of power; we'd traded it in for hand tools an hour before. I thought I had a couple of boxes of Kraft Dinner in the pantry and offered to cook River supper on my little yellow Finlay cook stove but he said he had plans.

Still, I wanted to make sure I saw him again, a wee bit more formally than watering the garden or passing on the road. I was working hard on an excuse but what came put of my mouth was: "I think my cat is invaded by aliens; think you could drop by with your mum for a visit?"

"It's not your cat," he said, "it's you that's invaded by aliens." He looked at me sternly as though I should've been able to figure this out for myself. This was news to me but I felt a great relief that someone was at last taking an interest in my ennui, my feeling of unwellness, my healing, and so I said, "Can she do people too?"

"Of course," he said, "we'll go see her. Saturday, 'kay?"

" 'Kay." Saturday I worked but I thought I'd get my friend Hannah to fill in for me; this was too important.

When I saw Hannah at work the next day she said, "Don't go, Melneeda; everyone knows Gifted is crazy." She swung her wings of dark hair at me, ominously, I thought.

"You're usually a reliable purveyor of information, Hannah, but I'm going anyway."

"It's your funeral," she said, shaking and shaking that hair at me. I'd grow my own that long and learn to work it like she did; people would have more respect for me.

"Thanks for covering for me."

Hannah sighed and walked away.

Saturday morning, I followed the scribbled map, not even noticing how I didn't get lost once. When I arrived Gifted was having a yard sale; she had three tables set up and every single item for sale was gorgeously, stunningly beautiful. She was wearing a long paisley skirt and a green velvet jacket; her hair was long and grey. When I noticed her smoking she said, "I have to; it's a smoking jacket, isn't it?" I laughed politely, not knowing what to say but Gifted took my hand and shook it firmly. "You must be Melneeda, River's friend," she said.

"I've known him forever," I said, which was more or less true. "But I don't think you and I have ever met."

"Oh, we have," she said, "but you were just a baby. Your mother and I were friends. But after she died, you know, Peter and I never got along that well."

"Sounds familiar," I said and Gifted laughed, a cross between grateful and gracious.

"Nice stuff," I commented, looking at her sale tables.

"I'm selling the stuff people have bartered me for my alien exorcisms," she giggled, as if it was all a big lark. "This is my third weekend and I've made thirteen hundred dollars. Don't need that much myself, I only needed to pay for repairs on my van. I put half of it in your account," Gifted explained to River. "Figured you could use a little mad money."

"I noticed," he said. "Thanks." He didn't tell her he'd just paid my rent with it and was back to broke as usual. I was relieved; in spite of her eccentric flair she was still just a mum and he just her son.

"Your mother's generous," I said. "My father's relatively rich compared to most people but he won't even let me grow a garden on his land since I left."

"It was a good thing, maybe," River said. "Have you driven by there? The corn's still short, thin and spindly even though it's rained twice a week since April."

I nodded. "I used to hear there were barrels of PCBs buried under the corn fields; truth is it sure felt like that."

"I heard that too," River said.

"No one talked about it much."

"I guess not," he said.

"Now," Gifted turned to me. "River tells me you're here on business," and she led us inside. We walked through a kitchen crowded with beautiful objects both old and new and into a hallway where a torn green curtain was strung up in front of an alcove. There was a big rip in the middle she hadn't bothered to mend, and a Queen Anne chair upholstered in blue velvet facing it. "Sit down, my dear," she said. "This is where it all happens."

River played assistant, brought me a mug of steaming herb tea and I thought to ask whether it might make me hallucinate but stopped myself, on account of possibly seeming rude. I knew I was just being influenced by all those rumours again. I sipped the tea; it wasn't too hot, and fragrant and delicious as if made from a blend of a hundred flowers that grow on a much happier planet than this one. I drained it all in a big series of gulps. I guess I'd been thirsty and the tea had a strong and immediate effect; it made me cry. I cried so much and for so long that at last even River and Gifted asked me if that might not be enough.

I cried because my dad and I had fought so much before I'd left, because I'd injured my till then supposedly impermeable body so very badly, because my landlady had screamed at me, because I owed River six hundred dollars which at my present rate of pay would take me as many years to pay back, and because my mother had died when I'd turned fourteen. I'd cried about that before, of course, but a little extra releasing never hurt, I guessed. I also cried most of my famous sarcasm out, but I wasn't aware of that part.

"That's Teary Tea for you," Gifted told me when I'd subsided a bit, "doing its job just like it's supposed to. You can't heal if you don't vent first; no one can. Now listen up, child. Are you ready to listen?" I nodded my head, afraid I'd cry some more if I spoke. "The aliens are on the other side of the curtain," Gifted said, completely without apology. "In the alcove. All the aliens I've exorcised from people's cats, and from the people themselves, are behind the curtain."

Maybe it was the Teary Tea but I took her at face value, or if not that exactly, at least felt I wanted to go along with her story, see where it led. I already felt better than I had in a year, just from all the crying. "You already put your hand through," Gifted said, and I looked at her in horror as though the alcove behind the curtain really was populated by skittering, hostile, utterly alien beings. I was afraid then, like a child woken from nightmare, wanted only for Gifted to take the aliens that were in me out and stuff them in that hole where she stuffed the others, because she could, because she was the only one who wasn't afraid. I didn't know what she planned to do with them later, didn't really care. I figured if Gifted could exorcise aliens she could deal with them too.

"Alienation," Gifted said, "it's a common problem."

"I'm in love with your son," I told her hopefully, startling even myself, relieved he was back in the kitchen washing his mother's morning dishes. I'd had no clue those words were about to pop out of my mouth. It occurred to me later that was part of her healing; to make me a person brave enough to speak her heart's truth instead of always hiding it behind sarcasm.

Gifted looked at my untidy hair, ripped jeans, holey boots, and winsome smile as though I just might do. "Full of foolish bravado, you stuck your hand through the curtain and they cut you, that's all," she repeated implacably.

"You're talking about my accident?" I guessed, as I'd never been to her house before, and had never once stuck my hand through the curtain. I wasn't about to do it now, either, considering the spooky visions she'd just implanted in my impressionable, tear soaked mind.

"Yes. The important question is, what did you bring back through? They're hoarding the good stuff over there, the stuff that makes us feel better, not so alienated anymore. I hope you realise my little set-up here is symbolic." She glared at me, as though suddenly suspicious I'd run off and tell Hannah and everyone she was even crazier than everyone said she was. "All this mass hysteria about aliens abducting or invading people is missing the point," she added emphatically, "even if it does turn me a tidy profit." She lit a cigarette, continued. "If we can't be happy how can we learn to grow, love one another? Even my son. I tried my best to raise him right but the world's too cold, too alienated by far. In spite of all my hard work he's never been able to grow his own garden."

We all went back outside and Gifted resumed her work of rearranging beautiful objects on her yard sale tables. I went into a dream, or perhaps it was a continuation of the same dream I'd inhabited with River since the day I'd planted a garden at his house. I didn't know we were about to make a fair trade, that momentarily he'd be planting one at mine.

I thanked Gifted, not really understanding any of it. I remembered then how I'd seen her in town once, only a few years before, had guessed who she was. I'd turned my head away, pretending I didn't see, when a bunch of kids had thrown rocks at her van, cracking the windshield, screaming that she was a witch, a bitch, all the usual and crazy whore to boot. I'd been eleven, old enough to know better. Worse still, River had saved me from the corner bullies more than once when I'd been buying my drugstore candy.

I sucked on guilt; meanwhile she went on in her busy, competent, let's-get-this-job-over-with voice, as though it was all tea and cookies from where she stood, no harder than slaughtering chickens, which, admittedly wasn't easy but all in a day's work. "You're just a little scared is all, because you've so recently left your father's house. You're a good camper, a good traveller and that's the main point. But I still want to know, and you need to know too, what treasure you brought back from the other side, stole back from the aliens hoarding it, keeping most of us miserable all our lives. Hoarding our joy, our desire, our magic."

She seemed almost normal then, just a middle aged lady who had a firm grip on life and knew a lot of stuff and I said "I'll figure it out eventually, Gifted. I'm sure I will."

"Okay," she agreed as she thought this was good enough for now.

"Thanks," I said, "and what do I owe you?"

Gifted just waved her hand, said, "Take care of my son." I nodded cheerily even though I was a little concerned by how she might mean that. It would be a major disappointment to me if she had it in mind I should start doing his dishes and laundry.

River would drive me home, he said, because my carburetor had fainted the minute I'd arrived. He'd come back and take a look, he promised. But even his usually reliable truck stalled on the way and in spite of our best efforts to get it going again, nothing worked. We were still six miles from my place but River took his canoe off the back and made me help him carry it through the woods to the water. We paddled home down the river, stopping just this side of the bridge. I thought we'd get out and portage up the steep bank and across the road but River said, "Let's canoe under," and we did even though we had to keep our heads down, the bridge was so low. I liked it though; it was a cool, froggy, echoey minute. Hauled the canoe out, set it on my bleached, parched lawn of quack grass.

He stood, looking at the river, at the brown grass, while I mentally struggled for the umpteenth time this summer, with how I'd ever pay him back for all he'd done. "River," he said inexplicably, out of the blue, as though his mother's healing had made him feel dreamy too, "my name is River Garden."

"So why don't you garden then?" I asked yet again; I really was curious. I felt so much better at speaking my heart since I'd met his mother, yet I knew I'd have to make it a daily practise, a habit, or I'd lose it again.

"Because my garden isn't like other people's: it's a garden existing only in the palm of my hand, invisible, and I've never figured out how to get it out of my hand and plant it, grow it up, normal sized; right now it's microscopic."

"Not seeds?"

"Hard seeds. Hard cases." River looked like he was going to cry.

I thought of how he'd let me plant at his house, paid my rent, helped me fix my floor and taken me to meet his mother, who'd cured my existential angst, exorcised the metaphorical aliens possessing me; he'd driven me home and most importantly been good company, good conversation at every stop sign and every red light over the summer, not staring out the window as though what was on his mind couldn't be shared, like so many men I knew. I thought of how so many good turns must deserve at least one in return, and if he didn't want to be my boyfriend, ever, I'd just have to let it go. I put my hand on his; it was my left hand, the hurt hand, although only a scar remained, a bit of numbness in the cold. I kept it there for a long time, felt gradually a charge building up, a kind of pressure which then began to flow from my hand into his. It was the life force, I knew, the green force, the force that had been stuck, unused, hoarded by my own alienation on the other side of the torn curtain.

"How long do I keep my hand there, d'you know?" I asked.

"Till it stops flowing," River said, looking into my eyes; his were very large and brown indeed.

"I've never done this before," I said. "I don't even know what I'm doing."

"It sure feels like you do. Just keep doing it, whatever it is. I think maybe you're soaking my seeds."

"What?"

"If I'm right, Melneeda, you'll see in a minute. It'll be a surprise. But that's what happened, why you tore your hand. You were supposed to be using it and you weren't. You cut your hand so the healing force could come through. The dam would be opened, the clog unobstructed."

"But I almost lost my hand."

"Use it or lose it," River said.

"But I'm only seventeen," I said.

"Age has nothing to do with it. It's because you've played all your life. Most people don't, you know. I could see it in you when you were just a kid. Remember how you used to spend the fall sitting up in the apple trees, eating yellow apples, writing and reading and drawing?" he asked, with something like entreaty in his eyes. I'd always thought he was so self contained, moving through the world; not needing anything from anyone, always having some thing to give. "Your force was clogged and how could it not be, growing up on a toxic waste dump," he added. "You know the former owners made a shady deal when they closed the old General Electric plant. They made a fortune burying that stuff."

"I heard that, but it's such a big farm," I said guiltily.

"It doesn't matter how much, it matters how clean."

"Peter got it cheap."

"No kidding, Melneeda."

"They didn't tell him."

"Of course not," River said. "But he just pretended not to know; everyone knew."

"He said I needed a lot of land to grow up on, after mom died. For the mother you've lost I'll give you a big piece of land to mother you; woods and fields and ponds. He said he did it for me."

"He was just greedy. I've never had more than a few acres. It's enough. Neither has Gifted."

I thought our conversation was quite possibly the most interesting one I'd ever had, seeming to explain so many things I'd always puzzled about in my life. The flowing had stopped; suddenly drained, I got up and walked towards the house. In front of the window a small bed of scraggly Cosmos bloomed. In it sat my morning coffee, half drunk and abandoned there. I picked it up and drank. It was a pale blue cup, my favourite although already cracked, a house warming present from my town buddy Hannah.

"Those cabbages I grew at your place are weird," I said, offering the cup to River. I thought we needed coffee to restart our brains, lost to his mother's soggy healing rituals, and cold abandoned Cosmic java seemed better at that moment than me leaving him alone to go inside and make new. I felt fragile as I knew he did; our fragility linked us.

"Gifted knows how to make sauerkraut," River said. "We'll get her recipe. But more importantly, they're how I knew about you."

When I turned back River had placed his garden hand on the ground beside the river; the seeds had loosened and fallen in that scratchy gravelly hardpan, barely good enough for chickens and a few leggy Cosmos that had been self-seeding for years. But to River's seeds it was darkest loam.

Already you could see the seeds germinating, sprouting, growing at hyper speed like time lapse photography. Foxgloves, lupins, old single hollyhocks in every shade; tomatoes, beans, squash, corn, peas, sunflowers, chamomile, bergamot, cabbages, broccoli. Also a little patch with a beautiful white bellflower I didn't know, an orange milkweed of all things, and several grasses I'd never seen before.

"What's that stuff, the plants you invented?" I asked.

"No, it's my regeneration project. Eastern prairie; indigenous to Ontario. Like the Eastern Bison, it's been mostly wiped out by settlers and lawns and parks and all that. We're supposed to start it up again, so this is my contribution."

"Very pretty," I said admiringly, "But it's a shame it's here and not on land any of us own," I said.

River was leaning over, watching his tiny garden grow. It was as big as his hand now.

As my hand.

"Maybe it's better this way. If someone's driving by hungry they can collect some food, or dig up a bit of their favourite shade of peony to transplant; that's all I ever wanted my garden to do."

As it grew we could make out more and more varieties of food, flowers, herbs, teas. You name it; River grew it.

We sat there the whole afternoon watching his garden grow, felt the tickling of creeping thyme emerging under our behinds by way of purple fuzzy pillows.

"What about after I move? Who will look after your garden?"

"This garden will be here, self-seeding forever; you tore it through from the other side of the curtain where the aliens were hoarding it. Now d'you think your injury was worth it?"

"Only a little numbness in the cold," I said, looking at the scar, and River took my scarred hand in his now empty garden hand and kissed it. As we went inside together the last of the tingling faded away.

WAITING FOR THE ZEPHYR

Tobias S. Buckell

The Zephyr was almost five days overdue.

Wind lifted the dust off in little devils of twisting columns that randomly touched down throughout the remains of the town. Further out beyond the hulks of the Super Wal-Mart and Krogers Mara stood and swept the binoculars. The platform she stood on reached up a good hundred feet ending in the bulbous water tank that watered the town, affording her a look just over the edge of the horizon. She strained her eyes for the familiar shape of the Zephyr's four blade-like masts, but saw nothing but dirt-twisters.

The old asphalt highway, laid down back in the time of plenty, had finally succumbed to the advancing dirt despite the town's best attempts to keep it out. The barriers lay on their side.

Mara still knew the twists and turns of the highway she'd memorized since twelve, when she'd first realized it led to other towns and people.

"Mara, it's getting dark."

"Yes Ken."

Ken carefully put the binoculars into their pouch and climbed down the side of the tower. Pushing off down the dust piled at its feet she trudged down to Ken, now only a large silhouette in the suddenly approaching dusk.

"Your mother still wants to talk to you."

Mara didn't respond.

"She wants to work it out," Ken continued.

"I'm leaving. I've wanted to leave since I was twelve, come on Ken… don't start this again." Mara started walking quickly towards the house.

Ken matched her pace, and even though she could see him wondering what to say next, she could also see him examining the farm out of his peripheral vision. Their farm defied the dust and wind with lush green growth, but only because it lay underneath protective glass. Ken paused slightly twice, checking cracks in the façade, areas where dust tried to leak in.

"Their wind generator is down. They need help, Mara. I said I would go over tomorrow."

Mara sighed.

"I really don't want to."

Ken opened the outer door for her, stamping his boots clean and letting it shut, then passed through as she opened the second door. Dust slipped in everywhere and covered everything despite precautions. Brooms didn't quite get it all. Although Ken thought them a useless necessity Mara thought the idea of a vacuum cleaner quite fetching.

"I need your help, Mara, just for an afternoon. You wouldn't feel right leaving someone without electricity, would you?"

Ken was right, without the wind-generator her parents would be without power.

"Okay. I'll help." Ken, she noticed, ever the wonder with his hands, already had a dinner set for the two of them. Despite being slightly cold from sitting out, it was wonderful.

ooo   ooo   ooo

The Zephyr was six days overdue.

Mara shimmied up the roof and joined Ken. He already had parts of the wind-generator lying out on the roof. She had just managed to brush past her father without being physically stopped. Mother stood around, looking wounded and helpless.

Ken made a face.

"The blade is all right. But the alternator is burned out."

Simple enough to fix. The wind generators consisted of no more than an old automobile alternator attached to a propeller blade and swivel mounted on the roof. What electricity the houses had depended on deep cycle batteries that used the wind generators to recharge. Solar panels worked in some areas, but here the dust crept into them, and unlike wind generators, didn't work at night. Plus, it was easy enough to wander out to a car lot and pick an alternator out of the thousands of dead cars.

Mara half suspected her father had called them for help just to get her out to his farm. Damnit.

"Mara," her father said from the edge of the dust gutter. "We need to talk." Mara looked straight out over the edge, out at the miles and miles of brown horizon. "Mara, look at me. Mara, we spoke harshly. We're sorry."

"We like Ken," her mother chimed in from below. "But you're young. You can't move out just yet."

"Come back honey. We could use your help on the farm. You wouldn't be as busy as you are with Ken."

Ken looked up at that with a half-pained grin. Mara swore and slid off the low end off the roof, hitting the dust with a grunt. Her father started back down the ladder but Mara was already in the cart, pulling up the sail and bouncing out across the dust back towards the relative safety of Ken's farm, leaving her mother's plaintive entreaties in the dusk air behind her.

Damn, how could she have fallen for that? Her parents were so obvious. And Ken, she fumed on her way back. He shouldn't have taken her over.

Even after he showed up, sheepishly cooking yet another marvelous meal, she tried to remain angry. But the anger eventually subsided, as it always did.

∘∘∘   ∘∘∘   ∘∘∘

On the seventh and eighth day of waiting reception cleared up enough for the both of them to catch some broadcasts from further north. Ken had enough charge in the house batteries for almost eight hours of television shows, and they both cuddled on the couch.

∘∘∘   ∘∘∘   ∘∘∘

Mara began to wonder if the Zephyr would ever show. The last visit was two years ago, when the giant wheeled caravan sailed into town for a day. Traders and merchants festooned its various decks with smiles and stalls.

The Zephyr, Mara knew from talks to its bridge crew, was one of the few links the outer towns of America still had with the large cities, and each other. Ever since the Petroleum collapse, with the Middle East nuked into oblivion and portions of Europe glowing, the country had been trying to replace an entire infrastructure based on oil.

Almost two generations later it was succeeding.

The large cities used more nuclear power, or even harnessed the sewer systems, but small towns were hit the hardest. Accustomed to power, but dropped off the line, isolated, a minor Dark Age had descended on them. Life based itself here on bare essentials; water and wind.

Mara wanted to see a city lit up in a wanton electrical blaze of light, forcing away the dusk and night with artificial man-made day.

∘∘∘   ∘∘∘   ∘∘∘

On the tenth day Ken found her in the bedroom frantically packing.

"They spotted the Zephyr coming in from the east," Mara said, hoisting a pack onto her shoulders.

"Are you sure you want to do this?"

"What?"

"Go. You don't know what's out there. Strange places, strange people. Danger."

Mara looked at him. "Of course."

Ken looked down at the ground. "I thought we had something. You, me."

"Of course." Mara paused. "I told you that I would be going."

"But I'd hoped… "

"Ken. I can't."

"Go." His voice hardened and he walked into the kitchen. Mara sat on the edge of the bed biting back tears, then snatched the two packs and left angrily.

○○○   ○○○   ○○○

The Zephyr rolled through Main Street, slowing down to a relative crawl to allow people to run alongside and leap up. Kids thronged the sides of the street, and furious trade went on. The four tall masts of the Zephyr towered above the small two and three storey town buildings. The masts looked like vertical wings, and used the same principles. Air flowing across the shorter edge of the blade-like mast caused a vacuum, drawing the massive wheeled ship forward.

Mara followed the eager crowd behind the ship. She nodded to the occasional familiar face.

Plastic beads, more precious than gold due the rarity of oils were draped across stalls that slid out of the side of the hull. Mara aimed her quick walk for one of these, but instead found herself blocked by a familiar form.

"Uncle Dan?"

"Hi." He had her arm in a firm grip. Mara saw the bulk of the Zephyr slowly moving away.

She tried to pull out of his grip, but couldn't. Her dad pushed through the crowd.

"Dad! What are you doing?"

"It's for your own good, Mara," uncle Dan said. "You don't know what you're doing."

"Yes I do," she yelled, kicking at her uncle's shins. The crowd around them paid no obvious attention, although Mara knew full well that by nighttime it would be the talk of the area.

She begged, pleaded, yelled, kicked, scratched and fought. But the men of the house already had their minds made. They locked her into the basement.

"You'll be out when the Zephyr leaves," mom promised.

There were no windows. Mara could only imagine the Zephyr's slow progress out of the town. She tried to put a brave face on, then crawled into a corner and cried. After that she beat on the door, but no came to let her out.

○○○   ○○○   ○○○

The basement was a comfortable area. The family den, it held several couches and carpet. The door creaked open, and from looking out Mara guessed it to be dusk. Ken came down the stairs carefully.

"It's me, Mara."

"I suppose you're in on this too?"

"Actually, no. You're family wants me to speak some sense into you. I won't lie to you, Mara. I want you to stay. But holding you here like this is ridiculous."

"The longer we all stay out here, away from the cities, the crazier it gets."

"Maybe. Your family's scared. They don't want to lose you."

"That doesn't give them the right to lock me up like a damn dog!" Mara yelled.

Ken came closer.

"My sail-cart is outside. That's as far as you need to get. You're a better sailor than anyone else, once in you can outrun everyone. The Zephyr is still reachable on a long tack. Hey, I never did get along with your uncle anyway."

Mara looked up at him and gave him a long hug.

"Thank you so much."

"If you're ever back in town, look me up."

"Will you come with me, then?"

"Ask me then."

Ken pulled away and stepped up the stairs.

"Stay close."

He launched himself into her uncle and dad, tackling them with a loud yell. Mara ran past, losing only a shoe, pushing past her mom and out into the yard.

The cart's sail puffed out with a snap, and she was bouncing her way over the sand before she looked back to see two figures at the door watching her go. No one bothered to chase her. They all knew her skill with the sail.

∘∘∘   ∘∘∘   ∘∘∘

It took the better part of few hours before the four masts showed up. Mara could hear distant shouting as she overhauled the giant land ship.

"Ahoy Zephyr," she shouted.

Some one tossed a ladder down, and Mara hauled herself up. The small sail cart veered off and tipped into the dust, snapping its tiny mast in two. It felt faintly liberating to land on the deck with a smile.

The merchant with the ladder stepped aside, letting an officer in khaki step forward.

"We've been watching you approach for the past few hours," he said. "We like the way you handle the wind."

"Can you read a map?" asked a woman in uniform. She wore strange braids on her shoulders.

"No."

"You looking for a position on board the ship?"

"Yes." Mara felt her stomach flip-flop.

"Then we'll teach you how to read charts," the woman said. She stuck out a hand. "Welcome aboard, kid, I'm Captain Shana. Ever cross me or give me a reason to, I'll toss you off the side of the ship and leave you to the vultures. Understood?"

"Yes ma'am."

"Good. Give her a hammock."

Mara stood on the deck of the Zephyr, enjoying the moment. Then the man in uniform touched her shoulder.

"It isn't fun and games, it's a lot of hard work, but worth it. Come on."

Mara paused and looked out at the flat horizon, full of tempting futures. Then she followed him below decks.

Blue Train

Derryl Murphy

An explosion shattered the silence, and after a moment Andy saw a plume of smoke and dust rise up from behind a distant hill. "Anyone else supposed to be out prospecting in this area?"

"Negative," said his quad. "I'm attempting to patch into a network satellite, see if I can get a fix on what's over there."

Andy collapsed his sleeping bag and stuffed it into a saddlebag, took a last swig of strong Indian tea, then hopped onto the quad, battered cup still in hand. "To hell with the network. So many birds going down, that could take hours before you get an idea what's happening."

"What's over there is using explosives. If you insist on going to look, then I would ask that you please leave me behind. My sense of self-preservation has certainly not been depleted by your rough treatment."

"Shut up," said Andy, flipping open the control panel and tapping at a gauge. "Your battery is still at forty- five percent, so we'll run electric and leave the fuel for later. Quieter that way." He thumbed a button and turned the throttle, and the quad jumped forward with a rising hum.

"That hill will likely leave my battery at less than twenty percent, Andy."

"And the sun is already out. Start recharging and stop worrying."

They drove across the dry creek bed, the quad steering them to the part of the opposite bank that looked easiest to mount. From there it was a steady ride up the hill, tacking back and forth to avoid tipping over, Andy leaning hard uphill each time to help with balance. As they neared the crest, there was another explosion, much louder this time.

Andy let the throttle snap back to off, and the quad slid to a stop on a small plateau near the top, parked beneath a sickly stand of aspen. He reached back and grabbed his old binoculars, then jumped off and hurried up the hill.

He dropped to his belly at the top and, using a bush as cover, snuck a look. "Fuck," he whispered. "Last thing I wanted to see out here."

Less than fifty meters away, just past the bottom of the hill, sat a sniffer, settled down in a low crouch on all six legs. In front of its battered metal and ceramic body was a large gash in the earth. A look with the binoculars confirmed what the sniffer was looking for; moisture was beginning to pool, flowing from the water table that Andy had been scouting.

He crawled backwards down the hill until he was sure he would be out of sight of the device, and then stood and skidded the rest of the way down to the quad. "Find a network yet?" he asked.

"Nothing," replied his machine. "What's over there?"

"A sniffer. It found the water."

There was a pause. Then, "That isn't good. Without a network we can't register this find. Anything on the side or top of the sniffer to tell you to whom it belongs?"

"I didn't stay around long enough to really look. Figured I'd come down first and see if there was a way we could beat it to the punch."

"Go back up and look, see if you can make out any markings on the side. Come back down and tell me what you see, and I'll cross-reference that and then we'll know what sort of chance we stand to save this claim."

Andy nodded, turned and ran back up the hill. The sniffer was still sitting in place, which might have been a good sign, but might not have been one as well. It could have been using this time to recharge some batteries, or it could have been in contact with its own network. If the second was true, then it had access to much better resources than Andy, and besides already registering this claim would be able to cause Andy no end of trouble if he tried anything.

Some of the ID on the side of the sniffer was illegible, scorched by previous blasts or worn away by time and weather. He was able to make out a string of six letters and numbers, though, as well as what looked like a faded picture of a star riding above what looked like a bear, only with something wrong with it.

He was about to sneak back down out of sight when a glint of sunlight in the distance caught his eye. Leaning back down on his elbows, he maxed out the mag on his binoculars and focused in on a giant gleaming silver snake, riding on large wheels and coming slowly his way.

"Oh, shit."

Back down the hill, then, faster than the last time. He almost fell as he tried to stop by the quad, but he managed to grab the bag rack on the back, almost ripping his arm out of its socket in the process.

"What is it?" asked the machine. "Why the rush?"

Andy climbed on and throttled the quad up, driving downhill as fast as he dared. He was too busy concentrating on not tumbling over that he didn't answer.

"My battery is only at twenty-five percent, Andy," warned the quad. "If you don't switch over to fuel soon, we won't be going anywhere and I won't even be around to talk to you."

"Whiner," said Andy. The quad was silent, likely pouting in response.

They finally came to a stop after climbing and descending one more hill. Andy got off the quad and paced for a moment before finally sitting on the ground in front of the machine.

"There's a pipeline coming. Maybe two klicks away at the outside."

"Already? There's something wrong with that sort of speed. What were you able to read on the side of the sniffer?"

"A bunch of the numbers or letters were pretty much erased. I was able to get 7Q6-CA-6, as well as a picture of a star sitting above a bear that looked like it had a tumor on its back."

"Ah," said the quad. "That certainly explains a lot, as well as opening up some new questions."

Looking up at where the sun had managed to crawl in the past ten minutes, Andy opened his pouch and pulled out a small pot of sunscreen and started smearing it on his face. "Tell me just what it explains," he said, wiping an extra-thick layer across his nose.

"American," answered the machine. "Judging by your description of the seal, I'd say the animal was probably a grizzly bear, so this would have come up from California."

Andy stopped, cocked an eyebrow back at the quad. "Grizzly bear? What the hell's that?" But before he could get an answer, another thought occurred to him. "And there's no fucking way that can be an American sniffer and pipeline! Shit, nobody even pays attention to where the border is anymore, but we sure as hell aren't so close that the two of those would crawl all this way for water! Especially from, from… " He snapped his fingers, trying to remember.

"California. And you're right, Andy, they wouldn't crawl all this way. Likely a pumping station has been set up, in Montana or in Idaho Free State to get it over the Rockies, or even on our side of the border."

"Well shit," whispered Andy. "Couldn't be our side. Enough gunfire over water rights on either side of the border without bringing it an international flavor."

"Most states are now cooperating, Andy," replied the quad. "It is equally difficult for all of them these days."

"Hmph. No network yet?"

"Nothing. I begin to wonder if any incoming signals are being deliberately blocked or scrambled."

Andy sat back down on the quad. "Why would that be?"

"It is a good chance they aren't allowed to be here. Unlikely that they have signed any sort of agreement with the feds, but that's the only way they should be allowed to get an extraction deal."

Andy laughed. "I don't see the feds sticking their noses in anything out here anymore."

"A signal, Andy! Wait one moment," said the quad. Andy stood silent, nervously rubbing his fingers on his palms while he waited.

"That wasn't the network. The pipeline is almost in place, and was broadcasting its claim. Says it has permission of the Blue Train to be here."

"Son of a bitch!" Andy kicked at a rock, sent it caroming off one of the quad's tires and into some squat bushes nearby. "Who the fuck do those provincial assholes think they are, giving permission for something like this? They pull up stakes and head out for no one knows the fuck where, and next thing you know they're cutting deals they aren't allowed to cut to give away our water. My water."

"The message repeated twice and then went dead. Still no access. I'm now fairly sure that I'm being blocked from getting at it."

"Fine." Andy started rummaging through the field equipment box that sat strapped to the back of the quad.

"What are you looking for?"

"Gonna take care of this myself," he answered. "I don't give a shit if it's the Blue Train or not, and I sure as hell don't care about the Americans." He pulled out three chunks of explosive and detonators, slipped them into two different vest pockets, then pulled his old rifle out of its holster and shouldered it.

"You can't be serious," said the quad. "You have no idea what will come down on your head if you get caught. When you get caught. At the very least, you lose any chance you have to claim this water."

"Doesn't matter. I want you to be ready to broadcast this location to the network as soon as that block is dropped. Tell everyone there's a new lake been found." He dug out an extra box of bullets, tucked it into a pants pocket.

"A lake? Andy, I don't know what you are talking about, but any call like that will bring in prospectors from miles and miles around. Probably bring in ordinary folk, too, if they're stupid enough to still be living out on the land." The machine paused for a second. "And it occurs to me that if the Blues signed a deal to give up water rights, they might be bold enough to sign a deal to try and circumvent fed jurisdiction with extradition."

"There you go with the feds again. Look, the Blues don't run this province anymore; they gave up that right when they packed up and headed out on that goddamn Train of theirs."

"But they are still the nominal power in these parts, since no one sees any sign of the feds at all these days. And back to the topic at hand, all American and former American states have the death penalty for anyone who sabotages their water supplies. The feds historically wouldn't ship anyone south if they face hanging or the firing squad, but based on philosophy the Blue Train may not feel so concerned for their own nominal citizens."

Andy shrugged. "Still my fucking water. If I'm going to give it up, everyone gets it. Took years of looking through charts and maps and infrareds we cheated from those birds in orbit to find a spot where the table had come back up. And I'm not gonna lose it to some mechanical pirates from another country."

The machine made a sound like a sigh. "Very well. You can't do this alone, then." A small dark green metal box spit out of the side of the quad and landed on the ground. "That's my beacon. I've tied it to a… " The machine paused, made a sound eerily like a shudder. "To a deadman's switch I've just programmed. I can set it off if need be, but if I become incapacitated while following you around like a fool, it will start to broadcast a signal. It gives the approximate coordinates for this magical new lake of yours."

"You don't have to do this, you know," Andy told the quad. "I'm sure I can figure out some way of getting to them."

"Unlikely. The sniffer won't be expecting anyone, but it also won't just let you walk up and attach some plastic explosives to it, and those bullets won't do anything but ricochet off its body and maybe bounce back to put a big ugly hole in you."

"So what do you propose?"

"Leave your gun. How steep do you think that hill is leading down to the sniffer?"

"Fairly steep. No way you can ride straight down there. You'd tip and roll, likely squash me flat."

"Exactly what I thought," said the quad. "But what if I went around the side of the hill with my engine roaring? Do you think you could do a decent tuck and roll?"

Andy scratched his beard, picturing the process. "Not too many trees in the way, or big rocks. It'll hurt, but I think I could do it without too much pain. But I'm gonna be dizzy as hell when I get to the bottom."

"Good point. I keep forgetting that the limits on humans just don't seem to end."

"But I see where you're going with this," said Andy, "and I think I see a way around it. Just trust me on it, and do your level best to divert the sniffer's attention. Give me thirty seconds after I wave at you from the top, all right? I don't know how well I can time this."

"Climb aboard then," replied the quad. "I'll take you to the bottom of the hill. But don't you start until you know I'm in place."

The quad brought him back to the hill, then headed off to the east, leaving Andy to lean hard and run up the slope as best as he could. Just short of the top he pulled out one chunk of explosive and inserted a detonator into it, held on to it tight. Then he double-checked his pocket to make sure that the remote for the detonator was still there.

Finally, he peeked over the edge and down the hill. The sniffer was still sitting in place, and the pipeline was now set up by the hole the sniffer had made. It was drilling deeper, braces having dropped down to keep its front wheels from moving anywhere. Already he could hear the motors as the powerful miniature pumps inside the pipeline started pulling the water up from underground.

He stood and waved to the quad, took a deep breath, then dove headfirst over the top of the hill, hanging tight to the explosives and the detonator. The first roll on the rocky soil knocked the breath right back out of him, a big whoosh of air that he could feel but not hear; the only sounds he could make out were the rustling of his clothes and the thumps and bumps and cracks as his body and head hit dirt and rocks and dried branches. He tried to keep his eyes closed, but they kept opening on their own, giving him a stomach-churning view of harsh blue sky swiftly followed by baked brown earth, and then repeated again and again.

And then he hit a bigger bump and went spinning into the air, rolled to a stop face up on the ground, hot sun trying to burn its way through his eyelids. He stayed still, feeling every muscle in his body trying to twitch, feeling the agony of the bruises, but thankfully not finding anything that felt like a broken bone.

Andy could hear the sniffer walking towards him now as he played dead, steady thumps reverberating through the ground and into his skull with background accompaniment from the pipeline as it pulled his precious water from the below. He had kept a tight grip on the explosive and the detonator, kept his fists closed as the American machine approached.

There was a loud roar off in the distance and then a shuffling as the sniffer shifted itself to view the quad. Andy opened his eyes and saw that it was turned the other way now, about three meters from him, and he rolled quickly to his knees and then jumped up, with two quick steps getting to the sniffer and slapping the explosive charge onto its body and then turning and running as fast as his dizzy state would allow.

One quick look behind showed that it had turned and was following him; too close to set off the charge, really, but if he waited any longer it would be closer still, or would catch him and then put in a call for help. He thumbed the trigger button.

There was a loud bang and then a sort of double-whumpf, and Andy was thrown to the ground. Something slammed into his back, once again knocking the wind out of him, and immediately after he felt something slice through his forearm. The heat on his back was fierce, even worse than the sun at noon.

Rolling onto his back, Andy held up his arm and had a look at the damage; nothing too serious, more of a scratch than anything, he decided. A small cloud of smoke hung in the still air and some of the scrub was on fire now, but the flames were small and already burning themselves down.

He sat up, put his hands to his ears to try and block out the ringing that started there, and watched as the quad rolled up to him. There were some muffled sounds coming from it, but nothing he could make out.

"Shit, I guess that thing still had some explosives inside it," he said. His voice sounded muffled, like he was talking with his mouth full of cloth.

More sounds from the quad. He waved his arms and shook his head, winced and put a hand to his forehead. "Can't hear a damn thing, quad. The explosion must've done something to my ears." He looked over to the pipeline, which appeared to be undamaged. "You getting through to the network now? Roll backwards a bit if yes." The machine rolled backwards. "Sending out the message I wanted you to?"

It stayed still.

Andy reached forward and grabbed a handlebar, pulled himself up and leaned heavily on the quad. "Well why the fuck not?" He yawned, felt a popping in his ears. "Sounds like… " He grinned. "Good. Hearing's coming back. Now, why the fuck not?"

"Climb on me and I'll show you," said the quad, still sounding distant.

"In a minute." Andy reached into his pocket, pulled out the other two chunks of explosive and detonators, and started running for the pipeline. He heard the quad rev up and start following him.

There was a good point about fifteen meters away from the snout and drill of the pipeline, sitting just back of another set of giant wheels. He got there and bent over, trying to catch his breath and feeling all of the new pains from the past few minutes. When he looked back up the quad was back beside him.

"I'm sending out the message now, but I'm not happy about it," it said. "You need to hurry and do this, though. I've got something to show you and then we have to get out of here."

"Right." Andy reached up, but the pipeline was still well beyond his hand. He tried jumping, but couldn't get much height with all of his muscle aches. He turned to the quad. "Come here, closer."

The machine moved to a place under the pipeline, and Andy climbed up and stood on the seat. Reaching high and standing on his toes, he was able to stick the charge to the battered gray metal pipe. He squatted down and grabbed the handlebar, told the quad to move another meter down the line, then he stood up and attached the other explosive, just in case. In the distance, the pipeline marched on through a gap in the low hills that surrounded them. A perfect place for a lake.

"Okay," he said, sitting down and grabbing a handle with one hand, pulling the detonator out of his pocket with the other. "Show me what you think I need to see, and let's get this done with."

The quad gunned its engine and they tore back up the hill Andy had just rolled down. Halfway up he yelled "Stop!" and then turned and pressed the button. Two simultaneous blasts pierced the air, chunks of metal flying high into the sky, and then a great gout of water began to spew forth from the pipeline, spilling out onto the parched earth. More water than Andy had ever seen, and all of it pouring free.

He tapped the side of the quad's fuel tank. "Show me."

The engine roared to life again, and soon they were at the top of the hill. Andy sat for a second, mouth hanging open, watching what approached from the west, and then dismounted and stood beside the quad.

"Haven't seen that in twenty years, maybe more." His voice was almost a whisper. "How long do you figure we have?"

"Less than an hour, I would guess. Can't outrun it, though. It got a fix on us as soon as I found my way back onto the network."

In the distance, towering above the tallest trees this parched land had to offer, the Blue Train was coming. Too distant to hear, its visage wavered in the hot air, a mirage one moment, more solid the next.

Andy shrugged, suddenly aware that the fight had finally left him. "We'll stay here, then. Wouldn't want to leave my lake without seeing how it turns out, anyway."

He sat painfully on the ground and leaned against a tire. Sometimes Andy would turn his head and watch as the Blue Train continued its approach, growing ever-larger and more foreboding by the minute, but more often he sat and watched the water pour forth, already a good-sized pond, arcing out and then splashing down from the wrecked pipeline like some mythical fountain, sunlight reflecting brilliantly off the water, mesmerizing in its unfamiliarity. Soil was stirring up underneath, giving most of the pond a dark and muddy look, but now Andy could see that in the center, at its deepest, it was starting to reflect the pure stark blue of the sky.

Eventually a deep rumble began to overtake the sound of the dancing waters, something Andy felt in his bones and teeth before he could really hear it, but becoming more audible with each moment. Finally he had no choice but to turn and watch the Blue Train, remembering that when it was present there was nothing that could overwhelm it.

There were eight cars now; the last time he'd seen it there were only five, rushing past in the distance and still large enough to blot out the mountains that had sat behind it. Twenty years ago it had still carried that new sheen, sparkling and shining in the harsh light of the day, metal gleaming in a way that was both uplifting and vaguely threatening.

Today there was nothing vague about the feeling. The Train was huge, menacing, almost angry-looking. Any polish it had once carried had been lost to the elements and the years, and now, even from this distance Andy could see the rust and grease and soot that pockmarked its surface, the rusted-out holes that ran along the bottom.

"It looks nothing like the pictures I see over the network," said the quad.

Andy shook his head, trying to force away the fear he felt in the pit of his stomach. "I guess we all change, don't we? Maybe not on the inside, but sure as hell do on the outside."

The Train began to slow down now, hissing and screeching with angry blasts of steam as it broke its way through small stands of quivering aspen and dipped and rose over smaller hills. Dry earth split and cracked beneath its wheels, small boulders shattered under its weight, and as it finally came to a complete stop a blast of extra-hot air sent a wave of dry soil across Andy and the quad. It shuddered and roared for a few seconds, and then with one last string of noisy farts, the engine fell silent.

For minutes the only sounds were the gurgling of the slowly growing lake and the squeaks, moans and hisses of the Blue Train as it settled. Andy just sat on the ground, watching and waiting, wiping grit from his eyes, nervously drumming his fingers and chewing on his lip.

Although the Train had come to rest at the bottom of the hill where Andy was, its peak was almost equal to that of the hill. The engine was larger than the other cars, over eighty meters long, and its wheels, dozens of them, each stood three times his height. Every wheel had a flaw of some sort, and some were so badly worn down that they didn't even touch down to the ground, were held up by the others to spin fruitlessly in the air. Deadfall stuck out at odd angles from various holes, and there was even the rotting corpse of a deer impaled on a stray piece of rusting metal.

The car behind the engine was only a bit smaller, dozens of rows of windows reaching from bottom to top. From some windows Andy could see faces peering briefly out before hiding back in the shadows, the mysteries of their lives and tasks intact for the moment.

A loud squeal interrupted the silence, and a door opened at the bottom of the first car, metal grinding against metal. Two men, tiny figures dwarfed by the Train, jumped to the ground and then pulled out two slats of rust and white metal, laid them down to be a ramp. There was an echoing growl from inside the car, and then a real automobile exited from the darkness, descended to the ground and started up the hill.

"What is it?" asked Andy.

"A Jeep," answered the quad.

Andy stood and held his hand over his eyes to keep the sun out. A real Jeep, driving up the hill toward him. Two miracles in one day. He looked down at the quad, wondering if he should try to make a break for it now, knowing as the thought touched his mind that he wouldn't get halfway down the hill. He steeled himself and continued to watch its approach.

The driver gave the accelerator an extra touch as it crested the hill, and then spun the wheel and brought the jeep to rest beside them. Two men carrying guns immediately jumped out, muzzles pointing at the ground but with their threat clearly implied. Then the driver also climbed out, running around to the other side and opening the door for his last passenger, standing back as that man stepped to the ground.

The first three men were all dressed in gray and brown camo, but this last man wore the uniform of the Blues, gray pants with only one or two small patches, a similar jacket, a light blue shirt and a red tie. His hair was also gray, perfectly combed, and he was freshly shaved. His teeth were white and even; his smile never wavered, seemed to be pasted on his face. For a few seconds he stood and watched the lake, then turned and looked at Andy. "It is a beautiful sight, isn't it?"

Andy blinked. He hadn't expected polite conversation, even if this man was a politician. "The lake? Yeah, it is. Never seen anything like it."

The Blue seemed to find this amusing. His smile grew even more, and he glanced back at his driver and the two men with guns, who also smiled. "Then perhaps you should find your way further north some day. There are still some small streams there, and even ponds that have not gone stagnant. And yes, a nice lake or two."

Andy shrugged. "I've heard stories. I'm also told that high in the mountains there are still some crystal-clear lakes and streams, and even some animals to be found. Not as if that does either of us any good."

"Yes. Sadly, the Train won't let us take our government into the mountains," said the Blue. "Too big. Pacifica claims that land now, you know, and holds back what water they can."

"Then why give this water up to the Americans? If you can't get any of that water that used to belong to us, then why not take advantage of the water that we do find here?"

"Oh, we wrote off this area long ago. Most of the south. Since the Exodus boarded the Train we've concentrated on our resources north of the Dry Zone."

"You've given over the south half of the province," said the quad.

The Blue's smile faltered for a fraction of a second, but a blink of his eyes seemed to reset it. "Ah, his machine speaks. I keep forgetting that before the Train departed we still allowed intelligent machines." He looked back to Andy. "Your device is correct. We have ceded territory over to our friends to the south, in exchange for some future, ah, considerations." He smiled, as if at a secret joke. "So now we will wait until our friends can muster a replacement pipeline, as well as officers to take you south for your trial and likely execution. I think we will have plenty of room on a lower level of a rear car, and I'm sure that your ATV will have parts we can use."

"You have no jurisdiction," replied the quad.

Now the man frowned. "I didn't come here to argue with a machine," he said. "The feds have no business here anymore, no longer even poke their heads west of Lake Winnipeg. And as the Deputy Minister of External Affairs, it is my job to make sure things run smoothly between those of us on the Train and those governments outside that we still have dealings with."

There was a buzzing sound then, a droning that started at a higher pitch and got lower as it became louder. With a sudden screaming roar two more quads jumped over the far edge of the hill, they and their riders coming to a stop behind Andy.

"Son of a bitch," whispered one, pulling his goggles off. His eyes were tearing up. "It really is a lake."

His companion was grinning wildly. "And the Blue Train, too. Almost two miracles in one spot. Like maybe a whole new life is gonna start, right here."

The Blue looked panicked by this suggestion. He lifted his arms to wave off the thought, but then there were more distant engine sounds, coming from all directions. Andy turned in a circle, counted at least a dozen quads riding over distant hills on their way. "The network tells me at least three hundred patched into our announcement, Andy," said his quad. "Some of them are two or three days away, but they're all headed here."

Andy looked at the two newcomers; he didn't recognize either one, but there had always been too many prospectors. He reached down and picked up a couple of large rocks and dropped them into a saddlebag, then sat on the quad, smiling. "Well?" he said to the two of them. "What are we waiting for? Let's send out a few invitations."

The quad gunned its engine and jumped around the Jeep before the Blue could order his men to do anything, the other two following close behind. They raced down the hill, whooping and hollering. By the time they were at the bottom, water was coming through a small notch between two hills, spilling out and pooling underneath the wheels of the second Train car. A new stream beginning its life here, not letting anything get in its way.

Andy grabbed one of the rocks, flung it high and watched it bounce off a window of the first car. Faces started to appear, and some doors opened a crack. "A lake!" he screamed. The other two joined the chorus. "Water! Here for all of us!"

They splashed across the stream, and he hurled the second rock high, yelled more of the same. Now people were coming out, a few wearing Blue uniforms, but most just dressed as ordinary citizens. Some, judging by their age, who had maybe never been out of the Blue Train in their entire lives. At first they were silent as they stepped out, speechless at a sight many of them had only ever heard about. But then, almost as one, they were all yelling, some crying tears of joy, and right away more took over from Andy and the others, beseeching their fellow residents to come out.

Andy stopped the quad and watched as they splashed through the stream, mothers dipping infants into the flowing water, children kicking and splashing, one man in uniform even stripping off his coat and tie and rolling in it. More quads arrived, adding their steady buzz to the cacophony of joyful shouts and laughter, hundreds of people all out and together, under the burning sun, in one spot and sharing a purpose.

Andy gunned the quad, steered past a knot of old women who were crying and hugging each other, raced back up the hill to where the Blue stood by his Jeep. The driver and gunmen were no longer there. He looked down the hill, saw that some people were now making their way upstream, and finding the amazing source of the water.

"You can still lock me away," he said, "and get all those people back in the Train to go find some ponds that aren't too stagnant. But it will have to wait a little while." He patted the quad. "Keep broadcasting."

"Oh, I am," said the machine. "So are a few of the others, including two that still have working network cameras. We're causing quite the sensation."

"Good to know." Andy jumped from the quad and ran back down the hill, this time making sure he didn't lose his balance until he was right at the edge of the water. He knew before he got wet that nothing would ever feel this good again.

Natural Disaster

Jill Boettger

In a small farming community off the Highway 22 there is a well, and by the well there is a tornado spinning dirt, gravel and rodents. There is a man with a broken heart walking down the road from a farmhouse. He has left the woman he loves, and left the farmhouse his father owns. He wraps his heart in cold bandages, and consoles it in the voice of Tom Waits. He is distracted by the messy package of bandage and blood, and walks right into the tornado. He dodges the whipping grass and the windswept animals. All around him things fall apart - the dilapidated neighboring barn, massive stacks of manure, hay bales, fences, a tractor plow and crusted treads, and the man, miraculously, is not harmed. He is young, he has no plans, and no explanation for the heart in his hands. The wind blows dirt in his nose and grass in his ears, and the man continues down the road. He carries several women in his back pocket to replenish his heart with love, never mind that's not what they're serving. Women = Love. This is the broken-hearted man's equation.

°°°   °°°   °°°

There is a man who lives down the road from the man with the messy heart-package. This man lives in a small cabin he built himself almost thirty years ago, in the company of wind and dust. He understands that the equation Women = Love is false. He has lived hard enough to know better. He smuggled women in the early years, paid attention, and learned that Women = Tenderness. He used the tenderness until the women grew sore and tired, and then he released them. He canceled his phone, built a barn, and started painting. He painted pictures of the long lost women in brilliant colours and covered the enormous walls of his barn. Occasionally, he thought about the tenderness, wondered what else the women were good for. He kept his thoughts to himself. When the tornado came it destroyed his barn—stripping paint and splintering colourful acrylic bodies—and left the man alone.

°°°   °°°   °°°

When the women were released, so many years ago, from the man with the cabin, the wind found them traveling in a shriveled group on a small road into Sundre. They were skinny and bruised and spoke a language the wind didn't understand. The wind blew seeds and blew questions into their dry ears, pressed them for stories as they traveled, pressed them for a laugh. The women ignored the wind. The wind blew harder. The women slid their skinny bodies into the abandoned tunnels of prairie dogs. They held each others' hands, they spoke softly. Today, their skeletons remain in a huddle underground, hand bones clutched like tiny cages. Today, they are joined by more back pocket refugees: women who've escaped the loveless grip of the man of the road. It happens this way every year: women leave farmers and oilers, and visit the accidental grave for restoration. They chew grain and sip from the well, they soften their nails with mud, and their hair grows long past their shoulders, draping their original, dark bodies. They give birth in the prairie tunnels to tiny girls who understand everything from the beginning: there is no equation. Their lives are for the highest beauty. In the fall, the new girls braid the dead roots of trees, and moisten the braids with their saliva. In the winter, they carve kaleidoscopes from icicles suspended in the tunnels. In the spring, they surface to join the trespasses of the wind— crossing fences and invisible boundaries. They visit the lonely men, they visit the heartbroken men, and leave traces of their beauty behind: fingerprints and a strand of hair, a leaf of grass.

RIVERBOY

A.M. Dellamonica

Midway through summer vacation, Michael runs afoul of Barry Sandler and his cronies, who take him to the old Creek Campground, peel off his clothes and toss him out of the car. Idiotic way to express homophobia, but is Michael going to antagonize them by saying so? Not when he's twenty miles from town with road rash on his ass.

He does risk a beating for the sake of his feet, wrestling with Ken Zandrachuk to get his shoes back. His former friend broke a finger last winter playing basketball; now Michael lunges into the car window and yanks the digit back. Ken loses one sneaker, and the connection between them breaks with an elastic snap. Michael falls back, panting as the car pulls away.

It is July, a night with searing, breezeless air like the inside of a crematorium. A delicious sense of tension hums between land and sky, electric and ruthless.

But this is no time to sit around composing odes to the coming storm. Michael slides the lone rescued shoe onto his left foot and tracks a quiet splash, looking for Petal Creek. In town, the creek is almost wide enough to deserve the name, a shallow green-gray band of water which is Rosen's big claim to scenery. Out here it is so narrow he could miss it in the dark as it dribbles through countless sloughs and ponds, providing nesting turf for ducks, and watering the small cottonwoods on its banks.

There—moonlight mirrors from shivered water and he sees a muskrat watching him. Michael kicks pebbles and it backs away, rolling its slick wet shoulders.

"You could've helped." He speaks not to the animal but the presence which sent it. "Hello? Gonna get me out of this?"

Blank stare from the wildlife. It roots in the wet bank of the stream, digging up a crocus bulb. Taking dainty bites, it watches him carefully. No rescue, then.

"Great. Screw you." Just then he spots the trail—a band of flattened grass winding east between shadowy bushes—and starts marching grimly in the direction of town. Maybe he can make it home before it gets light.

He gives himself a sideache hiking the trail, his gait a stride-hop-stride to protect his bare foot. A crop of blisters comes in on the left ankle, and mosquitoes make dive-runs on his stomach and dick. As he plods onward the sky blackens, the air cooling slightly, thickening like soup. He wonders how Cinderella felt, walking home from the ball with a pumpkin under one arm and a slipper missing. Did she break down and cry? Or was she angry? Then he hears the whizz of bicycle tires.

A glance confirms there's nowhere to hide: the trail is lined in thistle and wild rose. Covering his groin with both hands, Michael edges as close to the thorns as he dares. A lance of light cuts through the creekside foliage; then the bike rounds the curve. He's caught in the beam just long enough to give the rider a good look.

One look is enough: the shadowy figure skids out. The headlight bobbles and the bike skates to the edge of the creek. The cyclist's bark of alarm is deep-voiced, male.

Thank God, he thinks. Not a woman: maybe the town won't label him a pervert. Then he recognizes the cyclist, and his heart lurches. It's Will.

Dale Willer is a rookie music teacher from out East, barely older than his grade twelve students and crush-inducingly gorgeous. Strip the man's shirt, shove a baby in his arms and take a black and white photo: you could sell it poster-sized to every fag in the world. The girls at school have a pool going to see who will marry him one day. Michael has never encountered this before: in his experience, teaching aptitude and great looks come from mutually antagonistic ends of the gene pool.

As if that isn't enough, the man is dedicated, directing a concert band, jazz band, choir, and two string quartets. Michael is his star pupil, playing sax in everything but the quartets.

Tonight Will is in civvies—jeans, a tank top, and a long flannel overshirt which is caught in the rosebush. Even wiped out and surprised, dark hair curls over his forehead like he's been touched up by a band of vigilante stylists. He gapes at Michael, who is wishing the creek was the kind of raging torrent a humiliated teen could fling himself into, with fatal results and a decent chance they'd never find the body.

"I'm training for the nude triathlon," he says finally. "Hiking, bare-hand fishing and bobbing for apples."

His words break the spell—Will untangles himself from the bicycle. The brambles surprise Michael by stretching and then pulling free of the overshirt. Squinting, he peers into the trees, finding nothing but shadows.

Luckily, Will is too flustered by his near-miss with a naked student to notice trivialities like moving foliage. He takes the shirt off—an image from Michael's daydreams—and, averting his eyes, extends it on the ends of his fingers.

"Thanks." He ties it around his hips, loincloth style. Now maybe he can look his teacher in the eye.

But Will is messing with his bike chain. "Barry Sandler do this, Mike?"

He shrugs. "Didn't see."

"Lucky for him." The words are dry, but mercifully Will doesn't try to press the issue. Pushing the bike, he turns back toward town. Michael shuffles to catch up.

"I, uh… hope you didn't hurt yourself when you fell."

"No, I'm good."

The trail curves away from the trees, meeting up with a narrow gravel road sliced between high fields of canola. The creek follows the ditch on one side of the road; the other side is grassy and smells of horse manure. Rocks bite into the ball of his bare foot, making his hopalong gait downright springy.

A gopher waits at the roadside, black eyes wide and watchful, as they emerge from the trees. Michael scowls at the thing, and this time Will catches him.

"Pests," Michael grunts. That's all you have to say about gophers in Rosen. The small ground squirrels inspire plenty of gunfire, but not much in the way of deep thought.

"You're too big for him to eat."

"Give it time." He slaps a mosquito. "They're whittling me down."

"There's another gopher up there," Will says, pointing. "Funny. I didn't think they were nocturnal."

There's lots you don't know, Michael thinks. Welcome to Rosen, population four thousand. Due to a high rate of mystic activity, swimming and fishing in the creek are prohibited.   "Maybe they're following your example."

"Pardon?"

"It's kind of late for a bike ride."

"I had some energy to burn." Will gives him a knee-melting grin. "Couldn't sleep."

"Way out here?"

"I live at old Grayler farm. It's only a couple miles."

"Oh. But isn't it… " Suddenly agony shrieks upward from the arch of Michael's bare foot, so intense that his knee buckles and he hits the road on all fours. Pain-blind, he rolls sideways, driving blunt rocks into the flesh of his thigh. His hands, flying to the injury, connect with metal, a short, nasty scrap of barbed wire. Distressingly hot blood spills over his fingers as he gropes, finding one barb buried deep in the curve behind his big toe. He gives it a tentative pull, hoping it will slide free, and the answering flare of pain burns to the top of his sinuses.

"Fuck!" Now he's crying and angry. Far-off thunder cracks as he pinches the wire between his fingers and thumb, giving a hard yank. It comes loose, tearing as it bounces to the creek bank, and he curses in fury, both hands clapped around the gash.

Will has turned on his bike light, providing a maddening view of the damage. Red wetness covers his hands and foot in sticky patches. The edges of the cut are crusted with road dirt, and the wire glints rustily.

At the edge of the circle of light another gopher is watching, as inconspicuous as a drug addict hailing his dealer.

Closing his eyes, Michael fights for self control.

"What a mess. You okay, Mike?"

"Fucking Barry." He wipes the tears away. "I'm realizing anew why so many Alberta-born queers curl for Vancouver teams."

"Turn him in."

"I'm not photogenic enough to be the Tolerance Poster Boy." Deep breath—then he lifts his bare thigh off the gravel, balancing on his good leg and both arms. Maybe he'll get lucky now, and Prince Charming here will peel his tank top off to make a field bandage.

Happy thought. Too bad the prince is in the grip of social conscience. "People have to pay for these stunts, Mike. If they're made to learn… "

"Barry's graduated. He's gonna go to university and make some nice fraternity very happy."

"They have gays on campus too, Mike."

"I'll worry about that if I survive grade twelve."

"If you stop him… "

But by now Michael is safely inside his calm again. "There's always another Barry."

The luscious mouth tightens, almost pouting. "You can't walk any further like that. I'll bike back for the car, okay?"

"Okay. Thanks." Will slings a leg over the bike and pedals once, carrying himself ten feet. Then he pauses, looking back with a puzzled expression before finally cycling away.

Overhead, the stars are bright and white overhead, the moon huge and pale. There's so much light he can see colors: bright green shoots of canola, red-brown patches of blood on his skin. He relaxes onto a clean patch of long grass and foxtails in the ditch. The gopher is still watching.

"Roadkill munching little prick— " he tosses a pebble at it. "Why am I out here?"

It cheeps once, vibrating with nervous energy while the dense pre-storm air hazes with a sense of expectation. Then he hears a low scratching across the road.

Levering himself up, Michael sees the scrap of barbed wire, twisting and curling like an earthworm at the edge of the creek. "Oh… another stupid magic trinket, maybe? As they say in French class, quelle surprise."

He crab-walks on three limbs across the road. Maybe this will be all right. His first find was a flat piece of willow that he uses as a saxophone reed; it brought his music alive, taught him grace and breathing and tone, made him the town prodigy. That had worked out all right; this could too.

Sure. He looks at the sharp barbs waving blindly in the moonlight and tries not to reckon the odds. His second find…

A rush of air above Michael's face heralds trouble—he drops to the gravel, flat on his back as a brown form dives over him. A near miss. Stiff tailfeathers graze his chest.

The owl's flight path curves low, so that it seems to skid through the air horizontally, inches above the road. The gopher tries to run, but there is a soft impact. The bird arcs skyward, the gopher in its talons struggling weakly, dust and drops of blood leaking down through the moonbeams. Then, with a random twist, it gets loose. Falling back to the gravel, it tries to drag itself to cover.

Unexpectedly, his throat burns. That's how it always goes, isn't it? Always another victim.

The surface of Petal Creek is disappointingly rippled, just plain water where he was hoping to see a face. "You're shy tonight," he says. No answer— with the gopher immersed in its own misery, Michael feels completely abandoned.

Pinching up the wire gingerly, Michael feels it twisting in his grip. The loose ends bend and twine gently around Michael's index finger, nestling the juncture of the barbs harmlessly against the web of his thumb. He closes the hand slowly into a fist; the points do not break the skin. Two sharp tines protrude between his index and middle fingers while the others poke out alongside his thumb.

Something happens to his hearing then, tuning him to a faint hint of choir music emanating from below. Wordless harmony vibrates the ground—violins, piano, and bells, vaguely distorted and far away. The murmur of Petal Creek takes on a percussive rhythm; the rub of grass on grass is like brushed cymbals. A discordant whisper of feathers through air reaches him just in time.

"Go away!"

The owl misses the injured gopher and rises a few feet, violent booms of timpani in its beating wings. Michael can smell the blood on its talons.

He rolls to the creek, flinging a handful of rocks which manage to make it angry. Mid-air, it pivots, eyes flat with menace, coming for him claws first. Michael curls an arm over his eyes and sticks the other one out defensively, too scared to put thought together, to do something useful. Cold feathers make first contact with his outstretched hand. He shrieks.

The owl cries out too, a brief note of inhuman whistling pain. Then it is gone. The wingbeats are silenced, and something heavy tumbles into the grass across the creek.

Shaking, Michael uncovers his face. The bird is under one of the cottonwoods, mauled in a bright silvery strand of barbed wire. Its feathered breast is a bloody rag.

He stares at the loop around his finger. Was it fear that set the thing off, or being attacked? He is about to pull it off his finger when a far-off hum makes him glance up. More owls are above, circling and rustling. His eyesight is so keen he can pick them out, great horned, barn and snowy owls.

He gapes at them, mystified. He had thought of the animals as one collective entity, the eyes and ears of a single sentient force. Now, he watches the gopher drag itself into a sheltering burrow, and wonders if he had it right.

Enlightenment doesn't come. Will does, though, driving a pitiful orange Toyota and brandishing Bermuda shorts. Michael maneuvers into them, hissing with relief as the thin fabric covers his genitals. Hobbling out of the glare of the car lights, he unwinds his makeshift loincloth, making it a shirt again and slipping it on. Then he hops to the passenger door, struggling to open it without displaying his wire-bound finger.

Fighting his gearshift, Will drives in the direction of Rosen as a sliver of searing egg-yolk sunshine appears at the far edge of the world. Brilliant pink light streaks the bottoms of the thunderheads growing on the horizon.

To Michael's right, the line of canola suddenly drops and disappears, giving way to uncultivated terrain. Short grass and dandelions flow towards a white house with a brick chimney. The music is louder here, but the song comes from another melody—brisk string instruments, booming hostile bass. Spiderwebs hang from all the gaps in the fence, heavy with tiny bugs. The splattered remains of a field mouse lie in the drive.

Despite the renewed heat of the morning, the chimney of the house belches smoke. Gray shadows and shapes swirl around the house—serpentine ribbons, sails without sailboats, floral explosions like muted, silent fireworks. Miraculous, but Michael's first reaction is horror. He has never seen the prairie dish up its wonder so openly. There's no way Will won't notice this.

Sure enough, the car slows and stops.

"You gotta be wondering… " Then he reads identical fear on Will's face. Michael bites his lip. "This is your place, huh?"

The teacher nods. Shadows twist and caper as they stare at each other, and eventually Michael's surprise ebbs, leaving a strand of hope. Maybe they can share the burden. A co-conspirator would be nice.

"You hungry, Mike? Breakfast and pow wow, what do you say?"

"I say fine." He can smell coffee from here, fresh and acrid. The Toyota proceeds up the drive while vibrations of bass notes hum through the car floor. Past the barn, two coyotes lurk near the raised spray of a gopher hole.

Will supports him as he limps up the farmhouse steps. This is something he never thought to daydream: close but impersonal contact, the press of hard muscles through the thin tank top, body heat and the sweet yeasty smell of the other man's perspiration. He is aroused and flustered when they reach the kitchen and he can fall into a chair.

"Be right back," Will says, disappearing down the hall.

Michael spreads out his hand, dismayed to see that the wire is embedding itself in his finger, squeezing grooves into the flesh. No fears about the owls here—he digs in with his nails, forcibly extracting it. There is no pain. The skin is dusted rust-red, but does not bleed. Avoiding the barbs, he deposits it in the pocket of the shorts. It twists against his leg as his eyesight and hearing dim. Outside, a smoke butterfly flits against the window, leaving a sooty, insect-shaped smudge.

He frowns. "Are you doing something to encourage them?"

"They like music," Will's voice rumbles from the depths of the house. "Souza and Wagner. I play for them at night."

"You could mess up some kind of balance."

"Or restore a better one, Mike."

"They're scary enough as it is."

Will reappears in a baggy t-shirt, which is simultaneously a disappointment and a relief. He has a bag of frozen bread in one hand and a photo album tucked under one arm. Throwing two slices into a toaster, he pulls up a chair. "I thought I was the only one who knew. Is it just you and me?"

Co-conspirators. Michael takes an almost guilty pleasure in answering. "Mostly people are clueless. But Livia Redwing told me once there are chantments in the creek."

"Enchantments?"

"Chantments. She said the first explorers brought men with them who killed off the land's medicine."

"Meaning its magic?"

"I guess. Anyway, people hid the medicine in reservoirs and in objects called chantments. They're like cosmic piggy-banks."

"But they do things, Mike."

Which implies that Will has at least one, Michael thinks. Wonder if he wants another?

"Stored magic," Will murmured. "She know where they are?"

"She's dead now." He remembers Livia, ancient and cryptic, hinting secrets and making animals from pipe cleaners and twist ties. Wires. She had hinted she knew how to make chantments. Is the barbed wire one of hers?

"How about you, Mike? You know where to find them?

"No." The wire contorts in his pocket, a sharp barb poking through thin cotton to scratch at his thigh.

"We'll have to track them down." Will opens the album to a collection of photographs, all portraits, of a gangling, nerdy youth. His features are distantly familiar. "They can do anything."

"It's not that simple—" Then Michael touches the album as realization dawns. "These are you?"

It's Will's turn to look embarrassed. "Not long after I moved here, I woke up feeling this... compulsion, I guess... to clear a bunch of brush that had blocked the stream behind the barn. It was spring. The water was ice-cold and I got soaked fast. Tugging on logs damn near ripped my arms out. I was going to give up when I saw a fox trapped in the dam. Barely had its nose above water. So I got it loose, it jumped out of the water and ran. Later... "

"You thought you saw a boy in the water," Michael says wearily. "You thought he asked your fondest dream."

Will pauses, jolted out of his rhythm. "It was a woman. A woman made of smoke."

"But she asked you?"

"I thought I was running a fever. Hallucinating. But... I'd grown up believing I was conspicuously funny-looking. I don't know why, just one of those weird ideas kids get. Anyway... " His hand rises to brush his chin. "She helped me find an old razor, said to shave with it. Pretty soon I looked like this."

"You're not going to say you're bitter." He can't help the jealousy. Newcomer gets movie star facelift. Old faithful Michael gets barbed wire in the foot.

"No," he shrugs ruefully. "I suppose that seems shallow."

"No." No more than getting kudos for being more musically gifted than I really am, he thinks. He tries to untangle the barbed wire from his pocket but gophers whistle outside, alarmed. "What did you tell your folks about the new look?"

No answer.

"You feel like you can't go home, right? Listen, Will. Chantments change you. They make you more like them. The riverboy and the smoke woman."

"You'd rather be like everyone else?" Mild tone of voice.

"Me? I'm all herd instinct and no herd. I'd love to be like everyone else." Michael stares at the table, stirring his cooling coffee. The whole night lands on him like Barry on a rampage. Energy drains from his muscles and he's left feeling weepy, with nothing but caffeinated strain to hold him up.

"I guess two doesn't make much of a herd," Will says. "But we can help each other, Mike. I had a feeling that someone was in trouble on the trail tonight. That's why I was there."

"Believe me, I don't want to seem ungrateful. But a big chantment hunt is not a good idea."

"We'll talk it through. I'm not an idiot, Mike. You've been here longer than I have. I respect your experience."

"Yeah?"

"Absolutely. What do you say? Herd of two?"

"Herd of two," he echoes, tasting it. Sharing a secret with Rosen's most eligible bachelor. They shake hands, making him flustered and tongue-tied.

"Now—am I taking you home? Or the clinic?"

"Clinic," he says. Stitches. Tetanus shot. Then explain his disappearance to the parents. It won't be the first time, he thinks, as they hobble back to the Toyota.

A mile or so down the road, they come upon Barry's car.

Michael tenses, but the car is parked—not crashed, not burned, not wrapped in barbed wire. Its motor is running and its windows are shut.

Will pulls over. "Perks, Mikey."

Michael hops to the car. Barry and his merry men are passed out inside, snoring. Their lips are dry and cracked, their cheeks red, their chins stubbly. They don't look innocent, the way some people do when they're sleeping. They look spoiled.

"They drove out here looking for you, Mike. Probably expected you'd hike to the highway when they dumped you."

"Hitchhike home naked? No chance."

"What do you think they'd have done when they caught up? Give back your clothes? Apologize?"

"Don't." Struggling for calm, his fists clench all on their own. "This isn't helping."

"It's not enough they leave you to walk home bare-assed. They came back for a second go-round."

"So they're idiots. It's nothing."

"You found a chantment tonight, didn't you?" Seductive musical voice, inviting him to violence. "Use it—teach them."

"They're helpless," he says, drawing in molten air.

"That wouldn't stop them."

"Or you?" With that, his temper finally breaks. Hot wind ruffles his hair and warm raindrops patter the dust. Clouds roll overhead, towering and black. He could bring down hail, pulverize the cars. Fry them with lightning, burn them. And for a moment, he almost wants to. Will's never going to get it, he thinks. I'm still alone.

Rain sluices through his hair and down his face. Tiny rivulets flow into the torn flesh of his foot. The violent atmosphere struggles against the constraint of his will.

You can have anything. The whisper is faint and female, not the boy's voice he remembers from the day he found his saxophone reed. Eyes form, briefly, in the smoke from Will's car exhaust. You can be anything you want.

Like a small-town despot with a cover boy face? No chance.

Opening the door, Michael retrieves his clothes from the back seat and shuts down the engine. Then he lifts Barry's hand, tucking it deep into Ken's shorts. He turns their heads so they are nose to nose, kissing close.

They'll have a heart attack when they wake up.

He allows himself one long glance at Ken, until thunder rumbles at the edge of his control and he has to turn away.

Will is jubilant. "What did I tell you?"

"This isn't new," Michael sighs. "When I was ten I rescued a rabbit from someone's burn pile, and I saw the boy in Petal Creek. Your dearest wish, he offered. I asked to make a thunderstorm. Just one. It had been hot, and I love rain."

"And now you can have storms whenever you want."

"Whenever I want, yeah." He doesn't share the details, doesn't say the boy gave him a robin's egg and the egg summoned the storm. When the Creek flooded, Michael crushed the thing out of terror and remorse, and tawny gold magic had oozed out of the chantment like blood, infecting him with something unstable and dangerous. "Storms come when I have nightmares. I barbecued a dog once for scaring me. I told Ken I'm gay last October. We were friends, remember?"

"And then lightning burned his house down," Will says. Incredibly, he smiles. Michael feels tears threaten and fights back the thunder.

"Eight years of friendship and he blows me off like I'm nothing. I couldn't get past it. So the house burns…"

"He paid. He paid, Mike."

"Him and his family. And you'll notice he took the lesson to heart." Wishing he could make it home on his own steam, Michael hops back, collapsing in the passenger seat of the Toyota. He leans across to honk the horn until he sees Ken stir. "Will. Were you really on the Creek trail looking for me?"

The gorgeous eyes narrow.

"Or were you looking for the piggy banks?"

Will yanks the gearshift and the car jerks back into motion. Tires purr as they roll away towards town. "I said I'd listen to your point of view."

"You don't want a herd, you want a hunting partner," Michael says. "I can't do that. Sorry."

The look the teacher gives him then is full of menace, like the low brass and strings in a symphony. A hunter's face. "You can't stop me from looking, Mike."

"I wouldn't try."

"So at least you'll stay out of my way?"

"Me?" Michael says. "You never know where I'll pop up."

Will wrenches the car off the gravel road and onto the highway, with its black surface and neat yellow lines. As he accelerates a gopher darts into the ditch, just dodging a quick and grisly death. Ten miles up, Michael can see Rosen, a small circle of buildings bisected by the creek, lights twinkling in the last dimness of night.

"You've still got a year in my school, Mike."

He burps laughter. "And you'll what? Make my life hell? Better install some lightning rods."

Will's face goes fury-white, and Michael slips his hand into the pocket of the Bermuda shorts. With Will on the search, the scrap is too dangerous to hide or throw away. He'll have to learn how it works and what to do with it. Another chip of his humanity gone, maybe. Just something else to accept, like losing Ken. Like solitude.

The barbed wire settles around his finger with a silent scrape of metal over metal and Michael's view of town sharpens. Streetlights blink out, block by block, and he hears the music again, voices of grain and roadside poppies crooning high, cheerful notes. Sunlight makes a golden ribbon of the creek and he catches a glimpse of the riverboy in a pocket of rising mist, pacing the car's journey to Rosen. Making sure I'm okay, Michael thinks. Watching over.

And maybe that shouldn't be comforting, but he leans into the vinyl seat anyway, closing his eyes and letting the hum of the tires soothe him into a doze.

Afterword

FAREWELL TO THE LITERATURE OF IDEAS

The prairies: where you can sit on the porch and watch your dog run away — for three days. There's one old hound that I've been watching recede for some time, and I recently realised that it has finally vanished over my mental horizon, that being the old dog about how SF (speculative fiction, science fiction, whatever) is "the literature of ideas". That puppy is gone.

I never completely believed in the literature-of-ideas defence anyway. The idea that character, language, literary values didn't matter because SF was about ideas never seemed true. It wasn't true to the kind of writing I was doing, and increasingly, as I applied it to the writing of others that I admired, it seemed to be misused often to self-justify those works that were not only badly written, but had badly thought-out ideas. The writers whose ideas had the elegance of perfect virtue tended to work harder and harder to express these ideas as elegantly as they had been conceived.

What I find, however, is that speculative writing more often than not, ideas notwithstanding, is instead a literature of affect. It is a literature of place, of feeling, of personality, of reaction, of effect, of emotional impact. It is, in fact, some of the most emotional literature in existence.

I'm using "SF" in this context as a short form of the wider term "speculative fiction" because I believe that much literature of the fantastic, whether that fantastic is high-tech or magical in nature, shares many of the same tenets — and passions.

SF believes passionately in affect. SF believes that humans (and other beings who often stand in allegorically for humans) are intensely affected: by setting, by culture (originally in the form of technology, but now also social, political and personal cultures), by the action of individuals and groups.

Even the early North American pulp literature with its awkward fledgling writers learning their trade at a penny a word was fueled by passion — for technology, for the human spirit, for a future, for the future, whatever that might be, for a profusion of futures. Speculative writers of all stripes reinforce and extend these passions to include a passion for justice, for mercy, for survival, for healing, for growth, for change, and for love.

SF believes passionately in the power of human achievement. Technological accomplishment is at the core of science fiction, while the ability of sapient beings to transform their worlds is common to both science fiction and fantasy. The quality of the transformation determines the degree to which the resulting narrative is utopian or dystopian in nature, but even in a dystopian narrative, the effect the writer hopes to have is to warn of errors, suggest solutions and approaches, and in all ways influence the outcome as much as might the actual change agent. Can the mistakes of previous generations of scientists and technophiles be corrected or avoided, can technology heal the ills of societies and individuals without causing greater ills, can science advance causes like freedom from famine or oppression, can it bring justice and fairness with its progress? Arthur C. Clarke famously remarked that any sufficiently advanced technology is indistinguishable from magic, and so even hard SF is working in the realm of the magical, the realm of the fantastic. Writers of what is more traditionally termed fantasy concentrate on ethical achievements along with their magical transformations: can their characters recognise what is right and triumph over evil, heal the people and the land, bring justice, restore the ecological order?

SF says a passionate yes! to these questions and many more. Unlike the flat, shallow, non-committal voice of postmodernism, with its hopelessness and cynicism, SF holds to the belief that humans can learn to be better than we are, than we have been.

SF believes that individual human action and the actions of small groups can change the world. Even the passionately conservative among its practitioners hold this radical notion sacred. The ideas that are housed within speculative fiction are often radical: things like world peace, the elimination of hunger, the healing of the ecosystem, journeys to the Moon and other planets, the elimination of disease and violence and crime, the guaranteeing of safety for children, women and minority cultures — goodness. It's Habitat for Humanity in literature. How ever do we prevent being locked up as revolutionaries?

Partly it's because as practitioners of this radical art called SF, we employ all the time-honoured tactics of fantastic narrative since narrative has been recorded. In other words, SF believes in allegory and parable. At least part of original intent of the "literature of ideas" remark, it seems to me, was to highlight the degree to which the thought experiment is at the core of human literature: not the photographic plate but the catalytic reaction has been the model for truly effective literature through the ages, and the science fiction writers among the practitioners of SF merely re-invented that model for the Industrial Revolution. It's no accident that 1984 described 1948, that Frankenstein and The Time Machine were cautionary tales of hubris and human responsibility rather than mere expositions of clever ideas. It's no accident that Canadian SF, even that designed most consciously for the genre markets, involves isolation, the predicaments of aliens and outsiders, struggles within rather than against harsh natural environments, and so on.

SF believes in justice and the power of right. In a markedly Christian culture, we have in our history monumental political struggles between those who believed in original sin and the seductiveness of evil, and those (eventually condemned for the Pellagian heresy) who believed in original blessing. Despite the preponderance of the cautionary tale in SF, I suggest to you that the original-blessing heresy is alive and well in our tradition. If it weren't for a stubborn belief that people will seek after goodness and what is good, and will strive to do good if given the chance, SF wouldn't survive as a genre or a literature. Even the dire dystopians, warning us of certain disaster, are doing so, I believe, because they (we) think that there is someone listening to the warning, someone who will try to do something about it. (C.f. the belief in the power of individuals and small groups to change the world, i.e. to fix things!)

Much SF also believes in the beneficent universe: the spaceship crashes rather than burning up in the atmosphere, people survive rather than dying horribly, cultures reassert themselves in order rather than descending into squalid savagery and bone-crunching: it's a universe of possibility, of possible good outcomes.SF believes in the future. It may seem self-evident with future fiction, with "science fiction" which sets itself near or far in the future, but it isn't.

What are all those futures doing there? They are making a statement: the future is possible. Even the On the Beach or The Wave type of tale, with its massive destruction, "the end of life on Earth [or a part of Earth] as we know it", there's a purpose: to say "Don't do that!" to a readership the author assumes is listening.

There's an assumption that determined individuals and groups (sound familiar?) can make a future happen, even when things look bleak, even when the Doomsday clock in the so-called "real world" is ticking its way to the last midnight.

And finally, SF believes passionately in setting. It is grounded in place, and the place is intimately ours. SF is probably the literature which most exemplifies the tenet that setting is another character in the story. This may not be obvious because the settings of speculative literature are sometimes so fantastical, but SF understands that setting is everything that we know: place in space, time, culture, politics, language, education and information, scientific and technological accomplishment, climate, geography, degree of development and urbanisation, social circle, experience, emotion, and all of the many many other definitive co-ordinates which locate people on the grid that is our lives. SF believed in the Butterfly Effect long before there was a name for it, that chaos theory principle that a butterfly can flap its wings in one part of the world and change the weather in another. SF believes that microscopic changes in our lives, a rainstorm one day, a sunset the next, can change our futures.

In SF, setting is not flat in the conceptual sense, It is intrusive, obtrusive, visible, changeable, critiquable, and powerfully influential. It is a constant, present, active player in the location of any narrative and the formation of any future.

Hence this anthology based on a particular place: the prairie where we live and write and dream. The prairie is often considered flat. You can sit on the porch and watch your dog run away — for three days. Gives the term "flattened affect" a whole new meaning. What we who live here know is that the land has chosen to present a muted initial impact — to make room for infinity.

On the prairie, especially at night, you can see not only for three days into the future, but light-years, forward and back, from the light originating at the universe's creation on to our mutual heat-death (and prairie people who live through our winters know all about the concept of heat-death!)

Tourists scorn the prairie, see its subtle palette and patterns and accuse us of living in the middle of nothing. Yet this supposedly non-existent landscape is rich in detail and diversity, and it has been hugely influential to the people who live there, the artists who create there, and the future being created. When Judy McCrosky came to ask me to participate in the editing of an anthology of prairie-originated speculative fiction, I had no trouble seeing how it fit into this SF-nal view of setting as the original and most important character in the story of a particular set of futures. And indeed, editing the anthology, we discovered that Judy's original thesis, that the prairie would grow a particular flavour of speculative literature, was right. Perhaps it's more accurate to say a particular set of flavours.

This is not genetically engineered, trademarked brain food. This is not the one-note fiddle or the one-trick pony. This is the natural prairie wool, wildflowers in profusion, wildfire in the spring, wild mind all the time, wild ideas.

Yet it is not "a literature of ideas", even as speculative fiction as a whole for me is not in any way a literature of ideas. (I think I have established the very redundancy of that phrase. In the same way, I often smirk up my sleeve when I use the redundant phrase "speculative fiction". All fiction is speculative. All fiction is fantastic. All literature is imaginary and imaginative.) Speculative literature is simply literature: literature is, it is true, ideas. But even more, and certainly more importantly, it is affect. It is how people live their ideas, their feelings, their beliefs. It is not dry, even when it is serious. It is not frozen, even when it is cold. It is about growth, even when the flowers are subtle and the seeds are small. It is not flat, even when it is spacious and leaves a lot of room for the sky.

I have said goodbye forever to the myth of the literature of ideas. In the cold prairie night, with a curtain of hissing aurora borealis arching overhead and the hard sharp snow underfoot, there are no ideas. There are only soul and spirit and passion — and the future, the sharp, clear future in every breath.

Candas Jane Dorsey

About The Authors

Alexandra Merry Arruin lives and writes in Calgary, Alberta.

John H. Baillie lives and writes in Winnipeg, Manitoba.

Martha Bayless teaches Medieval Studies at the University of Oregon in Eugene, Oregon. She is the author of *Kitty Kapers*, a book about cats (Ten Speed Press), and has published fiction in magazines such as *Seventeen* and *Realms of Fantasy*.

Ven Begamudre writes fiction, poetry, and creative non-fiction. His books include the short story collection *Laterna Magika*, which was a best book finalist in Canada and the Caribbean for the 1998 Commonwealth Writers' Prize, and the biography *Isaac Brock: Larger than Life*. His latest novel, a historical fantasy, is *The Phantom Queen* (Coteau Books, 2002).

Renée Bennett lives in Calgary, Alberta, and writes whatever she wants, golly gee-whiz. The results have shown up in such disparate places as *TransVersions*, CBC Radio, and *Year's Best Fantasy* anthology.

Judy Berlyne McCrosky is the author of two collections of literary short stories, *Spin Cycle and Other Stories* and *Blow the Moon Out*, Thistledown Press, 1990 and 1995; and one romance novel, *Lake of Dreams* (Pseudonym Jody McCrae) Silhouette Books, 1992; but is currently focusing on speculative fiction. Many of her stories have appeared in magazines and been broadcast on CBC Radio. She lives and writes in Saskatoon, and teaches Creative Writing at the University of Saskatchewan.

Steven Michael Berzensky's dream of Spinoza's canine reincarnation on the Canadian prairie became *Baruch, the Man-Faced Dog*. The award-winning poet, previously published as Mick Burrs, resides in Yorkton, Saskatchewan.

Jill Boettger is a contributing editor at *Geist Magazine*, and a graduate student at the University of British Columbia. Her writing has appeared in publications across Canada, including *Prairie Fire*, *Crank* and *Alberta Views*.

Donna Dowman grew up on the prairies in Saskatoon, Saskatchewan. She now lives in Regina with her husband, her dog, and his cat. *Little Sister* is her first published story.

Bev Brenna has published three children's books as well as short fiction and poetry for adults. She lives near Saskatoon with her husband and three sons, and works at a local school as a special education teacher.

Tobias S. Bucknell is a Caribbean-born speculative fiction writer who has published in various magazines and anthologies. He now lives in Ohio, which is why he feel comfortable writing about strange things happening to seemingly normal people.

Carolyn Clink: Carolyn's speculative poetry has appeared in *Northern Frights* (all five volumes), *Tesseracts* (volumes 4 and 7), *Packing Fraction*, *Analog*, *On-Spec*, *TransVersions*, *Star-Line*, and *Tales of the Unanticipated*. She is a member of the Science Fiction Poetry Association and the Algonquin Square Table poetry workshop.

Ron Collins lives in Columbus, Indiana with his wife, Lisa, their daughter, Brigid and the obligatory cat, Rika. His writing has appeared in *Analog*, *Dragon*, and several other magazines and anthologies. He is a Writers of the Future prize winner, and a CompuServe HOMer Award Winner. He has been named to the Science Fiction and Fantasy Writers of America's Nebula Awards® preliminary ballot twice, most recently in 2000 for his short story *Stealing the Sun*. He holds a degree in Mechanical Engineering from the University of Louisville, and has worked developing avionics systems, electronics, and information technology.

A.M. Dellamonica is from Vancouver, B.C. Her fiction can be found at scifi.com, and in the upcoming anthologies, *Mojo: Conjure Stories*, and *Alternate Generals III*.

Candas Jane Dorsey is the award-winning writer of *Black Wine*, *A Paradigm of Earth*, *Machine Sex and other stories* and *Vanilla and other stories*. She has co-edited several other anthologies, and is the publisher of Tesseract Books.

Nancy Etchemendy lives and works in the San Francisco Bay Area. She is the author of four novels and several dozen short stories, as well as numerous poems. For further details, surf to http://www.sff.net/people/etchemendy.

John Grey lives and writes in Providence, Rhode Island.

Gillian Harding-Russell is a poet who lives and works in Regina, Saskatchewan.

Geoff Hart lives and writes in Pointe Claire, Quebec.

James A. Hartley is an Australian-born writer based in London, England. His work has appeared in *On Spec, Challenging Destiny, Speculon, Fangoria,* and will soon be in *The Mammoth Book of Future Noir, Underworlds,* and *SFWorld in China.*

Carolyn Ives Gilman has been publishing fantasy and science fiction for fifteen years. Her first novel, *Halfway Human,* came out from Avon in 1998. Her short fiction has appeared in *Fantasy and Science Fiction, Bending the Landscape, Interzone, Universe, Full Spectrum, Realms of Fantasy,* and *The Year's Best Science Fiction.* She has been a finalist for the Nebula Award in the novelette category. Her work has been translated and reprinted in Germany, Russia, and Italy. She lives in St. Louis, where she works as a museum curator, and is currently developing a nationally touring exhibition about Lewis and Clark.

Mark Anthony Jarman was born in Edmonton, attended UVic and the Iowa Writers' Workshop His books include *Ireland's Eye, 19 Knives, New Orleans is Sinking* and *Salvage King Ya!* Published in the Journey Prize Anthology and Best Canadian Stories, winner of Event's Creative Nonfiction contest, Prism's Creative Nonfiction Contest, Prism's Short Fiction Contest, and winner of a National Magazine Award (Gold), he is currently teaching at the University of New Brunswick and the Banff Centre.

D.K. Latta has published scores of short fiction in magazines, webzines and anthologies and is a co-founder of the pulp flavoured webzine, www.pulpanddagger.com.

David D. Levine is a Midwestern boy who now lives in Portland, Oregon. He is a graduate of Clarion West, and his stories have appeared in *Year's Best Fantasy #2, Interzone,* and *F&SF.* His parents are alive and well and living in Milwaukee.

Sophie Masson was born in Jakarta, Indonesia, of French parents and spent her childhood in both Australia and France—experiences which inform all her work. She is the author of 30 novels, numerous short stories, articles, essays and reviews.

Derryl Murphy lives in Prince George, British Columbia. His fiction has been in *Realms of Fantasy, Tesseracts 4* and *6, On Spec, Prairie Fire, Northern Suns,* and more. *Blue Train* is part of a sequence of environmental disaster stories that otherwise bear no relation to each other.

Carole Nomarhas lives and writes in Melba, Australia.

Lia Pas is a poet, multi-disciplinary theatre artist and yoga instructor currently living and working in Saskatoon. Her poetry has been published in numerous literary magazines and anthologies and in 2001, her chapbook, *Vicissitudes* was published by Underwhich Editions. She is currently working towards publication of two full length poetry manuscripts; *Passage* and *The Pythia Poems.*

Ursula Pflug has published over thirty short stories in Canada, the United States and the UK, in print and on the World Wide Web, including her recent *Green Music,* published by Tesseract Books. She is the recipient of numerous Canada Council and Ontario Arts Council awards. She has had speculative narratives produced for stage, film, and television. She lives in rural Peterborough County with her husband Doug Back and their two children.

Holly Phillips lives and writes in the West Kootenay region of British Columbia, one of the most beautiful areas in Canada. She has sold several stories in Canada and the US, and is currently a junior member of the editorial board at *On Spec,* the Canadian magazine of speculative fiction.

Hugh A.D. Spencer: An original member of the Cecil Street Writers Group, Hugh writes short stories, radio plays and criticisms of speculative fiction. He was twice nominated for an Aurora Award, in 1992 for short fiction and in 1995 for co-curating the National Library of Canada's Canadian science fiction and fantasy exhibition. From 2000 to 2002, Hugh was President of SF Canada. He is currently working on *Amazing Struggles, Astonishing Failures and Disappointing Success,* a radio drama miniseries on the history of American SF. Hugh was born in Saskatoon, and currently lives in Toronto.

Anne Louise Waltz is from Minnesota, reads almost everything, but writes mostly science fiction. Her short stories have appeared in a variety of small-press publications.